"I love Julie James'
—USAToday.com

the
novels
of
JULIE JAMES
are...

"A tantalizing dessert—a delicious, delightful read
that all hopeless romantics will enjoy."
—*Chicago Sun-Times*

"Sexy and effervescent."
—*Kirkus Reviews*

"Packed with hilarious
situations and sharp dialogue."
—*San Francisco Book Review*

"A rare treat."
—*Chicago Tribune*

Praise for the novels of Julie James

"I love Julie James's voice . . . *Suddenly One Summer* is another jewel added to her basket of treasures." —USAToday.com

"*A Lot Like Love* kept me up way past midnight!"
—Nalini Singh, *New York Times* bestselling author

"Remind[s] me of Katharine Hepburn and Spencer Tracy movies: They have that funny edge."
—Eloisa James, *New York Times* bestselling author

"Read *Just the Sexiest Man Alive*, and you will be adding Julie James to your automatic-buy list!"
—Janet Chapman, *New York Times* bestselling author

"Fueled by equal measures of seductive wit, edge-of-the-seat suspense, and scorching-hot sexual chemistry . . . [a] scintillating novel of romantic suspense." —*Chicago Tribune*

"A tantalizing dessert—a delicious, delightful read that all hopeless romantics will enjoy." —*Chicago Sun-Times*

"A fast-paced romantic comedy . . . A talented writer . . . Expect a lot of sparks to fly." —*San Francisco Book Review*

"James's smart heroines and fun dialogue are becoming her signature elements." —*Booklist*

Titles by Julie James

the thing about love

JULIE JAMES

BERKLEY
New York

BERKLEY
An imprint of Penguin Random House LLC
375 Hudson Street, New York, New York 10014

Copyright © 2017 by Julie James
Penguin Random House supports copyright. Copyright fuels creativity, encourages
diverse voices, promotes free speech, and creates a vibrant culture. Thank you for
buying an authorized edition of this book and for complying with copyright laws by
not reproducing, scanning, or distributing any part of it in any form without
permission. You are supporting writers and allowing Penguin Random House to
continue to publish books for every reader.

BERKLEY is a registered trademark and the B colophon is a trademark of
Penguin Random House LLC.

Library of Congress Cataloging-in-Publication Data

Names: James, Julie, 1974–, author.
Title: The thing about love / Julie James.
Description: First Edition. | New York : Berkley, 2017.
Identifiers: LCCN 2016058820 (print) | LCCN 2017004215 (ebook) |
ISBN 9780425273777 (paperback) | ISBN 9780425273784 (ebook)
Subjects: | BISAC: FICTION / Contemporary Women. | FICTION /
Romance / Contemporary. | FICTION / Contemporary Women. |
GSAFD: Love stories. | Romantic suspense fiction.
Classification: LCC PS3610.A4426 T48 2017 (print) |
LCC PS3610.A4426 (ebook) | DDC 813/.6—dc23
LC record available at https://lccn.loc.gov/2016058820

First Edition: April 2017

Printed in the United States of America
1 3 5 7 9 10 8 6 4 2

Cover photo © Carlos Cossio / Getty Images
Cover and stepback design by Rita Frangie

For my grandmothers,
Arline and Margaret

acknowledgments

As always, I'm grateful to my friends and family who graciously shared their professional and personal experiences during the writing of this book. From the heartfelt conversations about divorce, to the amusing discussions with my male friends about "guy code" and whether they could ever forgive a friend who knew about cheating, to the answers to my many technical questions about everything from firearms to private equity, I'm so appreciative for all you do to enrich my books. Please never stop opening those random late-night e-mails from me with subject lines like "Just curious," "I was wondering . . ." and "HELP," because I would be lost without you.

I could not have written this book the way I wanted to without the insight of one such friend, Brent Dempsey. Thank you, from the bottom of my heart, for being so generous with your time and for helping me get it right. I solemnly swear to never again use the words *stakeout* or *perp*.

I'm also grateful for the support of my former editor, Wendy McCurdy, who worked with me on eight books and also helped me brainstorm ideas for this one. Thank you for giving me the opportunity to share my stories and for making me a better writer. Your voice saying, "These people like each other too much!" will continue to motivate me to push myself every time I sit down at a keyboard.

Special thanks to Elyssa Patrick, Kati Brown, Brent Dempsey, and Brian Kavanaugh for reading early drafts of this book and sharing your thoughts with me. Thanks as well to my agent, Robin Rue, and to Mollie Smith for her advice and know-how in all things digital marketing related.

Thank you to everyone at Berkley for your support of this book. First and foremost, to Kate Seaver, my editor, and also to Ivan Held, Christine Ball, Claire Zion (Go, Cubs!), Jeanne-Marie Hudson, Craig Burke, and Erin Galloway: I deeply appreciate all the discussions, strategy talks, and warm conversations we've had this last year. I'm thrilled, and humbled, to be working with such a wonderful team of people.

Finally, thank you to my husband, Brian, who doesn't bat an eye when I call him at work with questions like, "So, if you were going to bribe a politician, would you divide the cash into two payments or just give him the whole fifty thousand up front?" You're my first sounding board in all things, always. And thank you to my kids, just for being my favorite people to hang out with. Love you guys.

1 ∽

Three minutes after the plane took off from the runway, FBI Special Agent John Shepherd knew he was doomed if he didn't act immediately.

Next to John, the guy in the middle seat was in his early forties and dressed in a suit and lime-green shirt. "Man, it's a packed flight tonight." He held out his hand in introduction. "Steve Fox. Corporate motivational speaker, leadership consultant, and occasional author. When I can *motivate* myself to write, that is." He laughed at his own joke. "So . . . you heading to the Windy City for business or pleasure?"

Yep. Steve in the lime-green shirt was going to be a Talker.

Not that sitting next to a chatty passenger was uncommon for John. He accepted the fact that in his line of work, it was an occupational hazard. Occasionally, someone would notice the FBI badge clipped to his pants—specifically placed there in case someone also happened to notice the Glock 22 on his right hip, under his suit jacket—and that inevitably led to a few questions.

FBI? Cool! Are you watching someone on this plane? Is it the guy in 10C? It's totally the guy in 10C, isn't it? He got snippy when the flight attendant tried to help him with his carry-on. You saw that, right? Ooh, do you think he has drugs in there? Or something worse? Oh my God, it's not a bomb, is it? Whew. So, an FBI agent . . . what's that like?

But tonight, having just completed a rough eight-month undercover investigation, John was hoping to have a few quiet minutes to unwind before the plane landed in Chicago.

And also to start thinking about how he was going to get things back on track with his girlfriend, Alicia.

"I live in Chicago," he answered Steve. He took earbuds out of his briefcase and plugged them into the armrest, then smiled apologetically. "I'm a bit of a nervous flier. It helps if I listen to air traffic control." The lie rolled easily off his tongue—as an undercover agent, he was well practiced in the art of bullshit.

"You know what else helps for that?" Steve grinned. "Vodka. Lots of it." Moving on to another target, he turned his head and eyed the woman seated on the other side of him. She had her e-reader in hand and gave him an unmistakable *Don't even think about it, buddy* look.

Steve sighed resignedly and pulled out his laptop.

The Talker now successfully contained, John turned toward the window and watched as the bright lights of Detroit faded in the distance. With any luck, it would be the last time he would see this city for a long time—hopefully not until he had to testify in court about his investigation. Not that he had anything against Detroit. In fact, for three years he'd called it home, having been assigned to work in the Detroit field office after graduating from the FBI Academy at Quantico.

Joining the Bureau hadn't been part of John's original career plan. Actually, for a while, he hadn't had much of a career plan. After graduating from the University of Wisconsin, he'd joined the Army—both to help pay off his student loans and to buy some time to figure out what he wanted to do with his life.

As it turned out, that had been the best decision he could've made.

Army life had suited him. He'd always been an athletic guy, and he'd done well with the physical challenges of being an enlisted soldier. But being in the Army also required mental toughness, determination, and discipline. So he'd pushed himself, more than he ever had, and after Basic Combat Training and Advanced Individual Training, he'd gone on to Airborne School and then had volunteered for the Ranger Assessment and Selection Program.

Eight weeks later, he'd proudly joined the elite ranks of the 75th Ranger Regiment. And it was at Fort Benning, where his battalion had been stationed, that he'd first been approached by Sean Piser, an operator and recruiter for the FBI's Hostage Rescue Team.

"We're federal law enforcement's only full-time counterterrorism unit," Piser had told him when they'd met at a pub on base. "HRT has the ability to respond within four hours' notice to hostage situations, major criminal threats, and terrorist incidents anywhere in the U.S. Our motto, *servare vitas*, means 'to save lives'—and that's exactly what we do. We're badasses that way."

As John sat dressed in his ACUs across a bar table from the recruiter, his answer, admittedly, had been cocky. "With all due respect, sir, I'm a Ranger. If I wanted to put 'badass' on my résumé, I think I'm set."

Piser had cocked his head at that. "I hear you're considering a career in law enforcement after you finish your tour this summer." Now it was his turn to sound cocky. "We're the FBI, Shepherd. You want to catch bad guys for a living? We're pretty much the cream of the fucking crop. So you might want to listen to what I have to say."

An announcement from the cockpit interrupted John's thoughts.

"Good evening, folks. On behalf of the flight deck, we'd like to welcome you aboard. Looks like it's going to be a smooth flight into Chicago, with an on-time arrival of ten twenty P.M."

John checked his watch. Thirty minutes and they'd be on the ground, which meant he didn't have a lot of time to figure out the logistics of his current mission: Operation Get Out of the Doghouse.

It was a working title.

Originally, he'd planned to come home tomorrow, since a bunch of agents in the Detroit office were heading out to celebrate wrapping up the investigation with a round of drinks—an investigation that had resulted in the arrest of twenty-seven suspects, including one state senator. But two days ago, the last time John had spoken on the phone with Alicia, she'd been . . . distant. Actually, she'd been distant a lot this past month, but more so than unusual in their last conversation. So, as a start to getting back in her good graces, he'd decided to catch an earlier flight and surprise her.

Obviously, he was aware that Alicia wasn't thrilled with all the traveling he'd been doing as part of his investigation. And he got that; he *had* been gone a lot as of late. Officially, he now worked in the Chicago field office, having transferred to his hometown over two years ago, when his mom had been diagnosed with lung cancer. But he'd been called back to the Detroit FBI office to revive one of his undercover roles, part of a large-scale sting operation into a criminal organization involved in money laundering, narcotics and firearms trafficking, and murder-for-hire schemes. Although, technically, he had only a part-time undercover role, he'd spent the last eight months traveling to Detroit anywhere from two to five days per week.

The job itself was interesting—he'd been doing undercover work for three years and liked the challenge of taking on new roles, as well as the adrenaline rush that came with knowing that he was getting something over on the bad guys. But from a relationship standpoint, it wasn't an ideal setup.

He'd always been honest with Alicia about his lifestyle. And when he'd first taken on the Detroit undercover investigation, she'd been great about the situation. They'd texted several times a day whenever he was out of town, talked on the phone every night, and had hot reunion sex as soon as he walked through the door of the two-bedroom apartment they shared. But when it became apparent that his travel schedule wasn't easing up anytime soon, Alicia had become less enthralled with having a "part-time boyfriend," as she'd put it one night while they were talking on the phone.

"It won't be that much longer. Then I'll be home so much you'll be looking for ways to get rid of me," John had joked. He'd been trying to keep the conversation light, despite his frustration that she'd chosen to bring up this subject—again—at that moment. He'd been about to walk out the door of his rented fake apartment for a key undercover meeting with a guy who not only was selling him illegal firearms but had also hinted that he was willing to commit murder for a fee. The thugs he was dealing with were armed and undoubtedly dangerous, and seeing how he was *lying* to them with every word that came out of his mouth, it was pretty important that he have his head in the game.

"Whatever. How many times have I heard that this year?" Alicia had asked sarcastically.

Honestly, he'd had a couple of tough days and long nights, and he'd just wanted to call his girlfriend and hear her voice without rehashing the same damn argument. "I can't deal with this right now, Alicia," he'd said brusquely.

"Fine. Not that it matters to you, but I probably won't be around much this weekend, if you try to call," she'd said. "I've got a work thing on Friday, and then I'm going out with Beth and Mia the next night."

In his frustration, John had told her to do whatever she wanted, and that he didn't expect her to sit around and wait by the phone for him.

Two days later, he'd called back and they'd both apologized

and just let the argument go. But things hadn't been quite the same between them ever since.

Now that he was back in town, however, that would change. No more long-distance relationship, or being a "part-time boyfriend." From here on out, he would be in Chicago and they could get back to the good place they'd been in eight months ago, back to the days when they were just a normal couple doing normal couple things, like coming home every night after work and trading work stories, or spending lazy weekends together without it hanging over both their heads that he'd be leaving again on Sunday night.

Feeling good about this, after the plane landed at O'Hare, John stopped at a kiosk next to baggage claim and bought fresh flowers as phase one of his mission: Operation Sorry I've Been Gone So Long (But You Did Know the Score When We First Started Dating).

Still a working title.

Then he got a better idea. In the cab on the way home from the airport, he asked the driver to wait outside Sweet Mandy B's bakery while he ran in and picked up a half dozen of Alicia's favorite cupcakes.

It was after eleven o'clock by the time the cab dropped him off at home, armed with flowers and chocolate. He and Alicia had moved into their apartment a year ago, renting the top unit of a graystone on a quiet residential street. At the time she'd wanted to buy a place together, but he'd hesitated, thinking it had been too soon in their relationship for that.

But now, he thought, maybe it was time to revisit that idea. It wasn't easy being in a relationship with a guy like him, an undercover agent who always had a go bag packed and might have to travel to another state—or country—with no notice. Yet despite all the ups and downs these past eight months, Alicia had stuck by him.

John unlocked the door to their apartment and saw that all

the lights were off. Assuming she'd gone to bed already, he left his suitcase and carry-on by the door and moved quietly as he set the cupcakes and flowers on the kitchen counter, followed by his Glock. He yanked off his tie and walked down the hallway, thinking he'd slip in bed next to her and surprise her. He pictured the two of them naked and tangled up together all night, his mind quickly going to some very dirty places since they hadn't had sex in almost a month.

He frowned as the reality of that hit him, and paused just before the bedroom doorway.

A month? Had it really been that long since they'd slept together? He began mentally scrolling back in time, wondering if that could be right.

That was when he heard Alicia moaning in the bedroom.

He froze, recognizing that particular moan, the low, sensuous sounds she made during sex. And for a moment he thought, *Maybe she's just using her vibrator.*

But then a deeper, male voice joined in, adding his moan to the chorus.

Fuck.

Pushing past the sharp stab of hurt, John stepped into the bedroom doorway and folded his arms.

There was Alicia, in their bed, naked in the moonlight and riding some guy who had his hands on her hips, guiding her.

"Just like that, baby. I'm gonna come so hard in you," the man groaned.

"Yes, don't stop on my account, baby," John said dryly.

Alicia shrieked in surprise and sprang off her lover. "John! Oh my God, what are you doing here?"

Dick swinging, the guy scrambled to cover himself with the blanket. His expression was contrite. "John—oh shit."

No.

John took a step into the room, his jaw tightening as he stared into the eyes of the man fucking *his* girlfriend in *his* bedroom. A man who'd always had a thing for long-legged brunettes like Alicia.

A fact John knew well since, up until two seconds ago, he'd considered this man a friend.

"Rob," he said, on some level still unable to believe it, despite what he'd just seen with his own eyes. He and Rob had known each other for years, ever since they'd lived together their junior and senior years of college, with two other guys in an off-campus apartment they'd nicknamed the Pour House because of all the parties they'd thrown there. In fact, he and Rob had just hung out two weeks ago, grabbing drinks with their other buddies when John had breezed back into town for the weekend. Rob had asked how things were going between him and Alicia, and John had admitted that things were a little strained. He'd *confided* in the guy, never once suspecting there might be an ulterior motive behind the question, not having any clue that the friend he was talking to already knew damn well how things were between him and Alicia, because that *friend* was screwing her behind his back.

"Get out," he said to Rob.

Alicia was crying, standing naked between him and Rob. "I'm so sorry."

John couldn't even look at her.

"We wanted to tell you," Rob said. "But Lucas and Matt said it would be unfair to give you the news while you were in the middle of an undercover assignment. So we decided to wait until you were back."

John blinked, his head spinning with this newest information. Lucas and Matt were part of the same circle of friends as him and Rob. *They* knew that Rob and Alicia were sleeping together? And they'd never said anything to him?

The hits just kept right on coming.

"I said get out," he growled.

Rob stood there, still with that worthless look of contrition, then nodded. Silently, he grabbed his clothes off the floor, gave Alicia a quick glance, and then walked out of the bedroom.

John stayed still, waiting until he heard the front door shut. When he turned around, he saw that Alicia had put on a navy T-shirt and her underwear. It was her favorite T-shirt to sleep in, one he'd seen her wear more times than he could count.

Now all he could see was Rob pulling it off her as they fell into bed.

"John, I am so, so, sorry. I never meant for this to happen." She reached for him.

He flinched. "Don't."

She dropped her hand. He looked at her for a long moment, trying to get a grip on the rush of betrayal and disbelief he felt. "How long?"

She brushed tears away from her eyes. "Two months. You and I had a fight, and I went out with Beth and Mia the next night. We ran into Rob at the bar and he and I started talking, first about you and me, and then, I don't know . . . it just happened. It was supposed to be a onetime thing, but . . ." She trailed off.

Well, he'd been right about one thing—things really hadn't been the same between him and Alicia since that night.

Not having anything else to say, he went into the closet to grab the go bag he always had packed for work. Between that, and the suitcase and carry-on he'd left by the front door, he'd have enough to get by for the next few days.

"I'll come by Monday morning for the rest of my stuff." He headed out of the bedroom. "Make sure you're not here."

"John, if you would just let me—"

"I don't want you here!" he shouted, whirling around in the doorway. "I can't even look at—" He stopped, his throat tightening, then shook his head.

A silence fell between them.

"I'm sorry," Alicia whispered.

Right. He'd heard that part already.

On his way to a hotel, John decided to make a pit stop. He drove to his friend Wes's place in Lakeview and left his car out front in a tow zone.

Let someone try to give him a parking ticket today.

He strode up the front steps of the two-flat building and knocked on Wes's door, aware that midnight was late for an unannounced visit but not giving a shit about that right then.

"Did you know?" he demanded, as soon as Wes opened his front door.

Wearing jeans and no shirt as he stood in the doorway, Wes cocked his head. "Know what?"

"That Alicia's been sleeping with Rob for the last two months."

Wes's eyes widened. "What? You're kidding me."

"I already know that Matt and Lucas were in on it." After dropping that bait, John studied the other man's face and body language for any signs that he was hiding something. Granted, his FBI training hadn't done him a lot of good in terms of detecting deceit as of late, but of all the guys he hung around with, he considered Wes to be his closest friend. And after everything that had happened tonight, he just . . . really needed to know if that was still the case.

Wes held out his hands. "John, I swear. I had no clue."

After a long moment, John nodded. Then he exhaled and ran a hand over his jaw. "Right. Sorry."

Wes pushed open the door. "Come on in. Claire's upstairs, but I'll tell her—"

John held up his hand. "No, it's fine. I have to go anyway."

"John. Come on."

John managed a sheepish smile. "Tell Claire I'm sorry for all the drama tonight." He turned and headed down the steps, ignoring Wes as he called his name, and got into his car. He stopped at a convenience store and bought a bottle of Four Roses bourbon, then checked into the Guesthouse, an extended-stay hotel on the city's north side. The room had a full kitchen and a washer and dryer in the unit, which would tide him over until he found an apartment to rent.

He dryly wondered what the etiquette was in situations like this, whether he was expected to continue paying half the rent on his and Alicia's place until their lease expired in three months.

Dear Abby: The other night I came home and found my girlfriend going for a moonlight ride on my friend's dick . . .

After unpacking the few things he had with him, he cracked open the bottle of bourbon. He took a seat out on the balcony that overlooked the downtown skyline and poured himself the first of many shots he had planned for the night.

He looked down at the glass and thought about how, just two hours ago, he'd been the jerk buying flowers and cupcakes for a woman who was, probably at that very moment, getting naked with her lover. His friend.

"Bottoms up to that," he muttered.

He closed his eyes and tossed back the shot, welcoming the burn of the bourbon.

In the morning, he woke up to a wicked hangover and a dozen voice-mail messages on his phone. Several from Alicia and Rob, which he deleted instantly; two from Wes, checking up on him; and one each from Matt and Lucas, who apparently had been alerted that he was aware they knew about the situation and were trying to do some damage control.

"Shep, we gotta talk. I was stuck in the middle between you and Rob—what was I supposed to do?" Matt said in his message.

Here's an idea, jackass: Maybe choose the side of the guy not *fucking someone else's girlfriend.*

"Shep, listen. I know what you must be thinking," Lucas led in. "But I told Rob and Alicia that if they didn't tell you everything as soon as your investigation was over, I would tell you myself. I mean, how was I supposed to know that you'd walk in on them? Man, that must've really sucked."

You don't say, asshole. John hit delete again, leaving his phone on "do not disturb" when he headed for the shower.

The hot water helped clear his head of the alcohol, but the bitter taste in his mouth lingered. Naturally, he kept thinking about walking in on Alicia and Rob. But there was something else that had kept him up all night, something that unsettled him as much as the shock of finding his girlfriend and friend in bed together.

He'd never suspected a thing.

He was an FBI agent. He specialized in undercover work. It was his *job* to notice things the average person overlooked, to be on the alert for suspicious behavior, to be especially aware when someone was hiding something. And yet somehow, despite all that, despite the twenty-one weeks of training he'd had at Quantico and the additional three weeks of training he'd undertaken to become a certified undercover agent—not to mention, over five years of on-the-job experience—four people, normal regular people, had managed to pull the wool over his eyes.

He channeled his anger and frustration into a fifteen-mile run along the lake, then spent the rest of the day apartment hunting. On Monday morning he let himself into the apartment he shared—*had* shared—with Alicia and packed up his stuff. She'd left him a note in an envelope on the counter, which he ignored. He used the unopened envelope to write her a note saying that he and Wes would come by to move out his half of the furniture on Friday morning, while she was at work.

His car loaded with boxes, he parked at the FBI building and nodded at the guards as he passed through the metal detectors. His squad, organized crime, was on the fifth floor, and as he made his way to his cubicle he was greeted by several of his squad mates, who congratulated him on the arrests in Detroit.

"Heard you nabbed a state senator. You been moonlighting on the public corruption squad?" joked Ryan, one of his squad mates.

"Figured they could use some help," John shot back as he settled into his desk chair.

For the rest of the day he caught up on work, being careful not to show any signs that anything was off around his co-workers. He might have been the jackass who'd unsuspectingly walked in on his girlfriend having sex with his friend, but he'd be damned if he'd let his fellow agents know that.

He grabbed takeout on the way back to his hotel, cracked open a beer, and channel surfed while eating dinner on the couch. Not finding anything that caught his interest, he turned the television off.

The hotel room fell silent.

He felt . . . restless. Unsettled. That happened sometimes after an agent finished a long-term undercover assignment. It took a few days, or weeks even, before home seemed like home again.

Just as he was eyeing the stack of unpacked boxes containing his things, his phone chimed with a new e-mail message. He checked and saw that it was from Sean Piser, the HRT recruiter who'd visited his Ranger battalion at Fort Benning six years ago. They'd stayed in touch, exchanging e-mails a couple times a year, and he knew that Piser had been keeping an eye on him ever since John had joined the FBI.

Probably two eyes, knowing Piser.

Selection starts in a week. Got an open spot with your name on it, Shepherd.

Right . . . it was that time of year again. John had been so wrapped up with the Detroit undercover investigation, he'd forgotten all about it.

Every year, the FBI held a two-week selection program at Quantico for any agents who wanted to try out for the Hostage Rescue Team. Normally, agents had to spend at least three years in the field as investigators before they qualified for HRT, but because John had been directly recruited from the Rangers per the Bureau's Tactical Recruitment Program, he'd been eligible after only two years.

And indeed, that had been his original plan—to get through his time in the field and then try out for HRT as soon as possible. With the tactical experience he'd acquired in the military, that career path practically had been expected of him. But once he'd started handling his own cases—and particularly once he'd begun doing undercover work—he'd found that he really enjoyed the investigative side of the job. So he'd held off on trying out for HRT, thinking it was something he would do the following year. Then one year stretched into two, and then his mom had gotten sick and he'd transferred back to Chicago. He'd met Alicia after that and things had gotten serious between them, and since being picked for HRT would've required him to relocate to the team's headquarters in Quantico, Virginia, he'd waited some more.

But now, his situation was different. After losing his girlfriend, his apartment, and three of his friends in the span of three days, he probably would never be *less* attached to Chicago than he was right then. Sure, he would miss his father and brother if he had to move to Virginia. But there was a reason Piser had recruited him and had continued pursuing him these past few years. And that reason was, simply, because he thought John was good enough for the team.

Maybe it was time for him to finally prove Piser right about that.

John spent the next two days weighing his decision. When he finally wrote back to Piser, saying he'd be there for tryouts, he felt good. Pumped.

Life had thrown him a curveball this past week, no doubt.

But now he was going to knock that son of a bitch out of the park.

2 ～

three weeks later

Special Agent Jessica Harlow waited as the security guard studied her FBI identification card, comparing her face to the photo.

"Looks like a match to me," the guard said, with a friendly grin. "Welcome to Chicago, Agent Harlow."

Returning the smile, Jessica tucked the billfold that held her ID into her briefcase. "Thank you." She glanced at the ID clipped to the guard's jacket and made a mental note of his name. *Roger.* "Where can I find the Special Agent in Charge's office?"

"Twelfth floor. End of the hallway."

After clearing the metal detectors and exiting the guardhouse, Jessica followed a wide curving sidewalk to the main entrance of the FBI's Chicago headquarters, an impressive glass-and-steel building located two miles from downtown. Fenced off from the public, the three-building complex—the largest among all the agency's field offices—was surrounded by green parkways and trees.

She exhaled as she entered the building, feeling . . . not nervous, exactly. Chicago was home, after all, and after being in Los Angeles these past six years, it felt good to be back in this city. But professionally speaking, she was the new girl in town.

In L.A., she'd considered many of her squad mates to be friends, and she'd had good relationships with both her squad leader and the Special Agent in Charge. Here, however, her fellow agents and supervisors had no idea what to expect from her, nor she from them. In that sense, she was starting all over again.

Kind of a theme for her this year.

She made her way to the elevator bank, where two men were already waiting—agents, she guessed from their attire. The shorter man, African American and dressed in a well-tailored suit, gestured animatedly as he spoke.

"All I said was, if we'd already registered for the slow-flow, medium-flow, and fast-flow nipples, did we really need the variable flow? Isn't that just a combination of all the other nipples we'd already picked?"

The taller man, Caucasian with dark hair and eyes, grinned. "How'd that question go over with Rae?"

"Not well."

"Because you don't *ask* questions at Babies'R'Us," the taller man said. "Take it from someone who knows. You push the cart, you lift the heavy things, and whenever she asks your opinion on something, just cock your head, take a moment, and then point to the yellow one."

Jessica fought back a smile as the elevator doors sprung open. *Men.*

The taller man held the elevator door open for her. She nodded in thanks as she stepped inside.

"First day?" the shorter man asked her.

"It's that obvious?" Jessica said good-naturedly, as she pressed the button for the twelfth floor.

"I heard you talking with Roger as we walked in." The

shorter man held out his hand in introduction. "Sam Wilkins. And this is Jack Pallas. We're both in Violent Crimes."

"Jessica Harlow. Public Corruption."

"That's a good squad," Jack said. "Lots of talented agents. Like . . . Seth Huxley, for instance." He turned to his partner. "You know Huxley, don't you, Sam?"

"We're acquainted." Sam's voice was a touch dry.

"Sam and Huxley have a little rivalry going on," Jack explained to Jessica. "I think they both wore the same thousand-dollar suit to work one day, and everything spiraled from there."

"This is what you tell people, ten seconds after I meet them?" Shaking his head in exasperation, Sam turned to Jessica. "Huxley's a good agent. He just likes to talk a lot of smack about how Harvard is the best law school."

"Sam here is a Yale man," Jack told Jessica.

"Indeed." Sam flashed her a grin that said he was quite proud of this fact.

"Got it." Jessica considered this. "Well, obviously this Agent Huxley has no idea what he's talking about."

Sam nodded, satisfied, as the elevator reached his and Jack's floor. "Thank you. See?" he said to Jack. "And that's coming from an independent source—clearly a very wise one." He winked at Jessica.

"Because everyone knows that *Stanford* is the best law school," she continued.

Jack laughed as Sam's mouth fell open. He gripped Sam's shoulder as the elevator doors opened. "You walked right into that one, buddy." He nodded at Jessica as he left the elevator. "Enjoy your first day."

Sam pointed mock-archly at Jessica as he stepped out. "To be continued, Agent Harlow."

Jessica smiled as the doors closed between them, thinking she rather liked those two. Their friendly ribbing reminded her of the dynamic she'd had with Javier, her partner in Los Angeles.

As a female in a profession where over eighty percent of her colleagues were men—and an even greater percentage of her supervisors—she'd quickly learned that a little good-natured trash talk went a long way in getting others to see her not as a "female special agent" but as a special agent who happened to be a woman. Not that she tried to downplay her gender, nor did she have any interest in pretending to be one of the guys. For one thing, she firmly believed that in many situations, her gender could be a tactical advantage. People inherently trusted women more than men, something that came in handy when one was an undercover agent.

And for another thing, she just really liked wearing cute high-heeled shoes.

On the twelfth floor, an assistant greeted Jessica from a desk in front of the corner office at the end of the hallway. "Mr. McCall will be with you shortly." She gestured to a small waiting area.

"Thank you." Jessica took a seat in one of the chairs and put her phone on vibrate to make sure it didn't ring during the meeting.

Obviously, she wanted to make a good first impression with the man who was, as of today, her new boss. She'd done her homework and knew that Nick McCall had been appointed five years ago to the position of Special Agent in Charge—or SAC, as agents referred to the position around the office. Before that, he'd been on the public corruption squad, specializing in undercover work.

That was something they had in common, at least.

She set her briefcase next to her feet, watching the bustling office activity as she waited. Being back here reminded her of the many times she'd had to visit this office, several years ago, when she'd first applied to the FBI. There'd been the preliminary exam—three hours of cognitive, behavioral, and logical reasoning tests—followed by an initial interview, language and writing tests, a one-hour panel interview, two physical fitness tests, and a polygraph and security background check. And throughout the entire process, she'd had a real hard-ass of a recruiter guiding her.

But a hard-ass who'd believed in her.

Don't give them any reason to doubt you in the Academy. You go in there, Harlow, and you'd goddamn better show them what you're made of.

The door opened, and a tall, well-built man with dark hair stepped out. His sharp green eyes fell on Jessica, and he walked over.

"Special Agent Harlow." He held out his hand. "Nick McCall. I just got off the phone with your former SAC. If half the things he says about you are true, we're very lucky to have you on board."

Jessica smiled, hearing that. "Thank you, sir. It's good to be here." She followed him into his office and took a seat at one of the chairs in front of the desk.

"So, you couldn't resist the call of the hometown," Nick led in.

That was the reason Jessica had given the SAC in Los Angeles, when she'd put in for a transfer to Chicago. And it was true. What was *also* true, however, was that she'd needed a fresh start and figured Chicago was the best place to get it. "My family all lives here. When I heard that this office was looking for agents with undercover certification, it seemed like an opportunity I couldn't pass up."

"The U.S. Attorney for this district and I have made it one of our top priorities to crack down on government corruption at all levels. And the agents on the public corruption squad have absolutely stepped up to the plate. I try not to go overboard in praising them so that it doesn't go to their heads, but they're a very skilled group of agents. And I'd say that even if they weren't my former squad."

Jessica smiled. No matter the office, one thing was always true: Squad loyalty ran strong. "Of course."

"The one challenge is that with the increase in the number of investigations we're handling, the squad is running short on agents who can cover the undercover work," Nick said. "Which is where you come in."

And she was eager to get started. "You said there are two other agents on the squad who are certified?" All special agents in the FBI were qualified to do "light" undercover work—investigations in which the agent had only a few interactions with the target or targets. Anything more than that required an agent who was undercover certified, meaning he or she had attended the FBI's undercover school at Quantico. The problem was, because of the extra training required, there were only a handful of undercover-certified agents in any given field office—mostly on the public corruption and organized crime squads, given the nature of the work.

"Agents Huxley and Roberts," Nick said. "Given their workloads, they were very pleased to hear you're joining the squad. They're probably waiting at your desk with a big welcome banner and a stack of thirty case files to hand over."

She chuckled. "I'm happy to get started right away."

"Glad to hear it. In fact . . ." Nick handed her a case file. "This one needs your immediate attention. It's an out-of-town investigation, a partial undercover assignment. Apparently, the public corruption squad in our Jacksonville office is looking for two 'shady Chicago business entrepreneurs.'"

Jessica raised an eyebrow. "'Shady Chicago business entrepreneurs'?"

"That's literally how the request was worded. And the best part is, I get requests like this all the time from other offices. I swear people think we're all still running around this city with tommy guns and hanging out in speakeasies." Nick pointed to the case file. "I have to turn down most of the requests because we've been so short on manpower, but this one seemed like it might be worth your while." He winked. "Plus, it'll make me look like a team player with the other SACs if I finally say yes to one of these things."

Intrigued by that lead-in, Jessica opened the case file. It wasn't uncommon for an FBI office to use out-of-town agents for an undercover assignment. In fact, under certain circumstances—such as investigations that involved a high-profile target—that was the preferred course of action because it minimized the risk that the agents would be recognized.

And that, she saw as she skimmed over the request from the Jacksonville agents, was precisely the case here. High-profile target, suspected of bribery and corruption. Most of the groundwork for the sting operation had been laid; all the Jacksonville team needed now were two experienced out-of-town agents to play the lead roles.

She felt the spike of adrenaline that came with every new assignment. "I'll start working on my undercover legend right away." Going undercover in this kind of case required a lot more than a simple name change and a fake ID. For starters, as an "entrepreneur," she would need a fake business that had web presence.

She made a mental note to coordinate with Stagehand, the internal prop and tech squad who handled all details related to undercover operations, on that front.

Then she made a second mental note to ask someone where the heck the Stagehand squad even was in this building.

Nick nodded approvingly. "Good. I'll call the SAC in Jacksonville and let him know you're on board."

They chatted for a few more minutes, mostly about her new neighborhood and how she was settling into the condo she'd bought when her transfer had been approved. She took the

Jacksonville case file with her as she started to leave the office, but when she got to the doorway she realized they'd forgotten to discuss something. "The assignment calls for two Chicago entrepreneurs. Will I be working with Agent Huxley or Agent Roberts on this?" She figured that whoever it was, they could start discussing logistics right away.

"Actually, neither," Nick said. "They're both involved in other undercover investigations right now. You'll be partnered with an agent from the organized crime squad for this."

Organized crime? Now that was unexpected. Not to stereotype—okay, fine, she totally would—but generally speaking, the agents from the organized crime squad were considered a little . . . rougher around the edges than those from other squads. And this sting op in Jacksonville, like many run by the public corruption squad, would require a certain amount of finesse.

Nick grinned, seemingly catching the skeptical look on her face. "Don't worry. He's a good agent. One of the best in this office. In fact, he just finished up the HRT Selection course. Tomorrow will be his first day back."

Hmm. Rough around the edges or not, her soon-to-be partner must have been something of a badass if he'd tried out for the FBI's super-selective Hostage Rescue Team. Because from what Jessica had heard, HRT's Selection course was two weeks of near torture. Every year, roughly half the class dropped out before completing the tryouts. And even if a candidate was still standing at the end, there was no guarantee he would be picked for the team—*he* being the operative word, since, in the thirty-plus years since HRT had been formed, no woman had ever made the cut.

Not that she, personally, had any interest. For one thing— ha—there was no way she'd make it through the tryouts; she'd had to work her butt off just to pass the physical tests in the Academy. And for another thing, she simply wasn't one of those adrenaline junkies who got all jazzed up over rappelling out of a helicopter, or parachuting into shark-infested waters in the middle of a hurricane, or hiding out in a muddy ditch with a sniper rifle while wearing one of those camouflage helmets with a little bush attached to it.

Really, that just wouldn't work with her hair.

Kidding.

Okay, mostly kidding.

In her six years with the Bureau, Jessica had known only one person who'd planned to try out for HRT: a guy in her training class who'd been recruited for the FBI directly from the Army Rangers. And not to dwell on the past or anything—another good theme for this year—but she and that guy in her training class had . . . well, one might say they hadn't exactly seen eye-to-eye.

Or, one might also say that he'd irritated the hell out of her.

Hey, look at me, watch me fly through this obstacle course with one hand and two feet tied behind my back. This is child's play to what we did in the Rangers, bitches!

All right, fine. Possibly, those hadn't been his *exact* words, but there was no doubt that he'd relished being the shining star of their training class.

Fortunately, *that* guy was far away now, undoubtedly already headquartered at Quantico with the rest of the Hostage Rescue Team. And as for this other guy she would be partnered up with, the one from the organized crime squad, if her new SAC swore by him, that was good enough for her.

As the new girl in town, frankly, she didn't have the luxury of *not* being a team player with this.

She finished her meeting with Nick and agreed she would drop by his office at ten A.M. the next morning to discuss the Jacksonville assignment in more detail once she'd reviewed the file. The rest of her day flew by in a whirlwind of introductions, a meeting with her new squad leader, and a tour of the entire complex. In Los Angeles, the FBI had shared the Wilshire Federal Building with several other government offices, but here in Chicago, they had the whole place to themselves.

By the end of the day, she was exhausted from all the nice-to-meet-you small talk, and she still hadn't had time to review the Jacksonville file. She grabbed it on her way out of the office, and, figuring she would make a working dinner out of it, she picked up a salad from the Green Door Tavern, a pub just around the corner from her place.

Salad and briefcase in hand, she walked into the lobby of her high-rise building.

Luther, one of the doormen, grinned from behind his desk. "Agent Harlow. How'd the first day go? Catch any serial killers?"

When she'd moved into the building last week, she'd made a point of introducing herself to all the doormen. Luther, in his early sixties, had been very interested in her job—so much so that she didn't have the heart to tell him that the life of an FBI agent wasn't quite the same as that depicted on TV and in the movies.

"Mostly just paperwork and introductions," she said.

"Ah, well. Tomorrow is another day." He pushed the button that unlocked the glass door leading to the elevators.

Before heading up, Jessica made a pit stop at her mailbox. In addition to the usual junk mail and bills, there was a FedEx envelope inside. She pulled it out and saw that it was from her lawyer's office in California.

She tucked the envelope into her briefcase, along with the rest of the mail, and then locked her mailbox and headed for the elevators. After letting herself into her condo, she set the briefcase and salad on top of the breakfast table in her living room that doubled as her dining area and office.

In the bedroom, she ditched her work clothes for a T-shirt

and jeans. She headed next for the wine chiller in her kitchen and cracked open the most expensive bottle she owned.

Because, screw it.

She knew exactly what was in that FedEx envelope, and she figured she might as well cap off the end of an era—her last remaining connection to Los Angeles—with a good glass of wine.

Settling in at the table, she took the envelope out of her briefcase and opened it. *For your records*, said the Post-it note from her lawyer. She had called on Friday, after the court appearance, so it wasn't as if Jessica hadn't been expecting this. But seeing the words in black and white, and actually holding the papers in her hands, made it that much more official.

JUDGMENT FOR DISSOLUTION OF MARRIAGE

There it was, the court's order and the signed settlement agreement between her and Alex that had been incorporated into the judgment. As divorces went—especially in L.A.—this probably had been the easiest money Jessica's lawyer had ever made. From start to finish, the process had been completely civil. She hadn't wanted any maintenance from Alex, nor had she sought any part of the profits from the films he'd produced during their three-year marriage. All she'd taken, aside from the stuff that had been hers before they'd gotten married, were the clothes, shoes, and jewelry he'd bought her. And even that wasn't out of spite, more a matter of practicality since Alex obviously had no use for them.

"Well, at least I'll be a well-dressed divorcée," she'd tried to joke with her best friend, Tara, who'd flown out to L.A. as moral support the weekend after Jessica and Alex's settlement conference. "God, do I actually have to use the word *divorcée*?" she groaned. "It sounds so *Real Housewives*-esque."

They'd been commiserating over cocktails at Norah, an

eclectic American restaurant in West Hollywood. "I don't understand what happened. You guys used to be so crazy about each other," Tara had said.

That was the hardest part of this whole thing. In the beginning, she and Alex *had* been good together. Their whirlwind courtship had been exciting and romantic—they'd met at a restaurant, during a private party hosted by a mutual friend, and when Alex had found out that she was an FBI agent, he'd asked for her opinion on the plot of a suspense thriller script he'd been thinking about optioning. They'd spent the rest of the night talking, grabbing a spot at the bar after the party broke up and staying until the place closed. He'd asked if he could see her again the next day, and then just like that they were dating, and she'd loved the fact that he'd refreshingly played *no* games. Back then, their differing professional worlds had been a good thing: He'd liked the fact that she wasn't in "the industry," and she, in turn, had found his insider stories about Hollywood to be a fun change of pace from the seriousness she often faced on the job.

The problems began about a year into their marriage. At first, it was little things, like the fact that she never particularly warmed to his friends, whom they saw *a lot*. They were all film producers, and they barely spoke to Jessica, having zero interest in anyone or anything not connected to Hollywood. That she could handle—she'd married Alex, not his friends, and she could deal with a few douchebags for the man she loved. But more troubling was the way *Alex* changed when he was around them, going from a man who was wry and witty and passionate about films to a guy who was arrogant, concerned with appearances, and far more interested in trading snarky insults about actors, writers, and directors with his friends than actually discussing anything substantive.

In the end, however, it was her career, not his, that became the problem. She began handling undercover investigations and had a lot of success on that front. She genuinely enjoyed it, too, the seeds of her desire to work undercover probably having been planted when she was eight years old and had become obsessed with *Wonder Woman* reruns, the budding feminist in her loving it every time the bad guys made the sorry mistake of ever underestimating Diana Prince.

Now if only the FBI could invent a Lasso of Truth she could pair with her pantsuits . . .

The one downside to undercover work, of course, was its unpredictability. A lot of her meetings occurred in the evenings and were set up on very short notice. She'd had to cancel dinner plans with Alex on several occasions, and, once, a vacation they'd planned to Cabo San Lucas. She'd felt terrible about that and had tried to reschedule the trip, but shortly afterward Alex began filming a movie in Toronto and somehow it just fell by the wayside.

The final straw broke eight months ago. She'd been asked to help out with an investigation into a Los Angeles city councilmember who they suspected was taking bribes for his reelection campaign. As part of that, she and a male undercover agent pretended to be a couple while attending several of the councilmember's fundraisers, so they could observe which donors were getting extra-special treatment.

From the start, Alex had been against her involvement in the investigation. "Are you sure you're just *pretending* to be a couple?" he'd asked, right before one of the fundraisers, leaning against the bedroom door and watching as she'd zipped up her dress.

"Of course it's just pretending." He'd asked the same question before the last fundraiser, and she was trying not to be insulted by whatever he was implying. He made movies, for Pete's sake—his whole business was about playing pretend.

Not wanting to have this fight right then, she zipped up the dress and smiled at him, going for a joke. "How do I look? Hopefully not like an undercover agent."

His eyes trailed over her. "I didn't buy you that dress so you could wear it with another man," he said coolly.

Right.

Apparently, long gone were the days when he'd *liked* seeing her get dressed up. She'd stepped out of the dress, leaving it on the bedroom floor and not saying another word as she changed into something else and then left.

Unfortunately, her assignment ran longer than expected, and the timing couldn't have been worse. One of Alex's films opened two weeks after the dress fight, and because she was still working undercover in a high-profile investigation, she had to bail on attending the premiere.

"There'll be paparazzi everywhere—I can't risk that someone would see my photo and remember me at one of these fundraisers. I'm so sorry, Alex." She was upset, too—of course she wanted to be with him on such a special occasion. But nothing she said seemed to make any difference; he was so angry he barely spoke to her for two days.

The night of the premiere he stayed out late, attending a party for the cast and crew. She waited up for him, wanting to get all the details, but when he got home he was in a subdued mood, said he didn't feel like talking.

After that, they never seemed to be able to get back on track. The tension between them increased, until finally, one morning over breakfast, she suggested they go to marriage counseling.

"I've already called a divorce lawyer," Alex said, not looking her in the eye.

She went quiet for a long moment, her throat tightening with emotion. "Fine. I'll move out this weekend, then." She stood up from the table, carrying her dishes to the sink.

"Jess, you don't have to—"

"Oh, I think I do, Alex." She cut him off sarcastically, wiping the tears off her cheeks as she left the room.

Jessica tucked the court order back into the envelope and set it off to the side.

Enough of the pity party, Harlow.

Her eyes fell on the Jacksonville case file inside her briefcase. This undercover role was exactly what she needed—something she could sink her teeth into. A distraction. After spending the last six months wondering how things had gone wrong in her marriage, it would be nice to just turn off that side of her brain for a while.

So she cracked open the case file and settled in at the table with her glass of screw-it-I'm-officially-a-divorcée wine as she began to take notes.

Time to show these boys in the Chicago office what she was made of.

3 ❧

When John walked into the office Tuesday morning, he found a small crowd of his squad mates waiting around his cubicle.

"Look who's back," Ryan said, doing a slow clap as John approached. "So? Was it as bad as they say?"

"Worse," John said. And he had the aching muscles to prove it, too. In the shower this morning, he'd cursed up a storm just trying to raise his arms to wash his hair.

"Was it nonstop drills?" asked Jin, another one of his squad mates.

"Let's just say they set the tone the first morning by waking us up at four A.M. for physical fitness tests. Swimming, running, and stair climbing while wearing a fifty-pound vest and carrying a thirty-five-pound battering ram—with no breaks in between. And that was the easy day," John said.

The Hostage Rescue Team selection process, as John and his fellow "selectees" had quickly discovered, was designed to break down the candidates both mentally and physically in order to identify the individuals who would perform the best in high-pressure situations. And indeed, the exercises and drills they'd been put through were no joke. During the course of two weeks,

John had scaled a narrow ladder to a grate seventy feet above the ground and crawled up the outside of a four-story building with no net to break his fall. He'd walked blindfolded underwater for seventy-five feet while carrying a thirty-pound weight, participated in a simulated hostage rescue in a shoot house while the evaluators observed him from an overhead catwalk, slept in cramped tents and barracks for no more than one or two hours each night, and been put through the "dog run," a training exercise where candidates ran with a large raft to a lake and paddled their asses off toward a target point while a helicopter flew low over the water to slow them down.

In other words, it had been two weeks of hell.

And John had thrived on it.

Still feeling like a fool for not knowing that his girlfriend and friend had been screwing around behind his back, he'd shown up for Selection angry and with a lot of energy to burn. But from that very first morning when the HRT evaluators had woken him up at four o'clock and told him to strap on a fifty-pound vest for a little "light" exercise, he'd stopped thinking about the shitty state of his personal life. Instead, he'd fallen back on his Ranger training, concentrating only on two things: (1) surviving and (2) executing the orders he was given to the best of his ability.

He had no idea what the evaluators had thought of him. To further mess with their heads, the candidates—who were known only by the number on their clothes, not by name—weren't given any feedback, positive or negative, during the entire process. But in some sense, it didn't matter. John had set out to prove something to Piser by showing up for HRT tryouts, but maybe he'd needed to prove something to himself, too.

And when he'd stood there at the end of those two weeks, sweaty, starving, exhausted, and with his muscles screaming in agony, but still ready to take on any other shit the evaluators wanted to throw at him, he'd felt surprisingly good. Spending fourteen days in constant crisis mode tended to put things in perspective, he supposed.

"Well, we're glad to have you back." Ryan grabbed John's shoulder in camaraderie. "And I think I speak for all of us when I say"—he feigned a quizzical expression—"Dude, what happened to your *hair*?"

The rest of the group laughed as John grinned and ran a hand through it. "Thought it was time to change up the look." Normally, he wore his hair a little longer, seeing how it was tough to play an organized crime thug if one looked suspiciously like a clean-cut FBI agent. But since having his hair in his face for two straight weeks of drills was never a smart idea, and ponytails didn't work with the combat helmets, he'd trimmed off a few inches before leaving for HRT tryouts.

Jin pretended to wipe away a tear. "But . . . I didn't even get to say good-bye to the man bun."

"Still with that?" John asked dryly. *One* time he'd made the mistake of wearing his hair tied back in a knot to work, and, boy, had his squad mates ever had a field day with that. For two damn weeks, all he'd heard was *Rapunzel! Rapunzel! Let down your hair!* every time he'd walked into the office.

Fortunately, all color commentary about his hair fell by the wayside when Brandon, a younger agent who'd recently joined their squad, walked over with a grin. "Guess who I just rode the elevator with?"

"The director?" Ryan quipped.

"The new agent," Brandon said.

Immediately, he had the group's full attention.

"And are the rumors true?" Jared asked eagerly.

"Do we have visual confirmation that she's cute?" Ryan wanted to know.

Brandon leaned against the cubicle, clearly enjoying having the inside scoop. "Indeed, we do."

John was obviously out of the loop. "Who are you guys talking about?"

"That's right, you were off yesterday," Brandon said. "A new undercover agent joined the public corruption squad. Rumor is she's a former lawyer—I heard she was giving Sam Wilkins crap about going to Yale."

"What is it with these former attorneys and their law schools?" Ryan nudged John. "Hey, how many postgraduate degrees does it take for a white-collar-crime agent to figure out how to use his pistol?"

John feigned surprise. "They let white-collar-crime agents carry pistols?"

He grinned as the rest of the agents cracked up. Yes, it was an old joke. And in truth, there were a lot of really good agents on the public corruption and other white-collar crime squads. Even the former lawyers, John could acknowledge, despite the fact that some of them seemed to fancy themselves a little more refined and intellectual than everyone else.

Not that he was biased against former-lawyer types.

Okay, maybe he was a *little* biased.

There'd been this one woman he'd met at the Academy, a former lawyer who'd worked at one of Chicago's top firms before joining the FBI. She and John were the only two trainees in their class from Chicago, and, normally, one might've assumed their local connection would foster some camaraderie between them.

But in this case, not so much.

Because in this case, said former lawyer had been a real pain in the ass.

Ooh, look at me, I'm soooo smart with my Stanford law degree. I should be teaching these classes instead of sitting here with the rest of you schmucks.

All right, maybe she hadn't said those *exact* words, but that had been the gist of her attitude. She was smart and quick on her feet, and a natural at interrogations, and there was no doubt that she'd been the shining star of their training class.

And she'd loved rubbing his face in it every chance she got.

Fortunately, *that* woman was across the country in Los Angeles, undoubtedly impressing the entire office with her wondrous brilliance or whatever.

"Any other intel on the new agent?" Ryan asked Brandon. "Like, whether she's single?"

"Going straight to that question, are you?" John said to Ryan.

"Hey, have pity on those of us who don't already have a gorgeous girlfriend waiting at home," Ryan shot back.

Right. John cleared his throat, adding "drop vague hints to co-workers about not seeing Alicia anymore" to his mental to-do list.

"Did you at least get the new agent's name?" Jin asked.

"As a matter of fact, I did. It's—" Brandon trailed off, looking sheepish as their squad leader, Special Agent Reece Gunnar, approached the group.

"As much as I hate to break up the sewing circle, gentlemen," Gunnar said wryly, "Shepherd here has a meeting with the SAC to get to."

This was news to John. "I do?"

"I just got off the phone with him, and he asked me to send you up." Gunnar's gaze settled on John's newly shorn hair, and the corners of his mouth curved. "Aw. Just when the man bun was starting to grow on me."

John looked up at the ceiling, shaking his head.

Seriously. *One* time.

At the end of the hallway on the twelfth floor, the assistant to the Special Agent in Charge waved John through from behind her desk.

"You can go in. Mr. McCall is expecting you," she said.

Nick looked up from his computer when John knocked on the door. "Agent Shepherd. Either you made it all the way through Selection—in which case, hats off to you—or you flunked out and have been on a very *un*authorized vacation these past few days."

John took a seat in front of the desk. "If that was a vacation, I really need to find a new travel agent."

Nick chuckled. "When do you find out if you made the team?"

"A few weeks." During his outbriefing, John had learned there were several steps to the decision-making process. *If* he'd earned the recommendation of the HRT operators, his candidacy would then be passed up the chain for approval by both the Bureau's Tactical Section and the Mid-Level Leadership Selection Unit.

"And when would you report to NOTS?"

NOTS, or New Operator Training School, was the eight-month-long program held every year at Quantico for new HRT recruits. "The Tuesday after Labor Day."

Nick nodded. "Then we'll keep you off any long-term investigations until you hear from headquarters. I spoke with Gunnar, and he says you have plenty of reports you can catch up with now that you're no longer traveling to Detroit every week."

John pictured the huge stack of paperwork waiting on his desk.

Probably, he'd rather be starved and tortured for another two weeks.

Nick grinned. "I had a feeling that would be your reaction. So I took the liberty of assigning you to a short-term investigation. Assuming you don't mind traveling again." He grabbed a file off his desk and handed it to John. "The Jacksonville office needs two Chicago agents to help out with a sting op. This one is a little different from your usual roles."

Intrigued by that, John took the file from Nick and opened

it. He quickly skimmed the summary provided by the case agents. "A private equity investor? That is a new one for me."

"I figured we should let you have a little fun, seeing how this could be your last undercover assignment."

Last undercover assignment. The words were a little bittersweet. "I see the sting op calls for two investors," John said.

"You'll be partnered with an agent from the public corruption squad. She's new—just transferred in yesterday." Nick checked his watch. "She should be here any moment, actually. I asked her to meet us this morning, so we could go over the details of the assignment."

Interesting . . . the new agent. Meaning, presumably, the new *cute* agent. John could only imagine the looks on his squad mates' faces when they heard about this. "Where'd she transfer from?" he asked conversationally.

"Los Angeles. But like you, Chicago is her hometown—which makes you both perfect for this job. Without even faking it, you two can wax poetic about deep-dish pizza, why the Cubs are America's team, and how putting ketchup on a hot dog should be a federal offense."

Hell yes, it should be, but John was focused on something else his boss had just said. "She worked in the L.A. office?"

"For the last six years." Nick cocked his head. "That puts her right around your year, doesn't it?"

Oh, indeed . . . it did. Which meant this was all either one hell of a coincidence, or John was about to come face-to-face with the one person who'd not only managed to get under his skin at the Academy but also succeeded in making him look like a total jackass.

Purposely.

Nick looked over at the doorway and smiled. "Ah. Perfect timing. We were just talking about you. Agent Harlow, I'd like you to meet Special Agent John Shepherd, your fellow 'shady Chicago business entrepreneur.'"

John closed his eyes momentarily, then stood up and turned around.

There she was, standing in the doorway with her tailored gray pantsuit and heels, looking sleek and stylish and so perfectly white-collar-crime-esque.

Her hair was different, he noticed. Still a warm blond, but instead of the long ponytails she'd favored at the Academy, it now fell to her shoulders in a straight, sophisticated cut.

"John," she said, her light blue eyes widening in surprise.

"Hello, Jessica."

Nearly fifteen thousand special agents in the FBI, spread throughout the United States in fifty-six field offices, and *she* had to show up in Chicago for what was quite possibly his last undercover assignment.

As his new partner.

And here he'd thought HRT tryouts had been hell.

4

John Shepherd.

Admittedly, Jessica was caught off guard at the sight of him in her new boss's office. For one thing, he was supposed to be in Quantico, already part of the Hostage Rescue Team and at this very moment engaged in a live-fire close-quarter battle exercise, or scaling a burning ten-story building. Probably while inverted and holding on to the bricks only by his pinky toes, just for extra kicks.

And for another thing, *wow*, he looked different from the last time she'd seen him.

Six years ago, John Shepherd had shown up at the FBI Academy looking every bit the former Army Ranger. With military-short hair, cobalt-blue eyes, and six feet, four inches of ripped muscles, he'd had the kind of clean-cut, all-American good looks that belonged on a Wheaties box.

But the man standing before her seemed . . . grittier. Gone was the buzz cut; instead he wore his deep gold hair in a semi-unkempt, textured style that was a bit longer and choppier. Also gone, apparently, was his razor—at least judging from the week's growth of scruff along his strong jawline.

No tie, she noticed. And an open-necked shirt underneath

his suit jacket. Technically, both were violations of the FBI dress code.

Just saying.

"Isn't this a coincidence?" she said, recovering from her surprise and putting on a smile for the benefit of her new boss as she walked into the office.

From behind his desk, Nick pointed between her and John. "Do you two know each other?"

"Jessica and I were in the same class at the Academy," John explained. From the easygoing nature of his tone, he, too, didn't intend to let the SAC in on their little personality clash.

"Funny. Small world, huh?" Nick asked.

"It sure is," John said.

"You can say that again," Jessica agreed, at the same time.

They looked at each other and chuckled, as if this were all *just so funny*. Ha ha ha, good times . . . Yeah, it would be a miracle if they made it through this assignment without throttling each other.

"So," Nick said, clapping his hands. "Since you two are already acquainted, I think we can just dive right in. Jessica, if you've had a chance to review the case file, why don't you bring John up to speed?"

"Of course." She refocused her less-than-equanimous feelings for the person sitting next to her and got down to the task at hand. She was a professional, after all, and an experienced undercover agent to boot. She could fake playing nice with the best of them.

Although she noted, for the record, that this dirty-hot, I-hang-with-unsavory-types look John had going on hardly screamed *private equity investor*.

And she also noted, for the record, that she was glad there was not, in fact, an actual record of her thinking of John Shepherd as *dirty-hot*.

Moving on.

"The target is Patrick Blair, mayor of Jacksonville, Florida," she began. "The son of a high school teacher and a Navy lieutenant, Blair attended law school at the University of Florida and, at age twenty-six, became the youngest city councilmember in Jacksonville history. The report the case agents sent over didn't include a photograph, so I snagged one off the Internet this morning." She handed one over to John. "A copy for your convenience, Agent Shepherd."

In response to her sweet tone, he threw her a look so dark and scowly she expected to hear an ominous boom of thunder outside.

Trust me, big guy. The feeling's mutual.

"Four years later, Blair ran for mayor and lost by only three thousand votes to a retired judge running on a nonpartisan ballot," she continued. "He then ran again in the next election with a campaign that emphasized his experience on the council and focused on Jacksonville's economic growth. He won that race, becoming the second-youngest mayor of a top-twenty U.S. city. His popularity continued to rise, particularly after he sponsored legislation designed to revitalize key neighborhoods through investment by the private sector, and earlier this year he was reelected to a second term by a whopping eighty-five percent of the vote. By all accounts he's quite charismatic and is especially popular among female voters." Jessica smiled. "I'm sure that has nothing do with the fact that he's single and was recently included in *People* magazine's 'Sexiest Politicians Alive' edition."

John snorted, flipping through the file on his lap. "So what's the catch?"

"The catch is that Jacksonville's golden boy is running a side business: taking bribes in exchange for political favors," she said. "The investigation started eighteen months ago, after a local lobbyist approached agents in the Jacksonville office with a tip that another lobbyist, Anthony Morano, was arranging bribes for the mayor. The tip turned out to be a good one, and after two agents visited Morano at home and had a chat with him about the advantages of cooperating with the FBI when one has been caught conspiring to engage in honest services fraud, he flipped on Blair and agreed to wear a wire.

"Through that, the Jacksonville agents learned that Blair has several real estate developers lining his pockets. And we're not talking penny-ante stuff here; these guys are paying Blair upwards of fifty grand a pop in exchange for his assistance with various zoning and permit issues. It's a nice little arrangement: For the right price, Blair makes a few phone calls to his friends on the city's Land Use Committee and, voilà, all the red tape and delays the developer would normally face magically disappear."

"Is there any evidence these other city officials are on the take?" John asked, his eyes meeting Jessica's.

She paused, flashing back six years to the many times she'd seen that focused, determined gleam in his blue eyes. Except, around her, that look typically had been accompanied by an irritated tightening of his jaw.

Ah, yes. *There* it was.

"That was one of the questions I asked Agent Leavitt in Jacksonville when I called this morning to introduce myself," Jessica said. "He says that, to their knowledge, Blair's the only crooked one of the bunch. There's no evidence that the other city officials are aware he's making money off this scheme— from their perspective, they're just helping out the mayor when he asks for a favor. Basically, being politicians."

"Do they have an estimate of how much bribe money Blair has raked in so far?" Nick asked Jessica.

"Around five hundred thousand. But the one concern the U.S. Attorney's office raised as a potential trial issue is the fact that, so far, all the individuals with firsthand knowledge of the bribes—Morano, plus the developers who've paid Blair off—are part of the scheme themselves. Once the arrests are made, we know how this will shake out: These guys will all turn on Blair in exchange for a deal. Which, while helpful, also leaves them open to impeachment on cross-examination that they're just saying what the government wants in order to save their own skins."

"An issue that's far less of a concern if the U.S. Attorney's office *also* has testimony against Blair by two undercover agents with firsthand knowledge of the scheme," Nick said.

"Cue the two 'shady Chicago business entrepreneurs,'" John said.

Exactly. "The specifics of the assignment are all there," Jessica said, pointing to the file John held. "You and I will pose as partners from a successful Chicago-based private equity firm interested in opening a restaurant in Jacksonville. Morano will set up a meeting with the mayor, under the guise that we'd like to discuss a few zoning and permitting issues with a property we have our eye on for the project. Then we go from there."

Nick rested his forearms on the desk. "I've already informed the Jacksonville office of your potential time restrictions," he told John. "They've assured me that you and Jessica will be able to wrap this up in a handful of trips. Frankly, either Blair takes the bait or he doesn't."

"I'll get started on my undercover legend right away," John said.

"Good." Nick grinned. "By the way, when I spoke to the SAC down in Jacksonville, he mentioned that, as part of your cover, they're going to put you up at some swanky hotel on Ponte Vedra Beach. So when you two are drinking mai tais by the ocean and swapping stories about the good old days at the Academy, don't forget who you can thank for this assignment."

Jessica and John laughed along as if that were just so darn *hilarious*. Ha ha, chuckle chuckle, ah . . . the "good old days" at the Academy.

Yeah, they were so screwed.

5

John left the SAC's office alone, seizing the opportunity to make his escape when Nick held Jessica back to ask how her first day had gone.

He headed straight for the elevators and jabbed at the down button a little harder than necessary. Staring at the closed elevator doors, he mimicked her confident voice in his head.

That was one of the questions I asked Agent Leavitt in Jacksonville when I called this morning to introduce myself.

Of course she'd already taken charge and called the Jacksonville agents to introduce herself. And of course she already knew the case backward and forward despite the fact that she'd worked in the Chicago office for all of about, oh, five damn minutes. That was Jessica Harlow doing her Jessica Harlow thing, because she put the *special* in *special agent*.

Sure.

"Shepherd."

Speak of the devil.

Steeling himself, he turned around and smiled as she approached. "Yes, Agent Harlow. How can I be of service?"

In response to his dry tone, she threw him a glare so cold it could've frozen all nine circles of Dante's Hell. Fittingly, just nine of the many places he would rather be than stuck working with her on this investigation.

"Look, I'm not thrilled about this, either." Keeping her voice low, she came to a stop next to him at the elevator bank. "I thought you were supposed to be on the Hostage Rescue Team already."

"And I thought you were supposed to be in L.A."

There was a quick flash in her eyes before she shrugged off his question. "Change of plans."

The elevator arrived at their floor, and they both stepped inside. She hit the button for the seventh floor, where the public corruption squad was located. Standing on the opposite side, he pressed the button for floor five.

They faced off as the doors shut. She folded her arms across her chest and studied him with those crystalline blue eyes that could so cleverly mask her emotions.

As he knew well.

"We're going to have to figure this out," she said. "We're supposed to be business partners in this."

Thank you, yes, being a *professional*, he was aware of that. He took a step closer. "It's called 'undercover' work, Harlow. If I can pretend to be a gun-buying, murder-for-hire thug, I think I can handle playing some rich investor type who wants to skirt a few measly zoning laws." Even a rich investor type who was apparently masochistic enough to get in bed with the likes of *her*.

Professionally speaking.

"Measly zoning laws?" she repeated.

Ooh, now he'd gone and pissed her off. How nice it was, really, that they could pick up like this, right where they'd left off.

She drew in closer, tilting her head back to meet his gaze. He was over a foot taller than her, although he noticed that she was heightening a bit with those expensive-looking three-inch heels she wore.

"Our target in this investigation is the mayor of the thirteenth-largest city in the United States. That's a pretty big deal in my book." She gestured to his facial scruff and hair. "And while I appreciate that this . . . *Sons of Anarchy* motif you've got going might ingratiate you with the gun-buying, murder-for-hire, organized crime thugs of the world, that's not quite going to fly with this sting operation."

"'Thirteenth-largest city in the United States'?" he scoffed. "Just how many hours did you spend reviewing the case files last night?"

She smiled sweetly as the elevator arrived at her floor. "Enough to get the jump on you."

Then the doors sprang open, and she gave him a friendly wave, once again stepping into the role of Ms. Congeniality. "So glad we got to catch up like this, Agent Shepherd. We'll talk again soon."

He watched her stride confidently down the hallway as the elevator doors closed between them.

Enough to get the jump on you.

Not for long, sweetheart.

Time for him to get cracking on that case file.

"*The* Ponte Vedra Inn and Club? Sounds nice," Tara said, from the living room. "Do they have a spa?"

In the bedroom, Jessica looked herself over in the mirror attached to her closet door. "They do, but I doubt I'll get to use it."

"Hey, if you're supposed to be a successful businesswoman, then I say you get to do it up," Tara called back.

Tempting, although Jessica doubted the old *But my character needed a warm bamboo massage* excuse would fly with the Bureau's bean counters in Pocatello, Idaho, where the finance division responsible for travel reimbursements was located. And now that she was single again, and living on a government salary, trips to a five-star resort spa weren't exactly in her personal budget.

She paused while looking into the mirror, suddenly remembering her twenty-ninth birthday, when Alex had arranged for her to have a whole day of services at a Beverly Hills day spa. They'd just gotten married and were still very much in the honeymoon phase, and when she'd come home eight hours later he'd acted like she'd been gone for eight weeks instead. With a hungry gleam in his eyes, he'd greeted her at the door with two glasses of sparkling wine and then had proceeded to strip off her—

Well. Anyway. No use crying over spilled Prosecco.

Taking a deep breath, she put on a smile and headed into the living room. "So. First impressions are key with these undercover ops. With that in mind, does this outfit say 'private equity director' to you?"

While holding her glass of wine, Tara took in Jessica's tan skirt suit and cream short-sleeve sweater. "Honey, that outfit doesn't say much of anything. More like it politely whispers, 'Hi, I'm boring.'" She cocked her head. "And possibly a little sexually frustrated."

Jessica gave her a look. *Ha ha.* Although that last part wasn't entirely off the mark. "Remember, these are business meetings I'm going to."

"Yeah, but suits like that are for lawyers and accountants. If you're supposed to be an entrepreneur, you need something that's professional, but with a little more flash."

Fair enough. "Hold on, I think I know just the thing." Jessica headed back into her bedroom. Probably, she was over-analyzing her wardrobe choices for this Jacksonville assignment. It was doubtful, particularly in a group of men, that anyone would notice if her character was dressed more conservatively than was the norm in the private equity world. But when it came to undercover work, she was something of a perfectionist, even with the smallest details. If *she* knew something was off, it didn't matter whether anyone else noticed.

"Lucky you, to be assigned such a fun investigation in your first week," Tara said from the living room. "Sounds like the Chicago FBI crew has welcomed you with open arms."

An image of John's scowling expression popped into her head. *It's called "undercover" work, Harlow.*

No shit, Sherlock.

"Most of them, anyway," she grumbled.

As she was belting her jacket, Tara popped her head in the doorway and nodded approvingly at the black slim-fit suit and fuchsia silk sleeveless top Jessica had changed into. "Now that, I like."

"I got it on sale at Saks." The three-quarter-length sleeves of the jacket and skinny fuchsia belt were too trendy for her to wear to work, but she'd picked it up for social events since it was one of those rare outfits that covered her pistol and was actually cute.

Tara took a seat on the bed. "Why did you say 'most' of the Chicago office has welcomed you? Did something happen?"

Jessica yanked the skinny belt out of its loops as she started to undress. Something had happened, all right—or better yet, some*one*. "It's not a big deal. Just this guy from my class at the Academy who hates me. Which is fine, since I'm not his biggest fan, either."

"A guy from the Academy?" Tara cocked her head. "You mean John Shepherd?"

Jessica pulled back in surprise. "How do you know his name?"

"Um, because you talked about him in quite a few e-mails you sent me while you were training."

"'Quite a few'?" Jessica scoffed, thinking that was definitely an exaggeration. "I mean, I suppose I might have mentioned him offhandedly once or twice . . ."

"Former Army Ranger, right? From Chicago, you said? Blond hair, blue eyes, built like Thor—"

"Great, so you're familiar," Jessica cut in brightly, figuring they were getting a little off track here. "The point is, he's back. Well, technically, I'm the one who's back, but regardless, he works in the Chicago office now and as luck would have it"— and by *luck*, she meant a cruel, evil twist of fate—"he's my partner in this undercover assignment."

Tara's eyes widened. "Really?" She started laughing. "How's that going to work?"

"I'll let you know as soon as I figure it out myself," Jessica muttered, as her cell phone chimed with a new text message. She walked over to the nightstand, picked up her phone, and saw that the message was from her brother, Finn.

You do NOT want to date a surgeon. Huge egos.

Her sister, Maya, also included in the group message, responded almost immediately. Your guy drives a Maserati. Yeah, he's real salt of the earth.

Jessica set her phone back down on the nightstand. Her two older siblings had been going back and forth like this all day. And while she normally was happy to join in the fray, on this particular subject she'd been adopting more of a keep-quiet-and-run-for-cover approach. "Maya and Finn are fighting over which one of them gets to set me up on a blind date."

Tara took a sip of her wine. "And how do you feel about that?"

"Eh, after thirty-two years, I'm used to all the bickering between those two. I think it's a twin thing."

Tara looked at her over her glass. "I meant, how do you feel about going on a date?"

Yes, Jessica got that, she'd just been going for a little humor. A deflection tool, her psychologist mother would say, along with her tendency to get a wee bit sarcastic when feeling defensive. "The divorce is final, so I guess it's time to get back out there." *Slowly* get out there, she emphasized in her head, while taking a seat on the bed next to Tara. "But a setup with one of these alleged Mr. Perfects my brother and sister want me to meet seems so . . . official." She jokingly rolled her eyes. "Plus, what if I actually like one of the guys? For the rest of my life, I'd have to live with the acknowledgment that either Finn or Maya was right."

Sweetie, you're deflecting again.

I know, Mom, thanks.

"You already know what I'm going to tell you," Tara said. "The hell with Mr. Perfect. You should be having fun right now, with some hot Mr. Wrong that you will shamelessly use for dirty, no-strings-attached rebound sex until you both realize your time together has run its course and part ways on guilt-free, wholly amicable terms."

"This actually happens?" Jessica asked.

"I've been told, in theory, this can happen." With a smile, Tara reached over and squeezed Jessica's hand. "So we'll take this in baby steps. We'll set you up on Tinder, you'll start with a few coffee dates, maybe drinks, and you'll go from there. It'll be good to get back out there, right?"

Actually . . . Jessica was starting to feel a little pumped. Maybe this *could* be fun. She'd never really played the field much, so this was her chance to live it up, enjoy her new single status, and get back into the proverbial saddle again. Besides, after the last six months spent feeling guilty, hurt, and wondering where her marriage had gone wrong, she could use a little fun in her life. "Yes. I *like* this plan," she told Tara. "But there's just one thing: I can't be on Tinder while working undercover. Or Match or anything like that. It'd be too risky to have my photo up on one of those sites with my real name."

Tara blinked. "Right. Of course." She sat back. "No online dating, then. Huh."

When she said nothing further, looking perplexed, Jessica

laughed. "Oh, come on. Dating can't have changed *that* much in the last four years. I mean, people do still meet each other without the help of dating websites and social discovery apps, right?"

Tara nodded slowly. "Sure . . . I've been told that can happen. In theory."

So not an encouraging response.

After Tara left, Jessica changed into her pajamas and settled in for some fine dining in front of the television: a bowl of Rice Krispies and the last glass of her screw-it-I'm-officially-a-divorcée wine. Remembering that she'd muted her phone with all the text messages flying between her brother and sister—*MY guy runs marathons; MY guy is a wine collector*—she switched off the "do not disturb" and saw that she had a few new e-mails.

Including one from Special Agent John Shepherd that was all of four words.

We need a website.

Interesting. Seemingly, a certain somebody was working late, reviewing the case file. Correct her if she was wrong, but hadn't that certain somebody just made fun of *her* this morning for doing the same thing?

She immediately wrote him back.

I took the liberty of setting up a meeting with the Stagehand guys for tomorrow at 3:00. Hope that works with your schedule.

Radio silence.

Shrugging off his failure to respond, she set her phone down, picked up her bowl of Rice Krispies, and tried to relax as she watched TV. But she found herself thinking back to something Tara had asked her earlier.

"Remind me: Why didn't you and John get along at the Academy?" Tara had frowned, trying to remember.

"Long story," Jessica had grumbled. A story, one might say, about a valiant, underdog heroine fighting to prove herself in the dog-eat-dog world of the FBI Academy while being continually challenged by a smug, uber-athletic, ex-Ranger villain who thrived on getting on her nerves every step along the way.

At least, that was *mostly* how she remembered it . . .

6

(she said)

Six years ago, Jessica had arrived at the Academy in Quantico feeling proud and excited—but also incredibly nervous. The FBI campus was located on a Marine Corps base, and that first time she'd driven through the double security gates and heard the sounds of gunfire in the distance and spotted a military helicopter flying overhead, there'd been a split second when she'd thought, *What have I gotten myself into?*

Shortly after arriving, she'd learned that she was one of only two women in a class of forty-one agent trainees. On top of that, because she'd applied immediately after graduating from Stanford Law via the FBI's law entry program—and thus had bypassed the minimum requirement of three years' work experience—at twenty-six, she was the youngest member of her class.

"You're a woman. You're fresh out of some fancy Ivy League law school with only a year's worth of job experience. And you're short." In their final meeting before she'd left for Quantico, her recruiter, Special Agent Stan Ross, had ticked off these characteristics on his fingers, looking particularly peevish about the last one. "Not to mention, you look like you just stepped out of a shampoo commercial with all this . . . flowy hair."

She'd smiled because, *aw*, in the eleven months she'd known Ross, that might've been the closest thing to a compliment he'd ever said to her.

He'd given her one of his trademark *I am a year from retirement and stopped suffering fools decades ago* looks, and she'd quickly dropped the smile.

Right. *Thou shalt not preen in the FBI.*

"There are going to be people who won't want to take you seriously. People who see a pretty, young blonde and make assumptions," he'd continued. "So you make them take you seriously. Don't give them any reason to doubt you in the Academy. You go in there, Harlow, and you'd goddamn better show them what you're made of. You do that, and you'll be fine. More than fine, actually."

Shockingly, then, his mouth had curved in a smile—she hadn't been aware those muscles on his face even worked—as he'd held out his hand to shake hers in good-bye. "Welcome to the FBI, Jessica. Now go give 'em hell."

That first day at the Academy, the trainees gathered in an auditorium-style classroom, all dressed in dark business suits. The instructors told them to introduce themselves, talk about their backgrounds, and describe why they wanted to work for the FBI. It was a chance for the trainees to size one another up, and Jessica had been relieved to see that all of them seemed a little nervous and unsure of what to expect.

All of them except one.

She'd noticed John right away—hell, they'd all noticed him right away. Taller and more built than anyone in their class, he was in a league of his own with his broad-shouldered physique and military-short haircut. Unlike the rest of them, who were simply praying they didn't get messed with too much on the first day, he looked confident and calm and ready for anything.

And for some reason, he kept looking at her.

Jessica first noticed it when it was her turn to introduce herself. As she stood before the rest of their class and talked about leaving her job as a lawyer to pursue a career with the FBI, out of the corner of her eye she could see John watching her closely.

Afterward, as they were being led on a tour of the campus, he approached her.

"Chicago, huh?" John winked and leaned in closer. "We should team up, Harlow. I say we take down the three trainees from New York first."

It was a joke; she knew that. And, actually, one of the trainees from New York was some blowhard linguistics PhD who'd bragged about how he spoke fifteen obscure languages or something, and, frankly, she wouldn't mind taking him down a notch or two in the spirit of healthy competition.

But she also remembered what Ross had said. *There are going to be people who won't want to take you seriously.* And she was hyperaware of the fact that, at that very moment, she and John were surrounded by their instructors and classmates, several of whom seemed to be watching them curiously.

She didn't want to be rude to John—at least, at that point she hadn't—but between the looks and the wink and this teasing whisper in her ear, she felt she needed to get something straight. As one of only two women in the class, she had zero interest in starting off her first day by giving people a reason to gossip about the fact that she and the incredibly *hot* former-Ranger trainee appeared to be getting chummy. So she gave John a neutral but polite response, and then she walked away and began chatting up the other female trainee.

Safety in numbers, she figured.

After that first introductory day, she and the other trainees were tossed into the proverbial fire. The program consisted of over eight hundred hours of training divided across four areas of concentration: academics, firearms, case exercises, and operational skills. Trainees, who were evaluated throughout the twenty-one weeks, were required to successfully complete all four parts of the program in order to graduate. Awards were given to the trainees who scored the highest in academics, physical fitness, and firearms.

No doubt, Jessica's strength was the classroom academics portion. As an attorney, she came into the Academy well versed in the fundamentals of law and ethics, and the advanced trial advocacy workshop she'd taken at Stanford, plus the year she'd spent at her firm, gave her a further leg up in interviewing techniques.

As it turned out, she was also pretty darn good at the practical exercises. She felt a rush of adrenaline every time she was handed a new case scenario, mock investigations that she and the other trainees worked from the initial tip all the way through the arrests. Most of the investigations took place at Hogan's Alley, the FBI Academy's mock town that had a hotel, deli, pool hall, post office, several shops, a bank that was "robbed" twice a week, and a whole cast of professional actors playing criminals, witnesses, and bystanders.

Yes, the case scenarios were often stressful, and, yes, occasionally trainees got injured—like the time Jessica learned the hard way, after taking a sharp elbow to the ribs, that some of the actors were told to be difficult and resist arrest in order to make the situation even more realistic. But despite all that, there was just something about being in the field and working an investigation that felt natural to her.

Not quite as natural to her, on the other hand, was the more physical half of the program—specifically, firearms techniques and operational skills. In those two areas, she had to work her butt off just to stay in the game.

If she had to put her finger on it, she'd say that was where the issues between John and her started: during their physical fitness training. Their PT instructors—aka *sadists* dressed in khaki pants and black FBI polos—were charged with the task of getting them into fit enough condition to (a) pass the physical fitness test required of all trainees and (b) withstand the physical rigors of being a special agent.

It was about as much fun as it sounded.

While being lectured and yelled at, Jessica and her classmates did sprints, long-distance runs, push-ups, sit-ups, and pull-ups. They also boxed, learned ground-fighting techniques, and ran the Yellow Brick Road, a six-mile Marine Corps obstacle course over hilly, wooded terrain where trainees climbed walls, scaled rock faces, crawled under barbed wire through the mud, and maneuvered across a cargo net.

Prior to showing up at the Academy, Jessica had run and practiced yoga regularly, and she'd considered herself to be in good physical condition. But the fitness training at Quantico was on a whole different level from any kind of exercising she'd done before. On top of that, *everyone* in her class was in good physical shape—or better. Which meant, at five feet, three inches, she was at a comparative disadvantage as the shortest and smallest among them.

She wouldn't lie; a lot of the days in those first few weeks were hard. Really hard. She would go to bed sore, bruised, and frustrated with herself that she'd finished last once again in some race or sprint, or had been taken down easily in yet another ground fight against one of her fellow trainees.

Because of that, it got a little . . . irksome, sometimes, to see how easy it all was for John. Here she was, constantly pushing herself and considering it a victory if she finished only *second* to last in a physical challenge, while he aced every race, drill, and competition without even breaking a sweat. Which would be all well and good—hey, more power to him—if the guy hadn't been so irritatingly up in her business about the whole thing.

Take, for example, the first time they ran the Yellow Brick

Road together. It was only their second week of training, and they'd been assigned to the same four-person team in a timed competition. So here she was, running up and down rocky terrain, slogging through mud, jumping over fences, and sloshing through cold, dirty creek water—all the while hoping that her stupid tampon wasn't leaking since, for extra fun, she'd gotten her period that day—and the entire time, all she could hear was John's deep, rich voice shouting at her.

Let's go, Harlow!

Step it up, Harlow!

Grab the rope, Harlow!

Pick yourself up, Harlow! Now move, move, MOVE!

For Pete's sake, she was perfectly aware that she was bringing up the rear on their team. Did the man really have to keep announcing it to the whole forest?

Needless to say, by the time they got to the cargo net, she'd been feeling a little testy.

"Maybe you'd rather just tie a rope around my waist and drag me the rest of the way?" Unfortunately, the sting of her sarcasm was lessened by the fact that she was panting so hard she barely got the words out.

Not even winded, John shrugged matter-of-factly. "I was going to suggest throwing you over my shoulder, but if bondage is your thing, Harlow, I'm fine with plan B."

Ha ha, wasn't he such a *riot*? She'd glared at him while climbing onto the cargo net.

Try doing this with cramps, buddy, and then we'll see who's so tough.

And then she'd dug even deeper to finish the course as strong as possible.

Or, take another example: that time, in their fourth week, when John had decided to single her out in front of their entire class during a physical fitness training session. Their instructor had been pulled out of the session to take an emergency phone call, so he'd asked John to supervise the sit-ups drill in his place.

And, man, had John ever eaten that up with a spoon.

"Get your back perpendicular to the ground, Harlow; otherwise the repetition doesn't count. And stop moving those hips," he'd barked, walking by her.

She'd shot him a dirty look, because, really? Was that necessary? She already had a whole slew of instructors telling her everything she was doing wrong; she could do without his voice chiming into the chorus.

Ultimately, though, it was the firing range where the low-simmering tension between them heated up into a full-fledged boil.

She didn't start out completely inexperienced with guns. In preparation for the Academy, she'd taken a class at a shooting range outside Chicago, as well as some individual lessons. But she certainly wasn't the best shooter at the beginning of the program—heck, she probably wasn't even in the top ten—and their instructors made it clear that the firearms portion was where the vast majority of trainees flunked out.

No pressure there.

Her class was at an outdoor shooting range that day, all of them positioned side-by-side in a line as they fired at targets fifteen yards away. By happenstance, she stood next to John, and, for whatever reason, she was having a particularly tough time hitting the target that afternoon. Probably, she was exhausted, and on top of that her increasing frustration wasn't helping her accuracy.

As she was reloading her Glock, she heard John's voice from her left.

"You're anticipating the blast and flinching when the shot fires. Plus, your stance is wrong," he said matter-of-factly.

Gee, thanks for the tip. She slapped the magazine into place, thinking she'd just ignore him and talk to an instructor after the session, when John suddenly moved in close.

Real close.

He rested his hand on her shoulder. "Spread your legs and lean into it," he said, standing behind her.

When the trainee on her right—the blowhard PhD from New York—snickered at John's words, Jessica blushed. *Great.* Now *this* was all she'd needed today. Feeling oddly unsettled by the weight of John's palm on her skin, she jerked away from him. "Hey. Easy there, big guy."

John pulled back, as if surprised by her tone, and then his expression hardened. "Don't flatter yourself, Harlow," he said. "I was just trying to help. But if you want to keep on sucking at this, hey, that's your prerogative."

Jessica blinked.

Right.

Not wanting to make a further scene, she forced herself to maintain a cool expression as John returned his spot. Without batting an eye, he fired off six rounds that hit the dead center of his target.

"Oh, I bet he'd like for you to keep on sucking," the blowhard PhD said, with a smirk.

Not at all in the mood, Jessica simply stared until the other trainee cleared his throat and went back to his own business.

She looked down at her gun, needing just one moment to shake off John's comment. Then she picked her head up, raised her Glock, and aimed for the target.

When she fired, she felt a surge of adrenaline mix with her anger.

And in that moment, something changed.

Over the last few weeks, she'd felt continually frustrated with herself for her performance in the physical challenges. But now, for the first time since she'd arrived at Quantico, she felt something beyond frustration.

She was *pissed off*.

John Shepherd thought she sucked, did he? Well, she might not have been built like a Viking god with those stupid big biceps and dumb washboard abs, and his pec muscles that looked sculpted out of rock, but she did not *suck*. She was smart, decisive, and coolheaded in a crisis, and she knew how to work information out of witnesses and suspects so that they never even realized they were being worked.

So the hell with John Shepherd. *She* knew she was good, and she also knew how much she wanted this.

And she planned to prove just that.

From that point forward, she kicked it into high gear and stopped wallowing in her frustrations. Yes, she wasn't where she needed to be with her firearms skills. Fortunately, there was something she could do about that; the FBI Academy had nine shooting ranges and a whole team of firearms instructors who were more than happy to work with any trainee who wanted to get in extra time on the range.

"Just tell me when and I'll be there," her instructor, Agent Balinski, had said without hesitation, when she'd dropped by his office to ask about additional practice. "Hell, I'll keep the place open all night if you want." Then he'd cocked his head. "For starters, we should work on your stance. You need to spread your legs and lean into it more."

So she kept hearing.

For the next several weeks, instead of grabbing a drink with her classmates at the Boardroom—the "bar" on the second floor of the Academy's main building that was, essentially, a cafeteria that sold beer—she spent most of her evenings on the firing range. She fixed her stance, got comfortable with shotguns and carbines in addition to pistols, and, after learning how to shoot off the reset, significantly improved her accuracy. And all the practice paid off: Not to toot her own horn, but by the midpoint of the course, she would dare say she was among the top five shooters in her class.

It didn't take a rocket scientist to figure out who was best.

Determined though she may have been, she was also realistic. There was no way she was ever going to shoot better than John, who'd been training with every kind of firearm under the sun for years. Which meant that if she wanted to kick his ass at something—and, oh, did she ever for that *if you want to keep on sucking* comment—she'd have to do it another way. Specifically, in classroom academics and the case exercises.

In terms of the case exercises, the real-life scenarios they ran through at Hogan's Alley were primarily about controlling the situation and not letting it escalate into violence. And, as it so happened, that was something for which she apparently had a knack.

"Shepherd! You're supposed to be *politely* escorting the guy out of the bar to answer a few questions, not going into the damn place with guns blazing like he's bin Laden holed up in a Pakistani compound!" their instructor had shouted, after one such exercise that ended with half the bar's mock patrons lying facedown against the pavement, bewildered and with hands cuffed behind their backs, because somebody had apparently gotten a little "fresh" with John.

"Shadow Harlow this next time," the instructor had barked at him. "Watch how she handles the same scenario."

Ah . . . seeing the look on John's face after that instruction very well might have been Jessica's favorite moment of the entire twenty-one weeks.

In the classroom, they studied law, forensic and behavioral sciences, ethics, and advanced interrogation techniques, and learned the skill every special agent most needed to master: report writing. Relatively fresh out of law school, Jessica fell easily back into the classroom routine and even tutored a hand-ful of her fellow trainees who felt less confident with some of the material.

Not that John was any slouch when it came to academics. As much as it killed her to admit it, the guy was smart, he picked up new material quickly, and he obviously put in a good amount of study time.

So she, in turn, put in *more* study time.

It wasn't only about competing with John, although this was not an unwelcome side benefit. Rather, it was about prov-ing something to herself and highlighting her strengths to her instructors. Yes, as the weeks progressed, she grew stronger and quicker and improved in the physical challenges. But so did everyone else in her class. Which meant, as the shortest and skinniest kid on the block, comparatively speaking, she re-mained near the bottom of the pack on that front.

She needed something to balance that out.

There was no award for high marks in operational skills, and John was already a shoo-in for the high mark in firearms. Which meant that her only shot at finishing first was in aca-demics. And if John Shepherd thought she was going to let him walk away with a trifecta of *all* high marks in their class, he had another think coming.

She would take that man down in the classroom even if it meant she had to duct-tape her eyeballs open at night to keep studying.

And so it went for their remaining weeks at the Academy. Since neither she nor John wanted to get a reputation of not being team players, they kept their mutual dislike just between them, feigning politeness when others were around and even working well together when required to do so.

On the sly, however, they traded insults and jabs every chance they got. And there were, indeed, plenty of chances. As part of the same class, she and John ate together, trained together, and even slept in rooms right down the hall from one another. It was like she could never escape the guy. They would be in a classroom, or at the shooting range, and there would be thirty-nine other trainees present, and still she'd be just so . . . *aware* of him.

Seventeen weeks into the Academy, it all came to a head.

Their class was in the gym, waiting to be paired up for their next fight. At the start of the Academy, they'd been informed that each trainee would spar against everyone else at some point. So Jessica had always known that she'd have to face John on the mat eventually, but nevertheless there'd been this teeny-tiny part of her that had hoped the instructors would just over-look that since John so obviously outmatched her.

That hope died a quick death on a sunny Friday afternoon.

"Shepherd—you're up. And you, too, Harlow," their defensive tactics instructor ordered them.

Jessica's heart began to pound, and so help her if she didn't nearly lose her lunch right there.

Her fighting skills had improved since joining the Academy, and she was scrappy enough to have *almost* beaten a few of the shorter and lighter male trainees. But John Shepherd?

She'd seen him fight many times, and the raw power and strength behind his punches—combined with the way his hands and feet worked together in graceful fluidity—was truly impressive. And that was despite the fact that he obviously held back in his matches, since, in a real-life scenario, the guy could probably kill them all with his bare hands if he wanted to. Un-doubtedly while inflicting a whole world of hurt along the way.

And now she had to face him one-on-one. The person he disliked most in their class.

She so was toast.

Quietly taking a deep breath, she headed over to the mat where their instructor waited. He reminded her and John of the rules as they strapped on their grappling gloves, headgear, and mouth guards: no hits to the groin area or other dirty moves, and the fight would end as soon as one of them tapped out. Out of the corner of her eye, she could see the other trainees gathering around to watch, probably taking bets on how many fleeting seconds it would take for John to get her down to the ground and trapped in a hold.

Then the instructor blew his whistle.

John came charging straight for her, all six feet, four inches and two hundred fifteen pounds of solid muscle—*oh shit*— and she put up her gloves, thinking that everyone had better start betting in nanoseconds instead.

But when John got within arm's reach, he slowed down and started circling around her, moving lightly on his feet. He was fully aware he'd just scared the crap out of her, his blue eyes crinkling at the corners as he waited for her to make the first move. And that was when Jessica realized something.

He was toying with her.

And just like that, a fire lit inside her.

Yes, she had no hope of winning this fight—between John's training and the fact that he had a full foot and over a hundred pounds on her, this was a foregone conclusion. But if he wanted to be cocky and dance around the mat like a cat playing with a mouse before swallowing it whole, perhaps she could work with that.

Her eyes met his and she quickly devised a plan.

Game on, John Shepherd.

Jessica's phone buzzed with a new e-mail message, abruptly snapping her back to the present. Realizing that she'd been sitting there on the couch with a bowl of now-soggy Rice Krispies, she shook off the memory and checked her phone.

Another e-mail from John.

You can cancel tomorrow's meeting with the Stagehand guys. The Jacksonville agents already took care of the website. All they need is a photo from each of us.

She frowned, surprised by this information.

When did you talk to the Jax agents?

His reply came moments later.

Just a few minutes ago. I called Agent Leavitt on his cell phone, figuring I should introduce myself, too.

Jessica rolled her eyes. So that was how it was going to be: John getting all huffy any time she tried to take charge in the case. Well, the guy was just going to have to get used it. This was a public corruption investigation, not organized crime, and as far as she was concerned that made *her* the lead undercover—

Her phone chimed again almost immediately.

She picked it up and saw another message from John.

By the way, I took the liberty of telling Agent Leavitt that we're free to fly down to Jacksonville next Wednesday. Hope that works with your schedule, he added, throwing back her earlier words.

Yep. It was going to be a long few weeks.

7

Sunday evening, John headed over to his dad's house for dinner, a weekly tradition that started when he'd first moved back to Chicago. It had been a convenient way for him and his younger brother, Nate, to check in on their mom without looking like they were checking in on their mom, who'd insisted that she didn't want anyone "hovering" over her as she went through chemotherapy.

Because they knew it was what Barbara Shepherd would've expected of them, John, his brother, and their father had carried on with the tradition after she'd died—at least to the extent that John's travel schedule had allowed. Although, admittedly, now the Sunday dinners consisted primarily of takeout—of which his mother most definitely would not have approved—and the table, with its empty seat to John's right, was a little quieter.

"So when do you find out if you've made the team?" John's dad, Eric, asked.

The three of them ate a deep-dish pizza John had picked up on the way over. It was the first time he'd seen his family since he'd been back from Quantico, so he'd told them about the tryouts—the parts he was allowed to talk about, anyway. Fascinated by the process, Nate had asked a bunch of questions. But their dad had been oddly quiet.

"A few weeks," John told him. "If I make it, I'd have to be in Quantico by Labor Day."

In response, his dad merely grunted and took another bite of pizza.

Okay, then. John shot a look across the table at his brother, who shrugged. The three of them ate in silence for several moments, until his dad grabbed another piece of garlic bread from the take-out container in the middle of the table.

"Just seems like this decision is coming out of the blue. I thought you were enjoying undercover work," he said.

"I waited six years to try out for the team," John said. "I wouldn't exactly call that a spur-of-the-moment decision."

His father tore off a piece of garlic bread and popped it in his mouth.

And . . . back to the silent treatment.

Frankly, John had been expecting a much different reaction from his dad, who'd been in the Army, just like him, before joining the Chicago Police Department. Many times over the last six years, his father had brought up the subject of the Hostage Rescue Team, bragging to his friends and other family members that John had a "standing invitation" to try out for the team whenever he wanted. But now that John had actually gone and done just that, his dad's reaction was tepid, at best.

He shot his brother another look across the table. *A little help here? I'm going down in flames.*

Nate nodded, on it. "Did you guys see that the Cubs traded Doyle?"

"About time," their dad said. "He's been awful this season."

The tension at the table eased as the three of them talked sports, and then his dad asked Nate, who managed a popular Irish pub on the north side of the city, how work was going.

Seemingly more relaxed after Nate finished regaling them

with this week's edition of crazy-bar-patron stories—of which he had a seemingly infinite supply—Eric turned back to John. "How about you? They got you working on anything interesting these days?"

"Actually, they just put me on a new undercover assignment. For one of the white-collar crime squads," John said.

"White-collar?" His dad grinned, resting his arms on the table. "Aren't you moving up in the world? What kind of assignment?" The former homicide detective in him was always eager to hear about John's investigations.

"Public corruption, a sting operation being run by another office. My partner and I are playing private equity investors trying to buy our way around a few zoning laws."

His dad raised an eyebrow. "You have a partner for this?"

While always protected by a team of backup agents, John typically didn't have a "partner" in his undercover roles. It was difficult enough for one agent to infiltrate an organized crime ring, let alone two. But things worked differently in the white-collar world.

"The case agents thought it would be more realistic if there were two of us." And John agreed with that assessment. Rarely did these private equity types work alone on an investment project—and in a case like this, they would be particularly inclined to put on a big show with the mayor, in order to underscore how important it was that the real estate "issues" they faced be resolved favorably.

"So this new partner of yours, what's he like?" his dad asked.

An image of Jessica popped into John's head, of her in that gray tailored pantsuit she'd been wearing the other day, when they'd met in Nick's office. They hadn't seen each other since, both of them opting instead to correspond by e-mail if there was something they needed to discuss about the case. For the most part, however, everything was being handled by the case agents in Jacksonville—as long as both he and Jessica were prepared for their undercover roles, there really wasn't too much they needed to say to one another.

Which suited him just fine.

"*She* is new to the office. She just transferred here from Los Angeles." *Most unfortunately*, John silently added, taking a sip of his beer.

His dad waited for more. "And? Does *she* have a name?"

John had a few nicknames for her, all right, but none that would be appropriate to share with his father. "Jessica Harlow."

Across the table, Nate cocked his head. "Jessica Harlow. Why does that name sound familiar?"

John shifted uncomfortably in his chair. "It's probably just one of those names that has a ring to it."

Nate didn't look entirely convinced. "Maybe."

His dad gestured impatiently. "Come on, this is a big deal— it's been a while since you've had a partner. Tell us more about her."

Really, John would rather not. "Having a partner is different in the FBI, Dad. It's not like you and Uncle Don." His "uncle" Don had been his father's partner on the Chicago police force for years. They were godfathers to each other's kids, had taken yearly family vacations together, and to this day still hung out every Friday night at the local tavern.

In the FBI, however, being partners with someone was a looser, less formalized concept. Young agents new to the office would be paired up with a more senior agent for training purposes, and, obviously, there were times when two agents worked as a team on a particular investigation. But those were typically short-term arrangements, not the kind of extended, almost family-like relationship his father recalled from the good old days when he was on the force.

His father waved this off dismissively. "Don't give me the 'it's different in the FBI' line. A partner is a partner. Someone who has your back, someone you trust. Let me tell you something: There are few greater bonds than that between a man and the guy—or girl—who will be standing next to him if the shit hits the fan. You know what I'm saying?"

John figured it was best just to be agreeable. "Sure, Dad." He took another sip of his beer, hoping that would be the end of it.

His dad nodded, seeming satisfied. "And you said she's from Los Angeles, right? Well, then, she probably doesn't know too many people in town. You should bring her by for dinner sometime." He waved his hand, as if that was settled. "You know, as a nice gesture."

John nearly choked on his beer. Invite *Jessica Harlow* to a family dinner?

He'd rather eat barbecued shoe.

Still, he played it cool, seeing no reason to get into his history with Jessica. "That's a nice idea. But she has family here in town, so I think she's set. And besides, this isn't a long-term arrangement. Especially since there's a good chance I won't even be working in Chicago much longer."

Immediately, he realized that it was the wrong thing to say.

His dad wiped his mouth with a napkin, his tone turning curt again. "Well. I guess you know what's best, right?"

Another silence fell around the table.

Nate looked between them and then smiled brightly. "So. How about those Blackhawks?"

A half hour later, John and his brother walked to their cars, parked in front of his parents' house. "I think it's safe to say Dad isn't thrilled I tried out for the Hostage Rescue Team."

"He'll come around," Nate said.

"It's not like I haven't left Chicago before," John felt the need to point out. "Between college, the Army, and Detroit, I've lived in another part of the country for most of my adult life."

"Come on, you know it's different now that Mom's gone." Nate held up a hand when John opened his mouth. "I'm not saying you should feel guilty about leaving if you make the team. Of course you should go—how many people get the opportunity to do something like that? And Dad knows that. He just got used to having you around these past three years. We both did."

John smiled, touched by that. Rare was the occasion that his brother, the jokester of the family, openly expressed sentimentality.

Then Nate continued. "Although I don't know why. It's not like you're all that interesting. I mean, clearly these attention-getting stunts like becoming a Ranger, and joining the FBI, and climbing the outside of a four-story building without a net are an attempt to compensate for the fact that you've been living in the shadow of your much cooler younger brother for years."

And . . . there it was.

Before he could answer, Nate pointed, as if just remembering something. "Speaking of attention-getting stunts, I ran into Lucas and Matt on Friday night. They came into the bar and asked about you. Matt gave me this big speech about how he's just a victim in this, getting caught up in all the drama between you, Rob, and Alicia. And then Lucas said he thinks it's bullshit that you've cut him out of your life, when he wasn't even the one screwing your girlfriend."

John's voice was almost a growl. "Is that what he said?"

The shithead.

Nate held up his hands. "Hey, don't shoot the messenger. You know me, I'm a people person. I just listen and take in everything that everyone tells me, even if it's bullshit." He grinned. "And then, in this particular case, after taking it all in, I told them both to go fuck themselves and threw them out of my pub."

That got a slight smile out of John. "Good for you." He almost wished he'd been there to see the looks on Matt's and Lucas's faces when his brother had tossed them out on their asses.

Nate's expression turned more serious. "Have you talked to Alicia at all?"

"No." And John had no intention of doing so. That was done. Both she and Rob had tried calling him while he'd been in Quantico for HRT tryouts, but he had nothing to say to either of them.

He was moving on. Moving forward, in fact. Sure, he'd lost his home, his girlfriend, and three of his closest friends in one fell swoop, and on top of that, he was currently renting a small, somewhat crappy loft in Bucktown since he didn't want to invest in anything permanent until he knew if he was staying in Chicago. And, probably, if he thought too hard about all of that, he'd feel pretty shitty about the whole situation.

So he wasn't thinking about it. Simple enough.

They got to their cars, but before climbing into his, Nate paused and looked at John, as if musing over something.

"Why *does* the name 'Jessica Harlow' sound so familiar?" he asked.

"I told you. It's probably just one of those names that has a ring to it."

"Still going with that, are you?" Nate asked.

Damn right, he was.

John got into the office early on Monday morning, coffee in hand. He had a couple of big days of research ahead, which he kicked off by checking out the fake website that the Stagehand squad down in Jacksonville had launched over the weekend.

"Looking sharp," Ryan said, passing by John's cubicle and checking out the picture on his computer. "Where they'd get the photo?"

It clearly wasn't a recent picture, since John—while clean-shaven in the photo—was currently sporting a two-week-old beard. Admittedly, some of that was out of laziness: Given the nature of his undercover roles, he'd gotten used to not shaving regularly. But on top of that, seeing how his so-called *Sons of Anarchy* motif seemed to irk a certain sleek public corruption agent, he figured he'd keep the look as long as possible. "I had it taken a few years back, for a sting op that fell through at the last minute."

"You look like you should be on the seventh floor, comparing cuff links with the rest of the white-collar guys and dropping pseudo-self-deprecating references to your Harvard MBA degree," Ryan said.

John grinned. Precisely the point.

He continued clicking through the website, impressed with what the Stagehand squad had put together. Clearly, they'd been working behind the scenes for some time prelaunch, because the website looked professional, clean, and, most important, real. It was all there, an "About Us" section that had fake bios for both him and Jessica—or "Dave Rosser" and "Ashley Evers," as they would be known while in their undercover identities; bios and photographs for two senior associates who also allegedly worked at the firm; several "Investment Strategy" pages dedicated to their firm's current and former projects; a "News" section with phony press releases the firm had put out regarding some of their biggest projects; and, last but not least, a "Contact" page that included a business address, an e-mail address, and a phone number that, in reality, connected to an administrative assistant in the Chicago FBI office who'd been recruited to play the part of Dave and Ashley's receptionist.

Yeah, they were sneaky like that.

For the next two days, John immersed himself in the world of private equity. He and Ashley ran Lakeshore Capital Partners, a small but lucrative firm that was headquartered in Chicago and focused on the hospitality sector, mostly restaurant and bar investments that fell within the $5 million to $25 million range. According to their website, their motto was to be "value creators who set ambitious goals while partnering with great talent in an opportunistic and cooperative approach to investment."

And, trust him, it would take *all* of his undercover skills not to literally gag on the words if he ever had to refer to himself as a "value creator" during this sting operation.

Total white-collar-speak.

The setup of the undercover op was relatively straightforward. He and Jessica would pretend that their firm was considering investing in a couple of restaurants and bars in Jacksonville, which, according to the case agents from the Jax office, had been gaining national recognition over the last couple years for its booming culinary scene. They wanted to test the market by opening an upscale wine bar and pizzeria in the Riverside neighborhood, and they'd identified the perfect location for the project: a vacant brick building that formerly had been a bank. Unfortunately, there were a few problems with the space.

Because the building was located in a historic district, there were several zoning and parking issues. Currently, the space wasn't zoned for outdoor seating in the back courtyard, which Lakeshore Capital Partners felt was a key part of the restaurant's future success. They would also need to obtain a variance for additional signage and landscaping, as well as a permit for short-term street parking dedicated exclusively to the restaurant since another key part of their business plan was to allow customers to call in take-out pizza orders.

With any luck, however, Jacksonville's golden-boy mayor would be willing to make all of their zoning and parking problems go away. For the right price, of course.

Wednesday morning, John got up before sunrise to pack his suitcase. He took a cab to O'Hare airport, which, not surprisingly, was crowded despite the early hour. After bypassing the general security lines—one of the privileges of being an FBI agent—he killed some time grabbing coffee at Starbucks and then took the neon-lit moving walkway to United's Concourse C.

At the gate, he spotted Jessica already sitting in the waiting area, checking her phone.

His eyes held for a moment, watching as she tucked behind her ear a lock of blond hair that had fallen forward as she looked down at her phone. It was funny—in an irritating kind of way—how he could still remember practically every quip, sarcastic line, and dirty look she'd ever thrown him despite all the time that had passed. Which was no small feat, considering the plethora of quips, sarcastic lines, and dirty looks there'd been over the course of their twenty-one weeks together.

But now . . .

With a sigh, he braced himself and headed over. When she spotted him approaching, her expression turned wary as he sat down next to her and parked his suitcase.

He looked sideways at her, and neither of them spoke for a moment.

"Ready for this?" he finally asked.

"Probably not," she said.

Well, that made two of them. His gaze flickered over the black slim-fit suit and pink silk top she wore, with a skinny pink belt and black high heels that completed the ensemble. "Are all your suits this snazzy?" He wasn't even sure why this made him cranky. He was an FBI agent; he was around women in suits all the time.

Just none that looked like Jessica Harlow did in them.

"Yes, they are all this 'snazzy.'" In return, she checked out his jeans and blazer, and then her eyes came to rest on his unshaven jaw. "So this is the look you're going with, then?"

Not exactly, but she didn't need to know that yet. "You don't approve?"

She was cut off from responding when the airline attendant announced that their flight was about to begin boarding.

Jessica tucked her phone into her briefcase. "There are a few remaining details of our backstory we should probably lock down before we meet with the Jax agents. Maybe we should plan to discuss those during the drive from the airport to the hotel?"

John stood up, preparing to board. "I was thinking the same thing." Obviously, a public airplane wasn't an appropriate place for two undercover agents to discuss the details of their covert sting operation, so they would have to wait until they were alone.

"Good. Okay." She took a deep breath, as if relieved to hear it, and stood up.

Seeing her reaction, he felt a quick flash of frustration. Did she really think so little of him that she was worried he would be anything *other* than professional in this? He opened his mouth to say something sarcastic, but then she paused where she was standing, pretty close to him. She cocked her head, and something about the way she was looking at him right then made the curt words die on his lips.

"What?" He shifted uncomfortably, his tone suspicious. "Why are you looking at me like that?"

Her mouth curved at the edges. "Just trying to picture you with a man bun."

For chrissakes. Apparently, word about that had spread far and wide throughout the office.

"The remarkably clean-cut John Shepherd I knew six years ago never would've gone for that," she continued. "I guess a lot has changed."

He leaned in, lowering his voice as they stood close. "Or maybe you only *think* you knew me six years ago, Jessica."

Satisfied by the flash of surprise in her eyes, he let her stew on that as he turned around and walked toward the gate, giving her a nice, long look at his man buns since she seemed to be so interested.

8

The flight attendant stopped by their aisle with the beverage cart. "Can I get either of you anything to drink?"

With a smile, Jessica gestured to the bottled water she had tucked into the seat pocket in front of her. "I'm good, thanks."

John sat next to her on the aisle. "I'm fine, too," he told the flight attendant.

"Well, if you change your mind and there's anything you need, just let me know." The flight attendant held John's gaze for an extra-long moment. "Anything at all."

Observing this from her seat by the window, Jessica resisted the urge to roll her eyes as the flight attendant moved on to the next row.

It was possible, she supposed, that the flight attendant—who was aware that both Jessica and John were armed federal agents via a code word on the passenger manifest—was just checking out John out of curiosity. But since Jessica herself had received little more than a passing glance, she suspected it had more to do with the fact that John looked . . . well, like John Shepherd always looked. He was definitely a man that people noticed—as she'd witnessed firsthand. Before takeoff, he'd stood up to help an older woman lift her carry-on into the overhead compartment and there'd literally been *sighs* of appreciation coming from the women in the nearby seats when he'd picked the thing up like it weighed nothing.

Yes, fine, he's good-looking, people. And oh-so-strapping. She got it.

Although, for the record, she noted that his facial scruff was quickly approaching that fine line between dirty-hot and "MAN LOST AT SEA, SURVIVES ON KELP AND RAINWATER FOR THREE WEEKS!"

Just saying.

She checked the clock on her iPad mini, which doubled as her e-reader, and saw that a mere five minutes had passed since the last time she'd checked it.

Crap.

They were only a half hour into the flight, and this lack of conversation between her and John was beginning to grate on her. Granted, she came from a boisterous family—some probably would say "loud"—in which her lawyer father and psychologist mother had always encouraged her and her brother and sister to express their opinions and feelings. So, even under the best of conditions, she didn't do well with awkward silences.

In this particular case, however, she was trying to stifle her natural urge to fill the void, seeing how John clearly had zero interest in talking to her. The moment the plane had hit the runway, he'd pulled out of his briefcase a small stack of newspaper articles about Jacksonville's culinary scene and had barely looked up since.

Which was fine. The two of them would just sit here, mere inches from each other, partners but not talking.

Nope, that wasn't weird. Not at all.

After Jessica had read the same paragraph on her e-reader five times and still had no idea what it said, she gave in and decided she would just have to be the bigger person here.

"So have you been to Jacksonville before?" she asked politely, breaking the silence. She kept her voice down, just as a precautionary measure, even though she and John had the only two seats on their side of the aisle and no one was paying any attention to their conversation.

John glanced up from the article he was reading and looked at her like she'd just said she wanted to yank open the emergency exit door and go for an impromptu skydive. "Of course I have. With *you*, Ashley, when we visited to look at possible locations for the restaurant we want to open. Remember?"

Jessica stared at him. *Ashley?*

Oh, for Pete's sake . . . what was this, some kind of method-acting shit he did to get into undercover roles?

She was never, ever working with anyone from organized crime again.

"Right. Okay there, *Dave*," she emphasized dryly, humoring him. "Not sure how I could've forgotten that." She turned back to her e-reader, thinking she and Daniel Day-Lewis here were going to have an even longer couple of days than she'd imagined.

After a few moments, she glanced over and saw John covering the side of his mouth with his hand as he read the article.

She put down her e-reader. "You're messing with me."

"You should've seen the look on your face." He stretched out his legs, appearing far more comfortable than any man his size should when stuffed into an economy seat. "And in answer to your question, no, I've never been to Jacksonville before."

Jessica waited. When he went back to his reading, she cleared her throat pointedly. "And this would be the part of the conversation when you ask *me* if I've ever been to Jacksonville," she said sweetly.

He looked up. "Oh. All right. Have you ever been to Jacksonville?"

"No."

Another silence fell between them.

"Not much of a conversation starter, is it?" he asked.

Cute. Fine, since inane pleasantries seemed to be beyond them, there was something she would, in fact, like to address. "What did you mean when you said that I only *think* I knew you six years ago?"

"Been stewing on that, have you?"

Not stewing. Just . . . interested. "I found it to be a curious statement. Especially since I think I got to know you pretty well six years ago."

He let out a bark of wry laughter. "Right."

Hmm. Rising to the challenge, she began ticking off the facts. "Born and raised in Chicago. Your father was a homicide detective, which got you interested in a career in law enforcement. You played football, well enough to get a scholarship to the University of Wisconsin, which I assume is where your huge competitive streak started—"

"See, right there." Cutting her off midsentence, he pointed and angled his body to face her. "That's what I'm talking about. You say *I'm* the competitive one—because in your mind, you think that *I* was the bad guy with everything that happened at the Academy."

Jessica stared at him, thinking this was self-evident. "Well . . . yeah."

He shook his head. "And here I'd thought maybe, just maybe, you'd gained a little perspective over the last six years. But apparently, you're still deluding yourself with this revisionist history."

Oh my God—revisionist history?

Hell, no.

She leaned in closer, being careful to keep her voice calm despite her rising temper. "What I remember—and, please, do correct me if I have any of this wrong—is you spending most of the training program hounding me, correcting me, telling me that I sucked, and then getting pissed off when it turned out that I didn't."

As soon as the words were out of her mouth, the most incredible thing happened.

John Shepherd blushed.

"I only said you sucked that one time," he grumbled. "And of course those are the parts you remember."

She threw up her hands in exasperation. "What other parts should I remember? If *you* weren't the problem six years ago, then how do you explain all our disagreements?"

He gave her a long, pointed look.

"Wait. You're saying *I* was the problem?" she asked incredulously.

"Sucks learning that you aren't perfect, doesn't it?"

Jessica opened her mouth to fire off a snarky reply, and then thought, no, she wouldn't give him the satisfaction. "Okay, Shepherd. Let's hear it. Lay out all your grievances. Because I'd love to know how, exactly, *I* was such a bad guy."

"As tempting as that might be," John said smoothly, "we only have an hour and a half left in this flight and that barely gives me enough time to make it through week one of the training program. But if you need me to give you a specific example . . ." He looked her dead in the eyes. "Come on, Jessica. You know what you did."

It took her a moment. "Get out. You're not still pissed about *that.*"

"Of course I'm still pissed about that," he said matter-of-factly. "Why wouldn't I be?"

"Seriously?"

"Yep."

She looked at him in disbelief.

He smiled charmingly. "Want to ask me a third time, just to be super-sure?"

Jessica peered up at the airplane ceiling. On second thought, maybe it wouldn't be so bad to do a little method acting in preparation for their roles. Especially seeing how, in real life, she wanted to *throttle* her partner. "You know what? Let's not do this, after all. I think dredging up the past will only make things worse, and you and I have got to be in sync these next couple of days."

"That's fine with me," he said. "I wasn't the one who started chatting about the good old days in the first place."

"Trust me, I won't make that mistake again." She leaned back in her chair and gestured to the stack of newspaper articles on his tray. "Besides, you obviously have some reading you want to do and I don't want to hold you up."

"I appreciate that," he said faux-politely.

"I'm glad you're appreciative," she said mock-nicely, before turning to her e-reader.

So much for lessening the tension between them.

Sheesh.

"You do realize you still make the sassy head movements even when you only think the words, right?" John said.

Jessica glared but remained silent.

After a few moments, John cleared his throat and held up the article he was reading. "There's some pretty interesting stuff in here about this Riverside neighborhood you and I are going to be driving through today. You're welcome to look at it when I'm done," he added begrudgingly.

Jessica smiled. "Actually, I already read that over the weekend. And the second article on your tray has a nice quote from the *Financial Times* describing Riverside as 'the closest thing to Greenwich Village you'll find in Florida.' I've been thinking of ways I can drop that into a conversation with you-know-who."

She winked.

John scowled—ah, yes, once again she was one tiny step ahead of him—as she proudly turned back to her e-reader.

Okay, fine. Perhaps she had a bit of a competitive streak, too.

John watched out of the corner of his eye as Jessica turned off her e-reader and leaned back in her seat, getting comfortable. When she closed her eyes, he shook his head and turned back to his reading.

Unbelievable. The woman was exactly the same as she'd been six years ago. Still a pain in the ass, still determined to rub his face in it every time she got the drop on him, and always convinced that she was right.

You're saying I was the bad guy?

The best part was, her surprise was no exaggeration—she genuinely believed that he was the cause of all the problems between them six years ago.

Welcome to reality, sweetheart.

She seemed to forget that *he* had been there, too. And the way he remembered those twenty-one weeks at the Academy, he sure as hell hadn't been the villain of their story.

Far from it.

(he said)

Six years ago, after finishing up his tour with the Army, John found himself in the middle of the toughest summer of his life. He was in Chicago, single and living with his parents at age twenty-seven, and waiting for FBI training to start in August.

And he was bored out of his ever-loving mind.

Admittedly, some of this had been expected as he readjusted to civilian life. Being a "Batt boy"—a soldier assigned to one of the three battalions of the 75th Ranger Regiment—definitely had kept him on his toes. Like the rest of his squad, he'd rotated through several combat deployments, and in between deployments, he'd trained. Constantly. The physical rigors of being a Ranger were no joke, so he'd continually pushed himself, beyond the point where common sense would tell others to stop.

In addition to the PT, there'd been parachute jumps, battle drills, and shoot house exercises, and days when his squad would load up their vehicles, head out to the range, and spend hours shooting their way through all the ammo they'd brought. Even the "down" moments at the garrison had been spent doing some form of physical activity: platoon football games, ultimate Frisbee, and planning assaults on other squads, just for the heck of it.

Not that it was all fun and games. In fact, a good chunk of those four years had straight-out sucked. But he'd say this: He'd grown up fast living in that kind of high-pressure environment, and it had instilled in him a strong work ethic. He'd always known exactly when he had to report for duty, but he'd never had any clue what time he would finish. Simply put, Rangers worked until the job was done.

After finishing his tour, he had a four-week break before heading off to Quantico. He'd decided to stay at his parents' house because he thought it would be nice to be someplace familiar—and it sure as hell beat bunking on a friend's or his brother's couch for an entire month. He'd been excited when the plane touched down at O'Hare airport, picturing the break as being one long vacation of catching up on some much-needed sleep, refueling on his mother's cooking, and hanging out with friends and family.

And it was like that . . . for all of about three days. What he hadn't anticipated, however, was just how *much* time he would have on his hands. Apparently programmed after four years of military life, he would find himself waking up at the crack of dawn despite all his attempts to sleep in. Used to doing PT first thing, he'd then go for a long run along the lakefront, get back home just in time to see his dad heading out the door for his shift, and have a leisurely breakfast of pancakes, eggs, and bacon with his mom.

Then he'd check his watch and wonder what the heck he was going to do with himself for the next twelve hours.

He was used to going nonstop from dawn to dusk and having virtually every moment of his life scheduled. Also, he was used to being around people—lots of them. But in Chicago, his brother and his friends all had jobs, so none of them were around during the day. And his parents' house seemed much quieter than he'd remembered.

On the fifth night of his break, he got an e-mail from one of the guys in his platoon, who'd also just finished up his tour.

Who knew the suck could be so much fun?

Yeah. He could relate.

Never one to wallow, John decided to take charge of the situation. After quickly blowing through the list of household tasks his mom asked him to do, he began inventing projects on his own. He cleaned out his parents' garage. Then he cleaned out their attic. And then he even organized his and Nate's old rooms.

"Dude, it is way too early for a visit," his brother groaned when he answered the door to his apartment, blinking at the daylight and with his hair sticking up in every direction.

"It's *noon*," John said, stepping past his brother to unload the two boxes he was carrying.

"When you work until four A.M., noon is too early." Nate was bartending in the evenings while taking business courses during the day, with the goal of getting into restaurant management. "What is that, anyway?" He pointed to the boxes John set down on the kitchen counter.

"I cleaned out your old room. Mom was telling me how she's been taking a few art classes, so I thought she could use the space for painting or whatever," John said.

"What's wrong with using your room?"

"Aside from the fact that I'm currently sleeping in it, I'm turning it into an office for Dad." Granted, in twenty-seven years, John had never seen his father do anything particularly officelike, but, hey, at least now he would have the space should inspiration strike.

Nate seemed to be fighting back a grin. "Don't take this the wrong way, John, because these are all very nice projects you're working on. But I'm thinking we need to get you a hobby. Quickly."

No kidding. "It's only three weeks. I'll be fine." Actually, there were two weeks, six days, and twenty-one hours left until he had to report to Quantico for his first day of FBI Academy. But who was counting?

Despite his edginess, John was careful to keep his feelings to himself. His college friends had all settled into big-city life, working hard at their careers and then playing hard in the evenings, going to a different swanky bar every night where someone knew somebody who could get them in. They would toast John's homecoming over glasses of ridiculously overpriced bourbon and ask about the things he'd seen and done as a Ranger. And he would tell them the exciting parts—because, really, that was what they wanted to hear—but they would never truly understand what he'd been through or was still going through, how everything at home simultaneously felt so familiar and also completely foreign, or how wound up he felt a lot of the time, like he needed to be doing *more*.

And so, consequently, he did more. He volunteered to power-wash and stain his aunt's back deck, added a second run to his daily exercise routine, dropped groceries off for his grandmother at her retirement home, and mowed his parents' lawn. Every other day.

And six of the neighbors' lawns, too.

"Mrs. Murray down the block called. She asked if you do gardening, too," his mother said as they finished up with the dishes one evening after dinner.

As she handed John a casserole dish to dry, he caught her eyes twinkling with amusement. So, perhaps, he'd overdone it today. "Depends on what she's paying," he kidded.

"Knowing Mrs. Murray, probably a glass of heavily sugared lemonade and a plate of stale wafer cookies."

"Tempting."

His mom smiled as she went back to her washing. A few moments later, she looked over. "I imagine it's a big adjustment, being home. Any regrets that you didn't sign up for another tour?" She kept her tone casual, but there were worry lines around her eyes.

Apparently, he hadn't been doing as good a job disguising his edginess around his parents as he'd thought.

Not wanting her to worry about him, seeing how she'd already had enough of that while he'd been in the Army, he gave his mom a reassuring smile. "No regrets. I never saw myself as a lifer." And that was true—he'd given a hundred percent every day he'd been a soldier, but he'd always planned to return to civilian life after those four years were over.

Now he just needed to get to the FBI Academy, so he could actually start that life.

Needless to say, that day in August when he finally arrived at Quantico Marine Corps base to the sounds of gunfire in the distance and saw a military helicopter flying overhead, he grinned and felt a rush of adrenaline kick in.

Yes. Now *these* were his people.

After too many days of so little to do, so much time, he was pumped and ready to be sweaty and tired and challenged, to have people barking orders at him and telling him to get his ass moving, and to be back on the shooting range. Hell, he was so stoked, he was even looking forward to being in a classroom again.

That first day, when his class had to introduce themselves and talk about their backgrounds, John discovered two interesting pieces of information. First, that the group was more highly educated than he'd assumed going in—a full thirty-one out of forty-one of the trainees in his class had a postgraduate degree. Several of those were lawyers, but they also had, among others, a biomedical engineer with a doctoral degree in pathogenesis, a guy with a PhD in linguistics, a college professor with a doctorate in forestry, and a guy with degrees in both chemistry and chemical engineering who'd left behind a lucrative job in Silicon Valley to come to the Academy.

Then there was the second bit of interesting information he gleaned upon walking into that classroom.

One of his fellow trainees was *hot*.

Admittedly, this was a new experience for him. There'd been no women in his Ranger regiment, so he wasn't used to looking around a group of people with whom he'd be eating, sleeping, sweating, shooting, and fighting over the course of several months and seeing one with long blond hair and light blue eyes that could stop a man dead in his tracks.

Her name was Jessica Harlow, he learned when it was her turn to stand and introduce herself, and in a funny coincidence, she was from Chicago, too. When she mentioned she was a trial lawyer, John wasn't surprised. Unlike some of the other trainees, who'd seemed anxious about this first day, even fumbling their words as they introduced themselves, Jessica appeared perfectly at ease as she described how she'd become interested in the law as a kid, listening to her father, a successful civil litigation attorney, talk about his cases at the dinner table.

"He had all these great courtroom stories," she said, speaking dynamically, "with words that sounded very impressive and dramatic to an eight-year-old . . . like *motion to quash* and *cause of action* and *res judicata*. But when my father had finished the story—obviously quite proud of himself—I'd sit there, waiting on pins and needles, until I'd finally ask, 'Yeah, but where's the good part, when somebody gets thrown in *jail*?'"

She smiled as that got a laugh out of everyone, easing some of the tension in the room as she then shifted gears and spoke in earnestness of her desire to work in a profession where she could serve her country and community and make a positive difference in people's lives. It was an eloquent speech, and one that well articulated sentiments shared by everyone in that room.

The class clapped when she was finished, more enthusiastically than they had after anyone else's speech, and John watched as she took her seat.

If these introductions were the trainees' first test—and he suspected they were, given the fact that several of their instructors had taken seats in the back of the room to listen in—then Jessica Harlow had just thrown down the gauntlet.

Interesting.

Given their shared hometown, he decided to walk over when the speeches were finished and personally introduce himself.

"Chicago, huh? We should team up, Harlow. I say we take down the three trainees from New York first." He winked to let her know he was kidding. She'd been funny in her speech, so he figured he'd open with a joke, too.

In return, she merely gave him a polite smile. "They're probably plotting the same thing against us." Then she moved along to talk to the other female trainee, leaving him standing there.

Huh. That hadn't gone the way he'd imagined.

He shrugged off the interaction at the time. Maybe she was a little on edge, like a lot of the trainees seemed to be, after the assistant director's announcement that the class would have a PT test the next day. It would be the first of three PT tests they'd be given over the course of the Academy, and all trainees had to pass at least once in order to graduate.

For several of the trainees, that first test served as a wake-up call.

"Thirteen of you failed," the assistant director said in a sober tone when they gathered the following day in the classroom. "That's not acceptable. We expect more of you—your country expects more of you. Push yourself. Be demanding of yourself.

Because, believe me, *we* are going to demand a lot from you over these next twenty-one weeks."

John wouldn't lie; when it came to the PT part of the program, the things they asked him to do were, well . . . pretty easy. He wasn't trying to show off, but given his background, doing sit-ups and pull-ups and running a six-mile obstacle course was not going to be a problem for him. Heck, as Rangers, they would do that kind of thing wearing full combat gear and carrying loaded packs.

That said, he was aware the PT wasn't a breeze for everyone. In fact, some people were flat-out struggling. Including Jessica.

He could see how frustrated she was, always finishing near the bottom of the pack or bringing up the rear. But he'd say this: The woman had determination. She'd be covered in mud and sweat while running the Yellow Brick Road, looking like she might drop from exhaustion any moment, and yet she'd find a way to dig deep and keep going.

He could relate to that feeling. Granted, the physical demands had been on a different level, but there'd been a couple of times in the Army when he'd been pushed so hard he'd been on the brink of crashing and burning. And what had always gotten him through was a little tough love from his drill sergeants, or from the other guys on his squad.

So that, in turn, was what he gave Jessica, any time they were partnered up or grouped together and she appeared to be struggling.

Let's go, Harlow!

Step it up, Harlow!

Grab the rope, Harlow!

Pick yourself up, Harlow! Now move, move, MOVE!

Of course, since this *wasn't* the Army and he was not, in fact, her drill sergeant, she had quite a few saucy things to say in response.

Actually, he kind of liked that part.

"Since you're obviously in need of something to do, instead of shouting at me through this whole drill, isn't there some tree you could fell with your bare hands, or a boulder somewhere that needs tossing?" she'd asked in a sweet tone during their Point Run, a seven-mile run around Quantico base during which they'd stopped every half mile to do calisthenics.

"A tree I could fell? How un-green of you, Harlow," he'd shot back, before they both took off at a run again.

They fell into a routine those first few weeks, lots of back-and-forth quips that he assumed, at the time, were all in good fun. And in the meantime, he had his own issues to worry about. Sure, he was rocking the PT and firearms half of the program, but on the academics side, he was very much in the middle of the pack.

That did not sit well with him.

He couldn't remember the last time he'd been just *average*. He'd done well at the University of Wisconsin, and not just "well" for a football player—he'd graduated with honors and worn the fancy stole with all the other smarty-pantses at the commencement ceremony and everything.

But the other trainees in his class were smart, too. Real smart. Every year, the FBI received nearly one hundred thousand special agent applications, but less than a thousand of those applicants would be chosen for the Academy. Which meant, as John was quickly learning, that *everyone* had been the best in their fields before coming to Quantico. And while he certainly wouldn't complain about being the top marksman or fighter in his class, out in the real world, FBI special agents rarely discharged their firearms or got into street fights. The academics side of the program was where he would learn the skills that he would use every day as an agent.

Kind of important, that.

One of the things they particularly focused on in the classroom was interviewing and interrogation techniques. For the practice exercises, the Academy hired professional actors and actresses to play witnesses and suspects, and the agent-trainees would be given an objective—for example, to get as much information as possible out of the witness in thirty minutes. The practice exercises were videotaped, so the trainees could review their performances, and their interview and interrogations instructor would often show the trainees' videos and critique them for the entire class.

John got a nice wake-up call of his own the first time he reviewed his videotape.

It wasn't that he was terrible. But he'd never interrogated, cross-examined, or deposed anyone before, and it showed. He'd spent too much time letting the witness talk about nonrelevant information, and he must've said *Okay* about fifty times during the interview. By contrast, the lawyers in the class, and some of the guys who'd come from law enforcement backgrounds, looked polished and comfortable working with the witnesses, established a good rapport, knew how to get the most important information faster, and didn't have any verbal tics or nervous habits. And when the class moved on to more advanced situations, like trying to get a confession, the lawyers and law enforcement officers already seemed to have a cache of tricks for dealing with an adversarial witness.

Jessica, in particular, was a standout. And John would know, because throughout those weeks, their interrogations instructor played almost every single one of her videos as a "good" example of what to do in whatever scenario they'd been given that day.

John, on the other, had yet to find his groove. Given his military training, his natural inclination was to be a little tough and demonstrate who was in charge, but all that did was get the witness hollering about Miranda rights and demanding to see a lawyer.

"I said 'take charge' of the situation, Shepherd, not scare the crap out of the guy," their interrogations instructor said after John had completed an exercise with an actor who'd pretended to be a defense contractor suspected of stealing a blueprint he planned to sell to a foreign intelligence agent.

John held out his hands innocently. "You said we should move in at this point in the questioning and invade the guy's comfort zone. That's what I was doing."

The instructor—a short, bald man in his early fifties—gestured to John. "Yes, but when *you* do that, it comes off particularly intimidating."

John grinned. Well . . . yes. That was Ranger blood running through his veins, and the good citizens of the United States weren't spending their hard-earned tax dollars to teach the most elite battalion in the Army to be a bunch of wusses.

"That wasn't a compliment, Shepherd."

Right. He nixed the grin stat.

The instructor stood there for a moment, scrutinizing John. "Is there any way you can make yourself seem . . . smaller?"

Needless to say, John's video was *not* one of the "good" examples shown to the class that day.

Later that afternoon, his class headed off to PT. They were sparring again, and when John found out whom he was paired against, he braced himself for the onslaught of douchebaggery.

Not that he was worried about the fight—candidly, he wasn't worried about any of the fights—but there was an unspoken etiquette to these matches. No one wanted to get seriously injured and be forced to drop out of the program, so with the exception of the "Bull in the Ring" day—the day they were specifically told to fight as hard as possible by the instructors, who wanted them to know they could take a punch and keep going—the trainees typically didn't go all-out, *Rocky*-style. The purpose of the exercises was to learn the techniques and know how to control an opponent in a hand-to-hand confrontation—

not to beat the crap out of one another. But of course, there was always one jackass in the class who pulled no punches, literally, and went for the throat every time.

Cue the guy with the PhD in linguistics.

Now, normally, John tried to be generous while sparring and not take advantage of the fact that he had considerably more training and experience than his opponent. But when their defensive tactics instructor blew the whistle and Linguistics PhD came charging at him—fists flying and trash-talking John in some foreign language as an attempt to psych him out, John had no choice but to (a) take a moment to try his hardest not to laugh and (b) take the guy immediately down to the ground and get him into a handcuffing position.

After the PT session, John got caught up talking to his instructor, and he was late getting back to the locker room. Just before he rounded the row where his locker was located, he overheard Linguistics PhD talking.

"It's bullshit that they pair us against him," he ranted. "Everyone knows Shepherd's only here because they recruited him for HRT. The guy's a fucking grunt. You think he would've made the cut otherwise, with a bachelor's degree from *Wisconsin*?"

As John stood on the other side of the lockers, his jaw tightened.

While the idea of storming over and handling this situation *grunt*-style was very tempting, he kept his cool as he walked around the corner.

Linguistics PhD instantly fell quiet and pretended to be looking at something in his locker. His sidekick, the Silicon Valley guy with double degrees, went pale and suddenly became very interested in tying his shoes.

John opened his locker and stripped out of his shirt. He tossed it into his gym bag, holding Linguistics PhD's gaze. "Is there something we need to discuss?"

The guy went red in the face and looked away. "Just blowing off steam, Shepherd."

"Maybe blow it off a little quieter next time."

Apparently having nothing to say to that, Linguistics PhD hastily got dressed and made a passive-aggressive show of slamming his locker as he left. His sidekick from Silicon Valley managed a nervous smile at John before following him out.

Moments later, one of the other trainees in their class, a detective from San Francisco, came out of the shower with a towel wrapped around his waist. "Can we just give the guy a good ass-kicking and be done with it?"

John half chuckled, appreciating the camaraderie. In the Army, guys with attitude problems like Linguistics PhD quickly found themselves zip-tied, covered in shaving cream, and stuffed in an empty locker. "Unfortunately, I think they expect us to be gentlemen here."

"So we'll put on suits and ties before we kick his ass." The homicide detective nodded at John as he headed to his locker. "Don't pay any attention to that bullshit he was saying, Shepherd. The guy's just being a sore loser."

That was John's take on it, too.

Mostly.

For the rest of the evening, there was a small part of him that wondered whether other people in his class felt the same way. That he, with a "mere" BA from the University of Wisconsin, wasn't intellectually on the same level as many of them, that he was a jock who'd been recruited not because the FBI believed he would make a good special agent but because they thought he'd be handy to have in a gunfight.

He got his answer to that question the very next day.

During firearms training, John was lined up next to Jessica at the outdoor shooting range. He noticed that she was having a hard time hitting the target and getting more and more frustrated with every shot. Their instructor was currently working with someone else down the line, so John figured he'd help her out.

"You're anticipating the blast and flinching when the shot fires," he offered. "Plus, your stance is wrong."

She glared at him, slapped the magazine into place, and got into position again—the wrong position.

John fought back a smile—*So stubborn*—and moved in closer to demonstrate. "Spread your legs and lean into it," he said, resting a hand on her shoulder.

She jerked away from him. "Hey. Easy there, big guy."

The look on her face completely took him by surprise.

Back off, it said, in no uncertain terms.

In that moment, John realized that he'd been very wrong in his interpretation of the dynamic between him and Jessica. These past few weeks, he'd thought they'd had a fun, playful vibe going with the quips and the teasing, possibly a way to cover up some sexual tension they both knew they couldn't act on given the fact that they were in the Academy and would be sent off to different field offices after graduation.

But nope.

Apparently, Jessica Harlow just thought he was a dick.

Feeling like an idiot, he snapped, "Don't flatter yourself, Harlow. I was just trying to help. But if you want to keep on sucking at this, hey, that's your prerogative."

Yes, it was a shitty thing to say. But in his defense—what the hell? He'd been trying to *help* by offering her shooting advice. These past weeks, *all* he'd done was try to help her. And if she'd had some problem with his approach, or didn't like the way he acted around her, she easily could've pulled him aside and talked to him in private. Yet instead, she chose to call him out in front of the whole class. As if he was . . . what? Hitting on her?

Pfft. He had better things to do with his time.

They didn't speak a word to each other for the rest of the firearms class. But later, when he got back to the dorm-style suite he shared with three other guys in his class, he thought more about his interactions with Jessica.

And now he saw them in an entirely different light.

Easy there, big guy.

Maybe you'd rather just tie a rope around my waist and drag me the rest of the way?

Isn't there some tree you could fell with your bare hands, or a boulder somewhere that needs tossing?

Sure. Because he was the grunt who relied on brute strength, right?

With that in mind, he set a new goal for himself. He might not have had a postgraduate degree, and he might not have come to the Academy with legal or law enforcement experience, but he was a damn fast learner. And anyone who thought he was all brawn and no brains was about to get a serious reality check.

He was going to get that high mark in academics.

To execute his plan, he stopped by their interrogations instructor's office the following day to ask how he could improve his interviewing technique.

The instructor seemed surprised by the question. "You're doing fine, Shepherd."

Jaw set determinedly, John stood military-straight in the doorway. "With all due respect, sir, 'fine' isn't good enough."

The instructor looked him over for a moment. "All right." He gestured to the chair in front of his desk. "Have a seat."

The following evening, they walked through some of John's videotapes. It reminded him of the postgame review they used to do when he played football, except instead of focusing on ways he could run a route better or his tendency to transfer his weight to his back foot before taking off from the line of scrimmage, they worked on refining his "neutral, nonaggressive approach" to interviewing.

"Try making more small talk," the instructor advised. "You military guys are used to coming in hard and fast—you get in, do the job, and get out. Here, you need to slow down. Establish common ground with the witness. Ask about his job or hobbies, or if the interview is at the witness's home or office, ask about any pictures of his family that might be sitting around. Start soft, and most important, let the witness *talk*. Agents can get hung up on getting a confession, but that's not always going to happen. And a really detailed lie is the next best thing."

The extra practice paid off. Over the next few weeks, John fixed his *Okay* problem and became much more comfortable going with the ebb and flow of the interview instead of being fixated on following a set list of questions. And with that, he finally found his groove. He'd originally assumed, given his build and background, that he'd be more of a bad-cop type in interrogations, but he discovered that playing against type and creating a "bond" with the witness could be much more effective.

"You seem stressed, Karen. Tell me what's going on," he said, in a sympathetic tone, to the "suspect" the next time their class was given an interrogation exercise. In the evenings, while the rest of the trainees were grabbing beers at the Boardroom, he'd been doing extra research into the interviewing techniques they learned in class, like "emotional labeling"—a technique used by FBI crisis negotiators—statement analysis, and how a person's body language, or even certain linguistic markers, could indicate deceit or suspicious behavior. Fascinated by the subject, he soaked up as much information as he could get his hands on.

And in turn, he became *good* at the practice exercises.

The only problem was, Jessica kept getting better, too. No

matter what he did or how much he studied, he couldn't shake the damn woman. And the instructors loved her—loved how much she'd improved her shooting, how instinctive she was at Hogan's Alley, how she did such a great job keeping the practice exercises from escalating into violence, *blah, blah, blah.*

Whatever.

Sure, under different circumstances, he might've found her skills and determination admirable—along with the fact that she somehow magically managed to look cute even when sweaty and wearing nylon gym shorts. But his views on Jessica had changed ever since that day at the shooting range. Now that he properly understood their situation—that she considered him Public Enemy Number One—he, too, had taken off the proverbial gloves. So if Jessica Harlow wanted that high mark in academics, she was going to have to get through him first.

And this grunt wasn't going down without a fight.

Seventeen weeks into the program, that mantra took a rather literal turn.

"Shepherd—you're up. And you, too, Harlow," their defensive tactics instructor called out as the trainees lined up in the gym to be paired up for their next sparring match.

As John put on his gear, he caught sight of Jessica on the opposite side of the mat. She adjusted her ponytail as she got ready for the fight, then took a deep breath, as if nervous.

Seeing that, he felt a mixture of things. Annoyance, for one. Yes, they didn't get along. No doubt, she was a burr up his ass. But did she really think there was a chance he would actually *hurt* her?

Christ, he hadn't thought her opinion of him was that low.

And second, knowing she was nervous made him feel . . . uncomfortable or something. Jessica Harlow was sassy and sarcastic and confident—she didn't get nervous. So she needed to snap out of it, because by now she should've thrown at least two dirty looks at him and whispered one snarky comment, and the fact that she hadn't was starting to seriously weird him out.

As they faced each other across the mat, he knew what to do.

When the instructor blew the whistle to start the match, John charged straight for Jessica, as if he planned to take her down hard. Her eyes widened as she put up her gloves, but she held her ground. Stopping just short of her, John changed course and gave her a cocky smile as he began circling her on the mat.

A spark of attitude and anger flashed in her eyes when she realized that he'd been messing with her.

Now *that* was the Jessica Harlow he knew.

Game on.

Throughout their training, the instructors had emphasized that there was no distinction between the genders, and that the men should fight the female trainees the same as anyone else. Nevertheless, chivalry was not dead. So instead of ending the match in two seconds, as John obviously had the ability to do, when Jessica made her move he let her get in a few punches so she could demonstrate that she'd learned the proper techniques.

Of course, his generosity only seemed to aggravate her more.

Big surprise there.

"Stop dancing around, Shepherd." Her speech was slightly slurred from the mouth guard, but her irritated tone came through loud and clear.

"Wait. You mean this is supposed to be a fight? And here I'd been brushing up on my tango." He heard a few chuckles from the class, but he remained focused on Jessica as he closed in, ducked her punch, and grabbed her.

She shifted her weight into a strong stance and shoved him off, but instead of retreating, as he'd expected, she lunged and struck the base of his throat with her forearm, channeling all her strength against that one vulnerable spot.

He stumbled back, coughing, and had to catch his balance.

Now it was *her* turn to smile. "Looks like your tango needs some work," she said as they circled each other.

"Eh. I've got a few moves you haven't seen yet."

"That's what they all say, Shepherd."

The class chuckled again, obviously enjoying the show. John feigned looking in their direction, knowing that Jessica would try to take advantage of his momentary distraction.

She stepped forward to strike his solar plexus, another weak spot, but he deflected the hit and got her in a hold. She tried to escape, so to maintain control he took her down to the mat in a mount, straddling her and pinning her on her back.

Their eyes met, and for the briefest moment, it occurred to John that he had a very beautiful woman trapped beneath him, between his legs. Granted, one wearing a mouthpiece and headgear.

He smiled, just slightly—because it *was* pretty cute how determined she was to try to beat him—and her eyes narrowed. Using the self-defense techniques they'd gone over in class, she bridged her hips, trying to throw him off, and managed to get on her side. She hooked his foot, pulling it over her leg while simultaneously elbowing his knee in an attempt to scoot out from underneath him.

It was a good move. And indeed, against a lesser man that maneuver very well might have worked.

But not against this man.

John grappled with her, getting her onto her stomach and into an arm-bar hold, ending the fight in a way that inflicted no damage. Except, perhaps, to her pride.

Pinned beneath him, her cheek pressed against the mat, Jessica swore under her breath and tapped out.

And . . . his work here was done.

John sprang up and pulled off his gloves. He resisted the urge to strut, but out of his many sparring victories, this particular one—while obviously expected—had a certain sweetness to it. Jessica had given him a run for his money in so many ways these past four months, but the fighting ring was *his* turf, and Ms. *Easy There, Big Guy* was—

—still on the mat.

He stopped the moment he noticed that, watching as Jessica slowly rose onto one knee. Breathing hard, she slid off her gloves and removed her mouthpiece, as if needing more air. Then she winced and touched the side of her rib cage—right on the spot where he'd pinned her with his knees.

She was hurt.

Feeling something soften inside him, he went over to her. He leaned down, reaching out a hand to help. "Jessica, I'm so—"

He never got a chance to finish that sentence.

She grabbed his wrist with one hand and ground the blade of her opposite forearm into his triceps, using it as a fulcrum to knock him off balance as she turned her body and pulled him down on a diagonal.

He hit the mat face-first.

He blinked, stunned, and then clenched his jaw when Jessica dug one knee into his shoulder blade. She used the other knee as a lock against his outstretched arm, getting him into a straight arm-bar hold.

"Now, remind me, Shepherd. From this position, would I handcuff the suspect before or after I read him his rights?" she asked, feigning innocence.

The entire gymnasium had fallen dead silent. Presumably, like John, everyone needed a moment to process what had just happened.

Then their instructor let out a bark of laughter.

The entire gym erupted, an enthusiastic mix of clapping and cheers. Wisely not pushing her luck—there was, after all, a lot John could do with one free arm and two legs—Jessica let go of him and stood up. Ignoring all the clapping, John hopped to his feet and spat out his mouth guard. Then he looked around for his gloves, which had gone flying through the air when she'd yanked him to the ground.

He turned around and saw Jessica holding them.

Eyes sparkling with amusement, she walked over and handed him the gloves. His hands brushed against hers as their eyes held.

"I didn't tap out," he said.

Her lips curved in a smile. "It doesn't matter." She turned and was greeted by a round of high fives as she joined the rest of their classmates.

A month later, it undoubtedly came as a surprise to no one when Jessica got the high mark in academics, officially decreeing her Cleverest of Them All. And John, too, became something of a legend at the Academy: the badass Army Ranger who not only got high marks in firearms and PT, *and* finished second in his class in academics, but also was pinned only once throughout the entire fighting program.

By a five-foot, three-inch lawyer.

10

Jessica glanced over and saw John's jaw twitching once again. He'd been silent for nearly the last hour of their flight, obviously brooding.

Fighting back a smile, she had a feeling she knew exactly what had him all worked up. "It was a joke, Shepherd."

He acted nonchalant. "What was?"

Please. "I can practically see the steam coming out of your ears. I know you're thinking about our fight."

They were interrupted by an announcement from the cockpit, letting them know they were entering their final descent and would be on the ground shortly.

John moved closer to her, his deep voice lowered in a heated whisper. "Spare me the innocent act—we both know it wasn't just a 'joke.' You wanted to prove a point, and you did. But don't try to say now that you weren't every bit as competitive as I was during those twenty-one weeks. Because you never saw *me* fake an injury and face-plant another trainee in front of the entire class."

Of course not. The mighty John Shepherd didn't have to rely on those kinds of tricks. Still, Jessica shifted in her seat, feeling a little uncomfortable when he put it that way.

Having made his point, John turned back to his reading. An awkward silence fell between them.

Don't engage him, she told herself. *There's no point.* But his words continued to nag at her, until she finally gave in and angled her body in his direction.

"Believe it or not, my objective that day wasn't to embarrass you." Like him, she kept her voice down so no one could overhear. "What I wanted was to show the instructors that I could think on my feet, even when incredibly outmatched. That I wouldn't give up. That despite my size, my future partners and squad mates could count on me to stay levelheaded and strong in a physical confrontation. So yes, I saw an opportunity and I took it. And if *you* ever find yourself fighting a seven-foot, five-inch giant who's double your weight, I would expect you to do the same."

John said nothing for a long moment, just kept shooting her pissy glares, as if trying to think up some retort and coming up empty-handed.

When he finally spoke, his tone was begrudging. "Fine. But I still say you didn't have to be so damn sassy about it." He imitated her voice. "'Remind me, Shepherd. From this position, would I handcuff the suspect before or after I read him his rights?'"

Jessica grinned, not remembering that part. "That's what I said? Ooh, that *was* sassy." When he scowled, she pooh-poohed it with a wave. "Oh, please. You had it coming for telling me I sucked in front of our whole class."

His jaw went taut, and just as Jessica braced herself for his retort, the plane suddenly dipped to the right. She grabbed the armrest—which happened to be occupied by John's forearm—and felt his strong, solid muscles beneath her fingertips.

She blushed and let go. "Sorry."

Oddly flustered by the memory of just *how* good a body John Shepherd had under those street clothes, she covered by watching out the window as they approached the airport. There was a long silence between them, until he spoke.

"I wasn't 'hounding' you during the PT," he said quietly.

Jessica turned around.

"I was trying to motivate you," he continued, speaking intently despite his hushed tone. "And if you hadn't been so stubborn and defensive and quick to decide that I was the enemy, maybe you would've realized that."

Gee, thanks. "I'm glad we cleared the air on that," she said dryly.

"And as an aside, the whole 'big guy' thing? Kind of lame. How about I start calling you 'little lady' during this assignment and we see how that goes over?"

She raised an eyebrow. *Not well.*

"Exactly. But regardless . . ." He paused, as if needing a moment. "That day at the shooting range . . . I never should've said you sucked. Especially since it was so far from the truth." He looked her in the eyes. "That was rude and uncalled for, and I apologize."

Jessica blinked.

Oh.

When she fell quiet with surprise—both from the apology itself and because John Shepherd had given her an actual *compliment*—he nodded, as if glad that was done, and put away the newspaper articles he'd been reading in his briefcase.

As if by mutual agreement, for the remainder of the flight neither of them brought up the subject of the Academy again. After deboarding the plane, they followed the signs to baggage claim. There, a woman in her midthirties, with long brown hair and dressed in a navy pantsuit, held a sign with the names *EVERS/ROSSER* written on it.

She shook both John's and Jessica's hands when they approached. "Mr. Rosser, Ms. Evers . . . nice to meet you. I'm

Sandra, from Sunshine Limousine. Do either of you need to collect any bags?"

Jessica gestured to her and John's carry-on suitcases. "Nope. We're all set." In actuality, "Sandra" wasn't the woman's name, nor was she a driver for a car service. Rather, she was Special Agent Jasmine Chopra from the Stagehand squad of the Jacksonville FBI office, whose job was to make sure John and Jessica had all props, personal items, and credentials needed for their undercover roles.

Wheeling their suitcases, they followed Agent Chopra through a door marked *Pre-Arranged Ground Transportation*. Outside, a black town car waited for them. After packing their suitcases into the trunk, Jessica and John settled into the backseat, where a duffel bag waited for each of them.

Jessica's bag contained a burner cell phone as well as several personal items: a wallet—complete with a driver's license, credit cards, and insurance cards all in the name *Ashley Evers*— a watch, purse, and sunglasses. As a wealthy private equity investor, Ashley would be expected to sport expensive versions of such items, and, as with all parts of an undercover assignment, the FBI was a stickler for details.

"Your own purse will work fine, if you prefer to use that," Agent Chopra said, as she drove. She glanced at Jessica in the rearview mirror and smiled. "I wasn't expecting you to show up with a Miu Miu bag."

John looked at Jessica curiously, and she blushed. Yes, typically, government-salaried special agents didn't carry eighteen-hundred-dollar purses. But she'd kept the bag as part of her divorce settlement and saw no point in letting it sit on the shelf, collecting dust.

Especially since it was a really awesome purse.

"It was a gift," she said to John, simply. Changing the subject, she gestured to the new "Dave" watch that he was putting on his wrist. Like her, his accessories had been upgraded for the job. "Nice Rolex." She leaned closer, peeking in his duffel bag. "Any chance there's a beard trimmer in there?" She feigned innocence when he gave her a dirty look. "No judgment. Just asking."

A few minutes later, they turned onto an access road that led to a small, abandoned airfield. Parked next to a nondescript white building was a sleek gray Mercedes roadster.

After the three of them got out of the town car, Agent Chopra handed Jessica a set of keys to the convertible. "The car is in both Ashley's and Dave's names. Everything's been taken care of—just drop it off in the rental parking lot at the airport when you head back to Chicago." She spent a few minutes talking with them about the undercover assignment, then shook both their hands in good-bye. "If you think of anything else you need while you're here, don't hesitate to ask."

As she drove off in the town car, Jessica and John walked over to the Mercedes.

"I'll say this, Harlow, you white-collar-crime agents do have nice toys," he said.

She smiled at that.

Damn straight, they did.

During the forty-minute drive to their hotel, Jessica and John locked down the remaining details of their cover story.

According to the profiles put together by the Jacksonville agents, Lakeshore Capital Partners was a complementary relationship, with each of them bringing different strengths to the table. Dave had a background in construction and was the more hands-on guy. Once a project had been green-lit, he handled all the real estate logistics and worked with contractors and subcontractors on any construction or remodeling of the space.

Ashley, on the other hand, focused on the big picture. With an MBA from Stanford (a detail Jessica appreciated, since she could talk with familiarity about the university) she came up with the concept and vision for a new project, knew the economics of the city and neighborhood in which they were looking to buy, and was in charge of pitching to investors and getting them on board.

After agreeing on a story explaining how Dave and Ashley had met, and why they'd decided to go into business together, John brought up one last topic they needed to cover.

"How about Ashley's personal life?" he asked, as they exited the interstate and turned onto the highway that led to the beach. "Is she single? Married? Any kids?"

In the driver's seat, Jessica stepped on the gas, thinking she definitely could get used to having this kind of horsepower at her command. "Single." Unless otherwise required by the assignment, she always said she was single while working undercover. No sense faking a family and having to worry that someone might ask to see pictures of them on her phone. "You?"

"The same. It's easier that way."

Apparently, there was at least one thing on which they could agree.

With the time change, it was nearly noon when they reached the hotel. Chosen by the Jacksonville agents, the Ponte Vedra Inn and Club was an upscale beachfront resort located just outside the city. According to Jessica's online research, the hotel had a picturesque lagoon, private golf course, and spa—and seemed to be the perfect place for two wealthy investors in town on business.

Or in this case, two *supposed* wealthy investors.

She drove along the lush green grounds to the main building, where several valets waited attentively. Instantly, any lingering tension between her and John was put on the back burner.

From this point forward, when in public, Jessica Harlow and John Shepherd didn't exist—nor did their disagreements or problems. Now, they were Ashley Evers and Dave Rosser, two savvy, shrewd businesspeople with one agenda for this trip: to do a little schmoozing with Jacksonville's mayor.

"You ready for this?" John asked, with a sudden gleam in his eye.

It was the same question he'd asked her at the airport, but this time there was no sarcasm in her response. "Absolutely." Feeling a rush of adrenaline—dozens of undercover assignments, and still, this never got old—she brought the car to a stop and smiled at the valet as she stepped out.

"Checking in?" he asked, holding the car door open for her.

"Yes, thank you."

Side-by-side, she and John walked into the hotel, wheeling their suitcases behind them. The lobby had an old-money feel to it, with marble floors, dark mahogany crown molding, and paintings of beach scenes on the walls. After checking in under her pseudonym, Jessica confirmed the time she and John would meet in the lobby and headed off to her room. Given their time constraints, she grabbed a sandwich and coffee from the hotel's gourmet shop along the way.

Not wanting to push it with the Bureau's bean counters, she'd booked herself the cheapest room available, one with a "mere" partial ocean view. After setting her suitcase on top of the king-sized poster bed, she took a quick moment to step out onto the balcony. To her left stretched a white sand beach interspersed with lounge chairs and umbrellas, and beyond that, the waves of the sparkling blue Atlantic Ocean crashed peacefully against the shore.

She took in a deep breath of the warm seaside air.

Now this was her kind of assignment.

Feeling a little nostalgic for California, she went back into the room to unpack her suitcase. With fifteen minutes to spare, she then changed into one of Ashley's outfits: a gray pencil skirt, short-sleeve ruffled white blouse, and gray heels. For a little flair, she added a chunky necklace and put her hair into a loose bun with a few wisps framing her face.

Satisfied that she looked the part of a sophisticated entrepreneur, she locked her Glock in the room safe, grabbed her purse, and headed out. Being only on the second floor, she took the stairs down and followed a walkway that led to the main building, where she'd arranged to meet John.

Standing in the lobby next to a table with a sculpture of a sailboat, he had his back to her as she approached. He turned around, presumably at the sound of her heels on the marble floor, and she nearly did a double take at the sight of him.

Holy smokes.

Gone was the dirty-hot organized crime agent with his scruffy facial hair and jeans, replaced by a clean-cut—and exceedingly handsome—businessman in a well-tailored suit. He was clean-shaven now, accentuating the angular lines of his strong jaw, and had tamed his thick, deep-gold hair into a brushed-back, groomed style that somehow made his eyes seem even more strikingly blue.

Recovering quickly, Jessica came to a stop in front of him, determined to act nonchalant.

"I take it you approve of the new look," he said.

So much for nonchalance.

"All right, so you clean up well. Let's not make a whole thing of it." Ignoring his sly expression, she took her sunglasses out of her purse and walked out the door into the bright Florida sunshine.

Time for Ashley and Dave to get to work.

11

Because out-of-town undercover agents generally avoided the local field offices—on the remote chance they might be spotted coming in or out of the building—John and Jessica drove to a generic-looking office in downtown Jacksonville that was covertly owned by the FBI and used for a variety of under-cover purposes. After taking the stairs to the second floor, they were greeted by the two agents in charge of the Blair investiga-tion, Special Agents Leavitt and Todd, both of whom were part of the public corruption squad. Todd, in his midforties, gave off a reserved, all-business air, while Leavitt, the younger of the two agents, had an athletic build and easygoing demeanor.

"Whose idea was it to give Ashley an MBA from Stanford?" Jessica asked, as the Jax agents led the way to a small conference room. "That was a nice touch."

"I thought you might appreciate that. Although, being a Duke man myself, a little part of me died inside putting that in," Leavitt joked.

John glanced at his watch. Impressive. Three minutes in, and the guy had already managed to sneak in a comment about his alma mater. Now all they needed to complete the white-collar package was the pseudo-self-deprecating reference to his postgrad degree.

"Did you go to Duke for business school?" Jessica asked.

"Actually, I did the joint MBA/JD program there," Leavitt said. "Because, apparently, three years of grad school student loans just wasn't enough."

Bingo.

After the four of them settled in at the conference table, Leavitt started off the meeting by thanking Jessica and John for their assistance, then gave them a brief overview of the investigation—most of which Jessica and John already knew from the case files. Once that was out of the way, they dove right into the details of tomorrow's sting operation.

"What's the plan for backup?" John asked.

Because the mayor was considered a low-risk target, everyone agreed that the security detail could be kept to a minimum. No SWAT team or special operations group, just Leavitt and Todd in a car parked a few blocks from the restaurant, using radio channels to listen in via the minuscule microphones John and Jessica would be wearing.

"I assume neither of you will be carrying tomorrow?" Todd asked Jessica and John.

Jessica looked at John. "I don't see any reason to take the risk that Blair would notice."

Typically, John was armed during his undercover assignments—one of the "perks" of playing organized crime thugs. But Dave the Value Creator was hardly the type to bring a pistol to a business dinner. "I agree. Any issues with the restaurant we need to be aware of?" he asked Leavitt.

"You'll be dining at Bistro Aix," Leavitt said, pronouncing it "X." "It's one of the mayor's favorite places. He gets the same table every time, a booth in the back of the restaurant that affords him some privacy. The acoustics are lousy but no worse than any other restaurant. The upside is that Blair should feel comfortable speaking openly, without worrying about being overheard."

They spent the next twenty minutes covering other logistics, until Agent Todd got a phone call.

"That's Morano," he said, referring to the lobbyist who'd been flipped by the FBI. "I told him to call when he arrived."

After Todd stepped out, Jessica looked at Leavitt. "Morano's been prepped on the cover story?" she confirmed.

Leavitt nodded. "We went over it so many times he could tell it in his sleep."

The plan, if Mayor Blair asked how Morano knew Ashley and Dave, was to say that the three of them had a mutual acquaintance, Morano's old college friend who now lived in Chicago. When that friend heard that Ashley and Dave were looking to invest in restaurants in Jacksonville, he told them to reach out to Morano, who knew "everyone and anyone" in northeast Florida.

"He did seem a little revved up when Todd and I met with him yesterday," Leavitt continued. "I'm sure it's just pregame jitters. Morano's been very cooperative throughout the investigation."

John refrained from commenting, but the cynic in him noted that if Morano had *not* been cooperative, he'd be looking at ten to twenty behind bars for his role in a major political corruption scandal.

Funny how people tended to play nice with the FBI under those circumstances.

He'd read the report on Morano, which painted a picture of a down-on-his-luck man who'd made the foolish decision to find an easy—meaning illegal—way out of his problems. After making a series of bad investments and subsequently going through a contentious divorce, Morano was emotionally and financially "in a bad place" four years ago, when a local restaurant developer approached him about a problem with a liquor license that had been held up by the city council. In a panic with the restaurant's opening scheduled for the following week, the developer suggested to Morano—who'd been a close advisor to Mayor Blair for several years—that perhaps they could find some "mutually beneficial arrangement" if the mayor would be willing to use his clout to lean on the city council and push the liquor license through.

And thus the seeds of bribery and political corruption were planted.

While publicly viewed as a charming, charismatic golden boy, Jacksonville's mayor was quite a different man behind closed doors: a man who was greedy, power-hungry, and narcissistic. After agreeing to push that first liquor license through the city council—and scoring a quick ten grand in the process—Blair realized there was an opportunity to make some real money just by schmoozing and making a few phone calls. If these people had money they wanted to throw his way, he rationalized, who did that hurt, really?

He and Morano agreed they had to be careful. They worked out a scheme: Morano, using all the right buzzwords and subtle innuendos, would suss out other deep-pocket types who also might be interested in a "mutually beneficial arrangement" that would make certain bureaucratic problems go away. Once an interest had been established, they would agree upon a price, and after the cash had changed hands, the lucky deep-pocket would suddenly find himself free of that pesky red tape in which he'd been so annoyingly enmeshed. Morano took twenty percent of the cut—his "finder's fee," as he called it—and within three years, both he and Blair had amassed healthy little nest eggs.

It all seemed so easy. That is, until Agents Leavitt and Todd showed up on Morano's doorstep one evening with an arrest warrant.

According to the agents' report, Morano literally *sobbed* when they confronted him about the corruption scheme, and instantly confessed—much to the dismay of his lawyer. Fortunately for Morano, however, the FBI had its eye on the bigger fish.

Mayor Blair.

And so a deal was struck. Eager to make amends, Morano told Leavitt and Todd everything he knew about Blair and agreed to wear a wire. Over the course of the next year, the FBI quietly built its case, gathering evidence of a corruption ring that involved not just the mayor but several of the city's most successful businessmen and women. All that was left now was the coup de grace, this last sting operation, and the FBI would move in and make the arrests.

Obviously, John had nowhere near the time and effort invested in the case that Leavitt and Todd did. But nevertheless, this was an important assignment for him, too. If he made HRT, he'd be in Quantico by September—and this stint with Jessica in Jacksonville would be his last job as an undercover agent.

And he had zero intention of going out on a loss.

When Morano arrived, escorted to the conference room by Agent Todd, John's first impression was that the lobbyist seemed wired and jittery, like he'd had too much coffee. A short, stocky man in his late forties with thinning brown hair, he had beads of perspiration scattered across his forehead as Todd made the introductions.

"Anthony Morano, semiprofessional snitch at your service," he said to Jessica. His voice booming through the room, he spoke with a Southern drawl. "We've got a big day ahead of us tomorrow, huh?" He chuckled, then turned to shake John's hand. Eyes widening, he took in the ten-inch height difference between them. "Damn. Glad I'm on your side."

When the five of them were seated around the conference table, Leavitt began to walk through tomorrow's plan. Morano had made arrangements to meet Mayor Blair at his office, and the two of them would drive together. John and Jessica would get to the restaurant early, giving them time to confirm that everything was working properly with their microphones.

Morano interrupted Leavitt here. "I'm glad y'all are taking care of the mics this time," he said to Jessica and John. "Every time I had to wear one of those things to a dinner, I'd worry that I'd rub my shirt the wrong way and—*plop*—the damn thing would fall onto my steak. Try explaining that one, right?" He slapped Agent Todd on the back, laughing, and then leaned in. "By the way, I've been thinking: Maybe we need a code phrase. You know, just in case something goes wrong tomorrow. Something innocuous that Blair would never pick up on. Like"—he paused dramatically—"'cherries jubilee.'"

John caught Jessica's eye as they both fought back a smile.

Ah . . . civilians.

For the next half hour, Morano continued to interject with questions and ideas, obviously both nervous and really, really excited to be working with undercover agents. Referring to himself, Jessica, and John as "the A-Team," he wanted to know everything from who would sit where in the booth (didn't matter), to whether a backup squad should establish "a perimeter" around the restaurant (somebody clearly had seen too many episodes of *24*), to how to react if someone recognized him or the mayor and came over to the table to say hello (just say hello back).

Leavitt looked embarrassed by all the interruptions, Todd seemed annoyed, but Jessica never so much as batted an eye. Patiently answering all of Morano's questions, she was polite and professional and managed to diplomatically steer the conversation away from his numerous suggestions without ever causing offense.

Watching from the sidelines as she did her Jessica Harlow thing, John found himself reluctantly impressed.

"I see you're still working that good-cop routine," he said, walking to their car after he and Jessica had finished the meeting with Morano. The next item on their agenda was to check out the property Dave and Ashley supposedly wanted to buy.

Jessica's smile was both coy and confident. "When the occasion calls for it." Sunglasses on, she held out her hand as they approached their rented Mercedes.

John dug into his pants pocket for the keys. "We're really going to do this? Alternate driving every time?"

Her fingers brushed against his as she took the keys. "If you prefer, Agent Shepherd, I'm happy to take all the times." She turned and walked around to the driver's side of the car.

John's eyes lingered, taking in her high heels and the way that slim-fit skirt hugged her hips.

Get your mind out of the gutter, asshole. She's your partner. And do you really need a reminder of what happened the last time you thought—

Oh no, indeed, he did *not* need a reminder. The disdainful look on Jessica's face when he'd touched her that day at the shooting range was a memory that remained quite clear in his head. Because of that, he planned to pay no attention whatsoever to the way she looked in her Ashley attire.

She climbed into the car, giving him a glimpse of several more inches of sleek, bare leg.

Starting now.

The drive was short, less than fifteen minutes, taking them over the St. Johns River and into the historic Riverside neighborhood. From the passenger seat of the Mercedes, John checked out the scene, an eclectic mix of funky coffee shops, trendy boutiques, antiques stores, and nightclubs. Jessica headed to King Street, the center of the restaurant and bar scene, and found street parking a couple doors down from the vacant brick building that Ashley and Dave were hoping to make the future home of their wine bar and pizzeria.

Unbeknownst to anyone outside the Bureau, in actuality

the FBI owned the building via a dummy corporation, having snagged it for the sting operation for a very reasonable price given its zoning and permitting issues. Since they obviously didn't want to deal with the hassle of faking that the property was on the market, the story was that Ashley and Dave had heard through a developer friend that the owner of the building wanted to sell and would cut them a deal if they could work it out among themselves and save the real estate agent commissions. Frankly, John doubted Mayor Blair would even ask about the specifics, but as with all aspects of an undercover investigation, the FBI was exceedingly thorough in making sure that everything appeared legit.

Using the key Leavitt had given them, Jessica unlocked the front door and John followed behind. The space looked, not unexpectedly, like a vacated bank—empty teller windows were framed by bulletproof glass, and along one wall was a row of abandoned cubicles, some of which still had desks.

"Doesn't exactly scream 'trendy wine bar and pizzeria,' does it?" Jessica asked.

"Depends how you look at it." John walked through the place. "Here's what I'm thinking: You put a big open bar in the center, with lots of seating. On this side of the restaurant, we'll have banquettes along retractable windows, which can open in nice weather, and four or five highboys here that'll be an extension of the bar area. Then on this side"—he crossed the space—"we do a row of half booths along the wall and create a section of tables here, behind the bar, that could be used for private events." He pointed toward the back. "Open kitchen, with a massive stone pizza oven as the focal point, restrooms over there, and in this corner we build a glass-enclosed wine cellar. Designwise, I'm thinking arches and lots of oak to give it a Tuscan-wine-cellar feel, but with red leather on the banquettes and bar stools for a touch of sexiness."

Jessica stared at him. For once, she appeared to be speechless.

"I'll take that as a sign you agree," he teased.

"How the heck did you come up with all that?" she demanded.

He shrugged, feigning innocence. "Just doing my job, Ashley. I am the design guy on the team, remember?"

Raising an eyebrow, she waited.

All right, fine, he'd spill his secrets. "There was a blueprint of the building in the case file. I showed it to my brother, who works in restaurant management, and asked him what he would do with the space."

"Oh." She shifted her weight, her tone begrudging. "That was actually quite resourceful."

He winked. "Not my first rodeo."

After checking out the "courtyard," presently just a paved lot the bank had used for parking, they locked up and walked around the neighborhood to get a better feel for it. By the time they got back into the car, it was nearly six o'clock. Dying in the ninety-six-degree heat, John took off his jacket as he walked to the driver's side of the Mercedes. After hanging the jacket in the backseat, he climbed into the car and caught Jessica watching as he rolled up his sleeves.

Assuming her look was one of disapproval, he cut her off at the pass. "I realize this probably breaks Section 2, Clause C of the special white-collar dress code, but let's see you try wearing long sleeves and a jacket in Florida in July."

"It's Clause D, actually. Clause C says that all our suits must meet the required level of snazziness."

Cute. He started the car and headed back toward the hotel. "Any thoughts, now that you've seen the neighborhood?" he asked, turning back to business.

"I think the question we most need to be prepared for with Blair is 'Why Jacksonville?'" Jessica said. "Meaning, why does a lucrative private equity firm from Chicago want to invest in this particular area? And, oh my God, I'm going to melt if this air-conditioning doesn't kick in." She cranked up the fan full throttle and adjusted the passenger-side vents so they were all pointed straight at her. "Ah . . . much better," she sighed.

With her eyes closed and a blissful look on her face, she looked more relaxed than John had ever seen her.

Aware that he was staring, he turned his attention back to the road. "You don't think we can sell our cover story? That the neighborhood has a booming culinary scene and we want in on the action?"

"I think we *can* sell it, but a few of the details Leavitt and Todd came up with feel a little . . . thin."

"Such as?"

"Well, supposedly, Ashley and Dave want to invest in several restaurant projects in Jacksonville, not just this one. I get that—we want Blair to think we're willing to sink a lot of money into his city if this first project goes well. According to the story Leavitt and Todd came up with, if Blair asks what other restaurant concepts we're interested in—which I think is likely—we're supposed to say that we're also thinking about opening a gastropub in the area."

John looked over. "And that's a problem?"

"Don't get me wrong, I like a quality burger and glass of wine as much as the next girl. But I counted while we were walking around, and there are already *three* gastropubs within a six-block radius. If I'm a successful investor looking to break into a hot culinary scene, I'm looking for fresh, new concepts to bring to the market—not something's that been done several times over."

He considered this. "All right. What restaurant concept would you suggest instead?"

"That I don't know. *Yet*," she was quick to add. "I'll do some research this evening into the newest restaurant trends and cross-check that against what Jacksonville doesn't have a lot of right now. Maybe vegan, or farm-to-table . . ." she mused.

"Anyway, I'll dig around and e-mail you my thoughts on a better concept by the end of the night."

Not his way of doing things. "If there's research that needs to be done, count me in. I'm not going to chill at the hotel bar drinking a beer while you get stuck with all the work."

"Aw, that's nice of you. Although I feel like I should mention that this falls within Ashley's territory. She is the big-picture girl, after all."

"We're partners now, Jessica. We work as a team," he said in no uncertain terms.

Her lips curved in amusement. "Oh, I was just pointing out that *I* should probably be in charge tonight since this is my character's side of the business." She paused cheekily. "Partner."

John shook his head. Here he was, trying to do a nice thing, and *bam*, he got smacked upside the head with the sauciness anyway. "Just to clarify, are you trying to get under my skin as much as possible, or is it simply an inherent talent of yours?"

"Probably a little of both."

He grunted, having suspected as much, and focused on the road as he changed lanes. A few moments later, he glanced over and saw her smiling as she looked out the window.

Aware that his eyes were lingering again, he turned back to the road. "So, about this research . . . to save time, why don't we make a working dinner of it?"

She checked her watch. "Actually, I was going to suggest the same thing." She shot him a sideways glance. "We'd have to order room service, obviously."

Yes, that had been implicit in his suggestion. After all, two undercover agents involved in a covert investigation into the city's mayor could hardly pull out their laptops in the middle of a restaurant and start talking shop.

Which left John with only one question.

"Your room or mine?"

12

Having changed into a casual top and jeans, Jessica scurried around the hotel room, putting away all personal items. She shoved her suitcase into the closet, along with the fuzzy purple slippers she always traveled with because she didn't like walking around barefoot in hotels. Then she canvassed the room one more time, just to be sure.

All clear.

She checked her watch and saw that she had two minutes. Good. Just enough time to catch her breath, get her game face on, and calm the butterflies that had been fluttering around her stomach every time she thought of John being in her hotel room.

Your room or mine?

It was ridiculous that she was even thinking about this. She was an undercover agent, he was an undercover agent, and in that line of work one quickly got used to meeting behind closed doors. Given the disparity in gender among special agents, she almost always worked with men, and not once had she ever thought twice about being alone with a male agent in a situation that, under different circumstances, could be construed as intimate.

Then again, none of those male agents had been John.

It was the same problem she'd had at the Academy; she just kept . . . noticing things about him. Like the fact that he was actually a pretty darn good partner: quick-thinking and decisive, but never overbearing or dismissive of her ideas. Or the controlled, smooth way he walked with just the right amount of swagger. Or how confident and prepared he was, despite the fact that this sting operation was a far cry from his usual fare on the organized crime squad.

Or the fact that he also happened to be stupidly hot.

That tailored suit he was wearing hardly helped the situation. Seeing him all buttoned up and businesslike was oddly quite provocative. Having witnessed John firsthand in a sweaty T-shirt and gym shorts at the Academy, she knew exactly what he had going on underneath that suit and tie—and it was nothing short of hard, sculpted perfection. There'd been a moment earlier, in the car, when he'd rolled up his shirtsleeves and the mere sight of his forearms had her nearly blushing.

Seriously. His *forearms*.

Thankfully, he hadn't seemed to notice that *she* was noticing these things. And she had every intention of keeping it that way. She had a job to do here, and ogling her partner's bare body parts wasn't part of the assignment her boss had given her. Most unfortunately.

A knock on her hotel room door interrupted her thoughts. Feeling better now that she'd resolved these things in her mind, she glimpsed through the peephole and then opened the door.

John stood there, wearing jeans and a white T-shirt that stretched tight across his toned chest and broad shoulders and showed off what had to be the sexiest biceps she'd ever seen.

Okay, she took it back: He could put the suit and tie back on. Or perhaps a baggy, shapeless hoodie. Maybe some sort of head-to-toe rain slicker. Because now there was *more* tanned skin, and *more* muscles, and suddenly her inner pragmatic voice—the one that had previously been telling her *not* to notice these things—was holding up its hands in surrender. *Yeah, even I've got nothing in response to that.*

His eyes moved over her, his voice low enough so only she could hear. "You're wearing *jeans*. Those sophisticates on your squad would have your badge if they saw this."

Ah, good. He was annoying her already. Just like that, they were back on course. "I'll have to trust you to keep my secret," she said dryly, stepping back so he could come inside. She closed the door behind him and handed him the room service menu. "Let me know what you want and I'll call in the order."

Once that was out of the way, they got down to business. Her room came with a small kitchenette, and next to that was a table and chairs where they could work. Being only a two-person table, it was a tight fit, with the backs of their laptops touching each other.

"I spoke to Leavitt about sending us the real estate listings for other properties that Dave and Ashley might've considered as potential locations for their restaurant," John said. "He said he'd e-mail those to us within the hour."

Jessica nodded. This was another detail in the cover story that she and John had agreed felt thin. On the off chance Blair inquired about other possible locations they'd looked at for their restaurant, they wanted to know what else was on the market. "Good. Thanks."

Getting comfortable in front of her laptop, she tucked her legs underneath her. "So. Hot restaurant trends." After running a Google search, she scrolled through the results while absentmindedly chewing on the end of her pen. "Ah. Here's something interesting . . ."

Peering up from her laptop, she trailed off when she noticed that John was staring at her.

Or, more specifically, at her mouth.

Blushing, she stopped chewing the pen and put it down. Bad habit, she knew. "This article says that 'upscale family dining' is on the rise. Maybe that's something we can work with." Continuing on with her research, she jotted down some notes on the hotel notepad she'd swiped from her nightstand. She was reading an article by some supposed food expert who proclaimed that "scrambled eggs" were one of this year's hottest trends (as opposed to last year, when they were so passé?) and was about to make a joke about that when John's voice cut across the table.

"Do you have to do that with the pen? It's distracting," he said, with an edge to his voice.

Oops. She hadn't even realized she'd had the tip in her mouth again. "Sorry. I have a slight oral fixation." Or so her mother, the psychologist, was always telling her. *Sweetie, it's a stress reliever. Try uncovering the source of the stress, instead of gnawing away at your problems.*

"An oral fixation," John repeated.

His jaw twitched.

She shrugged matter-of-factly. "That's what it's called."

He looked at her for another moment, then turned back to his laptop and began typing furiously.

Okay. Somebody seemed to be in a bit of a mood.

Their food arrived a half hour later. While eating dinner, they decided on a concept that Ashley and Dave were considering for their second Jacksonville restaurant project: a neighborhood farm-to-table American bistro that served locally sourced produce and meats and featured a weekend brunch that offered a rotating daily special of—wait for it—gourmet *scrambled eggs.*

"You're so proud of that detail," John said, before taking a bite of his blackened fish tacos.

Jessica smiled as she spread more mayo on her club sandwich. Actually, yes, she was. "I hear they're all the rage these days." As she uncrossed her legs to sit more upright, her right leg brushed alongside John's underneath the table.

A flash of heat spread low across her stomach.

"Sorry." She adjusted her position in the chair to put more space between them.

"No problem." He continued eating, suddenly seeming very interested in whatever he was reading on his laptop.

For Pete's sake, she was acting like she'd never been around an attractive man before. Her ex-husband, quite cute in his own right, was a film producer; she'd been to numerous parties and events with some of the most famous, best-looking actors in the business. Spend any length of time in Hollywood and hotness became as much a part of the scenery as palm trees. But one accidental touch of John Shepherd's leg and she was as flustered as a preteen at a Justin Bieber concert.

Get it together, Harlow. Focus on the assignment.

Fortunately, Leavitt's e-mail arrived while they were eating, keeping them busy with several real estate listings they needed to review. While perusing the photos of one of the properties, Jessica pulled out the bobby pins she'd used to secure her hair. The darn things had been digging into her scalp all day.

"I realize that Chicago is a pretty expensive city to live in, but can you believe how cheap—" John paused as Jessica's hair fell around her shoulders, wavy and wild from being in the bun all day. He cleared his throat and continued. "—how cheap some of these properties are?"

"I know. You can buy a building big enough to fit an entire restaurant for less than I paid for my one-bedroom condo." She was running her fingers through her hair, trying to tame it, when her cell phone chimed with a new text message—her personal phone, not the burner she'd been given for the assignment. A few seconds later, it chimed a second time.

"Excuse me." She got up from the table and went to the

nightstand, where her cell phone lay. As she picked it up, it chimed with yet another message.

My guy says you haven't texted him yet, her brother wrote. Did I mention the Maserati?

Jessica sighed as she scrolled through the messages. Not this again.

Only six times, was the quick retort from her sister. Jess—just come to the gym with me. Once you see my guy in his workout clothes, you won't give a crap about some stupid car.

Says the woman whose wife drives an Audi R8, Finn quipped.

Before Jessica could even jump into the fray, her phone vibrated with a smug reply from Maya.

And looks damn good in it.

Shaking her head, Jessica typed her reply. She loved her brother and sister, and knew they were just feeling protective and looking out for her postdivorce—a fact she found a bit amusing since she carried a Glock and could drop-kick them both to the floor should the mood ever arise. But sometimes, it was exhausting being the "plus one" to the conversation while they did their twin thing.

In the middle of something right now, she wrote.

Naturally, her sister was all over that. Ooh . . . something risqué?

Please don't answer that, her brother texted immediately.

Jessica stole a quick glance at John. His perfect biceps tightened gloriously as he took a sip from the bottled beer he'd ordered through room service.

She swallowed, her mouth suddenly having gone dry. It's a work thing, she told her brother and sister. Now stop texting me before you blow my cover and get me shot.

Her phone went dead silent.

She smiled. After waiting a few moments, she decided to put them out of their misery. Just a little FBI humor, guys.

Their responses came fast and furious.

You SUCK. I was freaking out.

What he said. ☹☹☹☹☹☹☹☹

Jessica chuckled as she walked across the room and retook her seat at the table. Eh, it served them right. Now maybe they'd back off with their plans to set her up on a date. Not that she wouldn't be interested down the road, but right now she needed to settle into single life at her own pace. Heck, the ink was barely dry on her divorce papers.

John raised an eyebrow. "Everything okay?"

"Hmm?" She gestured to the phone. "Oh yeah, everything's fine."

"Boyfriend checking up on you?" he asked lightly.

Boyfriend? Ha—that was a good one. "No, just my brother and sister."

He nodded, then took another sip of his beer. "So . . . is there a boyfriend?" He leaned back in his chair, his tone casual. "You weren't wearing a ring around the office, so I'm guessing there's no husband."

That hit a little close to home—not that she blamed John for asking. They were partners now; frankly, it would be weird if they didn't talk occasionally about their personal lives. "No boyfriend." She paused. "There *was* a husband. But he and I finalized our divorce a week ago."

"Sorry. I didn't mean to pry."

She smiled slightly at that. "Yes, you did."

His lips curved in acknowledgment, and then his expression turned more serious. "Is that why you left Los Angeles?"

She shrugged, taking a sip of wine and setting the glass on the table next to her laptop. "It seemed like a good time for a fresh start." Not a fan of being in the hot seat, she used humor to deflect and turn the conversation around to him. "What about you? Girlfriend? Wife? Kids? Perhaps a gaggle of tow-headed, extra-large boys who already excel at sports and know how to make fire with the ass end of a lightning bug?"

He laughed at that—a genuine laugh this time, as opposed to the wry mock-chuckles she was used to hearing. "Guess I missed the day they taught us that at Ranger school." He toyed with his beer bottle. "Nah . . . no wife or kids. There *was* a girlfriend. But she and I broke up a few weeks ago."

Judging from his tense body language, Jessica sensed there was a story. "That's when you tried out for HRT."

"I guess it seemed like a good time for a fresh start."

She half smiled at that. Fair enough.

Neither of them spoke for a moment, their personal revelations seeming to hang in the air between them. To cover, Jessica took another sip of wine and then turned back to work. "So, where are we with the property listings Leavitt sent us?" Checking the e-mail the agent had sent her and John earlier, she set the wineglass down on the edge of the table.

Apparently, *too* close to the edge.

The glass tipped and fell, shattering as it hit the tiled floor of the kitchenette area. Red wine splattered across the floor and the cabinets.

"Shit." She sprang out of her chair, as did John.

Embarrassed by her boneheaded move, and probably moving too hastily, she picked up one of the larger shards of glass and sliced her finger. She swore under her breath as blood flowed from the cut.

Crouched next to her on floor, John looked over and frowned. "You're hurt."

"It's fine." Not wanting to get blood everywhere, she went to the kitchenette sink and ran some cold water over the wound.

John was on his feet, coming over to examine her finger. "Let me see."

"Really, it's fine."

"Let me see," he repeated, more firmly. Without further discussion, he took her hand out of the water, holding it in his palm so he could get a better look.

After the chill of the water, his hand, slightly rough, wrapped like a warm blanket around hers.

"You don't think I'll need stitches, do you?" Their heads nearly touched as they examined the cut. Jessica peered up and realized her mouth was just inches from his.

Goddamn if his lips weren't as perfect as the rest of him.

She blinked, snapping out of it when John moved her hand back into the cold water.

"Let's see how quickly it stops bleeding." He grabbed some paper towels from the kitchenette counter and folded them over. After shutting off the water, he took her hand again and covered the wound with the paper towels, using his other hand to apply pressure.

Jessica glanced up, something softening inside her as she watched him work.

"Does that hurt?" he asked.

Her own voice was husky. "Not much."

"The illustrious Jessica Harlow, taken down by a wineglass." He pointed, and his tone turned firm again. "Hold the paper towels exactly like that, until I say otherwise."

"Yes, sir." She smiled sweetly when he gave her a look. Then her smile turned to a frown of protest when he grabbed more paper towels and started cleaning up the mess on the floor. "John . . . you don't have to do that."

"I think it's best if my partner has all her fingers for our sting op tomorrow."

Ha ha. She stood there, feeling useless as he picked up the remaining glass and wiped up the wine that had splashed across the floor and cabinets.

He came over to the sink to dampen a few paper towels. "Besides, it's fun seeing you squirm."

She pulled back, not sure what *that* meant. "Why would I be squirming?"

"Because you can't stand accepting help. At least not from me."

"That's ridiculous," she scoffed. "When have I ever had any problem accepting help from you? And don't tell me"—she paused when he pointed to her hand, indicating that she should apply more pressure to the cut—"that you're counting all the times you tried to 'motivate' me by yelling at me throughout the PT drills. We can agree to disagree on the supposed helpfulness of that technique."

He ignored her wry tone. "Actually, I was talking about the day on the shooting range."

Oh. That.

You're anticipating the blast and flinching when the shot fires. Plus, your stance is wrong.

She fell quiet, shifting uncomfortably at the memory. As she'd learned from her firearms instructor the following day, John had been completely correct in his assessment. Yes, he'd surprised her when he'd touched her shoulder, and, certainly, the whole problem would've been alleviated if he'd just *asked* if she wanted help. But nevertheless, in hindsight, perhaps her *Easy there, big guy* comment had been a teensy bit . . . harsh.

"Careful with the glass," she warned as he knelt on the floor to finish cleaning. "The little pieces are hard to see."

He looked amused, although it was tough to say whether this stemmed more from her suggestion that the mighty John Shepherd could be hurt by mere glass, or from his awareness that she'd dodged the subject of their argument at the shooting range. After throwing away the last of the paper towels, he came over to the sink to inspect her hand. "Do you have any Band-Aids?"

"There's a small first-aid kit in my makeup bag."

"Where's that?"

"On the bathroom counter. Just bring the bag out here and

I'll grab the kit," she added when he headed toward the bathroom.

After he returned with the makeup bag and set it on the counter, she unzipped it with her free hand and pulled out the first-aid kit. Without further ado, he set about the business of dressing the cut.

As she watched him, something compelled her to explain. "Maybe I was a little defensive that day at the shooting range," she acknowledged. "Before I left for the Academy, my recruiter gave me this speech about not doing anything that would give people an excuse not to take me seriously. It's bullshit, but the reality is, there's a double standard about these things; we all know that. As one of only two women in the class, I had to be careful not to do anything that, rightfully or wrongfully, could've been viewed as unprofessional." She paused. "Like flirt with the best-looking guy in the class."

His head shot up, his eyes wide with surprise.

She scoffed. "Oh, please. It's hardly a state secret that you're hot."

And for a moment, the mighty John Shepherd actually seemed speechless.

Then, with a coy curve to his lips, he went back to his ministrations and wrapped a large Band-Aid over the gauze. "How much did that pain you to say?"

"Even more than nearly slicing my finger off," she muttered.

With a smile, he finished up with the Band-Aid. "There." Holding her hand, he inspected his handiwork. "Keep the gauze dry," he lectured. "And don't go peeking at the wound until the morning—you might make it start to bleed again."

She was about to say *Yes, sir* again—just to needle him—but then stopped herself. Just once, maybe they could do without the sarcasm and quips.

"Thank you," she said genuinely.

His eyes met hers. "You're welcome."

Perhaps it was the low, sexy tone of his voice. Or maybe the warm look in his blue eyes. But suddenly, Jessica realized just how close she and John stood—only inches apart.

And he still held her hand.

He seemed to notice this at the same moment she did. She stepped back, and he instantly let go of her.

"Well. We should probably get back to work," she said brightly, trying to calm the flush rising to her cheeks.

Scooping up the Band-Aid wrapper and tossing it in the trash, she took a seat at the table in front of her laptop. She felt John's eyes on her but ignored it as he sat down in the chair across the table.

"Looks like there's only two listings left for us to review." When John remained silent, she peered up from her computer. Under his scrutinizing gaze, she kept her tone deliberately light and nonchalant, per their usual. "Don't fade on me now, Shepherd. We're almost at the finish line."

He cocked his head, as if about to say something, and then seemed to change his mind. "Right." He cleared his throat, turning to his own computer. "So. Where were we?"

13

Game day.

Not having anything on the agenda until that evening, John slept in and then headed to the hotel gym. After an hour of lifting weights, he still had time and an abundance of energy to burn, so he went for a run along the beach.

As his feet pounded against the wet sand, he ran through the plan for tonight's meeting with Mayor Blair. Probably, this was unnecessary—nothing had changed in the last twelve hours and he already knew the plan backward and forward— but focusing on work kept his mind off other matters.

After he'd sweated up a storm in the midmorning heat, the wide, blue expanse of the Atlantic Ocean beckoned him. Stripping off his shoes and T-shirt, he dove into the water and swam lazily along the shore, letting the waves do most of the work. Then he stretched out on one of the hotel's beach chairs and closed his eyes as the warmth of the sun drained all the remaining tension out of him.

There could certainly be worse undercover assignments.

A half hour later, having dozed off to the sound of the waves crashing against the shore, he threw on his T-shirt and running shoes and began walking back to the hotel's main building. A short distance ahead of him was a class of about ten people, all women, doing yoga on the beach. His eyes landed on a familiar five-foot, three-inch blonde who stretched, barefoot, on the mat.

Jessica.

And just like that, all the tension poured right back into him.

Just keep moving. Pay no attention to the limber woman in the tight black stretchy pants and purple tank top.

While *not* noticing Jessica was, in fact, a futile endeavor, he'd at least become something of an expert in faking it—especially after last night. First, there'd been the rubbing of their legs underneath the table. Then she'd done that sexy move with her hair, taking out the pins one at a time and letting it fall wild around her shoulders. If he'd ever wondered what Jessica Harlow looked like with tousled, I've-just-been-sexed-up hair, that question had been officially laid to rest last night: fucking *hot*.

And then there was the thing with the pen.

He couldn't even with the pen.

As if it hadn't been titillating enough to watch her slide the damn thing over, along, and between her lips, she'd had to go and declare that she had an "oral fixation."

Uh-huh. Sure. Like *that* hadn't had his mind going in all sorts of prurient directions.

The problem was, "prurient" were not the kind of thoughts a special agent should be having about his partner. And they definitely weren't the kind of thoughts a man should be having about a woman who'd once gotten extremely pissed off just because he'd touched her *shoulder*. He and Jessica were actually semi-getting-along now—sarcastic comments and dry quips notwithstanding—and he planned to keep it that way. He had a job to do here in Jacksonville, possibly his last undercover assignment, which meant he needed to stay focused on work and—

Christ, now she was doing some yoga pose that had her bent over, doggie style, with her cute, round ass sticking straight in the air.

She had to be kidding him with this shit.

Using her hands to push off the ground in a graceful move, she rolled to a standing position, arms rotating outward and extending to the sky. Opening her eyes, she went still when she saw him approaching in his jogging shorts and T-shirt.

Playing it cool, he threw her a nod—'*Sup*—and kept walking, forcing his eyes not to linger on the Sweet Round Ass of Torture or any of the other parts of Jessica Harlow that were on display in that tight outfit. Then he headed straight to his room, took a cold shower, and spent the rest of the afternoon in front of his laptop, catching up on some reports he'd fallen behind on in his other investigations.

It was the least sexy thing he could think of.

With rustic brick walls, a curved copper chef's bar, and large accent mirrors, Bistro Aix had a high-energy, bistro-in-a-big-city feel to it. The noise level wasn't optimum for the microphones John and Jessica had hidden on them, but since John had yet to find *any* restaurant that was optimum for an undercover agent surreptitiously recording his dinner companions via a small recording device adhered to the back of one of his shirt buttons, they would deal with it.

Right on schedule at seven o'clock, Morano walked into the restaurant, accompanied by the Honorable Patrick Blair. Following the mayor were two police officers from the sheriff's department—his protective detail—who gave the mayor a nod before taking seats at the bar. They likely would remain there for the rest of the evening, available if necessary but otherwise staying out of the way.

From his vantage point in the booth he shared with Jessica near the back of the restaurant, John watched as the mayor went straight into politician mode, schmoozing it up and gripping the restaurant host's shoulder as if they were old friends. And perhaps they were; Agent Leavitt had mentioned that this was one of the mayor's favorite restaurants.

At first blush, it wasn't hard to see why voters—and, apparently, *People* magazine—found Blair appealing. With a charming smile, perfectly styled sandy-brown hair, and a lean build, he appeared to be channeling a young, Southern John F. Kennedy. Albeit without the Ivy League education and wealthy family.

John had a sneaking suspicion that was exactly the vibe the ambitious politician was going for.

Following the host to the back of the restaurant, Mayor Blair stopped and shook hands with several of the restaurant's patrons, joking and chatting his way through the crowd. Then Morano leaned in and whispered something in Blair's ear, gesturing in the direction of John and Jessica's table.

As Blair turned in their direction, his eyes passed briefly over John before landing on Jessica. Cocking his head, he smiled and headed over.

John stood up to greet him, as did Jessica.

Showtime.

"There's my two favorite Chicago investors!" Morano said in a booming voice, showing his usual flair for subtlety. "Ashley Evers and Dave Rosser, it's my honor to introduce the esteemed mayor of this city, Mr. Patrick Blair."

Blair stepped forward to shake Jessica's hand first. "It's a pleasure to meet you, Ms. Evers."

"The pleasure is all mine, Mayor Blair. And please, call me Ashley."

"Ashley it is." He held her gaze for another moment before turning to John. "And Mr. Rosser."

John extended his hand. "Mr. Mayor. It's an honor."

They took their seats, with Blair helping himself to the chair across from Jessica. "So . . . the Windy City," he led in, immediately taking charge of the conversation. Like Morano, he spoke with a relaxed Southern drawl. "I visited there once, nine years ago. After taking the bar exam, I rented a car and spent three weeks driving across the U.S.—including two days in Chicago. Great city. Hot and humid as hell in August." He winked at Jessica. "It was like being home again."

"Three weeks? That must've been some trip," she said.

"Where else did you visit?" John asked.

Breaking only to order his drink—vodka on the rocks—the mayor spent the next ten minutes regaling them with tales of his cross-country journey. It was, as with most politicians' stories, partially a canned speech, peppered with prepared jokes and lofty phrases like, "in the great state of Oklahoma," and even contained a few poignant, memoir-worthy anecdotes.

It was a good charade, John observed. Blair was charismatic and dynamic and knew how to draw in his listeners. But having read the files, including the summaries of the conversations Morano had had with Blair while wearing a wire, John knew that lurking behind the charming politician's façade was a conniving, corrupt man who got his rocks off on using his power and influence for personal gain.

"Look at me, jabbering away here," Blair said, when the waitress stopped at the table to take their dinner orders. "How's the pork chop today, Charlotte?"

"The same as it always is, Mr. Mayor," the waitress shot back.

Blair grinned at John and Jessica over his menu. "Charlotte loves to give me crap for always ordering the same thing. But if it ain't broke, don't fix it, right?" He handed the waitress his menu. "And I'll start with the beet salad."

After the waitress left, Jessica folded her hands on the table, ready to get down to business. "Let me start by saying, Mr. Mayor, how much Dave and I appreciate you taking the time to meet with us."

Blair nodded graciously and gestured to Morano. "Anthony

said you were two people I needed to meet, and Anthony is always right about these things."

"I told the mayor that your firm is considering investing in some projects in Jacksonville," Morano said conversationally.

"That's great to hear," Blair said. "I strongly believe that by encouraging and leveraging both public and private investments in this city, we can create exciting new business and job opportunities. That's been one of my top priorities since the day I took office."

"I certainly think we bring that to the table," Jessica said. "I'm not sure how much Anthony has told you about Lakeshore Capital Partners, but we're a private equity firm that seeks out investment opportunities in the hospitality industry that fall within the five-million to twenty-five-million-dollar range. Now, obviously, it's all about finding the *right* opportunities. To do that, we look for concepts and markets that we believe have significant growth potential. And after doing our research, Dave and I believe that the Jacksonville culinary scene has a lot of potential."

The mayor leaned forward in his chair. "What is it, exactly, about Jacksonville that you find so appealing?"

Jessica's smile was sly. "You mean, other than the fact that it's 'the closest thing to Greenwich Village you'll find in Florida'?"

Blair let out a bark of laughter. "You really have done your research." As he took a sip of his drink, his eyes once again lingered on Jessica.

Seeing that, John tightened his grip around his own glass.

Considering his own struggles with the issue, he could hardly fault Blair for noticing that Jessica was a beautiful woman—especially tonight. With blue smoky eyes, blond hair tumbling to her shoulders in loose waves, and wearing heels and a knee-length black dress that seemed tailor-made for her figure, she looked both sophisticated and incredibly sexy. But there was something else in Blair's gaze . . . something predatory and calculating that seemed to go beyond mere frank, male appreciation.

"From a design perspective," John said, interjecting himself into the conversation, "I can tell you that the restaurant concept Ashley and I have come up with would be a perfect fit for the neighborhood."

"I hear you've been looking at properties in Riverside. Charming neighborhood, isn't it? Lots of culture and history—but not pretentious," Blair said.

"That's exactly the vibe we're looking for," John said.

The mayor nodded, then looked again at Jessica. "So tell me, Ashley, what kind of restaurant do you have in mind?"

And so it went. For the next half hour, Jessica did the majority of the talking, running through Ashley and Dave's pitch. Completely convincing in her role as a private equity investor, she described for Blair their pizzeria and wine bar concept and their enthusiasm for the project, and also mentioned their plan to follow up this initial investment with several more restaurant ventures in the city. John did his part, too, contributing his ideas as the design guy, but it was clear that Blair responded more receptively to Jessica, even finding a way, on several occasions, to draw her into a side conversation.

The undercover agent in John was pleased with this development. Business was business, and as long as their target seemed to be opening up and trusting them, he didn't give a crap about being sidelined while his partner handled the brunt of the conversation.

The man in him, however, was oddly tempted to handle things *grunt*-style if the esteemed mayor of America's thirteenth-largest city didn't stop ogling the V-neckline of Jessica's dress.

"Have you settled on a location for your restaurant?" Blair asked Jessica, after the waitress cleared away the entrées.

"We're trying to." Jessica glanced at John, as if this were a subject they'd discussed significantly. "Actually, we've found the perfect property on King Street, just south of Forbes. A former bank building. But there are a few issues with the space we'd need to resolve before we can commit."

"What kind of issues?" Blair cocked his head as if this were news to him, despite the fact that Morano had already apprised him of this fact.

All part of the dance.

Jessica laid out the problem, telling Blair about the zoning and parking problems they faced with the bank building. "Otherwise, it's an ideal location. As a matter of fact, Dave and I just did another walk-through yesterday, and we locked down a design concept. We're thinking a Tuscan-wine-cellar feel, with lots of arches and oak. Although I'm not entirely sold on the idea of 'sexy' red leather on the banquettes." She shot John a look of wry skepticism.

Playing off her lead, John flashed her a cocky smile, as if they'd had a lot of debates just like this one. "Eh. You'll come around by the time we open."

Shaking her head in exasperation—funny how art imitated life—Jessica turned back to Blair. "Anyway, we'll obviously apply for the necessary zoning variances and parking permits with the city's Land Use Committee, but . . . well, you know how these things go. It could take months before anyone even looks at our application. And unfortunately, we need to be able to make a decision faster than that. Our investors are very eager to move forward as soon as possible."

Steepling his fingers, Blair considered this. "Hmm. Let me give some thought to your situation. Sometimes, the right phone call to the right people is all it takes to smooth over predicaments like this. And in this city, obviously, I have all the right people on speed dial," he added, with no small amount of boastfulness. "Although, as I'm sure you understand, I can't just pick up the phone on behalf of everyone who asks for a favor. I have to choose those causes I feel most . . . motivated about."

Bingo.

John mentally grabbed the popcorn and sat back to watch as Jessica reeled in their big fish.

"Of course—which is why Dave and I appreciate you taking the time just to meet with us," she said. "And, as you're giving thought to our situation, if you think of anything *we* can do to help facilitate getting those zoning variances and parking permits, please let us know." She held the mayor's gaze, suddenly looking quite shrewd and calculating herself. "There certainly is no shortage of motivation on our end to get this resolved as quickly as possible."

"I think we understand each other quite well, Ms. Evers," Blair drawled, with a hint of a smile. He tipped his glass to Jessica and took a sip.

Shortly thereafter, the waitress stopped by the table to take their dessert orders. As the busboy set espresso cups around the table, Jessica excused herself to go to the restroom. Ever the gentleman, Blair stood up with her, taking the opportunity to put his hand on the small of her back as he told her where the restrooms were located.

Then he stared at her ass as she walked off.

John looked away, managing a polite tone as he thanked the busboy for the espresso cup.

Blair retook his seat and rested his arms on the table. "I've been wondering something, Dave. What, exactly, is the deal with you and Ashley?"

Next to the mayor, Morano suddenly seemed very interested in the alignment of his dessert fork and spoon.

Having a feeling he knew exactly where this was headed, John leaned back in the booth and fixed his gaze on Blair. "Meaning . . . ?"

"Meaning, is this just a professional relationship, or are you two involved personally, as well?" Blair asked.

Oddly, and in direct opposition to his undercover training, John was tempted to give some vague nonanswer to that question, something that dropped just enough of a hint to make the mayor rethink those lingering looks and "innocent" touches.

But.

As he knew better than anyone, Jessica was an extremely capable agent. She didn't need his protection in this situation—or his interference—and she'd given him no indication that she wanted to change up their cover story. Which meant he would stick to the plan: They'd agreed that Ashley was single, so single she would be.

"It's just a professional relationship," John said with an air of easy nonchalance, as if the idea of anything else had never even crossed his mind. "I don't mix business with pleasure."

Blair grinned, teeth flashing as the predatory gleam came back into his eyes. "Fortunately for me, I don't suffer from the same scruples."

Now there was a fucking surprise.

14

"I think that went well for a first meeting," Jessica said, as John drove the Mercedes out of the restaurant parking lot. They headed to the rendezvous spot, an abandoned warehouse, just three miles east, where they were meeting Leavitt and Todd. "Blair seemed to take the bait." Before parting ways at the restaurant, she and "Dave" had offered to show the mayor the proposed restaurant site so they could more fully explain their plans for the property and had reiterated their desire to get the zoning issues resolved expeditiously.

"We even managed to make it through dinner without any mention of a 'cherries jubilee' from Morano." John grinned.

"True." Adrenaline running through her, Jessica felt charged after the success of the dinner. *This* was why she put up with the unpredictability, the travel, and the crappy hours. In these moments, when all her hard work and preparation came together, and she'd just pulled off a con on a bad guy who was that much closer to getting his comeuppance, the thrill of undercover work was not unlike the high of really great sex.

If memory served.

"Can you believe how restrained Morano was? Leavitt and

Todd must've talked to him after we left the office yesterday," she said.

"I'm sure they put the fear of God in him that he'll be spending the next twenty years behind bars if he screws up this investigation with his antics." John looked over. "By the way, I think you picked up a new member of your fan club tonight."

Jessica made a face at the reminder. Unfortunately, yes, she'd noticed that, too—it would've been hard not to notice. "I think Blair spent half the dinner talking to my boobs. Which, given the circumstances, isn't entirely a bad thing." With a satisfied grin, she reached into the V-neckline of her dress. Given her line of work, she'd had a special modification made to a few of her bras: a small pocket hidden in the lining. From there, she pulled out the wireless microphone, a dime-sized metallic disc that looked similar to a camera battery, and tucked it into the case she'd left in the glove compartment.

"While you were gone, Blair asked if you and I were a couple." John glanced over, saw she was readjusting the neckline of her dress, and looked back at the road.

"Did he, now?" Jessica's mind began running through ways they might possibly use this development to their advantage. "What did you say?"

"That I don't mix business with pleasure." John's tone took on an edge that Jessica assumed was one of disgust. "He made it clear he doesn't share the same principles."

A few minutes later, they pulled up to the abandoned warehouse. Leavitt and Todd were already out of their car, waiting.

"'Sexy red leather on the banquettes'?" Leavitt joked, as John and Jessica got out of the Mercedes. "Who came up with that?"

John grinned, grabbing Leavitt's outstretched hand in a congratulatory shake. "Jessica and I added a few details to the script last night."

"You guys were great." Todd's expression was two parts approval and one part relief. "When Morano checks in, I wouldn't be shocked if he says Blair's already decided on the amount of money it'll take for him to pick up the phone and call one of his 'right' people."

They rehashed the highlights of the dinner, the camaraderie thick among them. While talking, John undid his shirt just above his navel and removed the microphone adhered to the back of the button.

Catching a glimpse of his smooth skin, Jessica felt a heated flush rise to her cheeks. *My God, woman, get a grip.* Looking away, she smiled along as Leavitt imitated Blair's comment about choosing those causes he felt most "motivated" about.

"So, Jessica, we couldn't help but notice that Blair seemed to be . . . well, flirting with you. Any thoughts on how you want to handle that situation?" Leavitt asked.

She appreciated that they were looking to her to take the lead on this—although, from her perspective, there was really only one way to handle it. Her job required that she play nice with Blair, and if that meant she had to put up with the jerk hitting on her over a couple of dinner meetings, well, unfortunately, she would hardly be the first woman to find herself in that predicament. "If stroking Blair's ego and letting him think his 'charms' are working on me moves the ball along in the investigation, I say we just go with it." She turned to John. "Don't you think?"

He paused before answering, then nodded. "I agree."

Jessica looked back at Leavitt and Todd. "Sounds like we have a plan."

During the fifteen-minute drive to their hotel, Jessica told herself that she was overthinking things.

The meeting with Blair had gone off without a hitch. She was pleased with the way things were moving along, Leavitt and Todd were pleased, and everyone anticipated that Ashley and Dave soon would have a follow-up meeting with the mayor. By all accounts the night had been a success, and now the only thing she should be thinking about was which glass of wine she was going to grab at the hotel bar before heading up to her room for a long, relaxing bath.

But instead, she kept dwelling on John's reaction when she'd asked if he agreed with her call on how to handle Blair's flirting.

He'd hesitated.

Yes, it was momentary, and quite possibly it meant nothing, but she'd never seen John Shepherd hesitate about anything. Ever. As part of his military training, he was assertive, authoritative, and decisive. If anything, his one flaw at the Academy had been his tendency to storm into a situation full throttle and ask questions later—after everyone was facedown on the ground and in handcuffs.

And yet tonight, when she'd asked for his opinion on the situation with Blair, he'd held back before answering.

This did not sit well with her.

Even during the height of their rivalry at the Academy—as much as it would've pained her to admit it back then—she'd had a lot of respect for John's intelligence and tactical skills. Working side-by-side with him over the course of the last thirty-six hours had only increased that respect. She trusted him to have her back, and, just as important, she trusted his judgment. So if he had any doubts about the call she'd made, she wanted to know about it.

She was still debating whether to say anything as she pulled up to the hotel's main entrance and handed the car over to the valet. On the one hand, her head told her that John, of all people, wouldn't hesitate to tell her if he thought she was wrong about something. Heck, he'd spent most of their time together at the Academy doing just that.

But her gut nevertheless said that something was up. And in the six years she'd been a special agent, her gut instincts hadn't been proven wrong yet.

In the lobby, where they normally would part and go their separate ways, she made her decision. "Actually, I think I'll follow you to your room, if you don't mind. There's something I forgot to ask you about tonight's dinner."

John studied her curiously for a moment, then gestured in the direction of the outdoor walkway that led toward the rooms. "I'm in the second building."

As they followed the walkway along the beach, she glanced over and looked for any sign that something was off—and noticed that he was similarly trying to get a read on her. They made small talk while walking to his building, and then, once inside, he directed her to his room.

"You're being awfully mysterious." At the door, he pulled the key card out of his pocket.

"Am I?" With a vague, noncommittal smile, she was careful not to give anything away. But then he opened the door to his room, and she became momentarily sidetracked by what she saw inside.

"You have an oceanfront view?" Her mouth fell open in indignation as she stepped into the room and set her purse on the bed. "How did you manage that on our budget?"

"I got a free upgrade at check-in." He flashed her a grin as he tossed the key card onto the desk. "I think the receptionist was flirting with Dave the Value Creator."

For some reason, the thought rankled Jessica. *Of course she was—just look at you*, she nearly said dryly, and then she thought better of it. After all, she wasn't supposed to notice how John looked—at least not in that way. She was his partner, they were working together undercover, and that meant she needed to continue chugging along with this charade, pretending as though she were somehow oblivious to the things that every other woman saw.

Like the deep blue of his eyes. Or the stubble that was already forming along his angular jaw. Or the thick, dark blond hair that begged to have a woman's fingers running through it.

Or how, right now, as he stood across from her in that hotel room, with the top button of his white collared shirt undone in a ruggedly sophisticated look, and his tall, broad-shouldered frame perfectly filling his gray tailored suit, he was—bar none— the most attractive man she'd ever laid eyes on.

She exhaled quietly, steeling herself as she met his gaze.

Yes. Good thing she hadn't noticed any of that.

Watching her, John cocked his head. "What did you want to talk about?"

Right. She was there to discuss work. Having decided that a surprise approach was her best chance of catching John off guard—if he was indeed hiding something—she came right out with it. "Why did you hesitate when I asked if you agreed that I should humor Blair's flirting?"

There was a flicker in his eyes. It was a momentary change, nearly imperceptible if she hadn't been looking for it, but it was enough to tell her that she was on to something.

"I didn't hesitate. I was thinking," he said matter-of-factly. "You asked for my opinion, so I took a moment and then gave it to you."

Hmm. A convincing response. But the tense position of his shoulders told her that something was off. "Why do I have a feeling there's something you're not telling me?"

"Maybe . . . because you're being paranoid?" He folded his arms across his chest. "Please tell me I'm not the first person who's ever dared to *pause* before agreeing with the illustrious Jessica Harlow."

The dig was a nice attempt to sidetrack her, but she ignored it and hit him with a question that was even more blunt. "Do you think it's inappropriate for me to encourage Blair's flirtation?" There was a firm rule that agents working undercover were not permitted to have any sexual contact with the target of an investigation, but she hoped it went without saying that she would never come close to crossing that line. In fact, as a woman in a profession dominated by men, she was especially careful not to even be within *miles* of that line.

John's expression softened. "That's what you're worried about?" He took a step closer to her. "Jessica . . . I think you're handling Blair perfectly. I never once thought that *you* are being inappropriate. He's the dickhead here."

She shifted her weight self-consciously. "You know how it is—you never know how these things will play out in court. Obviously, I can explain when I testify that I couldn't call Blair a 'pervert' and walk out during the middle of an investigation that took eighteen months to plan. But what if the jury sees it differently? What if they decide I was honey-potting the guy, and that I unduly influenced him to take the bribe?"

"'Honey-potting'? Really?" John asked, appearing amused.

She threw him a look. "It's a thing."

"Only in Hollywood." He put his hands on her shoulders reassuringly. "Listen, no one is going to think you did anything wrong. Given the circumstances, you don't have any choice but to play along with Blair's flirting." He squeezed her shoulders. "Okay?"

She nodded, giving him a relieved smile. "Okay." She waited a moment, then cocked her head. "So . . . if you don't think I have any choice but to humor Blair's flirting, why did you hesitate earlier?"

John's smile faded as realization set in.

Busted.

He let go of her shoulders. "Goddammit. I can't believe I fell for your damsel-in-distress trick again."

She grinned, pretty damn pleased to have pulled that off. "If it makes you feel any better, it is a very impressive trick."

He glared at her.

Okay, apparently somebody wasn't in the mood for jokes right then. "It's your own fault. If you'd just tell me why you hesitated, then I wouldn't have to resort to tricks."

"Christ, I forgot how you're like a dog with a bone when you've latched on to something," he muttered.

Now *that* ticked her off a little. "Hey. All I'm trying to do is figure out why my partner is holding back with me." Having established that he didn't think she was doing anything inappropriate with Blair—which had been her original concern—she couldn't fathom what the problem was.

"I told you, it's nothing."

She threw her hands up in exasperation, clearly missing something. "If it's nothing, then just tell me why you hesitated when I asked you about Blair!"

He whirled on her, his voice raised. "Because I don't like the way he looks at you!"

She blinked in surprise.

Oh.

John swore under his breath, and lowered his voice. "I had to sit in that restaurant, for two hours, as he ogled your chest and ass, and I couldn't say a thing about it. So when you asked if I agreed with a plan that would encourage Blair to do *more* of that, yes, Jessica, it took me a split second not to choke on the damn word before I said 'yes.'"

She took a moment before responding. "You're saying this because we work together," she clarified. "You don't like the way Blair looks at me because we're *partners*."

He looked away from her, his tone dry. "Yes, Harlow, because we're partners. What else would it be?"

He put his hand on the door handle, an indication that he considered this conversation over. And if Jessica was smart, she would follow his lead, say good night, and never bring up the subject again. He was in a mood, tempers were running hot, and they both had extra adrenaline coursing through them after the undercover job.

But nevertheless, something kept her standing there.

"I mean, I suppose it *could* be something . . . more," she said, deliberately keeping her tone nonchalant.

John went still, and then he let go of the door handle.

"More," he repeated. "As in, something more between you and me."

He crossed the room toward her, and her heart began to pound.

"I said I suppose it *could* be something more."

He gestured casually. "You were just . . . throwing the idea out there."

"Exactly."

He closed the gap between them. "Then why are you blushing?"

She opened her mouth to deny it, or make some quippy response, but when she saw the unmistakable heat in his eyes, the words fizzled and died on her lips.

Walk away, urged the pragmatic voice in her head. *Better yet—run.*

As if having the same internal debate, John stayed where he was for a moment, the air thick between them.

Then he reached up and cupped her cheek, stroking his thumb over her skin.

She closed her eyes, her breath catching at his touch.

Somewhere in the distance, she heard her inner pragmatic voice shouting through a bullhorn—*Put your hands in the air, Harlow, and step away from the hottie*—telling her that this was crazy, that she'd never so much as flirted with another agent before, and that a mere thirty-six hours ago, she and this particular co-worker barely had been able to speak two civil words to each other.

And since that was all indeed true, she reached up and put her hand against John's chest.

He shifted closer, his lips now mere inches from hers as he spoke in a low tone. "You should stop me."

"I know." She wouldn't have to push him away; all it would take was one word. But then she felt his heart beating hard and fast beneath her palm, the same as hers, and before she knew what she was doing, she curled her fingers around his shirt and pulled his mouth the rest of the way down to hers.

Screw it.

Her control of the situation lasted all of about two seconds. Immediately taking charge—of course he did—John backed her against the wall, trapping her there. With his hands cupping her face, he wound his tongue wickedly around hers as he claimed her mouth.

She arched against him, wrapping her arms around his neck. His hands moved to her waist, skimming down the sides of her dress and over the curve of her hips.

"John, we have to . . ." Her voice, a throaty murmur, trailed off as he slid his lips to her neck. *God*, that felt good. She dug her fingers into his thick hair, so turned on she thought she might melt right there, and impatiently pulled his lips back to hers.

Their kiss grew hotter and more intense with every breath, and judging from the sizable erection pressing between her legs, John was every bit as turned on as she was. Acting on instinct, she reached for the lapels of his suit jacket, ready to shove it off, just as she felt one of his hands part the slit of her dress.

She moaned softly when his fingers slid up her thigh.

There was a low sound deep in his throat, as his mouth

covered hers again. They began to move with an almost fever-
ish urgency as—

A phone rang.

No.

They both froze at the sound, as reality quickly set in.

"Is that your burner?" Her lips hovered just inches from his.

John's eyes closed briefly. "No. It's my cell."

Something seemed to pass between them, but then the
phone rang again and the moment just . . . slipped away.

Duty called.

Jessica slid out from her trapped position against the wall
and adjusted the skirt of her dress.

"Jessica," John said, from behind her.

Needing a moment to collect herself, she took a deep breath
and then turned to face John. "You should get that," she said
calmly, pointing to his phone on the desk.

John studied her for a moment. Yes, fine, she was trying to
hold her internal freak-out at bay, because kissing the man acting as her partner—no less, her partner in the first undercover
investigation she'd been assigned since transferring to her new
office—most definitely had *not* been on the agenda. While
there was no express policy prohibiting FBI agents from hooking up, even while working undercover, she, personally, had
always adhered to the *Don't shit where you eat* school of thought.
And in the six years she'd spent in the Los Angeles office, she'd
never once been tempted to break her own standards.

But a mere thirty-six hours with John Shepherd, and she'd
been ready to climb the man like a tree.

Internal freak-out commencing in three . . . two . . . one.

O.

M.

G.

John's phone continued to ring, and he walked over to the
desk and grabbed it.

He cleared his throat before answering. "Shepherd." He paused, his tone turning more colloquial. "Leavitt . . . what's the word?" He met Jessica's gaze. "Sure—try patching Jessica in."

They both waited while Leavitt tried to reach Jessica on her cell phone—which, obviously, was back in her hotel room, where she was supposed to be right now, drinking her celebratory glass of wine, instead of being *here*, with John, having just kissed the man like the world was about to end.

After what felt like an eternity, Leavitt finally gave up.

"No problem. I can fill her in when I see her," John told him, playing innocent on his end of the conversation. "So what did Morano say when he checked in?"

Jessica took a seat on the bed, watching as John listened to the other agent. His shirt gaped open at the chest, having become partially unbuttoned in the fray. And his left cheek bore a red scratch that she suspected was from the Band-Aid on her finger.

"We're thinking early-to-mid next week for that?" John locked eyes with her. "I don't want to speak definitively for Jessica without talking to her first, but we both understand the need to keep the momentum going on this. I'm sure we can make something work." He paused. "Of course. Will do."

He hung up the phone and gave Jessica the update. "Morano says that Blair bought it all. He's already bragging about how he could make our problems go away with one phone call to some buddy of his on the Land Use Committee. Leavitt anticipates that Blair will give Morano the go-ahead to set up another meeting sometime in the next couple of days."

She nodded. "I heard Leavitt ask about early-to-mid next week. I can be back in Jacksonville then."

"He also asked that I pass along to you his gratitude for a job well done. But I wouldn't be surprised if he tries to reach you again tonight, just to tell you himself."

An awkward silence fell between them.

"Don't freak out, Jessica," John finally said.

His knowing—and slightly amused—tone snapped her out of her haze. It was one thing for *her* to know that she was feeling, perhaps, a teeny-tiny bit caught off guard by their kiss. But as a matter of female pride, she refused to let *him* see that.

She who nearly climbeth the man like a tree must owneth it.

Or something like that, whatever.

She met his gaze. "I'm not freaking out."

He folded his arms across his chest and simply waited.

"Are *you* freaking out?" she asked.

"Hell, yes. I just fooled around with someone on the public corruption squad. My reputation as a badass might never recover from this."

She gave him a look.

"Give it time." He grinned cheekily. "That joke's going to seem a lot funnier tomorrow."

And despite everything . . . she caught herself fighting back a smile.

"Ah, there we go," he said. "Now all we need is one of your signature saucy comments and everything will be right as rain."

She looked up at the ceiling and shook her head. "I can't believe I kissed you."

"Please. I can't believe I kissed *you*." He walked over to the bed and sat down next to her. For a moment, she found herself thinking that it was kind of sweet how he was deliberately keeping things light to make this less awkward. Then she brushed that aside, realizing that this was hardly the time for sentimental thoughts.

First things first; she needed to make sure that their working relationship remained solid.

"So," she said leadingly.

"So."

All right, fine, she would be the first one to come out and

say it. They were both adults here, and professionals; they knew the score. "Well. As unexpectedly hot as that was"—she pointed to the place on the wall where they'd kissed—"I think we both know it's best if it doesn't happen again."

He cocked his head, looking at her for a moment. "You're probably right."

Although his expression remained unchanged, and his tone was casual, something about the way he paused made her, well, pause. Admittedly, there was a physical attraction between them—and, if she was being honest with herself, probably some pent-up sexual tension that stemmed from the twenty-one weeks they'd spent fighting each other at the Academy. But, obviously, that was *all* it was. She wasn't looking to get romantically involved with another agent; she'd just transferred to the Chicago office a mere ten days ago and had no interest in being the target of that kind of gossip. What had happened between her and John had been simply a crazy impulse, brought on by adrenaline and the heat of the moment. And he knew that, too.

Didn't he . . . ?

Her inner pragmatic voice did a face-palm.

And this *is why we don't hook up with other agents. Never dip your pen in the company inkwell. Don't get your nookie where you get your cookies. Don't fish off the company pier. Don't—*

Thanks, yes, she got the point.

Moving into damage-control mode, she was quick to explain. "I just think, with us having to work so closely together undercover, that it would be unwise for us to get involved in any sort of . . . emotional entanglement." *Oh shit, please don't let this get awkward.* "Plus, on a personal level, I just finalized my divorce, and I wasn't looking to dive right away into any sort of serious—"

With an amused expression, he held up a hand to stop her. "I appreciate the it's-not-you-it's-me speech, Harlow. Truly. But

I wasn't exactly about to get down on one knee here. In addition to having just got out of a long-term relationship myself, there's a good chance I'm moving to Virginia next month."

Oh. Sure, she'd completely forgotten about that. If he made the Hostage Rescue Team, he'd be heading back to Quantico.

For good this time.

Shoving aside a strange feeling inside her gut, she smiled sheepishly. "Sorry. I just thought I saw you hesitate there."

"I'm a single guy. Generally speaking, we like to review all other options before ever willfully taking the possibility of sex off the table."

Gotcha. Of course that was all it was. And that was good—great, actually. "Okay, so we're on the same page, then." She exhaled. For a moment there, she'd started to think . . . well, obviously it didn't matter now.

"We're on the same page." John leaned back on his elbows, stretching out his long, built frame on the bed. "Assuming, that is, you don't plan to make another move on me."

Ah . . . more revisionist history. "That's not exactly how I remember it happening, Shepherd. *You* moved in on me."

"After *you* opened the door with that 'It could be something more' line."

She stood up from the bed. "You know, as much as I'd love to do the he-said-she-said postgame analysis, it's getting late and we have an early flight tomorrow."

"I believe that's code for 'I know you're right, John, so I'm inventing an excuse to avoid having to admit it.'" He winked at her.

Frustrating man, looking so smug and confident and . . . seriously, did he have to be sprawled across the bed like that, with his shirt half unbuttoned, and those stupid, gorgeous blue eyes? And that *body.* My God, he might as well have a flashing neon sign over him: Awesome sexy times! Available here!

Refusing to take his bait, she opened the door. "Let's meet

in the lobby at six A.M. That'll give us plenty of time to get to the airport, even if we hit traffic on the way. Good night, Dave," she added sweetly, being careful just in case anyone was passing by in the hallway.

Without waiting for a reply, she ever-so-coolly made her exit. She headed down the hallway that led out of the building, getting halfway to the exit before she realized.

Dammit.

Turning on her heel, she went back and found John standing in the doorway to his room, leaning against the doorjamb.

He dangled her purse from one finger, whistling nonchalantly.

She stopped in front of him, and he handed the purse over. "Don't even say it," she warned.

His eyes crinkled at the corners. "Good night, Ashley."

Well, at least he was irritating her again.

Given the circumstances, she'd take it.

15

Friday evening after work, John pit-stopped at the loft condo in Bucktown he was renting. A small studio unit with a flyaway kitchen and a tiny bathroom, the place had zero bells and whistles, but it was clean and had an in-unit washer and dryer.

Between the Army and HRT Selection, he'd bunked in far worse conditions.

After driving around the neighborhood for twenty minutes, he found a parking spot on the street three blocks away. Carrying both his briefcase and his suitcase from the Jacksonville trip, he stopped off at his mailbox before heading up to the second floor.

Included among the junk mail and bills was a large envelope from Alicia.

He tucked it under his arm and carried his stuff up the stairs. After letting himself into the loft and dumping the briefcase on the pull-out couch that doubled as his bed, he shook the envelope from Alicia and heard paper sliding around inside.

A week ago, she'd sent an e-mail asking for his address so she could forward him some mail that had been delivered to their old place. Not wanting to encourage further communication, his response to her had been brief. Now, as he opened the envelope, he hoped he wouldn't find some note, or another apology, that she'd slipped in with the mail. These last few weeks, between his stint at Quantico and the investigation down in Jacksonville, he'd been able to keep his mind off the situation with Alicia and Rob, and he wanted to keep it that way.

He got lucky.

No note, no apology, not even so much as a Post-it saying, *Here's your mail—A*, using her initial as a signature, the way she used to do whenever she left him a note in their apartment. He'd always found that funny, that she bothered to sign them at all, because it wasn't like anyone else would be leaving him a Post-it reminding him that she would be home late that evening because she had a dentist appointment, and could he please remind the landlord to fix the burned-out light by the garage door?

XOXO—A, she'd write, at the end of every single one of those damn notes.

Crumpling the envelope into a ball, he tossed it into the garbage and then unpacked his suitcase. After changing into jeans and a short-sleeve henley that he left untucked to cover his Glock, he grabbed the suits he'd worn in Jacksonville and dropped them off at the dry cleaner around the corner.

From there, he hailed a cab and gave the driver the address for Sheridan's Pub, where he was meeting his friend Wes. Located on the north side and managed by his brother, the place had been one of John's standard hangouts for years.

The pub had a library-like decor, with dark hardwood, built-in bookshelves, and warm, ambient light. It was crowded that evening, and John looked around before he spotted Wes sitting on the far side of the bar.

"Hey, there he is," Wes said, grinning when John walked up.

John pointed to the four glasses lined up in front of Wes. "Did you save any for the rest of us?"

"Your brother insisted I try this new whiskey flight they just rolled out."

"Is it any good?"

A woman's voice cut into their conversation. "Very good. And I'd say that even if your brother wasn't paying me to." Nadia, the bartender, slid a napkin in front of John. "Welcome back. Nate says you've been at Quantico for some kind of superhero role-playing camp."

That brother of his . . . always a kidder. "Something like that. Is he working tonight?"

"He's around," Nadia said.

FBI agents weren't supposed to get intoxicated while carrying, so John passed on the whiskey flight and ordered a Koval bourbon instead.

"So? How was it?" Wes asked after Nadia walked away to grab them some dinner menus.

John cocked his head. "How was what?"

"Superhero camp. The Hostage and Rescue Team tryouts."

Had it really been that long since he and Wes had hung out? John mentally scrolled back and realized that the last time they'd seen each other had been the day Wes had helped him move his furniture out of his and Alicia's apartment.

Not exactly a jubilant occasion, that.

"It's just 'Hostage Rescue Team.' No *and*. They don't make us take the people captive first before rescuing them," John joked.

"That's funny. Speaking of funny things, what's with the new look?" Wes nodded at John's shorter hairstyle.

"It's for an undercover investigation."

"Ah. And judging from the hair product and clean-shaven jaw, I'm guessing you're . . . infiltrating a rogue group of men's cologne models?"

And so it went. For the next hour, they joked around and gave each other shit as they caught up over bourbon and meat loaf sandwiches, another new item on the menu that Nate talked them into. John regaled Wes with stories about HRT tryouts, and Wes told him about work and how his girlfriend, Claire, wanted them to run a marathon together.

John chuckled. "You still haven't told her that you hate running?" That had been Wes's "in" when he'd first met Claire at a party and had hit on her: She'd mentioned she was an avid runner, so he'd feigned an interest and had suggested they go jogging together sometime. A year later, he still hadn't figured out how to extract himself from the white lie.

"Well, I can't tell her *now*. I'm in too deep," Wes said.

"True. On the upside, after running twenty-six miles, the 10K races she's always signing you up for will seem like a piece of cake," John said.

"Twenty-six miles . . . who the hell thinks that's fun?" Wes demanded to know.

"Apparently, you do."

"Here's the other problem: The marathon training group she wants us to join does their long runs early on Sunday mornings." Wes gestured between him and John. "And since we have flag football on Saturdays starting in September . . ." He paused, shifting in his chair. "That, uh, means no more sleeping in either weekend day."

An uncomfortable pause fell between them.

Well, here they were.

All evening, John had been hoping to skirt by without any reference to his former "friends." Every fall, he, Wes, Rob, Lucas, and Matt played in a touch football league on Saturday mornings in Lincoln Park, and then they'd grab lunch at Sheridan's and watch college football on the pub's big-screen TVs. It was something John looked forward to every year: the good-natured competitiveness, getting sweaty in the crisp autumn air, and the easy camaraderie between old friends.

But now, that was done. *Finito. Poof.* His fun football Saturdays had disappeared into thin air, along with his girlfriend, three of his closest friends, and his apartment.

He took a sip of his bourbon before answering Wes. "Just move football to Saturday afternoons. I was the one always pushing to do it in the mornings." His tone turned wry. "And I think it goes without saying that I'll be sitting out this football season."

"Yeah . . . I figured that." Wes sighed, and both men fell quiet, awkwardly fiddling with their drinks. "God, our team's going to suck this season."

Despite everything, that got a half smile out of John.

Wes shared the smile. "I know. I'm terrible at this stuff. The whole situation is such a mess. The five of us have been friends for almost fifteen years, Shep. It sucks that it's come to this."

Yes, it did. And while John appreciated that Wes was doing what friends did—real friends, that is—and trying to commiserate over the shittiness of the situation, he'd been hoping to avoid any maudlin heart-to-hearts tonight. It was awkward, and every time he thought about Rob and Alicia sneaking around behind his back, he felt like a fool.

"It's the end of an era," he said sarcastically, hoping that would encourage Wes to drop the subject.

He didn't get so lucky.

"What Rob did with Alicia . . ." Wes looked at John. "I hope you know, I'm done with him, too. I've lost all respect for the guy. But as for Matt and Lucas . . . this past month, while you've been MIA with your HRT tryouts, I hung out with them a couple of times. And it was weird, because I felt like I was cheating on you or something." He shrugged, with a self-deprecating smile. "You know what I mean."

John appreciated Wes's sense of loyalty, but he wasn't trying to stick his friend in the middle of all this. "I don't expect you to stop hanging out with those guys. This is between them and me."

"You know they want me to try to talk to you, right?" Wes

asked. "They're hoping that if they give you some space, eventually this'll blow over."

John ran a hand over his mouth, debating whether to respond to that. Then he looked at Wes. "Two months ago, the five of us met for drinks at that bar in Lincoln Park—the Barrelhouse Flat. Remember that night?"

Wes nodded. "I remember."

"We were all hanging out, having a good time, and Rob mentioned that he'd sold a house that day, an expensive one that he'd had on the market for a while. So to celebrate, I bought him a drink." John leaned forward in his chair, his voice dipping lower. "And Matt and Lucas knew. They knew Rob was screwing my girlfriend behind my back—and they still let me buy him a goddamn *drink*." He paused. "Maybe they were caught in the middle at first. But that night, they chose a side. And it wasn't mine."

Not having anything else to say about that, John turned back to his drink.

And . . . now a really uncomfortable silence fell between them.

Then a hand rested on John's shoulder.

"So? What do we think about the meat loaf sandwiches?" his brother asked, standing behind him. "Good stuff, huh?"

Saved by the bell. John turned around, grateful for the interruption. "I'm a fan."

Nate moved his hand to the back of John's bar stool, as if planning to hang around for a while. "I've been meaning to ask—what happened with that stuff we talked about for your investigation?" He turned to Wes to explain. "I've been doing some consulting work for the FBI."

John fought back a smile, thinking that was overstating things a little. "You looked at one restaurant blueprint."

"And? Did you go with the sexy red leather on the banquettes, like I told you?" Nate asked.

"I did. The people I'm working with loved that part."

"Of course they did." Nate looked almost insulted, as if this had never been even a question. Then he turned to Wes. "Speaking of John's new investigation . . . does the name 'Jessica Harlow' mean anything to you?"

For chrissakes. "We're back to this?" John growled.

Nate gave him a careful once-over. "You get tense and shifty every time her name comes up. I find that curious."

Tense and shifty? John fought back a laugh as he adjusted his position on the bar stool.

He caught his brother watching him and froze. "I'm just stretching out my legs. You try being six-four and sitting on one of these damn stools."

"I'm six-three and sit on them every day."

"It's a crucial inch," John grunted.

"Anyhow . . ." Nate turned back to Wes. "Jessica Harlow is John's new partner. But I feel like I've heard that name before."

Wes considered this. "It does sound familiar. Although it might just be one of those names that has a ring to it."

John threw Nate a satisfied look. "I told you."

"A female partner? That's a first for you, isn't it?" Wes asked.

"I've worked with special agents who are women before. But yes, this is the first time I've been assigned one as my partner in an undercover op."

"So what's with all the shiftiness?" Wes grinned slyly. "Is she hot or something?"

Nate slapped the back of John's bar stool. "That's it! Jessica Harlow—the hot trainee from the Academy." He turned to John, pointing. "I *knew* that name sounded familiar."

John threw up his hands in disbelief. "How do you remember that? You don't even remember the names of our cousins."

Nate waved this off. "Only the second cousins. Those random ones in Minnesota."

"Missouri."

"Whatever.

Wes jumped in. "Wait, this is all coming back to me now. Jessica Harlow was the smart one in your class, right? You thought she was flirting with you, so you made some move on her at the firing range—"

"Uh, *no*. I was just trying to fix her stance." John quickly corrected him, having discussed this before, six years ago.

A month and a half into the training program, he and the other trainees had been given the weekend off to go home and see their families. John had spent that Saturday night hanging out at Sheridan's with his friends and his brother, who'd wanted to know all about the Academy. Somewhere in there, someone had asked whether there were any cute women in the program, and John had *offhandedly* mentioned Jessica's name in passing.

It was a comment he'd quickly come to regret, seeing how his friends and brother (a) had been all over him with lame-ass comments—*Just how cute is she?* (Very), *Are you tapping that?* (No), *Do you get to practice frisking techniques on her?* (Also no, but this may or may not have been the subject of a lurid classroom daydream he'd had during a snoozefest of a lecture on the behavioral analysis of gang graffiti)—and (b) had been all over him even more when he'd come home for a second visit ten weeks later, after he and Jessica had moved into the overtly hostile phase of their relationship and he'd pissily told his friends and brother to kiss his ass every time they brought up her name.

And now, here they were again.

"So, the two of you are working together undercover. Sounds cozy," Nate said.

Wes began to sway in his chair, singing, "'Reunited and it feels so good.'"

John looked up at the ceiling.

Shoot him now.

"For the life of me, I can't remember why I ever avoided talking to you two about this," he said.

Nate grinned. "All right, all right. We'll try to be more sympathetic to your hot-nemesis problem. Is she a nightmare to work with?"

An image popped into John's head, of him kissing Jessica against the hotel room wall in Jacksonville. He could still feel the softness of her skin and hear her breathy moan as he slid his hand underneath her dress.

Hardly the stuff of nightmares.

"It's been . . . interesting." Leaving it at that, he took a sip of his bourbon and deliberately changed the subject. "By the way, what's this crap you're telling people, that I've been at a 'superhero role-playing camp'?" he asked his brother.

"Somebody has to keep you grounded." With an easy grin, Nate sauntered off in the direction of the hostess stand.

After that, the conversation between John and Wes returned to normal, both of them avoiding any mention of Rob, Lucas, and Matt. The evening ended with Wes—who'd had several drinks by that point—declaring that he was heading over to Claire's place to put his foot down about running a marathon.

"Best of luck with that. Although you might want to save all that hot air for the twenty-six miles. You're gonna need it," John said, as Wes headed toward the front door.

Wes answered that with a middle finger as he walked away.

John planned to head out himself as soon as he finished nursing his drink. Alone with his thoughts, he found his mind drifting back to the past two nights he'd spent in Jacksonville.

I can't believe I kissed you.

Well, whether she believed it or not, that kiss had been *hot*. And if Leavitt hadn't called right then, John was pretty sure things between him and Jessica would've gone a hell of a lot further than a kiss.

And that was a rather intriguing notion.

Objectively, he didn't disagree with her that the safest course of action would be for them to pretend like the whole thing had never happened. Hooking up with a co-worker was always risky—and he and Jessica already had an incendiary enough relationship without adding sex to the mix.

That said, would he personally have stopped things if Leavitt's call hadn't interrupted them? Hell, no. That train had left the station, with its fireman gleefully shoveling every last bit of coal into the furnace to make it race down the track even faster.

But he'd seen the look of panic on Jessica's face afterward, and she'd made her feelings clear. *I think we both know it's best if it doesn't happen again.* And since he agreed that things would be simpler if they kept it platonic, going forward he would keep his mind out of the gutter whenever he was around her.

Or at least he'd fake the shit out of it.

16

The following afternoon, Jessica walked up the steps to her parents' house, an Arts and Crafts prairie-style home located in the Frank Lloyd Wright district of Oak Park, a suburb ten miles west of Chicago. Forgoing the doorbell, she braced herself as she pushed open the front door.

Her parents' security system chimed automatically, and all hell broke loose.

Two golden retrievers came barreling around the corner from the kitchen, with a huge black Newfoundland—her sister's dog—following right behind. Barking excitedly, they bombarded her, a tangle of wagging tails, panting tongues, and wiggling, furry bodies.

"Did you guys miss me?" Jessica asked, being sure to pet each of them equally as they jumped all over her.

Her gray sleeveless top and jeans now covered in fur, she brushed herself off and followed the dogs into the kitchen. Renovated a few years ago with sleek black granite and cream cabinetry, it was easily the most modern room in the house, the rest of which still maintained much of the original natural wood and art glass from when it had been built in 1906.

The dogs darted through the open sliding door that led outside. Hearing several voices out back, Jessica helped herself to a glass of ice water before stepping out into the eighty-five-degree heat.

Through the window over the sink, she surveyed the scene in the yard. From the look of things, someone had just turned on her parents' sprinkler—the old rotary one she and her brother and sister used to run through, in this same yard, when they were kids on hot summer days just like this. Her parents' dogs were going nuts, trying to attack the sprinkler; Finn's two kids were laughing as they ran through the spray; Maya was trying to dodge the water as she picked up the sprinkler and moved it farther away from the house—which, presumably, explained why the other adults on the patio were shaking off wet bags of potato chips and pretzel rods; Finn was yelling at a now partially soaked Maya to move the sprinkler even farther back and getting a glare of death in return; and Oliver, Maya's three-year-old son, sat under a tree in the corner of the yard, letting the Newfoundland lick his Popsicle before sticking it back in his own mouth.

Ah . . . she'd missed these guys.

Los Angeles had been an experience, no doubt. Professionally speaking, she was proud of the work she'd done with the field office there, and on a personal level, her life certainly had never been more glamorous. She and Alex had lived in a beautiful, classic estate in the Hollywood Hills, she'd gone to film premieres and private screenings, and she had dined with some of the biggest film and TV stars in the business. It had been a fun ride—well, some of it—and more than a little surreal at times, but she'd never stopped thinking of herself as a Midwestern girl at heart.

She headed outside. "Should I grab a hair dryer?" she joked to her mom, who was shaking water off a package of hot dog buns.

Her mother looked up, her face shaded by the wide-brimmed

hat she wore over her blond, bobbed hair. "Look who's here." She beamed. Hot dog buns in hand, she walked over and hugged Jessica. Her parents had been on a Mediterranean cruise for the last two weeks, so this was the first time she'd seen them since moving from L.A.

"AUNT JESS!!"

The kids shrieked and ran over. Jessica spent the next several minutes saying her hellos, including to Finn's wife, Kim, and Maya's wife, Camila.

"Yikes, did the dogs do that?" Finn teased as he greeted her, pointing to the frayed knees of her boyfriend jeans.

"Ha ha." She turned next to her dad, who'd left his perennial spot at the grill long enough to pull her in for a bear hug.

"Aren't you a sight for sore eyes?" he said, squeezing her tight.

Jessica smiled, noticing even more gray mixed in with his light brown hair. She cleared her throat, suddenly feeling really glad that she was back in Chicago. "Thanks, Dad."

She spent the afternoon relaxing and catching up with everyone as they ate lunch outdoors, under the pergola. Maya and Finn were in such good moods they managed to only get into three heated arguments (one political, one child-rearing-related, and one over the best filter to use on Instagram), and no one mentioned a word about Jessica's divorce, her reasons for moving back to Chicago, or anything related to her personal life.

At least until after dessert.

Her father launched the first salvo, when the two of them were alone in the kitchen, rinsing off their ice cream bowls.

"How's your new place?" he asked.

"I like it. It's fun being in the middle of everything. In Los Angeles, our neighborhood was so secluded." It felt odd, saying the word *our* in reference to her and Alex, although *my neigh-*

borhood didn't feel right, either. Just because she was divorced from the man didn't mean she was trying to pretend like he'd never existed.

Her dad stacked both their bowls inside the dishwasher. "It's a one-bedroom condo, you said?"

Jessica leaned against the counter. "Yep."

Her father frowned. "Meanwhile, that ex-husband of yours goes on living in his Hollywood mansion."

"Well . . . yes. We had a prenup, and Alex had bought the house before we started dating."

"Prenups are just opening offers in a divorce negotiation."

Her father was a former civil litigation attorney, not a divorce lawyer, but that was beside the point. "I wouldn't have wanted any of Alex's money anyway." Even when they were married, she'd always been aware of, and slightly uncomfortable with, the disparity in their incomes. They'd lived a certain lifestyle because Alex's film career paid for it, and since the perks of that lifestyle—including the Hollywood Hills house, the designer clothes, and the nice cars—were so far from anything she could ever afford on her own, none of it had ever felt like hers to begin with.

Obviously, it would've been a different negotiation if they'd had kids. Or maybe even if they'd been married longer than three years. But since that wasn't the case, she didn't need—or want—anything else from Alex. She might not have been rolling around in Hollywood-producer money, but she made a good income as an FBI agent. And in many ways, it had made the transition easier, knowing that she was starting over in Chicago on her own two feet.

"You could've at least taken his Porsche," her dad grunted.

"I'll keep that in mind for my next divorce." She smiled when her father gave her a look. "Kidding, Dad."

Hopefully.

Later, her sister accosted her when she was in the living room, checking her e-mail to see if there was any update from Agents Leavitt and Todd about a second meeting with Blair.

"Check it out," Maya said, in a hushed voice, holding out her own cell phone for Jessica to see. On the screen was a photograph of an attractive, dark-haired man on a treadmill.

Now *this* was getting out of hand. "You took a picture of the guy while he was working out?" Jessica asked. "Give the man a little privacy."

Maya dismissed this with a wave. "Do you see this body? And he's a *surgeon*. If we were back in the days when I still pretended to like boys, this guy totally would've been at the top of my fake-crush list."

Jessica doubted that, seeing how Maya had stopped pretending to like boys on the day she'd turned eighteen and the guy in this photograph looked about thirty-five years old. But before she could comment, Finn walked into the room.

Seeing Maya with her phone in hand, he pointed. "We're doing this now?" He gave his twin a smug look. "Well, then, *I* have a picture, too." He pulled something up on his phone and then showed the image to Jessica and Maya.

"It's a car," Jessica said.

"It's a Maserati." Finn gestured to the photograph like a model from *The Price Is Right*. "Seriously, Jess. Just picture yourself in the passenger seat of this beauty as my guy whisks you off to his Gold Coast condo for an evening of wine tasting from his collection."

"Screw wine tasting. My guy snowboards," Maya scoffed.

"That'll come in real handy for all those mountains we have in Chicago," Finn shot back. Then he smiled at Jessica. "You're looking for athletic prowess? *My* guy has a 7.4 golf handicap."

When Maya feigned snoring, Jessica thought it was best to intervene. "As much as this is all very informative, don't you think the things you two are highlighting about these men are a little . . . shallow?"

The twins both stared at her.

"Well, seeing how we're trying to set them up with our little sister, we assumed it went without saying that, as a baseline, they're both really good guys," Maya said wryly.

Jessica found herself surprisingly touched. "Aw . . . that's sweet, you two."

"Of course we're looking out for you, Jess." Finn threw his arm around her shoulders and squeezed.

Jessica leaned her head against him, soaking in the rare moment of overt sibling affection.

"Actually, my guy could be a serial killer for all the hell I asked," Finn said. "But you would look cool in his car."

He winked at her, and Jessica smiled.

It was good to be home.

Later, after everyone had left and her dad was outside cleaning the grill, Jessica sat at the kitchen counter and watched her mom make a pitcher of fresh lemonade.

"I heard Maya and Finn giving you the hard sell on their 'guys,'" her mom said, as she strained the pulp from the lemon juice.

"I think it's mostly just a competition between them at this point," Jessica said.

"Well, sure, partially. It *is* Finn and Maya. Those two were throwing elbows on their way out of the birth canal." Her mom smiled. "But they mean well. They're so used to acting that way with each other, they forget that it can come off a little smothering to someone outside their duo."

"More like a *lot* smothering," Jessica said, half grumbling and half affectionate because she knew their meddling came from a good place. She was thirty-two years old, had lived across the country for over half her adult life, and carried a loaded Glock 22 on her hip. But to her brother and sister, she would always be the "baby" of the family. Even if she could take those two clowns out in three moves.

Just saying.

Her mom studied her for a moment. "You know . . . if you told them you aren't ready to date anyone yet, they'd back off," she said gently.

Jessica smiled, appreciating her mom's concern. She'd missed the talks they used to have—often right at this very counter and not infrequently about boys and men—while she'd been in California. Sure, they'd talked on the phone, and she and her family had visited each other while she'd been in Los Angeles, but it wasn't the same as sitting here, leisurely drinking lemonade on a sunny Saturday afternoon and knowing that she did *not* have to get on a plane tomorrow.

"I am ready to start dating," she told her mom. "I'm just not feeling an interest in either of these guys, I guess."

Kind of odd, that. Successful, good personalities, attractive—obviously, these were positive qualities in a potential date. But for some reason, every time she'd been about to give in and pick one to meet for coffee—if for no other reason than just to get her brother and sister off her case—she'd found herself holding back.

Weird.

"I think it's because they're too perfect," she decided.

Her mom chuckled. "Is there such a thing?"

"Sure. I haven't dated in five years. I don't want to dust off my rusty skills with a guy who could be an actual contender."

"I think it's like riding a bicycle, sweetie."

"Tell that to Tara. I floored her when I mentioned that I couldn't be on Tinder because of my undercover work. Apparently, that's how all the kids are meeting these days."

Her mom gave her a look.

"Come on. That wasn't even that sarcastic," Jessica protested. "Speaking of Tara . . . she's the opposite of Finn and Maya. She thinks I need to stay away from serious relationships and have a fun rebound with a Mr. Wrong instead."

Her mom dumped ice into the pitcher. "I think the question is: What do *you* think?"

That, indeed, was the question of the day. Of the last six months, really.

In hindsight, Jessica realized that she'd been, perhaps, somewhat naïve about the impact of her career on her personal life. Not that FBI agents couldn't have happy, long-term relationships—in fact, most of the agents she'd worked with in Los Angeles had been married. But undercover work definitely presented some unique challenges. The investigations were unpredictable, she often had to travel and change plans on short notice, and, even when she was around, she was frequently distracted with work. She threw herself one hundred percent into every assignment—because that, simply, was what the job required. Any agent who phoned in an undercover role was putting her career, the entire investigation, and quite possibly her life and the lives of others at risk.

She didn't regret the choices she'd made. She was proud of the work she did for the FBI, and, frankly, she thought Alex could've been more flexible and understanding of the fact that there were times, unfortunately, when that work had to take priority.

But the fact that he'd given up on their marriage still stung. Getting divorced was hardly a party, even if she and Alex had remained civil during the proceedings. If anything, that had made it worse, *not* hating him, because he would make a joke or say something nice to ease the awkwardness of the settlement conference, and she'd find herself sitting there with a lump in her throat, wondering how things had gone so wrong between them.

Jessica saw her mom waiting for an answer, so she nodded. "I think having some fun could be a good thing."

Actually, she thought it could be a great thing. She was suddenly single again and back in Chicago, her hometown. Sure, it probably wouldn't be long before Ye Olde Biological Clock started chiming, but for now, the idea of getting involved in any sort of serious commitment just seemed exhausting.

Honestly, Mom? After these last few months, I just want to treat myself to meaningless, make-me-forget-my-own-name sex with a man who will go his merry little way afterward.

Okay, she was close with her mom, but not *that* close.

"So, then. Fun it is," her mom said. That decided, she poured them each a glass of lemonade and asked how things were going in Jessica's new field office.

"Pretty good. I'll be traveling for the next couple weeks for an undercover investigation, but I don't mind. It's kind of nice to be busy." Jessica took another sip, keeping her tone deliberately casual. "I have a new partner for the assignment."

"What's he like? Or she?"

"He." So many things Jessica could've said about John. She could've talked about the fact that they'd been in the same class at the Academy, and how the two of them couldn't stand each other back then. Or how, when she'd first been given the assignment, she'd been convinced that Fate was playing a practical joke on her. *Or* she could've said nothing about John at all and dodged the question by speaking vaguely about the investigation instead.

But instead . . .

"He's cute."

She nearly thunked her head against the counter. *Oh my God . . .* what was she, *thirteen* again?

Her mom cocked her head. "How cute?"

An image came to mind, of John in the hotel room that night, his shirt half unbuttoned and his long, lean, broadshouldered frame stretched out on the bed. *Assuming, that is, you don't plan to make another move on me.*

"Too cute," Jessica grumbled.

"If you're only looking for fun, sweetie, I don't think there is such a thing as *too* cute." Her mother shrugged off Jessica's look, her eyes sparkling with amusement. "Just saying."

While Jessica was stuck in traffic on the highway during her drive back into the city, her cell phone rang. Seeing that it was Leavitt calling, she answered via the Bluetooth connection to her car.

"We're in," Leavitt said, sounding pleased. "Morano called me just a few minutes ago. Let me try to patch in John, and then I'll update you both."

The phone went silent for several moments, until Leavitt came back to the line. "Jessica, you still here?"

"Yep."

"John, how about you?"

His low, rich voice sounded through Jessica's car speakers. "I'm here, too."

"All right. So, Blair wants fifty thousand in cash to reach out to his friend on the Land Use Committee," Leavitt said. "Agent Todd and I discussed it, and we think you guys should do the exchange at the restaurant site. It's quiet, and private enough that Blair won't feel like he needs his security detail there."

A key factor, seeing how Blair obviously wouldn't want to do the cash exchange for his *illegal bribe* in front of two Jacksonville police officers. "That works well. While we're there, we can tell Blair about the grand plans Ashley and Dave have for the space," Jessica said.

"Dave has decided he's very committed to those sexy red leather banquettes," John said. "So I hope Ashley is prepared to go to the mat if she's not yet on board."

Jessica rolled her eyes, not that John could see it.

Leavitt chuckled. "Todd and I were talking earlier about this fake-competitive dynamic you two added to your under-cover roles. It plays really well—almost like you've been doing this for a while."

Imagine that.

17

Since one of the upsides of being an FBI agent was that John didn't have to wait in the notoriously long security lines at Chicago's O'Hare airport, he found himself quite at his leisure as he made his way to his gate on Tuesday morning.

He and Jessica were catching a ten fifteen A.M. flight, which would give them plenty of time, even with delays—also notorious at O'Hare airport—to check into the hotel and make their seven P.M. meeting with Blair and Morano. Blair had chosen the time, likely tied up for the rest of the day strategizing with his campaign team on how to maximize all the publicity he'd been getting over the last twenty-four hours.

The mayor of Jacksonville was the city's hero.

Over the weekend, the governor of Florida—from the opposite political party as Blair—had met with a small group of business and state government leaders and had said, per an audiotape that had been leaked to the press, that there wasn't anything "iconic" about Jacksonville. He'd joked that the most memorable thing about the city was the smell of roasting beans coming from the Maxwell House Coffee factory, and then went on to note that EverBank Field, home of the Jacksonville

Jaguars football team, was surrounded by a jail, abandoned buildings, and fifty acres of "polluted, old shipyard."

Needless to say, the proud citizens of the country's thirteenth-largest city were not pleased with this characterization.

Naturally, the governor had tried to smooth over the brouhaha caused by his leaked remarks, claiming that he'd been merely attempting to explain his support for a bill that would give tax credits to businesses that relocated to Florida. Nevertheless, on Monday afternoon, when the mayor of Jacksonville stepped up to the podium as the keynote speaker at a community action awards luncheon, the local press waited with collective bated breath.

Never one to miss an opportunity, Blair gave the media exactly what they'd been hoping for.

He took a moment to address the governor's comments before beginning his speech. Describing Jacksonville as a "big city with small-town charm," he spoke proudly of the city's many bragging points, including its 111,000 acres of parks, the largest urban park system in the United States; the miles of sandy beaches that gave the Jacksonville area its nickname, "the First Coast"; the booming restaurant and arts scenes; and its naval base that employed over thirty thousand active-duty military personnel.

"And if all that isn't impressive enough," Blair thundered away to a ballroom filled with people who were already on their feet and clapping, "how about the fact that we're also the hometown of Lynyrd Skynyrd? Perhaps the good governor needs to come over from Tallahassee and join me for a beer at one of our nine craft breweries—we'll listen to a little 'Free Bird' and 'Sweet Home Alabama' and have a talk about what is and is not iconic."

The crowd had gone wild. As had the rest of the city, after the press reported the mayor's comments in every local paper and television newscast. According to Leavitt, who'd called

John and Jessica yesterday evening to give them the update, it was a virtual lovefest for Blair in Jacksonville right now, and they were anticipating that his already-high approval ratings would go through the roof.

"I've been informed by my SAC that, in light of all the favorable publicity Blair is getting, the U.S. Attorney is paying particular attention to the progress of our investigation," Leavitt had told them during yesterday's call. "So I hope you guys aren't the type to buckle under pressure." He'd chuckled, then paused and lowered his voice. "Seriously, you're not, are you?"

After serving in combat, and having worked undercover with some truly bad guys as part of the FBI's organized crime group, John was pretty sure he could handle one charismatic douchebag mayor.

While walking to his gate, he spotted a Starbucks and decided to grab a cup of coffee before boarding. Suitcase in tow, he maneuvered around the crowd of people scurrying in both directions and headed for the end of the line.

Then he spotted her.

Jessica stood near the front of the line, her head bent as she checked something on her phone.

John's eyes moved over her, taking in the sophisticated look of her cream suit and heels. He wasn't sure whether to be amused or wholly unsurprised by this coincidence.

Two steps ahead of him, once again.

He pulled out his phone and texted her. I'll take a tall of the dark roast.

She looked up from her phone, glanced around, and spotted him at the back of the line. She made a big show of checking her watch.

Nice of you to show up this morning, she texted back.

Cute.

He got out of line and walked over. "Better make mine a

grande. I sense extra-quippiness in you today, and I think I'm going to need it."

He took the handle of her suitcase, since she would need both hands free to carry their drinks, and wheeled their suitcases over to an empty table. There he noticed a black backpack that sat unattended on one of the chairs. His eyes skimmed the crowd just as a frazzled-looking woman pushing a stroller hurried over, scooped up the backpack, and went on her way.

That resolved, John went back to semicasual people-watching as he waited for Jessica. Once she had their drinks in hand—hers appeared to be some iced mocha concoction—she headed to the sugar bar and waited while the two people ahead of her added sweetener and milk to their beverages.

He watched as she slid the straw of her drink between her lips and nibbled on it absentmindedly.

Christ, not this again.

I have a slight oral fixation.

So help him, if the woman did anything even remotely erotic with that damn straw during their two-hour flight, the iced mocha concoction was going out the emergency exit door.

Even a man who typically didn't crack under pressure had his limits.

After she finished at the sugar bar, she walked over and handed him his coffee. Side-by-side, they wheeled their suitcases in the direction of their gate.

"Our friend made CNN this morning," John said, keeping his voice low and his words intentionally vague. While not front-page news, Blair's verbal bitch-slapping of Florida's governor had been picked up in the politics sections of several national media websites.

"I saw that." Jessica slowed as they passed a bookstore, her eyes skimming over a display table of bestsellers. "I watched the video of his speech. Our friend definitely knows how to work a crowd." She picked up a paperback with a beach scene on the front cover and flipped it over.

John waited as she put down that book and picked up a second one.

Then he waited some more as she checked out yet another book.

"Forget to pack the e-reader?" he teased. He'd noticed it had been her trusty companion during both of their prior flights together.

"No, I have it. But I buy paperbacks, too." She shrugged. "Mostly for reading in the bathtub."

John carefully kept his face impassive.

Don't even think about picturing her in the bathtub.

He was picturing her in the bathtub.

Trying to distract himself from the image of her all wet and slick and naked, he grabbed the book closest to him on the table and thrust it at her. "What about this one?"

She flipped it over and read the blurb out loud. "'In hot pursuit of San Francisco's most deadly serial killer in two decades, FBI Special Agent Kit Mancini . . .' Yeah, no thanks." She put the book on the table and moved along to a nearby magazine rack.

John chuckled. He couldn't read books about the FBI, either. "But I'm sure it's very suspenseful. And accurate . . . ish."

She snorted. "I bet Special Agent Kit Mancini never once—" She trailed off, staring at the cover of some magazine on the rack in front of her.

Her expression turned serious as she hastily reached for a copy.

Frowning, John walked over. "What is it?"

She didn't answer. Instead she flipped through the pages, found whatever she was looking for, and began reading.

John glanced at the cover. *People* magazine. He lowered his voice so only she could hear. "Is it Blair? What, did they name him 'Sexiest Windbag Alive'?" He was only half joking, not having a clue what could have Jessica so riveted.

She shook her head, her tone quiet as she kept reading. "It's not Blair." After a few moments, she closed the magazine and haphazardly set it back on the rack. "Sorry, I was just . . . What were we talking about?"

She looked rattled.

Jessica Harlow never looked rattled.

John put his hand on the small of her back, leaning in. "Jessica. What's wrong?"

"It's nothing." She pointed to a photo on the bottom left corner of the cover. "I just wasn't expecting to see my ex-husband on the cover of a magazine."

Ex-husband? John took a closer look. In the photo, a couple held hands as they beamed for the cameras, at what appeared to be a movie premiere or some other kind of red-carpet event. He recognized the woman, a brunette, some twenty-something actress whose name he was blanking on. The man standing next to her—Jessica's former husband, apparently—was dark-haired, in his midthirties, and had a medium build.

Above the happy couple was a short headline: PREGNANT AND ENGAGED!

Jessica straightened her shoulders. "Well. We should probably head to our gate and stake out our places in line to board." She feigned a smile. "You know how it is, trying to get overhead bin space these days."

Without waiting for his answer, she turned and walked away.

He was the least qualified person for the job.

Rare was the occasion John could say that. Not to toot his own horn, but generally speaking, he had skills. He could adopt a variety of personas for undercover jobs and had a knack for reading people; he'd been deployed to combat zones fifteen times and was lethally accurate in all manner of firearms, including assault rifles, machine guns, sniper rifles, and grenade launchers; and he'd been trained to fight on every type of terrain from the desert to the mountains. Yes, he hadn't quite figured out how to start a fire with two sticks and the ass end of a lightning bug, but he did know how to survive ten days in a swamp with a minimum of food provisions and on less than three hours of sleep per night, all while carrying eighty pounds of weapons and equipment over two hundred miles in ninety-degree temperatures.

But in this particular instance, he was in over his head.

Sitting beside him, Jessica gazed out the airplane window. She'd been quiet, having said all of about ten words the first thirty minutes of their flight. Even her trusty e-reader couldn't seem to hold her attention—resting on her lap, the device had long since gone into sleep mode.

He should say something. Obviously. But what? He was hardly an expert when it came to talking about feelings and relationship issues. Hell, the last time he'd had a problem in his own personal life, he'd gotten drunk, then had avoided the situation entirely by running off to Quantico and subjecting himself to two weeks of pure physical and mental torture.

It had seemed like a perfectly reasonable solution at the time.

His brother, the charmer, would know what to say in this situation. His brother would've had Jessica laughing by takeoff, immediately defusing the awkwardness of the moment and making her feel better with a self-deprecating "Men suck" joke or something like that.

John doubted he could pull off a "Men suck."

But maybe . . . he didn't have to address the problem specifically. Instead, he could signal the flight attendant for a couple of those miniature bottles of whiskey, pour Jessica and himself a drink, and just . . . start talking about football. Men had been effectively communicating that way for hundreds of years; surely she would understand that by *not* saying anything, he was, in fact, speaking volumes.

He glanced over and saw that she was still staring out the window. Something inside him softened at the sight of her looking so vulnerable.

He always did have a weakness for that.

"I'm sorry you had to find out about your ex-husband this way," he said, genuinely.

She turned her head away from the window. "It's not what you think." She paused, conceding. "Okay, it's not *entirely* what you think. It's not that Alex has moved on. That was inevitable—for both of us. But the magazine said that his fiancée is five months pregnant." She let that hang in the air. "Alex and I separated only six months ago."

Ah. "And now you're thinking . . . ?"

"Of course that's what I'm thinking. I suppose it's possible they got together right after Alex and I separated. But I *know* that actress. She was working with Alex on a film right before our marriage ended, and now I can't help but wonder if—"

"Don't."

Jessica blinked at his interruption. "I'm sorry?"

"Don't go there," he said, matter-of-factly.

She sat back in her seat, sounding defensive. "Well, it's not like I *want* to go there. But it would certainly explain some things about our divorce."

"You still don't want to know."

She opened her mouth and then shut it, as if thinking better about whatever she'd been about to say. "I think I'm the better judge of what *I* want to know, thank you. Seeing how *I'm* the one who just found out my ex-husband was very possibly having an affair." After shooting him a glare, she turned away and fell silent once again.

So . . . this conversation was going well.

"Men suck," John offered.

She turned and looked at him as if he'd just sprouted a third ear.

"Yeah, I knew I couldn't pull that off," he muttered.

She shook her head, then turned back to the window.

A long silence stretched between them as John debated whether he wanted to go down this road.

"It's different for us," he finally said, his voice low enough that no one around them would hear. "You think you'll have some kind of resolution if you know whether your ex cheated, but you're not thinking about what happens after that."

"What happens after that? Enlighten me," she said dryly.

"You'll replay in your head every conversation you had with him—and her, too—going back through even the most meaningless interactions, trying to figure out if there was any sign of what they were doing behind your back." He looked at her knowingly. "Because there had to be *some* sign, right? Some look, some hint, something one of them said to you, something you missed that, if you'd only paid more attention to it, you could've at least saved yourself the embarrassment of feeling like a fool for not having suspected a thing. So you'll parse through it all, like a new case file, studying every detail and trying to figure out how the hell two people with no undercover training and no particular skills at deception managed to pull the wool over *your* eyes. And the short answer is . . . they just did. As much as people like us hate to admit it, we're not infallible. And if you go down this road, trust me, you won't find any answers to the questions you've been stewing over since you saw that magazine. All you'll end up with is a lot of needless self-doubt."

Jessica's expression had softened by the time he was done speaking. "It sounds like you have some experience with this."

"You could say that." He saw her waiting for more. Fine, he

supposed he had to share now, after opening the door with a speech like that. "Last month, I walked in on my girlfriend having sex with one of my friends."

Her eyes went wide. "*No.* Literally mid-act?"

"Judging from the fact that he was groaning, 'I'm gonna come so hard in you,' I'd say they were nearing the end of the act," he said wryly.

She covered her mouth with one hand. "Oh my God, what do you even do in a situation like that? Did you kick the guy's ass?"

"Unfortunately, no," John grumbled. And he still wasn't sure he'd made the right call on that one. "He jumped off the bed, buck naked, dick swinging everywhere. It was not a situation I wanted to get closer to."

She made a face. "Fair enough." She paused, as if proceeding cautiously. "Had you and your girlfriend been dating a long time?"

"Two years." John almost left it at that but then oddly found himself continuing on. "We'd been going through a rough patch for a few months. I was traveling back and forth to Detroit for a job, and she wasn't happy with the situation. She called me a 'part-time' boyfriend."

Jessica bristled at that. "Didn't she know what line of work you were in before you started dating?"

John pointed. "Thank you. That's what I said."

Another silence fell between them as one of the flight attendants stopped by to take their drink orders.

"For me and Alex, the undercover work became this constant source of tension," Jessica said, keeping her voice low after the flight attendant left. "First, he started getting jealous of my male partners." She looked him over. "He would've hated you."

John had a sneaking suspicion the feeling would've been mutual.

"Then we started arguing any time I had to cancel plans for work," she continued.

John snorted, well familiar with *that* argument. "Like you want to cancel plans. Because that's so much fun for you."

"I know, right? As if I wouldn't rather be on a beach in Mexico, instead of working. But what was I supposed to do? Blow an entire investigation just so I didn't have to reschedule a vacation?"

"Try explaining that to the SAC."

"'Sorry, sir, that the L.A. County Sheriff's Department will get away scot-free with multiple corruption and civil rights violations, and that I wasted taxpayer dollars on a now-meaningless thirteen-month investigation,'" she imitated. "'But this is *the* week to go to Cabo. Everyone who's anyone in Hollywood will be there.'"

John pulled back. "Hang on. Are you talking about Operation Pandora's Box?" Last summer, the investigation into the Los Angeles County Jail system had been one of the FBI's most talked-about sting ops, making national news and resulting in the conviction of five high-ranking members of the L.A. Sheriff's Department. "That was you?"

"That was me."

He looked her over. "Well done, you."

She smiled at the praise, then fell quiet again. Side-by-side they sat for several moments, until she tilted her head in his direction.

"I do feel bad about canceling the vacation," she said, more serious. "And I also had to bail last-minute on the premiere of one of Alex's movies. I think that might have been the night that he . . . Well, let's just say things weren't the same after that."

John nodded.

Yeah, he'd been there, too.

"Don't beat yourself up over these things. If your ex couldn't appreciate how important your work is to you—hell, how important it is to society—well, then, his loss is the Chicago FBI's gain." His eyes met hers. "You're a great agent, Jessica. One of the best—if not *the* best—I've ever worked with."

She blushed at his words, then cleared her throat and went for a joke, repeating his words from the other day. "How much did that pain you to say?"

"More than the time another HRT selectee dropped a thirty-five-pound battering ram on my foot."

"Ouch." With a smile, she glanced down at her e-reader, as if just realizing it was there. She picked it up off her lap and got comfortable in her seat, then looked sideways at him. "Thank you."

"For what?"

"You know what for." She held his gaze meaningfully.

John felt something in his chest pull tight.

"Anytime, Harlow."

18

Twenty minutes late, Blair and Morano walked through the front door of the vacated bank building that soon would be home to Ashley and Dave's pizzeria and wine bar.

Supposedly.

"Sorry to keep you waiting," Blair said, as he and Morano crossed the room to the wall of empty teller windows where Jessica and John stood. "It took me longer to wrap things up at the office than I'd anticipated." Without much attempt at subtlety, his gaze traveled over the fitted white sheath dress Jessica had changed into at the hotel.

"No problem," she said. "Dave and I passed the time by listening to 'Free Bird' and 'Sweet Home Alabama' on my phone."

Blair let out a bark of laughter. "Heard about my speech, did you?"

"Mr. Mayor, I think practically everyone in this country heard about that speech."

"All in a day's work." Blair winked at her, obviously enjoying the flattery, then gestured to their surroundings. "So. This is going to be your Tuscan-like pizzeria and wine bar."

Morano also checked out the space. "How long will it take to turn this into a restaurant?"

"Ideally, we'd like to open in late fall," John said. "Here, let me show you what we have in mind in terms of design."

Jessica leaned against the teller counter, watching as John gave Blair and Morano a brief tour of the space. He, too, had changed at the hotel, into a light gray checkered suit, white shirt, and tie that was almost the exact deep blue shade as his eyes.

Probably, she needed to stop noticing things like that.

"What do you think?" she asked Morano and Blair after they'd finished the tour.

"I think it's going to be a hit. I'll be sure to have my assistant book me a table for opening night." Blair strode back to where Jessica stood and rested an elbow on the teller counter. "Now. About your zoning and parking problems."

"Yes, about that." Jessica held his gaze. "Anthony says you've agreed to help us out."

"I have." Blair looked down at the briefcase at her feet. "Assuming you have what I think you have in that briefcase."

Actually, Jessica had a little surprise for him on that front. But first she wanted to get him to talk more about the bribe. She and John were wearing wireless mics again, with Agents Leavitt and Todd listening in from an unmarked car parked in an alley a few blocks away. "Before we get to the briefcase, Dave and I have a few questions."

Blair looked between her and John, who leaned casually against a nearby cubicle. "What kind of questions?"

"We just want to make sure everyone's on the same page. A couple years ago, Dave and I had a problem related to some zoning issues back in Chicago—an alderman we thought we had a deal with tried to scam money out of us by making promises he couldn't deliver. That's made us more cautious with these types of arrangements." She smiled. "I'm sure you understand."

Blair's eyes flashed with arrogance. "With all due respect, Ms. Evers, I'm no fucking alderman."

"With all due respect, Mr. Mayor, I wouldn't be paying you fifty thousand dollars for one phone call if you were. But since we plan to develop several projects in Jacksonville, we consider this more an investment in a long-term mutually beneficial relationship."

Blair studied her for a moment. "All right. What do you want to know?"

"Anthony mentioned that you have a friend on the Land Use Committee?"

"Not just *on* the committee, he's the director. Paul Ryu."

"And he'll make sure our zoning and parking applications get approved?" she asked.

"He will if I ask him to."

"What if he asks why you want our applications approved?" John said. "Obviously, this deal needs to remain between us."

"You think?" Blair snorted. "Paul's not going to ask *why*. I'm the mayor. I ask someone for a favor, and it's done. Simple as that."

"There are some timing issues here, not the least of which is making sure we don't lose this property," Jessica said. "How quickly after we give you the money can you reach out to Ryu on our behalf?"

"I'll call him tomorrow." He cocked his head confidently. "Is that quick enough for you?"

Jessica looked sideways at John, as if to say, *I'm good. You?* He nodded.

"Well, then." She reached for the briefcase at her feet and handed it over to Blair. His fingers brushed over hers as he grabbed the handle—not an accident, she was quite certain.

Blair unzipped the case, peered inside, and frowned. He gave the briefcase a shake. "Is this a joke?"

"That's half of the money now," Jessica said. "The remaining twenty-five thousand is yours as soon as our applications are approved by the committee."

Morano stepped forward, his expression one of genuine surprise. "Uh, that's not what we agreed. There was never any talk about splitting the payment into parts."

Indeed, they had not discussed this part of the plan with Morano. Despite the fact that he was cooperating with the FBI, he wasn't privy to the agents' strategy at all times. The Jacksonville FBI office was eager to wrap up their investigation of Blair, and this sting op was the last piece of that. While the mayor *said* he would act quickly to get Ashley and Dave's applications approved, the FBI was hardly inclined to believe the mere word of a man whom they were about to arrest for corruption, bribery, and honest services fraud. This way, by holding the remaining twenty-five thousand dollars over Blair's head, he'd be more inclined to finish the job as soon as possible.

"As you said the other day, Mr. Mayor, I think we understand each other. So I'm sure you can appreciate why Dave and I feel the need to have some sort of guarantee in this situation."

Blair zipped up the briefcase. Then he took a step closer to Jessica, lowering his voice. "Careful, Ashley."

Out of the corner of her eye, she saw John watching. Like her, he was ready to act if need be, despite the fact that he hadn't outwardly changed his relaxed position against the cubicle.

Blair stopped just inches from her, the edge of his briefcase rubbing against her leg. His voice dipped lower, turning coy. "If I didn't know better, I'd think you were trying to see me again."

Mindful of her obligations to play nice as part of the sting op, Jessica feigned a smile in return. "That's just a bonus, Mr. Mayor."

He boldly held her gaze before turning and heading toward

the door, as if this were all part of some cat-and-mouse game between them. Which it was, of course.

Except the mouse hadn't yet realized who was who.

"Leavitt and Todd seemed pleased with how things went," Jessica said as she steered the Mercedes away from the abandoned warehouse that served as their rendezvous spot with the Jax agents.

"As they should be," John said, next to her in the passenger seat. "When this investigation goes public, the media's going to jump all over Blair's 'I'm the mayor' speech. You have a knack for getting great sound bites out of the guy."

"*We* have a knack for it," she corrected.

He gave her a pointed look. "Come on. It's clear Blair responds better to you. I'm basically the undercover cock-blocker at this point."

Jessica laughed hard at that, thinking she wouldn't have put it *quite* that way. "Well, that *is* a very key role."

"Sure, it is."

She smiled at his self-deprecating tone, although she wasn't entirely joking. With John present during the meetings, she was free to act impressed and intrigued by Blair's braggadocio—which, in turn, got him to talk more on the record. If the two of them were alone, on the other hand, Blair very well might be tempted to take his flirtation up a notch and create some awkward situation that Jessica would have to finagle her way out of without (a) blowing her cover, (b) making Blair suspicious, or (c) rejecting him in a way that left him so pissy he clammed up and stopped giving her all these great one-liners the U.S. Attorney's office would undoubtedly use in their case against him.

Not that she couldn't handle herself in such a situation, if need be. But it was handy to have John around so it didn't come to that.

Actually . . . it wasn't so bad having him around, period.

She glanced over. The evening sunlight brought out the deep gold of his hair, hair that she'd sunk her fingers into just five nights ago, as they'd kissed against the wall of his hotel room.

The memory made her feel compelled to say something. "Obviously, it's just acting. It's not like I *enjoy* having to flirt with Blair."

He seemed amused by her comment. "You mean you're not secretly crushing on the corrupt, egomaniac politician who soon will be going to prison for the next fifteen to twenty? Yeah, I think I got that."

She smiled, because *of course* that should've been self-evident. But she had a feeling, had she still been married to Alex and he'd learned that she was flirting with a man as part of an undercover assignment, that his reaction would not have been so matter-of-fact.

Not that she was comparing the two men. She and John weren't romantically involved—heated, hair-gripping kiss notwithstanding—and the fact that he was an undercover agent, too, meant he *should* understand the position she was in.

But still, it was nice to be with someone who just got it.

Jessica turned from I-95 onto Butler Boulevard, the freeway that would take them to the beach.

Out of the blue, John broke the silence that had settled between them. "I still don't like the way he looks at you, though."

Hearing the low, almost rough tone of his voice, she looked at him. He held her gaze for a moment, then turned and stared at the road ahead of them.

After dropping off the car with the valet, she and John headed inside the hotel. Slowly, they came to a stop by one of the lobby's white-marble columns.

"You're heading up to your room, then?" he asked.

"I think I'll order a glass of wine and dessert from room service. It's kind of a thing I do, after a job." Undercover work always left her a little wound up from all the adrenaline. "You?"

He shrugged. "I'll probably go for a run."

She nodded, as an image popped into her head of John running along the beach at sunset, getting sweaty in the warm evening air, his T-shirt clinging to his muscular chest.

She cleared her throat, her mouth having gone a little dry. "Should we meet here tomorrow morning, then? Say, seven o'clock?"

"Sure. Seven o'clock," he agreed.

A silence fell between them, neither John nor her moving to leave. Finally, she gestured in the direction of her room, not sure why she was hesitating. "Well. I guess I should get going. Good night, Dave."

He gave her a nod, his voice husky. "Good night, Ashley."

As she walked back to her room, she told herself that she was being silly for feeling oddly unsatisfied with that good-bye. Yes, she supposed she could've suggested they grab a drink together—she'd certainly done that with other undercover agents after a job, to blow off steam—but she remembered in vivid detail what had happened the last time she and John had been together, in this very hotel, with all the post-undercover adrenaline running through them.

Better not to tempt fate.

So instead, tonight she would unwind with a hot bath, a nice glass of wine, and dessert, and curl up with her book. And if that suddenly seemed boring in comparison to her last night at this hotel, when she'd kissed John and had nearly climbed the man like a tree . . . well, that was just fine. She was an undercover FBI agent, traveling halfway across the country and staying in a beachfront hotel as part of a sting investigation into a high-profile politician. Probably, a little "boring" wouldn't kill her for one night.

Once in her room, she took off her dress and heels and threw on a tank top and yoga pants. Grabbing the room service menu, she flopped onto the bed and was debating between the cabernet and the pinot noir when her cell phone pinged with a new text message.

She stretched across the bed, grabbed her phone off the nightstand, and saw that the message was from Tara.

Have you seen this? Call me. Attached to Tara's message was a photo of the *People* magazine with Alex and his pregnant fiancée on the cover.

God, *that*. Jessica had completely forgotten about her ex-husband and his possible affair.

She sprang off the bed and grabbed her laptop out of her briefcase. Taking a seat at the desk, she settled in to do some down-and-dirty research. Alex's fiancée was a fairly well-known actress; somewhere on the Internet—TMZ, Perez Hilton, *Us Weekly*—there had to be more gossip about her pregnancy and engagement.

But just as she began to type the actress's name into the Google search engine, John's voice popped into her head.

You don't want to know.

But really she did, sort of.

Trust me . . . all you'll end up with is a lot of needless self-doubt.

With a sigh, Jessica sat back in the chair.

As soon as she'd spotted that magazine in the airport, she'd started racking her brain for any signs that Alex had been cheating on her. But maybe John had a point. Would it truly give her any sort of "resolution" if she had confirmation that Alex had been unfaithful? Their marriage was over, she'd moved on, and so had he, obviously. At least, unlike John, she still had the option of choosing to believe that someone she'd once trusted and loved hadn't betrayed her in that way.

Last month, I walked in on my girlfriend having sex with one of my friends.

She cringed at the thought. It was bad enough having to deal with the possibility that Alex had been cheating on her; she couldn't imagine having actually *seen* it.

As an aside, who the heck cheated on John Shepherd, anyway? And she wasn't even taking the stupid-hotness into account, although—*hello*—did his ex-girlfriend have *eyes*? Sure, he had a well-developed ego, and he definitely could be too cocky and sarcastic. But, having gotten to know him better these last couple of weeks, she had to admit that there was a lot more going on underneath the surface of the all-American, GI Joe exterior than she'd originally given him credit for.

He was funny, in a dry-humored way. Smart, too, and very thorough when it came to work. Not a bad listener, either. In fact, he'd been surprisingly easy to talk to during a very personal moment, after she'd seen her ex-husband on the cover of *People* magazine. He could've easily avoided the conversation, but instead he'd opened up about his own personal life and had even given her some pretty good advice.

And talk about being *capable*. She'd heard enough about HRT tryouts to know that the Bureau really put those guys through the wringer, but John had made it through. Of course he had. He'd dominated on the firing range and in every physical and tactical challenge at the Academy, and he'd been breathing down her neck in the academic portion. And if she was being honest with herself, even back then she'd found that kind of confidence, ability, and know-how actually quite . . . sexy.

Her phone suddenly chimed with another text message.

Jessica blinked at the sound, coming out of her reverie. Spotting the actress's name on her computer screen, still waiting in the search line, she deleted it and shut her laptop. Maybe, on second thought, it was better not to go down that road.

I told you, she could practically hear John saying.

Yeah, yeah. Apparently, even in her imagination, the man just had to be right.

She grabbed her phone off the desk, expecting the new text message to be from Tara again, checking up on her.

But instead, it was from John.

Can I come to your room?

Well, then. Jessica's heart skipped a beat as she tried to recall how cute the underwear she had on was.

Not for that, he quickly added.

Pfft. Well, obviously. Of course she'd known he hadn't been referring to *that*.

Moving on.

Not sure what was going on, she typed back her room number. She did a visual sweep of the room, making sure it was presentable, and scrolled through the possible reasons John would want to see her. Maybe Leavitt had called about something that had come up in the investigation? Although that didn't seem likely; the Jax agent had always conferenced in both of them whenever he'd called in the past. Maybe a problem in Chicago? Something personal, perhaps, and John had to jump on a plane tonight and get back home?

Worried it might be something like that, she wasted no time answering the door when he knocked barely two minutes later.

"Hey," John said, standing on her doorstep. He'd changed into jeans and a navy T-shirt, and his cheeks looked a little flushed, as if he'd literally run right over after texting her.

"Hey . . . is everything okay?" she asked.

He glanced sideways, checking out the hallway. "Can I come in?"

"Of course." She held the door open for him.

He stepped into the room and waited until the door shut. "So. There's been a development."

She cocked her head. "With Blair? What happened?"

"It's not about Blair."

Jessica waited. He had a very odd expression right then—one she couldn't read. "Okay . . . what is it about, then?"

His mouth curved into a slow grin. "I made the Hostage Rescue Team."

Oh.

Wow. Jessica felt a sharp twinge in her chest, which she quickly shoved aside. "You made it? Oh my God, that's incredible! Congratulations!" She threw her arms around his neck and hugged him.

When his hands slid to her waist, she closed her eyes, feeling little butterflies in her stomach as she pressed against him.

"Thanks," he said huskily in her ear.

After lingering in his arms one moment just shy of getting-awkward-now, Jessica slid out from his grasp and put on a bright smile. "You must be over the moon about this."

He ran a hand through his hair. "I haven't really wrapped my mind around it yet. I just got the call a few minutes ago." He exhaled and then grinned. "Crazy, huh?"

She teasingly dismissed this with a wave. "Eh. I'm not that surprised. Remember, I was there at the beginning, when you were running circles around me on the Yellow Brick Road and barking orders about the quality of my sit-ups."

"I keep telling you, I was being motivational."

"Sure you were." The inside joke hung in the air between them, and for a moment he just looked at her.

Feeling oddly exposed under his gaze, she glanced down at her clothes. "Well, clearly, I need to change."

He cocked his head at the non sequitur. "Actually, I'm digging the yoga pants, but if you feel a sudden need to start shedding clothes after hearing that I made HRT, by all means proceed."

She gave him a look. *Ha ha.* "I meant that I need to change before we head down to the bar to celebrate."

His expression softened. "Jessica . . . you don't need to do that. You're already settled in for the night."

She stepped closer, peering up into his eyes. "I just found out that my partner made the most elite counterterrorism team in all of federal law enforcement. I think that merits a drink or two. Just give me five minutes."

19

Their options, John discovered, were limited.

The resort's more casual bar, located on the beach, stopped serving drinks at sunset, which—as the bartender pointedly informed him—was in about five minutes. He directed John up a spiral staircase to the Seahorse Grille, the hotel's signature restaurant.

At the hostess stand, a fifty-something woman in a black pantsuit greeted him warmly. "How can I help you?"

He asked for a table for two, then did a quick survey of the place: white linens on the tables, a vaulted ceiling with exposed beams, and floor-to-ceiling windows that showcased a sweeping view of the Atlantic Ocean. He gestured to his jeans. "Am I okay dressed like this?"

The hostess looked him over. "Darlin', you could walk in here wearing a barrel and I don't think anyone would mind." She grabbed two menus and smiled. "Right this way."

She led him toward an open table along the window, in the center of the restaurant. John spotted another table in the far corner, where no one else was currently seated. There, he and Jessica would be able talk without being overheard.

"Could we have that one instead?" he asked, pointing.

She nodded graciously. "Of course."

After being seated, he texted Jessica to let her know about the change in venue, then ordered a bourbon on the rocks when the waitress came by. It was one of the rare nights he wasn't carrying his Glock, and he wasn't driving, which meant he was free to drink and celebrate with abandon, should the mood strike.

While waiting, he took in the view of the Atlantic Ocean, still trying to process everything.

The Hostage Rescue Team.

Holy shit, he'd made it.

"Hope you saved room to finally put 'badass' on your résumé," Piser had said, when he'd called to deliver the news. "You're on the team, Shepherd. Welcome to the best job in the FBI."

In some senses, John probably shouldn't have been so caught off guard. This was, after all, what he'd been recruited for. Then again, being recruited for HRT was no guarantee that one would actually make the team; only about ten percent of agents brought in to the FBI via the Tactical Recruitment Program actually ended up being HRT operators. In fact, in the thirty-plus years since HRT's inception, fewer than three hundred men total had been selected for the team.

And now he—the "grunt" with the mere bachelor's degree from Wisconsin—would be one of them.

Heady stuff.

It wouldn't be an easy lifestyle; he knew that. HRT operators understood that the team always came first—before, even, their own individual needs. He would be gone from home for extended periods of time and could be called away with little notice. But having no girlfriend, wife, or kids made him the perfect candidate in that regard. The upside of Alicia's cheating was that it had freed him up to seize this opportunity without worrying about uprooting anyone else to Virginia, or about the strain the HRT lifestyle would put on his personal life. He'd been free to think about just himself, probably for the first time since his mom had gotten sick and he'd transferred to the Chicago field office.

Our motto, servare vitas, *means to save lives—and that's exactly what we do.*

John could still hear the pride in Piser's voice that first day they'd met at Fort Benning to discuss HRT, pride that had been there for good reason. Despite John's show of cockiness that day, even he had to admit that HRT operators were an entirely different level of badass than Rangers—they were special agents whose only counterparts were Navy SEAL Team 6 or U.S. Army Delta Force. No other law enforcement SWAT team was its equal; they were an exclusive unit uniquely trained to handle terrorist and other high-risk incidents both in the United States and around the world. As part of HRT, he would be on the cutting edge of the FBI's capabilities, his every day focused on firearms, tactics, preparation, and specialized skills such as close-quarter battle, fast-roping out of helicopters, and parachuting.

"So? What do you say?" Piser had asked, when John had gone momentarily quiet after hearing he'd made the team.

He enjoyed working undercover—actually, he enjoyed it a lot. But this was the chance of a lifetime, an opportunity to do something few people *could* do. He'd proven himself during HRT selection, he was proud and honored to have been chosen for the team, and he knew, logically, that if he ever planned to take this step in his career, the time was now.

So he'd told Piser *yes.*

John's cell phone, resting on the table, buzzed with a new text message. He glanced down to read it.

Sorry—on my way.

Jessica. If anyone had told him six years ago that *she* would be the first person to buy him a drink in congratulations for making HRT, he would've laughed in their face. But now, here they were.

About time. How hard is it to take off a pair of yoga pants? he texted back.

His phone screen was quiet for a moment, and then he saw the three dots that indicated she was typing. He braced himself, waiting . . . and then the screen went quiet again.

Saucy quips eluding you tonight? he teased.

I really don't like you sometimes.

He smiled and set down his phone, the exchange reminding him of the many times she'd sassed him at the Academy. Only this time, he was pretty sure she didn't actually detest him, which was nice. Heck, she'd even hugged him when he'd told her he'd made HRT. A sweet gesture, that—albeit, also a torturous one, given how incredible she'd felt pressed against him wearing only a tank top and yoga pants.

As his hands had slid around her waist, he'd had to quickly remind himself that they'd agreed they wouldn't complicate their partnership by getting physically involved. Or, at least, she'd made some proclamations and he hadn't *dis*agreed. He'd said he wouldn't touch her again—unless she made a move on him—and he intended to stick to his word. But sometimes, when she looked at him a certain way, he remembered how hot their kiss had been, and how sexy it had sounded when she'd moaned his name.

John.

As if on cue, Jessica strode into the restaurant. Immediately, his grip tightened on his rocks glass.

The woman clearly loved to torture him.

Tonight, she'd shed her usual white-collar-esque attire in favor of a long, summery dress with a slit on one side. The breezy fabric parted as she walked, giving him peek-a-boo glimpses of sleek, bare leg all the way to her midthigh. And for the first time, with the heeled sandals she was wearing, he noticed that her toenails were painted purple.

No clue why that did it for him, but, man, it really did.

"That was *twelve* minutes," he growled when she got to the table. "Not five."

"You're cranky with me already? I just got here." She considered this for a moment and smiled. "That's impressive, even for me."

Cute. His jaw tightened as she took the seat across from him and flashed more peek-a-boo leg.

She ordered a mojito when the waitress came by the table, then leaned in and lowered her voice once it was just the two of them. "So. The Hostage Rescue Team." Her blue eyes sparkled. "This is going to do wonders for your ego, isn't it?"

"You should probably prepare yourself for obnoxious levels of bragging and insufferability tonight."

She laughed. "I appreciate the heads-up."

John smiled, thinking it was nice that they could joke around like this. It was a shame, really, their timing. Just when she'd finally stopped detesting him, he was leaving.

Feeling an odd pang, he brushed it off and took a sip of his bourbon.

No sense dwelling on that.

She lowered her voice again, a curious gleam in her eyes. "I've never worked with anyone who went through Selection. But I've heard a few stories."

John wasn't surprised to hear it. Despite the fact that the specifics of HRT Selection were supposed to remain confidential, somebody always talked. And in the thirty-plus years since the team's inception, the stories that ran around the FBI field offices had reached near-mythic proportions.

At four A.M. sharp that first morning of tryouts, they'd lined up John and his fellow selectees—buck naked—for a weigh-in, and then had put them through a grueling series of physical fitness tests. After that, there'd been a psychological test, and then the selectees had headed out to the shooting range for a preliminary qualification course.

Five selectees had dropped out by dinner that first day. By the end of the fourth day, they'd lost another six.

"What kind of stories?" John asked, playing coy and enjoying this rare moment of knowing something the esteemed Jessica Harlow did not.

Jessica paused as the waitress dropped off her drink, then took a sip of her mojito. "For starters, I heard they practically starve you and then give you only enough food for half the group, to see who will be greedy and who will take care of his teammates."

"Hmm. That would be an interesting exercise."

"I also heard they make you race twenty-two miles over the Yellow Brick Road, with full gear."

That had been day four and, actually, it had been twenty-two and a *half* miles. She was correct, however, about the full gear; the selectees had each carried backpacks and personal gear that weighed forty-five pounds combined, *and* had taken turns carrying an additional fifty-pound bag stuffed with medicine balls.

And John's dinner that night, after rations had been divvied up, had been a banana.

That had not been one of the easier days.

"The details are a little fuzzy. After about mile sixteen, they all start to run together," he joked.

Jessica remained undaunted. "And I also heard there's a claustrophobia test, where they make you crawl through the Academy's heating ducts while blindfolded."

Also true, but far worse, in John's opinion, had been the time they'd made him and the other selectees swim through rancid sewer water. That shit had been *cold*. Literally. "You've heard a lot."

She looked at him for a moment, then shook her head, her tone a mixture of admiration and disbelief. "How do you do this stuff? I barely made it through OC Spray Day."

He laughed, the reference bringing back another memory from their time together at Quantico. "OC Spray Day" was one of the most universally dreaded days for special agent trainees at the Academy, when their defensive tactics instructors hit each of them with a burst of pepper spray and then made them—while incapacitated—defend their firearm and get an attacker on the ground in a spread-eagle position.

John had been through a similar exercise as a Ranger, so he'd known what to expect. Others had struggled more, including Linguistics PhD, who'd gotten yelled at by the instructors for keeping his eyes closed while fighting—they had to have at least one open to pass—and then had thrown up in the grass afterward. But what John remembered most vividly about that day was Jessica, coughing, eyes red and teary, as she'd drawn her training pistol and had forced her attacker to the ground with authoritative command. *FBI! Don't move!*

Actually, he'd found that part of the exercise pretty hot.

"What are you talking about? You did well that day," he told her.

"*You* did well that day. I passed." She made a face, saying the word distastefully.

He grinned teasingly, leaning in. "You don't have to get an A-plus in everything, you know."

"Says the man who fought me tooth and nail for the one high mark he didn't already have in the bag."

Fair enough. John took another sip of his bourbon, then looked at her for a moment, noticing how the blue pattern in her dress was nearly the same shade as her eyes. He had a random thought then, that this was the kind of flirty, summery dress she would probably wear back home in Chicago if the two of them went out on a date.

She cocked her head at his look. "What?"

There was something he needed to know. "Did you really hate me back then?"

She seemed surprised at first by the question. Then she swirled the straw in her glass. "I was aggravated by you. Wanted to throttle you most days. And I was jealous of you, of course—we all were. But *hate* you? No."

His eyes held hers. "Were you attracted to me?"

Her poker face was stellar. "I've already admitted you were the best-looking guy in our class."

"That's not what I asked."

She conceded this with a slight smile. It was the kind of look that had him thinking again—this time, about the silky-softness of her skin as his fingers had slid up her thigh.

"Would you two like another round?" asked a voice, to his left.

John blinked at the waitress's interruption, then glanced at his and Jessica's near-empty glasses. His eyes still holding hers, he answered for both of them.

"Yes. We would."

After their second round of drinks had arrived, in keeping with Jessica's post-undercover tradition, they decided to order dessert. Over spoonfuls of dark chocolate brownie topped with warm salted caramel and vanilla ice cream, John played good cop, asking Jessica about her family, her new condo, and what she thought so far about the Chicago field office.

His motives in this were twofold. First, he was curious and genuinely wanted to know more about her. And second, when she talked, his gaze naturally fell to her lips.

He really liked looking at her lips.

They were interrupted at one point by a flurry of text messages from her sister and brother—Maya and Finn, he learned—

who, apparently, wanted to throw an anniversary party for their parents and couldn't agree on a location.

"How long will they do this?" John asked, fascinated, watching Jessica's phone, which rested on the table. She'd long since turned off the ringer once the twins had started texting, but her phone vibrated and lit up every time a new message came in.

"It usually lasts about a half hour, and then they burn themselves out." Her smile was affectionate. "It's annoying, I know, but you get used to it. Actually, when I was in L.A., I found myself looking forward to their daily text spats. I could practically hear them arguing—it was like being home again."

He caught her word choice there: that Chicago was *home*. Not Los Angeles, apparently, despite the fact that she'd lived there for several years.

After a brief skirmish between them over the dessert's one maraschino cherry, he asked Jessica how she'd gotten into undercover work. This was something else he'd been curious about, ever since they'd partnered up.

"My second year in L.A., the violent crimes squad asked me to help out in a kidnapping investigation," she said. "They'd tracked down the suspect and the three-year-old girl—his stepdaughter—to a room he'd rented at the Fairmont Hotel in Santa Monica with a stolen credit card. They had him under surveillance from the room next door, and they were trying to come up with a way to get him to open the door without taking any extreme measures that could possibly put the child in danger."

"Of course."

"So . . . they asked me to dress up as one of the housekeeping staff."

John let out a bark of laughter. "Get out. Of course that's what the L.A. office would do. That's like something out of a movie."

"Maybe. But it worked. I put on the uniform, rolled a housekeeping cart up to the guy's door, and told him I was there to do the turndown service. He let me into the room, and . . . well, let's just say, thirty seconds later, he was facedown on the ground wearing my handcuffs." She smiled at the memory, then turned more serious. "When we reunited the little girl with her mother . . . that's a moment I'll never forget. It wasn't even my case, barely more than a walk-on role, but I've had the undercover bug ever since. So much of what we do as agents is behind the scenes, but undercover work is on the front lines; it's up close and personal, actually meeting with the bad guys and getting them to trust you and tell you all their dirty little secrets. It's exhausting at times, and unpredictable, but every time I go out on an assignment I feel that same rush I did four years ago." She blushed, as if embarrassed for having gone on so long. "Well, you know how it is."

He nodded, feeling a twinge of nostalgia that this would be his last undercover case.

Yes, he did know.

She gestured. "What about you? How'd you get into it?"

He rested his arms on the table. Funny story, that. "I'd been in Detroit for two years, on the organized crime squad, when they roped me into a walk-on role. Another agent on the squad was trying to infiltrate a motorcycle club we'd been investigating for a laundry list of criminal activity, and we wanted to bolster the agent's credibility as a bad guy. So we decided to stage an altercation at a bar that the club members hung out at."

She cocked her head. "What kind of altercation?"

"Ah . . . how naïve you are, my white-collar-crime friend, that you even have to ask. See, life on the organized crime squad isn't about posh beach hotels and snazzy suits. We tend to be a little grittier. More real."

"I see we've entered the bragging and insufferability portion of the evening," she said dryly.

He chuckled. No offense taken. "The plan was that another agent would go to the bar, pretend to be a drunk patron, and start trouble with the undercover agent trying to get in good with the motorcycle club. Things would escalate into a fight, the second agent would lose—convincingly—and the club members would see what a tough guy the first agent was."

"And you were the second agent?" she asked.

"Yes."

"I see." Her blue eyes sparkled. "So . . . basically, your first job as an undercover agent was to get your ass kicked."

He looked up at the ceiling. "I sense I'm going to regret telling you this story."

"You know, instead of kicking your ass, the other agent could've just faked like he was hurt and then pulled you to the ground in an arm-bar hold. I'm told that can be a very effective maneuver against a man of your size."

John gave her a withering look.

"Give it time. In another six years, that joke's going to be really funny," she said cheekily. "So, how real an 'altercation' are we talking about here? Did you actually get hurt?"

"Not really. Just a black eye, some bruised ribs, and fifteen stitches in my hand."

Her eyes widened, her tone instantly turning serious. "Oh my gosh. What happened?"

Actually, this was his favorite part of the story. "The other agent and I had choreographed the whole fight, right down to a theatrical beer bottle smash that I would duck away from just in time. And that all went as planned, except, apparently, some glass from the bottle landed on the floor by our feet. So the other agent and I are going at it; he's acting like a tough guy, and I'm hamming it up, slurring my words and pretending to be

drunk out of my mind. Finally, he 'throws' me to the ground"—
he used air quotes, because the other agent had been all of about
five-eleven and 170 pounds and, well, *come on*—"and my hand
lands right on a chunk of glass from the beer bottle."

Jessica grimaced. "Oh, that's bad."

"No, it was perfect. It sliced my hand open, so there's blood
everywhere: on me, on him, all over the bar—it totally made
the fight look even more authentic. My squad leader was so
impressed, as soon as they released me from the ER, he took
me and the guys on the backup squad out for beers."

She stared at him for a long moment. "I think you organized crime guys might actually be a little crazy."

He flashed her a proud grin. "We prefer to think of it as
'dedicated to our craft.'"

She considered that, then beckoned with her hand. "All
right. Let's see this 'perfect' battle scar of yours."

He slid his left hand across the table. The scar ran across the
top of his palm, about two inches long. He'd worn it like a
badge of pride these four years since his debut undercover
assignment, a symbol of his dedication to the job and his will-
ingness to go all-in for a role.

Jessica picked up his hand to take a look, wrapping her
fingers around the back of his hand.

He went still at her touch.

She frowned, and then flipped his hand over as if looking
for something. "Are you sure this is the right hand?"

"Ha ha." He moved to take his hand back, but she held on.

"I'm kidding." She turned his palm back up and gently
traced her finger over the scar.

He drew in a breath.

She peered up. "Does that hurt?"

He met her gaze. "No."

A pink flush crept over her cheeks, and neither of them
moved or spoke as the air seemed to go still between them.

Then she cleared her throat, letting go of his hand as the waitress approached.

"Whenever you're ready—no rush," the waitress said with a polite smile, leaving the check on the table.

After the waitress walked away, Jessica looked over her shoulder at the empty restaurant. "I didn't realize we'd shut down the place."

He had.

He'd just been enjoying himself too much to care.

Since it was a nice night, they decided to walk along the beachfront path to their rooms. It was nearly a full moon, and a light breeze coming off the ocean cut through the thick humidity in the air.

"What did your family say when you told them the news about HRT?" Jessica asked.

John stole another look as the breeze parted her dress. Those *legs*. He pictured them wrapped around him, the heels of her sandals digging into his back as he—

She stared at him expectantly.

Right. They were walking and talking here. Probably he should pick up his tongue off the walkway before she tripped over it in those heels. "My brother mocked me, as expected, and asked if I would have to wear tights and a cape now that I've graduated to 'full-time superhero camp.' That's what he calls HRT. As for my dad . . . I haven't told him yet. I want to give him the news in person. He wasn't thrilled when I went through Selection."

Jessica sounded surprised. "He doesn't want you to be on the team?"

"I think it's more that he doesn't want me to move to Virginia. Ever since my mom died a year ago, it's pretty much just been him, my brother, and me." He frowned. "I need to figure out how to make that situation right before I leave."

"I'm sure he'll come around. He's a former cop; he knows

what kind of opportunity this is for you." Jessica glanced his way. "And I'm sorry to hear about your mom."

"Thank you." He smiled, realizing something. "She would've loved seeing me with you." As soon as the words came out, he rephrased that. "I mean, seeing you as my partner."

"What makes you say that?" The breeze had tangled a lock of Jessica's hair in the delicate gold necklace she wore, and she worked on the knot with her fingers as they walked.

"She was a big feminist. That's how she met my dad, in fact." John should know; he and his brother had heard the story only about a hundred times. "May tenth, 1980. She rallied in Grant Park with eighty thousand other activists in support of the Equal Rights Amendment. Betty Friedan and Gloria Steinem spoke, and they all marched down Columbus Drive wearing white sashes in honor of the 1920s suffragists."

"And your dad marched, too?" Jessica looked impressed. "How progressive of him."

"Actually, he was one of the cops assigned to cover the protest. He was lined up on Columbus, doing crowd control, and—so the story goes—as the protesters marched by, he saw this woman trip and fall down. Worried that she might get trampled, he shoved his way through the crowd and helped her up. Turns out, the woman—my mom—had sprained her ankle pretty badly, but she was stubborn and insisted that she wanted to keep going. My dad watched her hobble along the street for about a hundred feet before she gave in and sat down on the curb. He'd probably never given the Equal Rights Amendment a second thought before that day, but something about the disappointment on my mom's face got to him. So he walked over, picked her up, and carried her the rest of the way so she could finish the march."

Jessica put a hand to her chest. "Oh my God, that might be the most romantic thing I've ever heard."

He winked. "We Shepherd men have moves."

"You're a modest people, too, I hear."

He laughed. So *saucy.* "The point is, my mom would've loved your story."

Jessica gave him a bemused look as she tried to work her hair from the necklace. "I wasn't aware I had a 'story.'"

"Please. The whole one-of-only-two-women-in-our-class thing? Dominating in academics and all that extra training you put in on the shooting range and with the PT? You had a story. Hell, I could practically hear 'Maniac' playing in the background every time you stepped into the gym."

She went tellingly silent.

"It was your theme song at the Academy, wasn't it?" he asked.

She laughed like this was the funniest thing. "My theme song . . . right." She shot him a look, saw his grin, and threw up her hands. "Okay, *how* could you possibly know that?"

"Mind powers." He laughed when she poked him in the shoulder. "Fine. I could hear the song playing on your iPod every morning before PT."

She *hmph*ed at that, looking a little piqued. "You must've been hovering awfully close."

He shrugged, his tone sly. "I probably was." They walked in silence for a moment, the peaceful rhythm of the ocean waves the only sound between them.

He couldn't resist.

"'She's a maniac, maniac on the floor,'" he sang under his breath.

She shook her head, seeming to fight back a smile. "That's fine, laugh it up." Finally, she stopped struggling with her necklace and let her hands fall to her side. "All right, I give up. I'm stuck."

"Come here." He moved closer and they both stopped on the walkway. Bending his head, he took a closer look at the necklace. "Your hair is knotted around the clasp."

"Just yank it out. The rest of my hair will cover the bald spot." Despite her attempt at levity, her voice sounded throatier than usual.

"There's a joke somewhere in there about never harming so much as a hair on your head." And it wasn't a joke, actually—this particular agent had always brought out the protective side of him. Even if she'd never needed it.

Patiently, he began unwinding the tiny lock of her hair that was caught around the necklace. It took a few moments, and then he freed the last strands from the clasp. "There." That accomplished, he smoothed her hair back around her shoulders.

Standing just inches away, she peered up at him with those gorgeous blue eyes. "Thank you."

He moved even closer. "You know, normally, with this whole romantic backdrop—the moonlight, the beach—I'd probably kiss you right about now."

"Would you, now?" She raised an eyebrow.

But she didn't move back.

He shrugged, feigning nonchalance. "Well, with you being single, and me being single, and with all the laughing and joking around tonight, it just feels . . . expected."

"Expected?" Her lips curved, as she considered this. "What's stopping you, then?"

"I promised I wouldn't make a move on you. Actually, it wasn't a promise, per se. More like I agreed not to disagree with you."

"So you're saying the ball's in my court."

He bent his head, stopping just before his mouth touched hers. "The ball has always been in your court, Jessica," he said huskily. "From the first moment I walked up to you at the Academy."

She looked at him for a moment. Then she stood up on her tiptoes and leaned into him.

The instant her lips touched his, John slid one hand to her waist and threaded the other in her hair.

About damn time.

20

This time, Jessica and her inner pragmatic were in complete agreement.

If John kept kissing her this way, she could not be blamed for any indecent acts she committed right here, on the beach.

First, he tangled his hand in her hair, holding her close as he teasingly explored her mouth. Then he took it up a notch and deepened the kiss, leaving her weak in the knees as his tongue wound hotly around hers.

Yes. This. For too long, they'd been dancing around each other, but that ended tonight.

Hooking a finger into the waistband of his jeans, she tugged him closer, as close as she could get him, and felt the thick ridge of his erection pressing against her stomach.

That . . . was not where she needed it, exactly.

"You're too big," she murmured. She felt him smile against her mouth. "I mean too *tall*." Although, judging from the situation in his jeans, she'd been spot on with the "big guy" nickname.

His hands moved to the backs of her thighs and lifted her up so she could straddle his waist. "Better?"

"Much better." Eye-to-eye with him for a change, she cupped

his face in her hands and kissed him. Their mouths melded together as his hands curved around her bottom, holding her up as their lips and tongues tangled heatedly.

He pulled back to gaze at her for a moment, both of them slightly out of breath. Without discussion, he began walking up the path toward the nearest building.

She smiled. "You can't carry me to your room like this. If someone walks by, they'll know what we're up to."

He pointed with his chin. "Then we're lucky my room is right there."

She glanced over her shoulder, then turned back to him in indignation. "You got another oceanfront room?"

He grinned, tipping her toward him. "You can rail at me for that later." His mouth covered hers, his kiss commanding all her attention until they reached the outer door of his building. He set her down and reached into his back pocket for his room key card. Making quick work of the lock, he opened the door, grabbed her hand, and tugged her into the hallway—

Just as a man in his sixties, dressed in athletic pants and a T-shirt, stepped out of a room farther down the hall.

Jessica and John walked chastely in silence as the man headed their way. In tandem, they gave him a nod while passing by.

"Nice night for a walk," he said.

"Quite," Jessica said, with a casual smile.

"Sure is," John agreed.

They waited until they heard the outer door shut behind them, then reached for each other again.

Moving so fast her head nearly spun, John pinned her against his hotel room door. Bracing his hands on either side of her, he leaned down and kissed her, long and deep.

"John," she breathed. They needed to get inside the room. Now.

"It drives me crazy when you say my name like that." He

peered down into her eyes. "Why now? You said you didn't want to complicate things between us."

Yes, she did. "Well . . . you're leaving now." She paused, trying to remember if he'd ever actually said that he'd accepted the spot on the team. "You are leaving, aren't you?"

He looked at her for a moment and then nodded. "Yes."

Pride and admiration, along with her genuine happiness for what he'd accomplished, mixed with a more bittersweet emotion.

Latching onto the pride, she reached up and touched his cheek. Good for him. This was a once-in-a-lifetime chance—he *should* go. "Then that keeps things pretty simple between us, doesn't it?" Her words were gentle, but matter-of-fact.

Something flickered in his eyes. "Yes. It does." He lowered his head and kissed her. The heat of the moment took over, the two of them intertwined against the door as their hands began to move impatiently, almost desperately.

Reaching around her, he slid his key card into the lock and opened the door. They tumbled into the room, and she reached for the hem of his T-shirt before the door had even shut behind them. Stepping back to help, he yanked the shirt over his head.

Sweet Jesus.

She blinked, not sure where to look first. Chest sculpted like an armor plate; broad shoulders; strong, corded arms; rippling abs with a trail of dark blond hair that dipped invitingly into the waistband of his jeans.

"What time is our flight tomorrow?" she asked.

"Nine o'clock."

"Good." She gestured to his body. "I'm going to need some time with all this."

He smiled wickedly, his eyes a deep, smoky blue as he closed the gap between them. Sliding his hands up her back, he found the zipper of her dress.

She exhaled unsteadily as he pulled down the zipper, exposing her back to the cool air of the hotel room. Holding her gaze, he inched one dress strap off her shoulder, then the other.

The dress fell to the floor and pooled at her feet.

His gaze traveled up, taking in her heels, her cream silk thong, and her strapless bra. "Even better than I'd imagined," he murmured. Wasting no time, he unhooked her bra, which slipped to the floor next to her dress.

"What else have you imagined?" she asked.

His lips curved. Moving quickly, he pinned her against the wall, capturing both of her hands in his.

She smiled coyly as their eyes met. *Now* they were getting somewhere.

His mouth swept down on hers, his kiss demanding and possessive. He released her hands and lifted her up, so that she straddled him again. His lips found her breasts, and she dug her fingers into the back of his hair as he teased one of her nipples with his tongue. Moaning softly, she arched against the rock-hard cock that pressed between her legs.

He growled low in his throat. "I don't think I can do this the nice way, Jessica."

"Good. I don't want it the nice way," she breathed.

That decided, he carried her into the bathroom. Holding her up with only one arm, he continued kissing her while rummaging around in his Dopp kit for what she hoped was a condom. Once he found it, they made it only as far as the hallway, where he set her down against the wall.

Their hands began moving frantically. He yanked down her underwear as she undid the button on his jeans, pausing only to grip his forearms for balance as she stepped out of her thong, one leg at a time. Then she unzipped his fly and shoved his jeans and boxer briefs past his hips.

Both of them breathing heavily, he handed her the condom and kicked off his jeans and underwear, making equally quick work of his socks and shoes. She got a split second to marvel at the sight of him fully naked as she ripped open the condom, and then he was on her again, big and hard as she rolled the condom on.

Ready and *so* willing for what was about to come next, she straddled him when he lifted her up. She felt him between her legs, and then he gripped her bottom and pressed her against the wall for leverage.

She closed her eyes and moaned as he eased into her, filling her completely.

God, that was good.

Opening her eyes, she saw John's hot, fierce expression. Holding her gaze, he began to move in smooth, deliberate strokes. Their ragged breathing cut through the stillness of the room, until the intimacy of the moment became too much and she closed her eyes, throwing her head back and surrendering as he thrust faster, fucking her hard against the wall and giving her everything she needed as she climbed to the edge of her orgasm and then plummeted over, with wave after wave of intense pleasure flooding through her.

He spread her legs wider, completely dominating her now in deep, claiming strokes that pinned her to the wall. He groaned, and every muscle in his beautiful, powerful body seemed to draw tight as he swelled inside her, his breath ragged and strained until he shuddered, almost violently, and slowly, finally, came to a stop.

Her eyes met his as she tried to catch her breath.

Wow.

His voice was husky, still slightly shaky. "Did I hurt you?"

She felt her chest tighten. "Far from it."

His gaze softened, and then he bent his head and kissed her, pulling her off the wall to carry her to the bed. Carefully depositing her there, he gripped the base of the condom and pulled out.

Jessica checked out his ass appreciatively as he walked into the bathroom.

A few moments later, he came back out, his eyes roving over her as he walked to the bed. Sliding one hand down her leg, he gripped the back of her ankle and lifted it up. He undid the buckle of her strappy sandal and let the shoe fall to the floor, then did the same thing with the other shoe.

He climbed onto the bed, his arms planted on each side of her, trapping her in. Bending his head, he gave her a devilish smile.

"*Now* I'm ready to do this the nice way."

Afterward, they lay side-by side on the bed as he traced lazy lines along her arm.

"When do you leave?" she asked.

His fingers paused. "Labor Day weekend."

So soon. Only two and a half weeks away. She nodded, going for a joke. "Good. That's about when I was planning on getting sick of you, anyway."

"*Pfft.* I'm already counting down the minutes until I can make my escape from this room."

"It's your room."

"Shit. *Foiled.*"

She smiled, then turned her head to look at him. Gently, he brushed a lock of hair out of her eyes.

Suddenly wanting to be even closer to him, she shifted on the bed, resting on her forearms and leaning forward to kiss him. He palmed the nape of her neck, curling his fingers into her hair as he claimed her mouth. His other hand skimmed down her back, a light, seductive touch that sent a thrill up her spine.

She'd already had the man twice tonight, but she still felt like she couldn't get enough of him.

Seemingly of a similar mind-set, he gripped her by the hips and lifted her on top of him. She slid her knees forward, straddling him, and whimpered with pleasure when his erection pressed between her legs.

"Are you sore?" he asked huskily.

It should've been weird, hearing John Shepherd ask her that. But instead it felt intimate and erotic, and, actually, it turned her on even more. "I'll manage," she said throatily.

He rolled her onto her back, giving her a steamy kiss before climbing off the bed. Then he held out his hand. "Come with me."

She put her hand in his, and he led her into the dark bathroom. He flicked on the makeup mirror light so a soft, ambient glow filled the room, then headed over to the shower and turned on the water.

She said a silent prayer that her waterproof mascara would live up to its promise.

As steam filled the room, she followed him into the shower and shut the glass door behind them. She ducked under the spray, closing her eyes as she brushed back her hair and felt her muscles loosen under the hot water.

"Hmm." She was about to make a joke about their situation, that she still wasn't giving Dave his sexy red leather on the banquettes even if she was sleeping with him, but then she opened her eyes and saw John watching her.

His gaze was as hot as blue fire.

"Looks like we're going to need another condom," she teased. Her eyes traveled down to his erection. *Criminy.* No wonder she was a little sore.

He pressed her back against the marble tile. "I have something else in mind."

Then he got down on his knees in front of her.

Oh . . . she *really* liked where he was going with this.

"You might want to hang on to the soap dish," he warned.

Despite being utterly turned on, she smiled. "Because you're going to rock my world that much?"

"Yes. But also because of this." He took one of her legs and hooked it over his shoulder, spreading her open to him.

"John," she moaned, threading her fingers through his thick, wet hair as he licked her.

"I told you what it does, hearing you say my name like that." Splaying his fingers over her hips, he held her steady as his tongue flicked over her clit.

She leaned her head back against the marble, thinking he had a really good start on that promise to rock her world. "Why weren't we doing this six years ago?" she breathed.

"Because you didn't like me six years ago."

Well. *That.*

21

The following day, as soon as he was back in Chicago, John set up a meeting with the Special Agent in Charge. They met late that afternoon in Nick's office.

Nick stood up from his desk when John walked in. "Funny coincidence, Shepherd. I heard a rumor that HRT calls went out yesterday. Then this morning, my assistant told me you'd requested a meeting."

John saw no reason to beat around the bush with that lead-in. "I made the team."

"So you did." Nick stepped around his desk and shook John's hand earnestly. "Congratulations, John. It's an incredible achievement—and very well deserved."

"Thank you, sir." John took a seat in front of the desk, opposite Nick.

"You'll start NOTS in a couple weeks, then?" Nick asked.

He nodded. "The Tuesday after Labor Day. My plan is to head down to Virginia the weekend before." He'd thought about trying to rent an apartment in advance but had decided it wasn't worth the hassle. Instead, he'd booked a reservation at an extended-stay hotel just outside Quantico and figured he'd look for something more permanent once he got there.

"I'd like to tell you the easy part is ahead of you, now that you've made it through Selection. But I doubt any part of HRT can be called 'easy.'" Nick spoke jokingly, but his tone also held an unmistakable measure of respect.

"I suspect I'll be finding out how true that is in the very near future." John had talked to Piser about the HRT training agenda, so he knew what to expect. He would spend the next thirty-two weeks in New Operator Training School (NOTS), after which he and his fellow classmates would be divided among the sniper and assault teams, depending on HRT needs. If placed on a sniper team, he would then be sent to the Marine Corps' eight-week sniper school for additional training.

It sure as hell wouldn't be easy; John didn't need to be told that. But there was an adrenaline rush that came with the knowledge of what lay ahead—similar to, but even more powerful than, the thrill he'd felt when he'd been asked to join the 75th Ranger Regiment. Sure, after one tour, that thrill had subsided and he'd decided to leave military life and pursue a career in law enforcement. But *this* was the Hostage Rescue Team. The elite of the elite. He'd set out to achieve something few could, and he'd been accepted.

Frankly, the whole idea still humbled him.

"What's your caseload look like?" Nick asked. "Anything that can't be transitioned to someone else?"

"My only active undercover case is the Jacksonville assignment, and that should wrap up next week. Agent Harlow and I will be giving the mayor his final chunk of cash as soon as he pushes our zoning variances through the city's Land Use Committee. Everything else can be transitioned—which I'm sure my squad mates will be thrilled to hear."

Nick chuckled. "Good to hear about Jacksonville. Hope it hasn't been too rough for you, moonlighting on the public corruption squad."

An image flashed into John's head of Jessica in the shower

last night, naked, wet, gorgeous, and digging her fingers into his hair as he'd licked her to an orgasm.

Hardly rough, that.

"I'm getting by." He struck a nonchalant tone, not wanting his boss to get even a sniff of anything beyond a professional relationship between Jessica and him. What had happened in Jacksonville was their business alone. "At least I scored a few fancy suits out of the assignment. Not that I'll need them where I'm going." Unlike other FBI agents, HRT operators showed up for work in T-shirts and workout clothes. No sense bothering with a suit and tie when the day started with a two-hour training session in the gym.

Nick met John's gaze. "Well, I can't say I'm thrilled to lose you. Speaking as a former undercover agent, you either have what it takes to do this job or you don't. And you have it. When you first asked to transfer here, the SAC in Detroit personally called me to put in a good word for you. He said I'd be lucky to have an agent with your dedication to the job, and as proof of that, he told me a story about your first undercover assignment." He looked amused. "Something about a 'staged altercation' at a motorcycle bar?"

That story sure was making the rounds these days. "Heavy on the staged part," John said modestly.

"I probably shouldn't tell you this," Nick continued, "but the Detroit SAC said your squad leader had originally picked you for that assignment because of your size—he figured it would impress the motorcycle club even more if the other undercover agent took down a guy as built as you. But when he saw how much you committed to the assignment—how eager you were to take on a thankless role for a case that wasn't even your own—he knew he was working with an agent who was going places. You're talented and a true team player, John. Selfishly, I wish your time with this office could've been longer. In the two years you've been here, you've certainly impressed both your squad leader and me every bit as much as the Detroit guys promised you would. But if HRT is where your heart and aspirations lie, I can't argue with that. And I genuinely wish you all the best."

John swallowed, not having expected all that. "Thank you, sir. That means a lot."

A few minutes later, while riding the elevator down to his squad's floor, he mulled over his boss's words.

If HRT is where your heart and aspirations lie, I can't argue with that.

As with many things in life, it wasn't quite that simple.

Did he have mixed feelings about giving up a successful career as an investigator and undercover agent? Of course he did—this was a big decision, one involving a move halfway across the country and a job completely different from the one he held now. Sure, he would get to play "full-time superhero," but anyone who focused exclusively on the swagger of being an HRT operator and didn't give serious thought to the realities of the job—the grueling missions, the life-and-death stakes, the nonstop training—probably wasn't sane enough to hold the title.

There would be no more "up close and personal" work, as Jessica had called it. No more getting the bad guys to trust him and tell him their dirty little secrets. The Hostage Rescue Team didn't play "nice," and they certainly weren't trying to gain the bad guys' trust. It was a different line of attack for a specific kind of situation. HRT operators rolled into a mission full-bore, wearing body armor and armed with submachine guns, automatic assault rifles, flash-bang grenades, breaching gear, and the confidence that they were the toughest and most prepared guys on the scene.

Yes, there was a lot he would miss about Chicago: his family and Wes, his job, his squad mates, and . . . other things. But he'd committed to this course of action the day he'd arrived at

Quantico for Selection, and he had great admiration for the Hostage Rescue Team and what they could accomplish.

He'd given Piser his answer, and now he would see that through.

When the elevator hit the fifth floor, John stepped out and headed to his desk. Two of his squad mates, Brandon and Jared, were hanging out at Jared's cubicle, discussing a drug-trafficking investigation and a new lead they'd uncovered during a wire-tapped telephone conversation. His other squad mates in the surrounding cubicles were relatively quiet, going about the daily business of reviewing files, conducting online research, and filling out interview reports.

Another reason to join HRT, John thought. Less damn paperwork.

Or so he hoped.

He took a seat at his desk and began organizing his case files, not expecting whichever of his squad mates inherited his cases to understand his "creative" filing methods. About ten minutes into that project, an all-office e-mail from the SAC popped up on his computer screen.

John's name was in the subject line.

I'm pleased to announce that Special Agent John Shepherd will be joining this year's class at New Operator Training School—

Several *whoop*s rang out from nearby cubicles before John had finished reading the e-mail.

Jin rolled his chair into the center aisle to gape at him. "Holy shit, Shepherd. You made HRT?"

"God*damn*, that's kick-ass." Ryan was on his feet, grinning as he headed over to John. "When did you find out?"

His squad mates circled around him, slapping his back and shaking his hand in congratulations. As they fired questions at him, their squad leader—to whom John had broken the news earlier—came out of his office and joined the fray.

"When was the last time someone from this office made the team?" Brandon asked their squad leader.

Gunnar thought about that. "It's gotta be five years now."

Ryan fist-bumped John. "Way to represent the squad."

John soaked in the camaraderie. Maybe the swagger alone wasn't a good enough reason to join HRT.

But it sure as hell was a nice perk.

That evening, Jessica caught a cab outside her condo building and gave the driver the address for Sepia restaurant. She was running late for her dinner with Tara, having gotten stuck in rush-hour traffic after being out in the northwest suburbs conducting interviews related to another bribery case—this one involving a clerk for the Cook County Recorder of Deeds who'd been accepting cash payments in exchange for preparing fraudulent quitclaim deeds.

As the cab weaved through the city streets, she scrolled through her e-mails, making sure she hadn't missed anything urgent while conducting her interviews.

When she saw the e-mail from the SAC with John's name in the subject line, she paused momentarily before clicking.

I'm pleased to announce that Special Agent John Shepherd will be joining this year's class at New Operator Training School, starting September 5. Agent Shepherd has given six years of exemplary service to this office and the Detroit field office and has been instrumental in several of our most significant organized crime investigations. Agent Shepherd's hard work and dedication has led to countless arrests and successful prosecutions. Our loss will be HRT's gain.

So, it was official.

Jessica could only imagine the celebration on the fifth floor when the news had broken. Probably, John's squad mates had cheered and preened collectively that one of their own had been selected for the team, and then had dragged him out to a bar for a night of drunken revelry. At least, she hoped that was what they'd done. Organized crime agents might be a little rough around the edges, but she assumed they knew when a few shots of whiskey were in order.

She thought about texting John, maybe a teasing comment about being partnered up with the office celebrity, but then thought better of it. If he was out drinking with his squad mates, there was too big a risk that one of them might somehow see her message. And on top of that, that kind of flirty-ish, out-of-the-blue text felt a little intimate, like something she would do if they were dating.

Which, obviously, wasn't the case.

When the cab pulled to a stop, she stuck her phone into her purse and paid the driver. Located inside a historical building and formerly an 1890s print shop, Sepia had a warm interior that blended both rustic and contemporary elements: exposed brick walls with vintage prints, an Art Nouveau tile floor, and ornate chandeliers surrounded by modern sheer drum shades.

The hostess led Jessica to a table near the back of the restaurant, where Tara was already seated with a glass of wine. When she saw Jessica coming, she stood up and gave her a hug.

"Sorry I'm late. Traffic coming back into the city was awful," Jessica said.

Tara squeezed her tighter. "Don't worry about it. I'm just glad you could make it."

"I'm really glad you suggested this," Jessica said as they took their seats. Tara had texted her earlier that day about dinner, and she'd been all too eager to accept. Given the events of the last twenty-four hours, she had some seriously juicy gossip to share.

Tara's tone turned serious. "Of course. I've been thinking about you all day."

Jessica cocked her head, thinking that was a curious thing to say. "You have?"

"Well, yeah. I still can't believe the news about Alex."

Right—*that*. Jessica had completely forgotten, again, about her ex-husband and his new fiancée. In her defense, she had quite a lot going on these days, between her undercover assignment, traveling back and forth to Jacksonville, her other cases, and a smoking-hot interlude with her partner last night.

Or, if one was being technical, *four* smoking-hot interludes with her partner last night.

Just saying.

Quickly, she mustered the proper level of indignation about Alex. "I know. You'd think he'd at least do me the courtesy of sending an e-mail as a heads-up, so that I wouldn't have to find out the news from a magazine in an airport."

Tara nodded in agreement. "What a jerk. It sucks that you were blindsided like that."

"No kidding. I was looking for something to read in one of the bookstores, and then I turned around and—*bam*—there was the magazine, right in my face." Jessica glanced down at the wine list, then nodded at Tara's glass. "By the way, what are you drinking?"

"The sangiovese."

Interesting choice. "Is it any good?"

"I like it. Here, try it yourself." Tara held out her glass.

Jessica took a sip. "Mmm. I think I'll go with that, too." That decided, she set the wine menu off to the side and steered the conversation toward something more pleasant than her ex-husband. "So, what's going on with you? With all my traveling, I feel like we haven't talked in forever."

Tara stared at her. "Um . . . is that it?"

"Is what it?"

"Aren't we going to talk more about this thing with Alex? Burn the man in effigy? Bitch about how men suck, then get drunk and make snide comments about how his fiancée's last movie stunk? Which it did, by the way. I saw it in the theater a couple months ago, and twenty minutes in, I was so bored I pulled out my phone and started playing Candy Crush."

Jessica doubted it was *that* bad, but she appreciated the loyalty. "I'll be sure to skip it when it comes out on iTunes," she said, a touch dry.

Tara pointed. "There. That's the sarcastic Jessica I know." She paused on that note when the waiter dropped by the table to take Jessica's drink order and tell them about the specials.

After the waiter headed off, Jessica returned to the topic at hand. "It's a slippery slope," she explained. "If I start talking about Alex, I'll start asking questions. Like when they first hooked up. Or how interesting it is that his fiancée is five months pregnant when *we* were still married six months ago. And if I go down that road, the next thing you know, I'll be scouring the Internet for every detail I can find about their engagement."

Tara shrugged. "That's what I would do."

Jessica half smiled. "It would drive me crazy if I thought I missed some sign that Alex was cheating. I think I'm better off not knowing."

Now you're stealing my lines, Harlow, she could practically hear John saying.

Apparently, even in her imagination, the man couldn't pass up an opportunity to gloat.

The waiter brought Jessica her glass of wine, and after she and Tara ordered dinner, their conversation turned to topics that were less fraught with peril: work, who went home on *The Bachelorette*, and Tara's most recent Tinder horror stories. Jessica bided her time, waiting until their entrées arrived before she ever-so-casually changed gears.

"So, a funny thing happened last night," she led in, cutting into her strip steak.

"While you were working? It's been a while since your last crazy FBI story. Do tell."

"Technically, this happened after we'd finished working." With a sly air, Jessica took a sip of her wine, just to prolong the moment.

Tara cocked her head. "What's with the look?"

"Are you braced?"

"I need to be braced for this? Why? What did you do?"

Jessica set down her wineglass. "I slept with John Shepherd."

"Get *OUT*." Tara giggled when Jessica shushed her. "But you can't stand him." Her eyes widened. "Ooh . . . was it hate-sex? I've always wanted to have hate-sex."

"It wasn't hate-sex." Jessica mentally scrolled back through their night together. "Just really, *really* good regular sex."

"Aw, look at you with your cheeky grin. Jessica's got her groove back." Tara lowered her voice conspiratorially. "Not that I give a crap, but are you two allowed to hook up? You know, since you're partners?"

"There's no official rule against it, and I guarantee this isn't the first time it's happened. It's more a judgment thing."

"Ah. And what convinced you more when you were 'judging' the situation: his handsome face or his Thor-like body?"

"That's funny."

Tara winked. "So, come on. Give me all the details: what, where, when—I think I know the *why* and *how* already."

Jessica thought about where to start. "Well, we got stuck on this undercover investigation together, and we've been traveling as part of that. And . . . I don't know, we just started talking and getting along. Last week, we had an argument—actually, I'd call it more a misunderstanding—and *that* led to a pretty incredible kiss"—she caught Tara's look of indignation—"I know, I've been meaning to tell you about that, but work's been crazy and I thought it was just a onetime thing. Then last night, we had a few drinks to celebrate some good news he'd received, and we were joking around and sharing work stories, and there was a beach and moonlight . . . and one thing led to another." She smiled coyly. "And then one thing led to another three times after that."

"Nice." Tara clinked her wineglass to Jessica's. "Okay, I have to mentally reset here, because all I've ever heard about this guy has been negative. So we don't hate John Shepherd anymore?"

"We don't hate John Shepherd anymore," Jessica confirmed.

"And . . . you *like* John Shepherd now?" Tara gave her a pointed look. "Putting aside the beach and moonlight and the really, really good sex."

Jessica immediately opened her mouth to say something quippy, but then she stopped herself.

So much had changed with John these last few weeks, it was hard for her, even, to wrap her mind around it. That first meeting in the SAC's office, there'd been so much anger between them, to the point where she'd had serious misgivings about their ability to work together.

But now, well . . . John was the guy who put a Band-Aid on her finger after she cut it on a broken wineglass. (Albeit, while being bossy, but still.) He was the guy who unwound her hair when it was caught on her necklace, being careful not to damage even a strand. The guy she talked to about her failed marriage after seeing a picture of her ex-husband on a magazine cover. The guy she shared funny work stories with over a brownie sundae; the guy who understood the pressures—and the rewards—of her job; the guy she trusted implicitly as her partner to have her back; and the guy who somehow had the ability to make her smile even when he was annoying the heck out of her.

And . . . you like *John Shepherd now?*

Her lips curved, thinking about how far they'd come since their days at Quantico. "Yes. I do."

Tara blinked, as if she'd expected a different answer. Then, slowly, she smiled. "Well, if you like the man, that's all I need to know." She leaned in, speaking excitedly. "So what does this mean? Are you guys, like, dating now? Could it turn into something serious?"

"No."

The word came out a little too quick, so Jessica regrouped and slowed down. "You know I'm not looking for anything serious right now. This is my rebound. My fun, hot, post-divorce fling. And even if, hypothetically speaking, I were looking for something serious, this wouldn't be it."

Tara frowned. "Why would you say that? You just told me you like the guy."

"Because he's leaving."

As the words fell between them, Jessica shrugged, matter-of-fact.

"Leaving? Where's he going?" Tara asked.

"Virginia. He made the Hostage Rescue Team and has to relocate to Quantico." She saw Tara's blank look and explained. "It's this elite counterterrorism unit. Basically, these are the guys the FBI sends in to handle major U.S. crisis situations: hostage and terrorist incidents, significant criminal threats, that kind of thing. They get deployed for overseas missions, too—a lot of times, HRT operators are embedded with Navy SEAL or Delta Force commandos. And when they're not on a mission, they train. Constantly. I can't even imagine the amount of testosterone flowing through that little corner of Quantico. Picture ninety super-alpha males running around with the coolest toys, guns, ammunition, and vehicles the U.S. government can buy."

"Wow." Tara took all that in. "So he's leaving for good, then."

Jessica swirled her wineglass. Technically, John wouldn't be an HRT operator for the rest of his career—most of those guys burned out after five or six years on the job. But it was unlikely he would ever be in her neck of the woods again. After HRT, there would be tons of options open to him, like leading a field office SWAT team, being an instructor at the Academy, or working at FBI headquarters. But instead of getting into that, she simply said, "Yes. For good."

She took a long sip of her wine, then noticed that Tara was watching her. "What? Oh, come on. Stop looking at me like you're waiting for me to burst into tears or something. First off, I'm happy for John. Truly. Second, this is what I want, remember? To use your words, 'dirty, no-strings-attached rebound sex' with a hot Mr. Wrong that I will shamelessly use until our time together has run its course."

"I did say that. But when you told me you liked John a few moments ago, you had a look on your face that I haven't seen in a while."

"What kind of look?"

Tara's eyes met hers. "Happy."

Jessica blinked, caught off guard by the words. But the undercover agent in her quickly recovered. "I guess that's what good sex after a six-month hiatus will do to you," she quipped.

"Hmm." Tara studied her for a long moment. "Let's go back to the hypothetically speaking part."

Jessica sighed. "Here we go."

Tara ignored her. "Let's say you *were* looking for something more than a rebound. There's always long-distance dating, you know. In the age of texting, FaceTime, and phone sex, it's actually quite possible."

Jessica humored her, just for a bit. "Okay, and then what? Hypothetically speaking, let's say that works for a few months. In between John's incredibly intense training schedule and my less-than-predictable work schedule, we manage to find a few stolen moments for FaceTime chats and steamy phone sex. How long until that gets old?"

"I don't know. I think the relationship would either fizzle out or it would grow stronger, and then . . . you'd have to make a decision about following him to Virginia, I guess."

And therein lay the rub. "There's no decision—moving isn't an option for me. I just transferred to Chicago. Under FBI policy, I'm not eligible for another transfer for two years." Jessica watched as Tara's expression lost its hopeful glow. Her voice softened, adding, "And that's just being eligible. Realistically, it would probably take at least three years."

"Oh. That *is* a problem." Tara fell momentarily quiet. Then she met Jessica's gaze and smiled gently. "I guess it's a good thing we were just speaking hypothetically, then."

Jessica returned the look. "Yes, it is."

The last thing she wanted was for anyone to start getting ideas that this interlude between her and John had legs. That line of thinking would almost certainly lead to disappointment and, quite possibly, heartbreak.

And she, for one, already had been through enough of that this year.

22

The following evening, John approached the target's house armed with two of the most lethal weapons at his disposal.

Cheeseburgers and French fries from Five Guys.

For extra ammunition, he'd also brought along a couple of chocolate shakes. Operation Butter Up Dad Before Breaking the News was officially under way.

Another working title.

His father opened the front door, his eyes lighting up when he saw the red-and-white checkered logo on the shakes. "This is a surprise. I figured you were just bringing pizza. Is there bacon on those cheeseburgers?"

"I assume that's a rhetorical question."

Thirty seconds later, they were seated at the kitchen table, cartons and paper wrappers spread out before them. As they chewed in silence, John surreptitiously studied his father, trying to get a read on his mood.

"You still working on that undercover assignment?" his dad asked. "The one with the public corruption squad?"

John wiped his mouth with the napkin. "It's almost wrapped up. We have one more meeting left, and then the case agents should have everything they need to make the arrest."

"How big's the target?"

"Big enough." With the investigation still ongoing, John couldn't say much more.

His dad raised an eyebrow. "Big enough that I'll be reading about the investigation in the papers?"

"Possibly." John pictured the look on Blair's face when Agents Leavitt and Todd showed up at his front door to make the arrest. Actually, it would be Leavitt and Todd *and* a backup squad. The FBI never took chances, and guys like Blair were highly unpredictable during arrests. The esteemed mayor of America's thirteenth-largest city was no hardened street criminal for whom prison was practically a rite of passage—for him, being arrested by the FBI was essentially the end of the world. When faced with the sudden knowledge that his career and once-bright political aspirations were over, and that, instead, he'd be spending the next fifteen to twenty behind bars, there was no telling what he might do.

Unfortunately, John and Jessica wouldn't be there for the party—as the undercover agents in the investigation, they would take no part in the arrest and receive none of the proverbial glory. Once the two of them wrapped up the sting op, they wouldn't see Blair again until they testified in closed court. And to protect their anonymity, their names would never be associated with the case in press releases and court documents. To the outside world, he and Jessica would be simply known as "UC1" and "UC2."

His dad reached for his shake and took a sip. "Nate mentioned that your partner on the case—this Jessica Harlow person—was in your class at the Academy."

Nate had talked to his Dad about Jessica? John had a bad feeling he knew where this conversation was headed. "Did he, now?"

"He also said you get 'tense and shifty' every time her name comes up."

Bingo.

John threw out his hands in exasperation. "Why is Nate so focused on this? Doesn't he have other things to worry about, like . . . whether to add a Buffalo chicken sandwich to the bar's brunch menu?"

His dad studied him. "Huh. You do seem a little tense."

Shutting up now.

John took a bite of his burger and chewed more forcefully than usual. After he swallowed, he saw that his dad seemed to be watching him with amusement.

He went for a more diplomatic answer this time. "Yes, there was some friction between Jessica and me at the Academy. But we're fine now." In his mind's eye, he saw her stretched across his hotel room bed, naked except for her high-heeled sandals.

Oh yeah. Just fine, indeed.

His dad nodded. "It was the same way with me and your uncle Don."

John fought back a grin. Well . . . probably not *exactly* the same. Either that, or his dad and Uncle Don had been a helluva lot closer than he'd realized.

"I couldn't stand the guy the first time I met him," his dad continued. "Thought he was a cocky SOB. But when you're partners, you find a way to work it out."

"That's true." John was still stuck on the vision of naked Jessica in his bed. Blond hair tousled, her gorgeous legs straddling his hips as they'd—

"What's with all the goofy smiles?" his dad asked, cutting into his thoughts.

Busted.

"This cheeseburger's just so *good*," John said, covering with another bite.

"Hmm." His dad eyed him suspiciously, then reached for a French fry. His tone turned more casual. "Anyway, it's good that you worked things out with your partner. It'd be a shame to end your career as an investigator on a bad note before heading off to HRT."

John froze at the words.

Fucking Nate.

His dad read the look on his face. "Don't go blaming your brother—he didn't say a word. You and I haven't done dinner on a weekday since your mom got sick, and then you suddenly show up with Five Guys. I was a detective for twenty-five years, John. I think I can figure it out."

John sighed. So much for gradually easing into the subject. "I got the call two days ago, when I was out of town."

"When do you leave for Quantico?"

"The weekend before Labor Day." John sat forward, resting his forearms on the table. "Look, I know you're not thrilled about this. But it's a good opportunity for me and—

His dad held up a hand. "I know perfectly well what it means to make the Hostage Rescue Team." He looked John in the eyes. "And if this is what you want, then I'm happy for you, son. And I'm also incredibly proud."

John blinked, having been braced for a much tougher conversation. "Oh. Well . . . thank you." He sat back in his chair, exhaling in relief. "Okay, then."

"I know I was hard on you the last time we talked about HRT. I was just being . . . well, selfish." His dad shifted in his chair, his tone gruff yet slightly sheepish. "When you transferred back from Detroit, I guess I figured you were here for the long haul. It's been nice having you around these last couple of years. I probably don't tell you and your brother this stuff often enough, but our Sunday dinners are the thing I look forward to most all week."

A dagger of guilt pierced John through the chest. "Dad—"

His father stopped him again. "I'm just explaining why I reacted the way I did last time. Look, I get that this is your life, not mine. You have to do what's best for you. Just because your mother and I chose to make Chicago our home doesn't mean you're bound to this city, too."

"It won't be forever. Who knows, in five or six years I could end up back here again." John tried to look at the bright side. "Plus, Virginia's only an hour-and-a-half flight away. I still get vacation time, and then there's the holidays . . ." He trailed off, not wanting to make too many promises. When on a mission, HRT operators worked until the job was done—there were no holiday breaks.

"You'll come home when you can. I know that." His dad paused, his eyes looking shiny. Then he cleared his throat, sounding gruff once again. "So, you got an address where I can come visit you in Virginia, or do I have to figure that out for myself, too?"

While finishing their burgers, they talked about the logistics of John's move. He'd spent the bulk of his day working on that: calling moving companies for estimates, finding a decent extended-stay hotel that was in his budget, and renting a storage unit outside Quantico where he could temporarily stash his furniture until he found a place to live.

"Sounds like you're moving full steam ahead," his dad said, as they cleared off the kitchen table.

John shrugged. "Not much choice. Labor Day weekend will be here before I know it." He immediately regretted his choice of words. *Way to be sensitive, asshole.*

His dad nodded, his voice subdued. "Yep, it will."

A silence fell between them.

His dad looked at him a moment, then walked over to the refrigerator and pulled out two beers.

He held one out to John. "Cubs game starts in a few minutes. Lester's pitching. Should be a good one, if you want to stay and watch."

With a slight smile, John took one of the bottles. "I'd like that." Shepherd men might have been good at a lot of things, but overtly expressing feelings wasn't one of them.

A couple of beers on a warm summer night, and baseball.

That was how they said good-bye.

Friday afternoon, Jessica wrapped up her second day of interviews in the county clerk bribery case and managed to beat the bulk of rush-hour traffic into the city. Once back at the FBI office, she saw that someone had left a message on Ashley's cell phone.

Judging from the 904 area code, the caller was from the Jacksonville area.

"Ashley, it's Patrick Blair. I've got an update for you—call me back."

The message caught Jessica somewhat by surprise. This was the first time the mayor had contacted either her or John directly. Prior to this, Morano had always acted as an intermediary between them.

Wanting to find a quiet space before calling Blair back, she headed to an empty conference room at the end of the hallway and shut the door. Instead of dialing up his office directly, she called an internal Bureau number that was answered by a computer. Using the keypad on her phone, she entered the code set up for the case, Blair's phone number, and the phone number she wanted to show up on Blair's caller ID—in this case, Ashley's cell phone number. Then she took a seat in one of the conference room chairs as the computer dialed Blair's phone number and began recording the call.

"Mayor Blair's office," his assistant answered.

"Hi, this is Ashley Evers, returning the mayor's call."

"One moment, Ms. Evers. I'll see if he's available."

A satellite radio station cut in as Jessica was put on hold, and the song "Take My Breath Away" began to play.

Oh man . . . she *loved* this song.

She hummed along, as images of hot men in aviator sunglasses and flight suits ran through her head. All too soon, the music cut out as Blair's assistant came back on the line. "The mayor will be right with you, Ms. Evers."

"Thank you."

Seconds later, Blair picked up on the other end of the line. "Ms. Evers. You caught me just before I left the office," he drawled.

"Glad I did—your message left me curious, Mr. Mayor. I hope this update means there's good news."

"Sure does. Tell your assistant to book you a flight down here for Thursday."

Jessica felt a rush of excitement. They were so close to wrapping up this case; she could practically taste it. "Why? What's happening Thursday?" She had a pretty good idea, but she wanted Blair to spell it out for the recording.

He chuckled, sounding smug. "The question you *should* be asking is: What's happening on Wednesday?"

When he fell silent, she realized he was actually waiting for her to ask.

Of course he was.

"All right . . . what's happening on Wednesday?" she said, playing along like a good little undercover agent.

"The Land Use Committee meets that afternoon. I played golf this morning with Paul Ryu, the director, and he says there won't be any problems getting your variances pushed through. Naturally, I played up my excitement for your project and reminded him how eager I am to create investment opportunities for out-of-state businesses. After hearing that, Paul was all in."

"That is good news."

"I would expect you'll get official word of the committee's decision late in the day on Wednesday." Blair's voice dipped lower. "And then you and I will have some business to settle."

"*If* we get that call from the committee," Jessica emphasized, because Ashley was hardly the kind of businesswoman to travel halfway across the country based solely on a man's word, "Dave and I will be on a plane the next morning."

"There is no *if*, Ashley—this is a done deal. I told you, in my city, I always get what I want." Blair left it at that and hung up.

Jessica checked to make sure the call was disconnected, and sighed.

Turning and returning to some secret place inside.

Yep. That song was going to be stuck in her head all day.

23

After leaving the conference room, Jessica bypassed her cubicle and headed for the stairwell, so she could update John and let him know that they likely would be traveling to Jacksonville on Thursday. Sure, she supposed she could call him, or even simply send him a text message, but she felt like giving him the news in person. It was . . . a chance to stretch her legs. Get some exercise. Very important, that, when one had a desk job.

She took the stairs two flights down and then followed the hallway into the main office area. Having never been on the fifth floor before, she looked around curiously. For the most part, it looked the same as her own floor: a large open space filled with cubicles that were broken into groups, floor-to-ceiling windows, and various whiteboards and bulletin boards with case information lining the internal walls. Tucked into the corner, with windows that looked out over the group, was a small, private office belonging to the squad leader.

She passed by several cubicles, looking for John's, and smiled to herself when she spotted his nameplate above a currently unoccupied desk by the window.

JOHN M. SHEPHERD
SPECIAL AGENT

Interesting . . . John *M.* Shepherd. She made a mental note to find out what the middle initial stood for. Michael, perhaps. Or maybe Matthew?

Inquiring minds wanted to know.

Tabling that issue for the moment, she headed over to see if John's squad mates knew where he was. There were five of them—all men—in the nearby cubicles. Busy working, they didn't notice as she approached.

"Excuse me. Do any of you happen to know if John is around?"

At the sound of her voice, all five agents peeked their heads over the tops of their cubicles. There was a split-second silence as they looked at her, and then three of the agents stood up, as if to introduce themselves.

The tall agent with light brown hair got to Jessica first, extending his hand with an easy grin. "You must be Agent Harlow. Ryan Hannigan."

Someone behind him cleared his throat.

Without looking back, Ryan gestured in the direction of the other guys. "Agents Choi, Samuels, Botsch, and Lanarrelli."

In turn, each of them smiled and said hello.

"Actually, we met a couple weeks ago, in the elevator." Botsch, the youngest-looking of the group, paused as if searching for more to say. "We were both going up."

Agent Choi rested his arm on the cubicle wall. "We heard you're from the Los Angeles office. What was it like there?"

"Warm," Jessica said.

The five of them laughed like this was the funniest thing.

She smiled with them. Yeah . . . she was quickly getting the impression they didn't have a lot of female agents on this squad.

"I was hoping to talk to John about a development in our

case." She checked her watch and saw that it was four thirty. "Is he gone for the day? I can always just try his phone."

"He took off a little early—said he was heading to the gym," Ryan said. "That was only about twenty minutes ago, so I'm sure he's still there."

"Thanks. I'll check it out." With a friendly nod good-bye, she headed in the direction of the elevators and hit the button for the second floor, where the building's state-of-the-art gym was located.

Currently, the gym was relatively quiet—not unexpectedly for this time of day. A few agents ran on the indoor track, and two more were using the cardio machines. No sign of John, so she headed toward the weight room.

She found him there, working the heavy bag.

Wearing a fitted gray T-shirt and athletic shorts, he moved around the bag while throwing different combinations. Each punch was powerful and controlled, a fluid movement of hips and shoulders and arms and footwork. Sweat made the T-shirt cling to his broad, toned chest, while his strong forearms and biceps flexed and strained gloriously with each hit.

And *she* had slept with this man.

Her lips curved in a private smile.

Damn right she had.

His eyes met hers in the mirror behind the heavy bag, and she regrouped. *Right.* Work first; ogle her hot partner later.

She crossed the room and leaned against a rack of dumbbells. "Your squad mates said you cut out a little early today."

He grunted in response and kept hitting the bag.

She spotted his phone on the mat, saw that he had the timer going, and assumed he was doing some sort of interval training. Forty-six seconds left, according to the clock.

She'd wait. The view wasn't half bad, after all.

He hit the bag with a punishing right hook, so forceful she half expected it to go flying through the air.

Actually, the view was pretty darn fantastic.

He moved the way he would in a real fight, his footwork active as he worked a variety of shots, hitting from different angles and changing speeds. He focused intently on the bag, striking hard in two- and three-punch combinations.

As she watched, she sensed that something was off. Granted, she hardly expected the man to smile and giggle as he kicked the shit out of a hundred-pound bag, but still, he looked . . . aggravated.

The timer on his phone went off and he ended the interval with another right hook that had some truly bad intentions behind it. Stepping back from the bag, he glanced her way, then yanked open the strap of one of his gloves with his teeth.

She walked over to his phone, bent down, and hit the button to stop the beeping timer. Next to his phone was a water bottle, so she picked it up and handed it to him.

"Thanks," he panted.

"You're welcome." She watched as he chugged the water, beads of sweat trickling down the sides of his face. "How many rounds do you do?"

"Ten. Three minutes each."

She waited for the expected teasing comment or quip, but instead he took another sip of water.

Something was definitely off.

"You seem irritated," she commented.

"Yes. Somebody interrupted my workout," he shot back.

Hmm. Good poker face, and he sounded flip enough, but she wasn't buying it. So she simply cocked her head and waited.

He scoffed. "What is this, the good-cop routine?"

"Do I need to break out the good-cop routine?"

He gave her a look, and she raised an eyebrow.

He sighed resignedly. "It's no big deal, Harlow. I handed over my biggest case to another agent today. Armenian street gang. Extortion, violent crimes, illegal firearms deals, narcotics—you name it, these guys are guilty of it. We've been running wiretaps on twenty-four different phone numbers, and I just convinced a man on the inside to flip. Took me months to make that happen—he put a lot of trust in me to keep him and his family safe." He shrugged. "The new agent will take care of him, I know that. It's just . . . very unsatisfying to walk away."

Jessica nodded. She'd recently been in this position herself, when she'd transferred from Los Angeles to Chicago and had to give up all of her cases. Agents spent months on investigations, often longer, and sometimes the work became very personal.

But there was a bright side. "There are plenty of bad guys where you're headed, John. And lots of people in really terrible situations who will be kept safe because *you* were there to make sure of it."

He seemed momentarily surprised by the sincerity of her tone. Then he looked at her, taking in her high heels and tailored suit, and held out the gloves.

"Want to go a round?" The teasing gleam was back in his eyes.

Cute. "The last time we faced off on a boxing mat, that didn't go so well for you."

"You distracted me last time. But now I know your tricks."

She smiled coyly at that. "I think I could still find ways to distract you."

Their eyes met, her words lingering in the air as two agents walked into the weight room.

Back to business.

"Blair called me this afternoon," she told John.

"He called you directly?" His less-than-enthused expression reflected his opinion on that, but he made no further comment. "What he'd say?"

She filled him in on the situation. "Blair seems confident the committee is going to approve our variances. I'll call Leavitt when I get back to my desk and bring him up to speed."

"I'm around this evening if he wants to talk to us both." John glanced at the two agents over by the bench press, then looked back at her. "You getting out of here soon?" His tone was casual—just an agent making chitchat with his partner at four thirty on a Friday afternoon.

But there was a warm look in his eyes as he held her gaze.

"I shouldn't be here too much longer. Probably another hour." She let that sit for a moment, and then she smiled. "I'll let you know if Leavitt says anything noteworthy. Otherwise . . . have a good weekend, Shepherd."

She turned and left the room, nodding at the two other agents on her way out. When back at her desk, she called Leavitt, who was understandably surprised to learn that he was out of the loop.

"Blair called you directly? He's stepping up his game," Leavitt said.

"Lucky me." They discussed the logistics of Thursday's meeting, and then Jessica booked her hotel room and began looking into flights to Jacksonville.

As she was checking out the available seats on the plane—a window for her, an aisle for John, per usual—it hit her that this was the last trip the two of them would take together.

When do you leave?

Labor Day weekend.

"Everything okay?"

Jessica blinked, realizing that she'd been staring at her computer screen for who-knew-how-long. She turned around and saw one of her squad mates, Vaughn Roberts, standing in the aisle with his briefcase in hand.

"Yes. Just finalizing some travel plans." She smiled—relaxed, not too bright. *Nothing to see here.* "Heading out?"

She chatted with Vaughn for a few minutes—nice guy, new dad, had lots of funny stories about all the ways in which his two-month-old daughter was keeping him and his wife on their toes—and then, shortly thereafter, she called it quits, too.

As she was walking across the parking lot, heading to her car, her cell phone buzzed with a new text message.

From John.

What's your address?

She didn't have to ask why he was asking—that was obvious. She glanced around the parking lot, feeling a little clandestine to be trading these kinds of messages with her partner while still at work.

500 W Superior, she typed back, and hit send.

She waited for her inner pragmatic to tell her this wasn't a good idea, that what happened in Jacksonville should stay in Jacksonville, blah, blah.

But instead . . . silence.

Jessica smiled to herself.

Apparently, her inner pragmatic had enjoyed the view of John in his sweaty T-shirt, too.

24

"*Ladies* and gentlemen, the captain has indicated it's now safe for you to use all approved electronic devices. In a few moments, the flight attendants will be making their way through the cabin to offer you . . ."

Next to John, Jessica pulled her laptop out of her briefcase as soon as the announcement was made.

"No trusty e-reader today?" he asked.

"Unfortunately, I have to write two 302s. I was supposed to do them earlier in the week."

"Falling behind in your paperwork? Tsk, tsk, Harlow. I think that's grounds to be stripped of your high mark in academics." He put a hand to his chest. "As the first runner-up, I happily accept the award instead."

Eyes on her computer, she was already typing away. "Never going to happen, Shepherd. Learn to live with the disappointment."

He fought back a smile, his eyes roving over her slim-cut black pantsuit and heels. They hadn't seen each other since he'd left her place early Saturday morning, and being with her again—just the two of them, trading jabs on a plane—felt good.

Really good, actually.

Between her work schedule and his personal commitments, he and Jessica seemed to have been going in different directions this week. On Saturday, he and Wes had driven two hours out of the city and camped at Starved Rock—a tradition of theirs, the same thing they'd done before John had left for basic training, and then again when he'd been assigned to the Detroit field office. Sunday, he'd gotten back into town just in time for dinner at his dad's house, and then he and his brother had spent the evening shooting hoops at Foster Beach, on one of the illuminated basketball courts.

During a break, John had sat on one of the benches by the water, checking out the nighttime skyline in the distance.

"Think you'll miss it?" his brother asked, sitting down next to him.

"Of course," John said. Just because there were bigger opportunities out there for him didn't mean it was easy to say good-bye to everything he was leaving behind.

Nate was quiet for a moment. "You know I only make the superhero-camp jokes because I don't like saying good-bye, right?"

"I'll be back." John paused. "And actually, I kind of like the superhero-camp jokes."

"Of course you do. Fucking egomaniac," Nate muttered, under his breath. He looked sideways at John, and then they both started laughing.

After a comfortable silence fell between them, John glanced at his brother. Despite all the joking around, and the fact that much of their relationship was based on trying to annoy the crap out of each other, they'd always been close. So as a parting gift, he decided to give Nate something he would cherish for years to come.

The satisfaction of being right.

"I had sex with Jessica Harlow."

Nate's eyes widened. "I *knew* there was something going on with you two. When?"

"Last week, when we were traveling. And then again a couple nights ago."

Nate gripped his shoulder. "Aw, this is huge. After six years, you finally got her to sleep with you." He squeezed John's shoulder in congratulations. "So? Was she worth the wait?"

John took a sip of water to cover his smile.

Clearly, his brother had never met Jessica Harlow.

Halfway through the flight, Jessica took a break from her writing and stretched her arms over her head. She looked at the files stacked on John's tray table.

"What's that?" she asked.

"I pulled the debriefing reports for some of HRT's biggest missions. Figured it can't hurt to know my history before I show up for NOTS," John said.

She leaned over, checking out the report on his lap. "Waco? Not exactly light reading, that."

No kidding. Eighty-six people dead, including four federal agents, in what was one of HRT's most well-known—and controversial—missions. "So, what's this new case you had to travel for?" he asked, more interested in talking about her than an operation that was over two decades old. He'd texted her on Monday to see if she wanted to get together, and she'd shot him back a message saying she'd gotten a last-minute assignment out of town and would be gone until Wednesday evening.

He'd understood, of course. But still, he'd been disappointed.

"It's an investigation being handled by the Columbia field office," she told him. "The solicitor of Lexington, South Carolina, reached out to them regarding a complaint he received against one of the city's police officers."

"Lexington, South Carolina?" That was a new one. "What's the complaint?"

"A woman claims she was sexually assaulted by a police officer who responded to her 911 call. Apparently, she and her boyfriend had gotten in an argument earlier that evening, he beat her in their home and then took off when she called the cops. She says that when the police officer arrived, instead of helping her, he took her into a bedroom, fondled her and exposed himself, and then arrested her for making a phony 911 call."

John shook his head in disgust.

"I know. It's awful," Jessica said. "The solicitor believes she's telling the truth, which is why he brought the case to the FBI—so we could investigate the potential civil rights violations. Unfortunately, there's no evidence to corroborate the victim's story. And to make things more complicated, she'd been drinking that night. You know exactly how that will play out in court—especially when she's testifying against a police officer with a clean record. So to alleviate that problem, the case agents in Columbia put together a plan to try to catch the cop red-handed. That's where I come in."

"What kind of plan?" John asked, even though he had a pretty good idea where she was going with this.

"I'll pretend to be a domestic assault victim—fake bruises, overturned furniture on the scene, the whole works—and we make sure this cop gets my 911 call. We'll put cameras and mics all over the place, I'll act like I've been drinking, and when the cop arrives . . . we'll see what happens."

He looked her in the eyes. "Meaning, you'll see if he tries to sexually assault you, too."

"Yes."

After a moment, she pointed. "I think your Waco file is toast."

He glanced down and realized he'd clenched his fist tight

enough to crumble the debriefing report. *Nice.* He set the mangled papers on his tray tables.

"The Columbia field office doesn't have any female undercover agents who could handle the assignment?" he asked, keeping his tone conversational. "Or . . . the Charlotte office? Atlanta? Is Chicago handling *all* the undercover assignments now, or just the ones where we send in our agents to be attacked by armed sexual predators?"

She cocked her head pointedly.

Fine. Perhaps that had been *slightly* sarcastic.

"Given the delicate nature of the assignment," Jessica said, "they were looking for an undercover agent with significant field experience. Apparently, my name was at the top of the list." She held his gaze, no hesitation. "And I'm glad it was. I want the assignment. This guy preyed on a woman who'd just been beaten up by her boyfriend. It was his job to protect her, and instead he took advantage of her in one of the worst ways possible. So now *I* am going to do *my* job. And I'll make sure this piece of shit never carries a badge again."

Seeing her blue eyes flash, John felt a warm feeling spread across his chest.

Well. Tough to argue with that.

He took a moment before answering. The man in him didn't like the idea of her being in a position where she might have to let some asshole expose himself to her or touch her. But the agent in him knew there wasn't anyone in the FBI better suited for the job. He'd seen Jessica in action, after all.

She would play this piece of shit like a fiddle.

"If this guy somehow gets you pinned down before backup arrives, use that leg breach you liked so much at the Academy. That's a good move—it almost even worked on me. *Almost*," he emphasized.

When her lips curved, he frowned. "What?"

"You're cute when you're protective," she said.

He snorted at that. "I'm not being protective. I'm simply giving you professional advice, one colleague to another."

"Ah. Well, thank you for that, then." She turned back to her laptop—her break was over, apparently—and started typing again.

As John watched her work, something compelled him to speak. "Maybe I'm being *a little* protective."

She looked up from her computer to meet his gaze. Suddenly feeling like he'd admitted more than he'd intended, he shifted in his chair. "Mostly because you make very questionable footwear choices." He nodded gruffly at her high heels. "You'll break an ankle chasing a bad guy in those things."

She smiled. "When's the last time you heard of a white-collar-crime agent getting in a foot chase?"

Fair enough.

25

On the way to the hotel, Jessica called Leavitt to check in.

"It'll be just three of you today," the Jax agent informed them, his voice sounding through the car's speakers. "Apparently, Blair told Morano he could sit this meeting out."

Jessica exchanged a look with John, who was driving. "That's a surprise."

"Morano was disappointed to miss it. I think he was hoping for one last chance to break out a 'cherries jubilee,'" the Jax agent joked.

After they hung up with Leavitt, Jessica mused over this newest information. "Do you think Blair is trying to cut Morano out of the loop?"

"Possibly. Blair thinks we're planning several more investments in the city. He's gotten comfortable with us," John said. "Why give Morano twenty percent of the bribes when Blair can work with us directly? That just cuts into his own profit."

Indeed, that sentiment seemed to be confirmed when they met Blair a few hours later, at the restaurant site.

"Did I tell you the Land Use Committee would come through, or what?" Blair asked as he strode through the front door of the abandoned bank.

John extended his hand, greeting the mayor with a grin. "For the record, I never doubted you. It was all Ashley's idea to split the payments."

Playing her part, Jessica threw him an irritated glance before turning to Blair and shaking his hand. "We're thrilled the problem could be resolved so expeditiously. Thank you, Mr. Mayor."

"All in a day's work." True to form, his eyes skimmed over her pencil skirt and short-sleeve white shirt. "And I think it's time you started calling me Patrick."

Leaning against the teller counter, John cocked his head as if just realizing something. "Where's Morano?"

"He had another commitment, a dinner with one of his clients," Blair said with a dismissive wave. "He sends his regrets."

Knowing this was a lie, Jessica watched for any changes in Blair's body language or demeanor. "Sorry he couldn't make it." She threw out a little bait to see if he would bite. "But I think the three of us can manage well enough without him."

An opportunistic gleam entered Blair's eyes. "I couldn't agree more." He eyed the briefcase that rested near John's feet. "Assuming you don't have any surprises for me today."

"No surprises here." John reached down and grabbed the suitcase, then handed it over to Blair. "Twenty-five thousand in cash, as promised."

After taking the briefcase, Blair looked between Jessica and John, as if debating whether to unzip it and count the money. Apparently trusting them by this point, he let the briefcase fall to his side and gestured to their surroundings instead. "When do you start renovations?"

"Hopefully in a few weeks," John said. "We already have the plans drawn up, so the next step is finding the right general contractor."

"Have you given any thought to what your next project in Jacksonville will be?" Blair asked Jessica.

"Actually, yes. We'd like to switch things up, conceptwise—we're thinking about a farm-to-table neighborhood bistro that'll bring in a big weekend brunch crowd. Something upscale, where the menu changes every week depending on the season and what's fresh in the market. I have this idea for a rotating special of gourmet scrambled eggs. Maybe pancakes, too. The kind of place that people keep coming back to because the food is great and they're curious to see what the chef has on the menu—but that still feels approachable and relaxed."

"Gourmet scrambled eggs and pancakes? Sounds very metropolitan." Blair considered this. "I like it." As he moved closer, his tone turned teasing. "Just don't forget the grits, Ashley. Jacksonville may be a big city, but it's still Southern at heart," he drawled.

She smiled. "Grits. Got it."

He paused, looking her over. "We should talk more about this project the next time you're in town. Maybe over dinner?"

With six years of field experience as a special agent—the last several of which she'd focused on undercover cases—Jessica had learned the value of paying attention to nonverbal cues. And right now, without even saying the words, Blair was telling her something quite interesting.

Dilated pupils. Increased blink rate. A slight flush to his skin that indicated an elevated pulse. The way he'd begun to speak a little faster ever since he'd lied about Morano. All of which led her to believe that the mayor was either afraid or excited about something.

And she highly doubted he was afraid.

"I'd like that. I'll call your office to set that up," she said.

Blair pulled his cell phone out of his suit jacket. He touched the screen a few times, and then Ashley's phone began to ring inside Jessica's purse.

"Call that number instead. It's my private cell." He winked, then ended the call and stuck the cell phone back into his jacket. "Until next time, then."

He extended his hand. When Jessica took it, she felt his thumb brush deliberately over the top of her fingers.

She so couldn't wait to see this guy in an orange prison jumpsuit.

"Until next time," she echoed.

Blair turned to John with a more disinterested air. "Dave." He briefly shook John's hand in good-bye, then turned and walked out the door.

John waited several moments, until they could be sure he was gone. "He's up to something."

Jessica thought back to the opportunistic gleam she'd seen in Blair's eyes. "Yes, he is."

At the rendezvous spot, Leavitt and Todd were in such a celebratory mood, Jessica half expected them to break out a bottle of champagne right there.

"And that, my friends, is a wrap," Leavitt said, as Jessica and John climbed out of their rental car.

Todd shook both their hands heartily. "Well done." He flashed them a wide grin, a departure from his usual reserved demeanor. "I'll be drinking the good whiskey tonight."

Jessica chuckled at that. She'd had a few long, intense cases herself and knew what a relief it was when they finally came to an end.

High on adrenaline and victory, the four of them went through the play-by-play as Jessica and John handed over their mics.

"Who came up with the scrambled eggs idea?" Leavitt wanted to know.

"That was all Jessica," John said.

Todd pointed at her. "When you gave Blair your pitch, I

turned to Leavitt and said, 'Hell, *I* want to eat at this restaurant.'"

Thunder boomed ominously above them.

"The sound of Blair's demise," Leavitt whispered faux-dramatically, getting another laugh from all of them.

"Speaking of which, when do you anticipate you'll make the arrest?" Jessica asked.

"We have a few odds and ends to tie up, and then the U.S. Attorney's office will want to review everything," Leavitt said. "But I know they're as eager as we are to get the ball rolling. I can't imagine it would be more than a few weeks."

The sky flashed with lightning as drops of rain began to fall.

"I think that's our cue." Todd shook both their hands, thanking them for their assistance with the case. Leavitt followed suit, promising to touch base by the following Monday if they hadn't yet moved forward with the arrest.

Jessica and John made it to the car a few seconds after it began to downpour. She scrambled into the passenger seat and slammed the door shut as rain battered the car.

"For chrissakes," John muttered.

Running her fingers through her damp hair, she looked over as John reached for the buttons to adjust the driver's seat, his knees practically touching his chin.

"Perhaps you might consider moving the seat back before you exit the vehicle?" he asked, a touch dry. "Just once."

She tried hard not to smile as his seat slowly inched back. "I told you, I'm happy to drive all the time, Agent Shepherd."

After his seat was finally in position, he started the car. She cocked her head, curious about something. "Why didn't you tell Leavitt and Todd you made HRT?" He'd had the perfect opening, when Leavitt had made the comment about calling them the following Monday.

"That tends to be a long conversation. People want to know

about Selection, they have questions about NOTS . . . it's a whole thing. I don't have time for a whole thing tonight."

"Big plans?"

John put the car in gear to head back to the hotel, the look in his eyes heated enough to fog the car windows. "Very big plans, Agent Harlow."

26

It was a little after eight o'clock by the time they reached the hotel grounds. Because of the storm, John decided to skip the valet and park as close to his room as possible—no way were they making that walk from the lobby in this downpour.

Apparently, however, everyone else staying at the resort had the same idea. He took the closest spot he could find, which wasn't saying much, and then grabbed the gift shop umbrella they'd stashed in the backseat earlier. Small and lime green, it was hardly an awe-inspiring weapon against the current elements.

"Stay here," he told Jessica, as rain cascaded over the car's windows in thick sheets. He pushed the door open and got the umbrella up, then climbed out of the car and strode around to the passenger side.

He opened her door and held out his hand to help her out of the car. Huddled close together under the umbrella, they made a run for the door through the driving rain.

Once inside, they both grinned as they assessed the damage. He was essentially soaked from the shoulders down, and Jessica hadn't fared much better; most of her left side and the lower half of her body were wet, her clothes clinging to her.

That part he didn't mind.

They hurried through the frigid, air-conditioned hallway, and he unlocked the door to his room. She made a beeline for the temperature control panel on the wall and shut off the air-conditioning. Apparently still not warm enough, she opened the door that led out to the covered balcony and let the humid, ocean-scented air fill the room.

John headed into the bathroom to grab a couple of towels. While there, he quickly shed his clothes and shoes, everything except his boxer briefs, and hung them over the shower door to dry.

He came out of the bathroom to find Jessica leaning against the balcony door frame, gazing out at the rain and the ocean. Her hair was wavy and wild from the humidity and she was bare-legged, having ditched her shoes and skirt.

She looked lost in thought as she worked on her shirt, her fingers toying idly with one of the buttons.

When she noticed him standing there, she smiled. "Towels. Good idea."

He walked over and handed her one. "What were you thinking just then?"

For the barest second, he could've sworn he saw a flicker of something he couldn't quite read in her eyes—but then it was gone.

Her tone was light as she dried off her legs and feet. "I was thinking how unfair it is that *you* get even better looking when wet, while I look like I'm trying out for an eighties glam rock band." She set the towel on the nearby chair, next to her skirt.

Closing the gap between them, he stood facing her in the balcony doorway. He reached over to brush a lock of hair out of her face—hair that, if he was being totally honest, was doing some pretty strange things right then and seemed to be getting bigger and wider by the minute. And yes, her makeup had run a little, her blue eyes smudged with black eyeliner and mascara. She even had a small smear of it on her right cheekbone.

But still.

"You look beautiful," he said huskily.

Her expression softened, and then she blushed, appearing momentarily unsure what to say.

He ran his thumb gently over her bottom lip. "I can see the self-deprecating quip just hovering here, begging to come out."

She smiled at that. "You know me well."

Yes, he did.

He lowered his head and kissed her. Slowly at first, but then her lips parted eagerly and he wound his tongue around hers, wanting more. Impatiently, he shifted her to the side—never breaking the kiss—and used one hand to slam the balcony door shut, giving them privacy.

Pinning her back against the balcony door, he slid one of his legs between her thighs and began unbuttoning the rest of her shirt. She was already breathing harder, and he was right there with her—after spending the last ten hours playing it cool for the sake of their assignment, he was glad to finally drop the façade.

He pushed the shirt off her shoulders and let it fall to the floor. She sank her fingers into the back of his hair and touched her tongue to his in a slow, erotic kiss that had his cock straining against his boxer briefs.

The woman always had driven him crazy with her mouth.

Cupping her ass in his hands, he lifted her up. Given their thirteen-inch height difference, it was easier to kiss her this way—not to mention, this position conveniently put his cock right between her legs.

As the full length of his erection pressed against her, she inhaled unsteadily. He pulled back from kissing her and saw the unabashed desire in her eyes.

Seeing that made him feel . . . things. Dangerous things.

"Take off your bra," he said in a low voice.

She unhooked the front clasp and slid the straps off her shoulders. She didn't say a word as the bra fell to the floor, but with the daring way she held his gaze, she still managed to make the gesture look saucy.

He sucked the rosy tip of one of her breasts into his mouth, relishing the sound of her ragged breathing as he teased her with his tongue.

"John," she moaned.

There it was again, his name on her lips, in that throaty voice that drove him fucking wild. Backing away from the door, he carried her over to the bed and set her down.

She watched with obvious appreciation as he shed his boxer briefs.

"Lay back," he told her.

Heat flashed in her eyes as she stretched across the bed. "You're a little bossy tonight."

"I can make it a lot bossy, if you prefer," he shot back.

He climbed onto the bed, moving alongside her for a long, heated kiss. His hand trailed down her breasts and stomach and kept going, disappearing into the waistband of her underwear.

She sucked in a breath when he slid a finger inside her. As he stroked her in a slow, smooth rhythm, her nipples tightened and she arched against his hand.

"Does that feel good?" he murmured.

"Yes," she breathed.

He added a second finger and then brushed his thumb against her clit. She gasped and spread her legs a little more.

Heat coiling in his abdomen, he sat up and yanked open the nightstand drawer, where he'd stashed a box of condoms earlier. As he pulled one out of the box, Jessica climbed onto his lap, straddling him.

Seeing her playful, naughty look, he slid his hands down to cup her round, perfect ass. "You need to take off this underwear."

"In a minute." Moving her hips, she rubbed his erection against her and closed her eyes in pleasure. "Mmm."

Christ. Palming the condom, he slid his hands to the lacy wisp of fabric at her hip. He gave it a sharp yank, and her underwear fell by the wayside in two pieces.

Problem solved.

With a somewhat wry expression, she reached between them to pull out the front half of her underwear, and dropped it to the floor.

He grinned wickedly. "I did ask nicely first." Sort of.

"Speaking of asking questions, I have one for you." She cocked her head, smoothing her hands up his chest. "Have I ever told you I have this . . . slight oral fixation?"

Oh . . . fuck, *yes.*

"I think you may have mentioned it," he said, trying to play it cool.

With a knowing smile, she climbed off his lap and stepped back from the bed. She curled her finger, indicating he should move closer to the edge. He did so, resting his feet on the floor.

Then she knelt down in front him.

"Jessica . . ." He trailed off. She hadn't even started yet, and he was already throbbing. Just seeing her, on her knees like this, was enough to get his blood pumping.

She took his cock in her hand. "Tell me what you like."

Everything about you, said a voice inside his head. "You can start by wrapping those pretty lips around me."

Groaning when she slid him into her mouth, he threaded his fingers into her hair. "Take me deeper . . . just like that." Leaning back, he watched as the sexiest woman he'd ever met licked, sucked, stroked, and teased him with her mouth and hands, bringing him treacherously close to his breaking point.

"Look up at me." When her eyes met his, he felt something raw and primal clawing at him. "You are the hottest thing I've ever seen."

Holding his gaze, she teasingly circled her tongue around the head of his cock.

He needed to be inside her.

Now.

"Come up here," he said.

She eased him out of her mouth and pressed a soft kiss against his inner thigh, then climbed onto the bed. He grabbed the condom and handed it to her, inhaling sharply when one of her hands brushed against his balls as she rolled the condom over him.

The saucy minx gave him a coy smile.

"Turn around," he growled.

She did so, getting onto her hands and knees. He smoothed a hand down her back and along the curve of her ass, then gripped his cock and pushed the head into her warm, wet entrance. Looking down, he watched as he sank deeper into her, not stopping until he was all the way in.

She moaned, her body clenching tight around him.

Fuck, she felt amazing. He gritted his teeth, forcing himself not to move as she adjusted to him. "Tell me if I go too hard."

"You won't." She gasped as he slid in and out.

When he sensed she was ready, he tightened his fingers around her hips and pulled back, then thrust fast and deep. She whimpered in pleasure, so he did it again, and then faster, smacking their bodies together as he took her hard. The sounds of her moans and his ragged breathing filled the room, and when she moved down onto her elbows, letting him take complete control, he groaned at the raw intimacy of the moment.

"John. Touch me," she said, her voice thick with need.

Feeling her body tremble, he leaned down and reached between her legs, the words pouring out of him in a low, possessive growl. "I love when you're on the edge like this. You're so goddamn sweet. So mine."

She cried out, clenching around him like a glove. He thrust hard and came with her, groaning as his body shuddered in release from an orgasm so strong he thought his eyes might roll back in his head.

Gasping, he sank against her. Feeling her legs shake, he flattened his hand against the bed to avoid crushing her as he collapsed.

After disposing of the condom in the bathroom, John washed his hands and gave himself a long look in the mirror.

You're so goddamn sweet. So mine.

So, that last part had just sort of slipped out.

Dirty talk, obviously. He was hardly the first man to get carried away with grandiose words when on the brink of an orgasm. Surely Jessica understood he hadn't been saying that he thought she was *his*, his. *Pfft.* Clearly, that wasn't the case. He knew their time together had an expiration date—in eight days, he would ride off into the sunset and start a new phase of his life in Virginia. He and Jessica hadn't had any conversations about what happened after that, nor did he expect them to. She, too, would move on, and this fling between them would become mere memory, a fun time they both looked back on fondly.

Hopefully, they would even stay friends. He would text her sometime when he was back in Chicago visiting his dad, Nate, and Wes, and he'd meet her for coffee, or a drink. He would tell her about HRT, and she would catch him up on life in the Chicago field office and her newest cases, and maybe even slip in a mention of some guy she was dating, a nice guy who took her to fancy restaurants and made her laugh and had met her family and—

John relaxed his jaw, which had suddenly clenched tight. Anyway.

He headed back out to the bedroom and found Jessica lying facedown on the bed, her head tucked in one arm. When he took a seat on the edge of the mattress, she propped herself up on one elbow.

"Everything okay?" she asked.

In light of the *So mine* slip-up, he was careful to sound as casual as ever. "After that"—he nodded pointedly at the bed—"everything is definitely okay."

Quick to get off that subject, he reached for the room service menu on the nightstand. "Don't you have some tradition about ordering a glass of wine and dessert after finishing a job? We should follow Todd's lead and splurge on the good stuff tonight. This was, after all, officially my last undercover assignment."

She glanced down at the menu and then smiled.

"That's certainly worth the good stuff."

Later that night, after they'd polished off a key lime torte and a bottle of wine (the latter of which had been consumed, in part, during a sexy tryst in the oversized bathtub), Jessica finished brushing her teeth and came out of the bathroom to find John already asleep.

With a slight smile, she shut off the lamp on her nightstand and climbed into bed. As she settled in, he rolled onto his side and draped an arm over her hip, his hand coming to rest against her stomach. Probably he was half asleep and barely aware of what he was doing, but still, the intimacy of the gesture felt nice. More than nice, even.

Ahem, her inner pragmatic said pointedly.

Relax, it's just a little cuddling, Jessica reassured the voice. She never claimed she didn't like John—okay, fine, at least not in the last week or so. They were friends and partners, and there was, admittedly, a strong physical attraction between them. But there was a limit to how deep her feelings could go—a limit to how deep she would *allow* them to go.

With him leaving, for good, in little more than a week, she didn't have any other choice in the matter.

27

Thursday evening, John surveyed the small loft condo he'd rented for the summer, satisfied with the progress he, Nate, and Wes had made in just a couple of hours.

The movers were coming at seven A.M. tomorrow morning to load all of the furniture and kitchen items, as well as most of his clothes and other personal effects, onto a truck that would arrive in Virginia on Wednesday, after the holiday weekend. Given how relatively little stuff he had, particularly after the breakup with Alicia, John doubted it would take the movers long—with any luck, he'd make it into the office by ten o'clock.

By this point, he'd been phased out of all his cases, so it wasn't like he had any actual work to do. But he had a cubicle to clean out, people he wanted to see before he left, and he also had a feeling, given the surreptitious conversations that ended as soon as someone spotted him heading back to his desk, that his squad mates had planned a going-away party for him. Which was exactly what he'd told them *not* to do, but, presumably, the assholes couldn't pass up the chance to embarrass him one last time.

Squad loyalty required nothing less.

In the flyaway kitchen, Wes taped up a box of glassware and

dinnerware and used a Sharpie to write *Fragile* on the top and sides. John had focused on packing his clothes—with the exception of a week's worth of stuff that he would throw into a suitcase and take with him—and his brother was in charge of boxing up photo albums, picture frames, and other irreplaceable items that John preferred to transport himself, just to be safe.

"Check out the dinosaur pajamas on this guy." Sitting on the living room floor, Nate held up a photo from an album their dad had given John after their mom died.

John moved closer, grinning at the picture of the two of them with their mom on a Christmas morning about thirty years ago. "Says the guy wearing a onesie with ducks on it."

"Dude, I'm, what, eighteen months old there? I make that shit work." Nate paused for a moment, taking in the photo. "Mom looks so young."

John nodded, his expression softening, too. "She does." Then he pointed to another photo on the opposite page. "Check out Dad's sideburns. He looks like Wolverine." As Nate chuckled, John grabbed the last of the garment boxes and stacked it along with the others in the corner of the room.

He'd gone over to his dad's house for dinner the night before, one final time before leaving town. That hadn't been an easy good-bye, but for the most part John had kept things light and positive. Indeed, that had been his modus operandi since he'd returned from Jacksonville: Instead of dwelling on everything he was leaving behind in Chicago, he was keeping his eyes on the prize. By this time next week, he'd be a NOThead, knee-deep in training and on his way to becoming either a sniper or assaulter on the only U.S. law enforcement unit capable of responding on four hours' notice to terrorist or criminal threats anywhere in the country.

Servare vitas.

Hope you saved room to finally put "badass" on your résumé.
Welcome to the best job in the FBI.

Hell, yes, he was pumped and ready for that.

"Well, what do we have here?" Nate said, interrupting John's thoughts.

John turned and saw his brother holding another photo album, one he'd dug out of God-only-knew-where, a random collection of photos John had taken while in the Army. Also tucked in there, because he hadn't known where else to put them—filing skills were hardly his strength—were two class photos from the FBI Academy. The first had been taken at the shooting range, the trainees all dressed in their new agent uniforms. The second was a more formal shot in the auditorium on graduation day, with everyone wearing dark suits, white shirts, and muted ties for the men.

His brother held one of the two eight-by-ten photos in his hand. "So this is the infamous Jessica Harlow." He looked slyly at John. "I'm guessing, of the two women in the class, that she's the noticeably hot blonde."

Before John could answer, Wes scurried across the room to check out the photo. "Let me see." Standing behind Nate, he grinned approvingly. "Ah, now I get why you were crushing on her so hard."

John shook his head as he walked over. At this point, it wasn't even worth responding to their comments. He took the photo from Nate and saw that it was the one taken at the shooting range. "I haven't seen this picture in years."

There they were, all forty-one of them, dressed in their blue polo shirts, khaki pants, and hiking boots. John's eyes lingered on Jessica, who stood off to the right in the front row.

Wes peered over his shoulder. "Isn't she a little short to be a special agent?"

John smiled. Now that Wes mentioned it, she did look

smaller than usual in this photo. It must've been the lack of high heels. "You don't notice it in person. She has a very commanding aura about her."

Nate and Wes exchanged a look.

Pretty sure he didn't want to know what that was all about, John handed the photo back to his brother. "Think you can fit the rest of that into one box? I'm running out of trunk space here."

Determined to keep moving, John grabbed his suitcase out of the closet and began packing the remainder of his clothes.

Two hours, three fist-bumps, and one joking—but solid—man hug later, John stood on the sidewalk in front of his building, watching Wes's car drive off.

It still felt weird sometimes, only seeing Wes. Two months ago, if John had been leaving, there would've been a bigger send-off that would've included Rob, Matt, and Lucas, probably at some trendy bar with a rooftop deck where Rob knew somebody who could get them a table. Rob would've made a toast to John that would've been funny but surprisingly touching—for all his many flaws, the guy was charismatic, at least—and Matt would've gotten drunk and hit on ten girls he had no shot of landing, while Lucas would've spent the entire night focused on one girl, whom he did, actually, have a shot of landing, if he hadn't waited so long to make his move that another guy had beaten him to the punch.

For a fleeting second, John wondered what the three of them were up to, and whether they'd heard the news, through Wes, that he'd made HRT and was moving to Virginia. He assumed—although he sure as hell hadn't asked—that Rob was still seeing Alicia, so presumably she knew as well.

That whole situation seemed like a lifetime ago.

In the eight weeks that had passed since he'd walked in on Alicia and Rob, he'd been through the hell of Selection, found

out that he'd made the Hostage Rescue Team, and had participated in a sting operation targeting the mayor of one of the
largest cities in the United States.

And then, of course, there was Jessica.

She would be his last good-bye, which, given their history,
was perhaps the most surprising turn of events of all. He hadn't
seen her for the past couple days—she'd been in South Carolina, preparing for the undercover op that was going down
tonight—but the plan was for him to spend the night at her
place tomorrow. He'd made a joke about it, naturally, claiming
that he needed a place to crash since his own bed would be
halfway to Virginia by then. But the truth of the matter was,
there was no one else with whom he'd rather spend his last
evening in Chicago.

Which reminded him . . .

He pulled his phone out of his jeans pocket. They'd talked
about the case before she left, so he knew Jessica wasn't scheduled to make her Lexington, South Carolina, acting debut until midnight, when the scumbag cop who liked to prey on
female victims was back on shift. Right about now, she was
probably with the case agents and backup, setting up the hotel
room the FBI had commandeered to use as the scene of the
alleged domestic assault.

John could practically see the determined gleam in her eyes
as she counted down the minutes until show time.

Text me when you're done tonight, he typed.

She'd be fine. He knew that. He just wanted to hear it
straight from her, when this whole thing was over. The undercover agent in him might have been cheering her on from the
sidelines, and might even have been a little jealous, professionally, over some of the details of her cover—apparently, they'd
hired a special effects makeup artist to give her fake bruises,
and that was some cool, sneaky shit—but the man in him
seemed to be more focused on the fact that she was over eight

hundred miles away and on an assignment where the *best* possible outcome was that an armed police officer tried to sexually assault her.

John took a moment to consider that, then added another sentence to his text message.

Doesn't matter how late it is.

He hit send, then headed back inside. There, he found his brother relaxing on the couch, beer in one hand and checking his phone with the other.

John grabbed another beer from the fridge and joined him.

"I've been doing some research on your superhero camp," Nate said, conversationally, as he put his phone away. "Honestly, I'd never heard of the Hostage Rescue Team until you mentioned it. Thought maybe you'd just made it up to sound cool."

John took a sip of his beer. "And you're satisfied now that it really exists?"

"Yep. And from what I read, it's the real deal." Nate paused. "In fact, I read that two HRT operators were killed just a couple years ago, during some training exercise off the coast of Virginia Beach." He glanced over. "I assume you know about that already."

John nodded, his tone turning more sober. "Yes." Apparently, the two operators had been fast-roping out of a helicopter that had encountered some sort of difficulty, and they'd fallen 150 feet into the water. There were no acceptable losses in the FBI, and every effort was made to prevent such tragedies from occurring—that was why HRT trained as hard as it did. Nevertheless, every operator who joined the team did so with a full understanding of the risks involved.

Nate looked over and held John's gaze. "Just be careful and all that."

John smiled slightly, not fooled by the faux-casual tone and touched by his brother's rare display of concern. "I will."

With a nod, seemingly glad to have that off his chest, Nate eased back and put his feet up on the coffee table. "Now, about this Jessica with the 'commanding aura' you keep talking about."

"I'm pretty sure the only reason we keep talking about her is because *you* keep bringing her up."

Nate ignored this. "Kind of a shame that things between you two seem to be heating up right when you're about to leave."

John considered that. "Most likely, it wouldn't have turned into anything serious even if I weren't leaving. She just got divorced and isn't looking for a relationship—especially not with someone she works with. Hell, she even told me she only slept with me *because* I'm leaving."

"Or maybe she likes your aura, too, but doesn't want to admit it," Nate said.

"How long before we drop the aura thing?"

"I've just never heard you talk about a woman that way," Nate said.

John took another sip of his beer, thinking it was best to let that one slide.

After watching him a moment, Nate shrugged. "Well, it sounds like you dodged a bullet there."

Of course that was what his brother would say. "You know, not all men think being in a relationship is this thing to be avoided at all costs, like chlamydia or serving time in a third-world prison."

Nate gave him a pointed look. "What I meant is, *if* Jessica had been looking for something more serious, you would've had to leave for Quantico knowing that you might've actually had a chance with her."

The words fell between them as John went silent.

Then he cocked his head, his demeanor as casual as ever. "You're right. I guess I did dodge that bullet." He pointed to his brother's nearly empty beer. "Want another?"

Without waiting for an answer, he stood up and walked to the refrigerator, ignoring the feel of his brother's eyes on his back.

Hope you don't get stuck with some lame-ass purple unitard and tights on the day they hand out uniforms—even a superhero can't get laid wearing that.

Those, of course, had been his brother's parting words as they'd hugged good-bye. A comedian till the end, although John had caught the way Nate's voice sounded thicker than usual.

Now alone, he exhaled while standing with his hands on his hips in what would soon be his former living room/bedroom. Everything was packed and ready to go, save for the few things he would need to get him through Saturday morning. He planned to hit the road early, since the drive to Quantico would take him at least twelve hours. Nate had offered to come by the condo on Saturday afternoon, after John left, and let in a cleaning crew before returning the key to the company that had handled the rental.

Really, at this point, there wasn't much left for John to do.

He checked his phone and saw that it was ten thirty P.M.—eleven thirty P.M. in Lexington, South Carolina. T-minus a half hour until Jessica placed a distraught call to 911 that would get the ball rolling.

John thought about the good undercover story she would have after this—yet another for her already impressive collection. With that in mind, he grabbed a second beer from the fridge and settled onto the couch for a long night of channel surfing.

Both the man and the agent in him knew there was no chance either of them was falling asleep until she texted to say she was all right.

"And then what happened?"

Jessica raised a trembling hand to push a lock of hair out of her eyes, feigning a wince as her fingers brushed against her "bruised" cheekbone. "He, um, ran out when I called 911. Probably took the car and left."

The cop—Officer Luttrell—stood a few feet from her while jotting things down in a small notepad. "What's the license plate of the vehicle?"

Jessica frowned, slurring her words. "It's SFK . . . 739, I think? Or maybe 793."

"Color, make, and model of the vehicle?"

"Red Chevy. A Silverado." Again, she slurred the *s* sound.

The scene had been set, and so far, everything was going according to plan. Earlier today, Jessica had used the name "Becky Sauer" to check into the Comfort Suites in Lexington, a town in central South Carolina located twelve miles outside Columbia. So the story went, she and her boyfriend, Jonah Reed, had driven down from Greensboro, North Carolina, to attend a surprise thirtieth birthday party for one of Jonah's former fraternity brothers. They'd had a few drinks—both at the hotel beforehand, and at the party—and had been having a good time, until Becky had gotten a text message from her ex-boyfriend, Ryder. It was just a meaningless thing—so her ex texted her sometimes, so what?—but Jonah, who'd always been possessive and particularly jealous of Ryder, had just *lost* it. They'd gotten into a big fight at the party, until Becky had stormed out and come back to the hotel.

Which, apparently, had only made Jonah even angrier.

Wearing a short dress that had one torn spaghetti strap, and with "bruises" on her cheek and arms, Jessica sat on the edge of the room's king-size bed. On the dresser that doubled as a TV stand was a half-empty bottle of bourbon.

Almost immediately after he'd walked into the hotel room, Office Luttrell—her target—had noticed the half-empty bottle of bourbon, as well as the hotel room telephone that lay smashed in pieces by the wall. What he had *not* noticed, nor would he ever, were the minuscule microphones and video cameras that had been hidden all over the room. Nor did he have any idea that in the next room, on the opposite side of an adjoining door that had been rigged to appear locked but was actually ready to open, was a six-man FBI SWAT team armed with Remington twelve-gauge shotguns and Glock 17 pistols. Jessica had two code phrases—one in case of an emergency, and the other that conveyed that she'd gotten everything she needed from the target. Either one would have the SWAT team bursting through the door in an instant, their movements quick and precise as they got Luttrell on the ground before he had the chance to even contemplate reaching for his gun.

But first, Jessica had *her* job to do.

Moving closer, Officer Luttrell picked up the overturned chair, setting it upright in front of the desk. "How many drinks did your boyfriend consume tonight?"

Jessica teetered slightly on the bed. "I don't know. A lot."

"And how much have you had to drink, ma'am?" Luttrell asked.

She sat up straighter. "Just a few." She peered at the cop, blinking as if she was trying to focus. "Maybe three . . . or four."

Luttrell considered this, then walked over to his partner, a younger police officer—around twenty-three or twenty-four years old—who stood by the door.

In case the cops were watching as they began to talk between themselves, Jessica ran her hands through her hair, letting her eyes well up with tears once again. *If* Luttrell was going to take the bait, this was the part where he would come up with some excuse to get rid of his partner, who was obviously junior in seniority.

"Why don't you go talk to the people in the nearby rooms? See if anyone heard or saw anything," Luttrell suggested to Junior Cop.

Hearing that, Jessica felt a rush of adrenaline.

Here we go.

Luttrell lowered his voice as he continued. "Ten bucks says we're gonna find this Reed guy in one of the bars on Main Street, with even more bruises than she has." He spoke quieter still, so Jessica could only partially make out his next words, something about "out-of-towners," "partying," and "sober up."

"Should I call in the vehicle?" Junior Cop asked.

"Check to see if it's in the parking lot, but hold off on calling it in for now. I'll meet you downstairs in the lobby, after I finish up here."

Jessica glanced over as Junior Cop left the room. The door shut behind him with a firm *click*, leaving her and Officer Luttrell alone.

"Sounds like your boyfriend isn't in any condition to be driving," Luttrell said, as he crossed the room. He grabbed the desk chair, turned it around, and sat facing Jessica, close enough that his knees brushed against hers.

He looked at her for a moment, his gaze traveling from the neckline of her dress to her bare legs. "You shouldn't let him treat you this way. A woman as pretty and nice as you can do a lot better."

Catching the predatory glint in his eyes, Jessica bent her head. "It only happens when he drinks," she said quietly.

Luttrell put a hand on her leg, just above her knee. "Talk to me, Becky. I'd like to help you, if I can."

Jessica watched as Luttrell's hand slid an inch higher up her leg. She took a deep breath, pretending to attempt to compose herself, but on the inside she felt as calm and steady as ever.

She raised her tear-stained face to meet the cop's gaze.

Game on, asshole.

28

"*Told* ya we'd be in and out in less than two hours. I wish all my jobs were this easy."

Mike, the head mover, handed John his copy of the paperwork. The two of them stood next to the moving truck, which was parked on the street in front of John's building. "So what's in Virginia?"

"New job," John said.

"Cool. Good luck with that." He shook John's hand and told him that his guys would be in touch on Tuesday to give him their approximate arrival time.

Standing on the curb, John watched as the truck drove off with his things. When it turned at the end of the street and disappeared, he exhaled as the finality of the moment sank in.

This was it.

Obviously, he'd known that this day—his last in Chicago— was coming. He'd been preparing for it these last two weeks. And part of him couldn't wait to be on the road tomorrow, driving to Virginia to get started with this next phase of his life.

Another part of him, however—a part he'd been doing his best to ignore these past couple days—felt a little . . . unsettled.

Particularly whenever he thought about the fact that this was the last night he would spend with Jessica.

Stumbling into a casual, no-strings-attached arrangement with a smart, funny, beautiful woman who had no problem with the fact that he couldn't offer her more was like striking gold for a single, thirty-something man in his position. He knew that. He was moving halfway across the country and was about to start a high-intensity job that would require all his time, energy, and commitment. It was hardly the time for him to be starting a new relationship. Especially a long-distance one.

Still, it wasn't like he *enjoyed* the thought of saying good-bye to Jessica. They'd gotten close in the five weeks since she'd started at the Chicago office, and as much as it killed him to admit it, even the saucy comments had grown on him. They worked great together, she challenged him, she made him laugh, and if he was being honest with himself, he would miss all that when he was gone.

Very much, in fact.

His loft now empty except for the suitcases and the few remaining boxes he would transport in his car, John locked up and headed to work. As he pulled into the parking lot of the FBI office, his cell phone buzzed with a new text message. He glanced down at the cupholder on the console, where he kept his phone, and could see that the message was from Jessica.

They'd exchanged a few brief messages at two A.M., after she'd texted to let him know that she'd finished the undercover op in Lexington and that everything had gone fine. Given the nature of the assignment, both the man and agent in him wanted to know more specifically what "fine" entailed, but she hadn't been able to talk at the time—she'd still been wrapping things up with the agents from the Columbia office. She'd promised, however, to text him in the morning with her flight information.

After John parked his car, he picked up his phone and saw that her message was longer than he'd expected.

The AUSA who will be handling the case wants to meet with the Columbia agents and me at 1:00. Told them I HAVE to be done by 2:30, to make the 4:17 flight. Lands at 5:29. I'm sorry I'm going to be late . . . I can tell my doorman to give you the key to my place, so you can let yourself in.

Immediately after that, she'd sent a second message.

But don't peek at the gift bag on the kitchen counter. ☺

He felt a warm feeling spread across his chest. You bought something for me? He grinned at the thought of her shopping for him.

Just a little going-away present.

His smile faded. Right—a good-bye gift. He should've guessed that. Text me when you board, he typed back. I'll probably just hang out at the office until you're home. It was his last day in the Chicago field office, after all. His last few hours as a special agent.

He might as well soak it in.

Once he got into the office, his last day at work flew by. His squad leader took him out for a lunch/exit interview, he tackled the dreaded packing up of his desk, and at four P.M., his squad mates "surprised" him with a going-away party. Despite his no-party protests, they even pulled out a cake decorated with the HRT insignia: an eagle carrying a broken chain over the words *Servare Vitas.*

Genuinely appreciative—and a little embarrassed by all the fuss—John said a few words to thank everyone. And as he looked around the room, at the faces of his squad mates, his squad leader, the agents on other squads that he'd worked with over the last few years, and even the SAC—who'd made a point of stopping by—he felt a sudden, strong mix of emotions.

To cover, he ended his speech with a joke about how much time he had left before they assigned his cubicle to someone else.

"About fifteen minutes," Nick, the SAC, shot back with a grin. Everyone laughed, John included.

Eyes on the prize, he reminded himself.

The crowd was big enough that the party spilled out of the conference room, with people mingling around the cubicles and in front of the squad leader's office. John made the rounds, wanting to talk to everyone, and didn't have a chance to catch his breath until well after five o'clock. By that point, almost everyone had cleared out except for the agents on his squad, who'd long since turned the party into a roast, telling stories about his cases and getting in their last jokes and jabs.

"Speaking of interesting cases, your white-collar partner-in-crime never showed up," Ryan commented.

"What's her situation, anyway?" Jin asked.

"What do you mean, her 'situation'?" John asked.

"Is she single?" Brandon asked bluntly.

John half chuckled at that, buying himself a moment before answering, and saw that all five guys standing around him were waiting with bated breath.

He threw a sideways glance at Ryan. "Don't tell me you're getting into this gossip now, too."

Ryan shrugged that off with a grin. "I wouldn't mind knowing if she's single. I only talked to her for a couple minutes the other day, but she made an impression."

An irrational wave of possessiveness swelled inside John.

Actually, she is seeing someone. Me.

Obviously, he couldn't say that. First off, he and Jessica were keeping their personal affairs private. And second, after tomorrow that statement wouldn't be true anymore. He would be in Virginia, and Jessica would be free to date anyone she wanted.

He doubted she would get involved with another agent. She'd had a lot of concerns about dating a co-worker, and he would have liked to think that she'd broken her rules for him because the connection between them was unique. But his squad mates' interest was a sharp reminder that other men were going to be pursuing Jessica—good guys, like Ryan, who could offer her a real relationship, not just a three-week fling.

Guys she could fall in love with.

John relaxed his hands, which he belatedly realized he'd clenched behind his back, and gave his squad mates a diplomatic answer. "She's never mentioned a boyfriend to me."

After steering them onto another topic of conversation, he excused himself from the group. Looking for privacy, he headed to the hallway by the restroom and pulled out his cell phone. He'd turned the ringer off during his speech, and he saw that he'd missed one call from Jessica, and two text messages letting him know that her flight had been delayed.

John dialed her number, wanting to get a full update.

Perhaps it was the fact that it had finally hit him that he was leaving tomorrow. Or, possibly, he was still feeling unsettled after the conversation about Jessica with his squad mates.

He just really wanted to know when he was going to see her.

Shortly after the flight attendant made her plea for everyone to stow their bags and take their seats as quickly as possible, Jessica's cell phone rang.

"Hey, you," she said. She'd been trying to reach John for hours. Unfortunately, she wasn't sure how much time she had to talk, so she got the most important information out first. "So the bad news is, some storm front moved in that delayed my flight. The good news is, I'm finally on the plane and we're pushing back any moment. They're saying we'll land in Chicago at six fifty-five." She lowered her voice, even though she'd scored one of the single seats on the left side of the regional jet and doubted anyone could hear her over the hustle and bustle of all the boarding activity. "I missed your going-away party, John. I'm really sorry about that."

Having become something of an expert in disappointing

people because of her job, she braced herself. And she deserved his frustration—this had been a big day for John, and she'd been a no-show.

But instead he said, in a teasing voice, "It turned into a roast. I know you—if you'd been here, you would've been tempted to regale the crowd with tales of a certain fight between us at the Academy. And I'm not sure our relationship can withstand that story going public."

She laughed. *God, I miss you.*

The words nearly flew out of her mouth before she caught herself.

Wow. That was quite a heavy sentiment there. Those were the kind of words a woman said to someone she was really, truly dating. Not to a man who was leaving, for good, *tomorrow*.

As she'd been doing all day, every time that thought set in, Jessica ignored the nagging feeling in her stomach and focused on the matter at hand. "Do you want to hang out at my place? I already called the doorman and told him to let you in if you come by."

"I'm good. I'll grab a beer at my brother's bar and hang out there until you land." He shifted topics. "You haven't told me yet how things went down last night. First and foremost: Are you okay?"

When Jessica heard that, something inside her melted.

She was running late—way late—on his last night at home. She'd just missed his going-away party. But the thing he was most focused on was whether *she* was okay.

Because John Shepherd was that kind of guy. A really *good* guy.

Jessica looked out the airplane window, trying to focus as her throat suddenly felt tight.

Get a grip, she told herself. Probably she was just overemotional and exhausted from the events of the past couple of days.

"I'm okay." She maintained a relaxed, confident tone. "My

target was mostly into exposing himself to someone he thought was in a vulnerable position. Needless to say, certain parts of him shriveled up right quick when six guys with body armor and shotguns came storming through the door."

The flight attendant signaled her to put her phone in airplane mode.

"I have to go," she told John. "We're about to take off."

"We'll talk more when you get home. I want to hear the rest of the story," he said.

"It might even top the one about being a hotel housekeeper." After saying good-bye, she hung up and looked at her phone for a moment.

We'll talk more when you get home.

Under different circumstances—circumstances in which John *wasn't* leaving town for good tomorrow—it probably would've been nice to have someone like him to come home to after an exhausting investigation.

Really nice, in fact.

Taking a deep breath, she forced herself to smile at the fifty-something male passenger across the aisle from her.

"Heading to Chicago for business or pleasure?" she asked him.

"Work conference," he said. "You?"

"Heading home. I'm with the FBI in Chicago," she offered.

"FBI? Wow." The man eagerly angled his body in her direction. "What's that like?"

Desperate times called for desperate measures. He wouldn't stop asking her questions the entire flight, and that was precisely what she needed.

Something—anything—to keep her thoughts about John at bay.

29

Two hours later, however, Jessica was about to seriously lose her shit. Along with every other passenger on the plane.

Another storm had rolled in almost as soon as they'd pulled away from the gate. Not wanting to lose their position in line, the pilot had kept the plane on the tarmac, with the hope of departing as soon as the skies cleared. But when lightning moved into the area, air traffic control grounded all flights and sent the planes back to the terminal.

"Due to the weather, unfortunately, air traffic control has canceled all outbound flights for the rest of the evening." The airline employee standing behind the desk at the gate looked harried as she repeated her speech, the same one she'd given to the five passengers who'd been in line ahead of Jessica. "I apologize for the inconvenience and I'm happy to reschedule you for the first flight tomorrow morn—"

"No, I need to be on a flight *tonight*," Jessica emphasized. "Any airline. I don't care. I'll pay whatever. But it's imperative that I get to Chicago."

The five passengers in front of her had been unsuccessful in their efforts to get on another flight leaving tonight. But she had a trump card.

She pulled out her FBI credentials. She'd never used her job to get her anything—not even to get out of so much as a parking ticket. But tonight, if it would help, damn straight she would use it to get on a plane. "I'm a special agent with the Federal Bureau of Investigation. I need to be in Chicago tonight."

The airline employee shook her head, barely glancing at the credentials. "I'm really sorry. But there's nothing I can do. The storm is anticipated to last at least another four hours, and all flights out of this airport have been canceled for the rest of the evening."

"Fine. Put me on flight out of Charlotte, then. Or Charleston. Myrtle Beach. Hell, I'll fly out of Atlanta if I have to." Jessica sounded a touch desperate even to her own ears.

"Charlotte is experiencing the same weather as us—they've grounded all flights, too. And both Charleston and Myrtle Beach are over a hundred miles from here. Given the late hour, even if you got in a cab now, you wouldn't make any of the flights leaving those airports tonight." The airline employee's expression was sympathetic. "I'm sorry, ma'am, but I'm afraid you won't be getting to Chicago tonight."

For a moment, Jessica just stood there.

"But . . . I have to make it back," she said. "A friend of mine is leaving tomorrow morning, and I need to see him. I don't know when I'll see him again after this. *If* I ever see him again."

She swallowed as the reality of that settled in.

Straightening her shoulders, she pointed to the computer. "Pull whatever strings you have to. I don't care if you stick me on a damn FedEx plane. Just find a way to get me home."

The speech didn't work.

Nor did it work fifteen minutes later, when Jessica repeated it to the employee behind the airline's customer service desk.

She was officially stranded.

Running her hands through her hair, she took a moment to calm herself before she called John.

"Your flight got canceled," he said quietly, as soon as he answered. "I've been checking the updates."

"Everything's canceled. I can't get out of here tonight." She shook her head. "John . . . I'm so sorry. I don't even know what to say—I can't believe this is happening. Although maybe I shouldn't be surprised." She bit her lip, trying to force out a joke. "If we ever wondered how I ended up divorced, I think that mystery has been solved."

"Don't do that," John said. "This is the job, Jessica. I get that."

She knew that, too. But right then, it didn't make her feel any better. "Where will you sleep tonight?"

"I'll crash at my brother's place."

She nodded, not that he could see that. "They can put me on a seven A.M. flight that arrives in Chicago at eight thirteen. I know you wanted to get an early start tomorrow, but if you can hold off until I get back, I'd really like to say good-bye in person."

"Well, I'd hate to leave without my good-bye gift." His voice turned more serious. "I can wait."

A few moments later, Jessica hung up the phone and stared at the window that looked out onto the tarmac. She'd checked the forecast, and it was supposed to rain for several hours. Yes, the weather was supposed to clear up by the morning, but as an experienced traveler, she knew there were never any guarantees when it came to the airlines. And if there were any delays in the morning, she'd lose her chance to say good-bye to John.

She couldn't risk that happening.

Carry-on suitcase in tow, she walked determinedly to the escalator and took it down to the lower level. Since time was of the essence, she headed to the first open rental counter she saw and pulled out her driver's license and credit card.

"I need a car," she told the Hertz employee standing behind the counter. "And also the location of the nearest Starbucks."

With over eight hundred miles to cross, it was going to be a long night.

Meanwhile, seated alone among a lively Friday night crowd at Sheridan's Pub, John set his phone down on the bar after finishing his conversation with Jessica.

A sharp pang of disappointment hit him right in the gut, but he immediately buried the feeling down deep.

Maybe, in the long run, this was for the best. All day he'd been counting down the hours until he and Jessica could be alone again, and that kind of attachment was dangerous. Probably, he'd gotten too close to her, and if they'd spent the night together, it would've been that much harder to walk away in the morning.

He needed to start distancing himself. For his own sake.

Nate grinned as he came around the bar. "That's a pretty gloomy look for someone who's about to spend the night with his dream girl."

As always, his brother had impeccable timing.

"I'm not spending the night at Jessica's. She's stuck in South Carolina until the morning," John said.

Nate's face fell. "Shit, John, I didn't realize. What happened?"

John shrugged. "Bad weather. They canceled all flights for the rest of the evening. Can I crash at your place instead?"

"Of course." His brother looked at him.

"Shit happens, Nate. We don't need to have a whole discussion about it." John took a swallow of his beer.

Nate seemed like he was about to say something. But then he sighed and simply nodded instead. "If you say so."

30

Fueled by caffeine, upbeat music from her phone, and sheer will, Jessica made it to Chicago in exactly twelve hours and twelve minutes. Knowing she was racing against the clock, she left her rental car parked with the hazards on in front of her building, breezed past Luther the doorman with a promise that she would only be a few minutes, and then took the elevator up to her floor.

Once inside her place, she brushed her teeth, did a quick refresher of her makeup so she didn't look *completely* like she'd been driving for twelve hours, and threw on a pair of jeans and a T-shirt.

On her way back out the door, she grabbed the gift bag off the counter.

She texted John to let him know she'd be at his place in ten minutes. In actuality, it took her eighteen minutes, the latter eight of which she spent driving around his neighborhood trying to find a place to park. Finally, she got lucky when someone pulled out of a spot across the street from his building.

Standing on his doorstep, she took a moment to pull herself together.

Of course it was bittersweet to say good-bye to someone

who'd become a friend—with benefits—over this past month and a half. But that was where her emotions had to stay. For her own sake, she needed to just . . . be levelheaded here.

She pushed the button on the intercom that rang his condo, and a few seconds later the door buzzed as it unlocked. After taking the stairs up to the second floor, she followed the hallway to his unit.

His front door stood wide open.

Heading inside, she found John in the furniture-less living room, taping up a box. From the looks of things, he was all ready to go.

The thought put a dull ache in her stomach, so she covered with a smile. "I could've been a burglar."

"Burglars don't ring the buzzer." Wearing jeans and a gray T-shirt, he set the roll of duct tape on top of the box. "You made it."

"The joys of airline travel," she quipped dryly.

A brief pause fell between them, and she felt oddly like he was studying her. Playing it casual, she looked around the condo. "So this is your place." Whenever they'd gotten together these past few weeks—aside from their hookups in Jacksonville—he'd always come to her condo.

"It was always temporary. I knew there was a chance I'd make HRT and have to move again, so I wasn't too picky."

"And now, here you are."

His mouth curved in acknowledgment. "Here I am."

Another pause between them.

Well. She held out the gift bag. "On that note . . ."

He took the bag from her. Jokingly, he feigned nearly dropping it. "What'd you get me, a bowling ball?"

"Hand weights, for the car ride." She demonstrated, lifting her right arm in a curl. "Can't have you showing up at Quantico not as pumped up and uber-manly as the other HRT guys."

He threw her a look—*cute*—and then reached into the bag. He pulled out the bottle of Elijah Craig 21-Year-Old Single Barrel bourbon she'd bought, and then looked up at her, seemingly taken aback. "Jessica. This is a *really* nice bottle."

She blushed, dismissing that with a wave. "I figured you could crack it open when you graduate from NOTS. Maybe share it with your classmates. I'm sure you'll all be ready for a good drink by then."

John glanced back down at the bottle, then nodded. "Thank you. This is great." He put the bottle back in the gift bag and set it on the ground next to his small stack of boxes.

She tried to sound bright. "So it looks like you're all set to hit the road."

"Pretty much. I just need to load these last few boxes into my car."

"You said you're staying in a hotel outside Quantico?" she asked.

"Only for the short term, while I house-hunt. Since I'll be there for a while, I didn't want to rush into buying something."

She nodded. Made sense. After all, as of today, Virginia was officially his home.

John's eyes met hers.

Looking at him—really looking at him—something inside her softened. "I'm so sorry about last night. I had this whole plan to take you out to dinner for your last night in the city."

He stepped closer. "It's okay. These things happen. I told you—I understand." He flashed her a wry smile. "On the upside, you did my brother a favor. He got in twelve extra hours of jokes about me wearing purple tights and a leotard at 'superhero camp.'"

She laughed as that image flashed into her head. "I better be the first person you text with a pic if that happens."

He chuckled, too, and then his expression turned more serious. "Come here." His voice husky, he pulled her in close.

When his arms wrapped around her, holding her tight, her eyes welled up. Relying on all her undercover skills to fight back the tears, she gave herself one more moment to soak in the feel of him.

And then she pulled away.

"Well," she exhaled. "I know you want to get on the road, so I should probably get going."

He nodded. "I'll walk you to your car."

Her car. Of course—he didn't realize that she'd driven all night in a rental. Undoubtedly, he assumed she'd come in on the seven A.M. flight, like she'd told him she was going to do last night.

It didn't matter now. The point was that she'd made it in time to say good-bye. But for whatever reason, standing here with him now, in their last few moments together, she felt self-conscious about the lengths to which she'd gone to see him.

So she lied.

"I took a cab. I didn't want to worry about parking." She made her way to the door, then turned around. "So listen: You be careful out there, big guy." Adopting a playful tone, she grabbed his shirt and tugged. "I know it's HRT, but that doesn't mean you have to go storming into every place like you've got bin Laden holed up in a Pakistani compound."

He shook his head at the joke, a reference to the day their instructor had made him shadow her at Hogan's Alley. "Six years later, and you still remember that."

"Of course I remember. That was my favorite day at the Academy." To cover up the wobble in her smile, she stood on her tiptoes and kissed him.

"Good-bye, John," she said softly.

Then she opened his door and walked away, through the hallway and down the stairs. Once outside, on the sidewalk, she kept going, ignoring her rental car in case John was watching out his window. If he saw her, he'd wonder why she'd lied about taking a cab, so she'd come back for the car later.

Right now, she needed to keep moving. Her heart was racing and she felt like if she stopped or slowed down, if she did anything other than keep moving forward, she might do something incredibly foolish.

So she just kept walking.

John shut the front door after Jessica left.

For several moments, he stood there with his hand on the doorknob.

Then, slowly, he let go. He turned around, away from the door, and his gaze landed on the remaining boxes of his things.

He needed to get out of there. Now.

After packing the boxes into the trunk of his car, he locked up the condo for the final time. He left the keys in the mailbox for his brother, who would come by later to let in the cleaning crew.

Then he climbed into his car and started the engine. On the front passenger seat was the gift bag Jessica had given him—he hadn't wanted to put it in the trunk, thinking the heat might ruin the bourbon.

He grabbed the bag and put it on the floor of the backseat, out of sight.

Jaw set, he shifted the car into drive and focused on the road ahead.

two weeks later

Jessica walked into Ombra, a restaurant in Chicago's Andersonville neighborhood, and spotted Tara sitting in one of the booths by the front door. Her mouth dropped open as she headed over.

"Oh my God, your hair. I *love* it," she said, greeting her friend with a hug.

Tara struck a pose. Previously long and wavy, her ebony hair now fell to her shoulders in a straight, layered style. "I got it cut yesterday. I felt like I'd had the same hairstyle forever." She checked out Jessica's suit and shoulder bag as they sat down in the booth. "Don't tell me you just got off work. It's eight o'clock on a Friday."

Jessica took a seat across the booth from Tara. "I know. I got this new case and it's a total time suck."

"That's what you said last Friday, when I asked if you wanted to go out," Tara said.

"I did say that. This is another new case."

"Wow." Tara cocked her head. "Sounds like you're working a lot lately."

"You know what they say: 'Justice never sleeps.'" With a wink, Jessica changed the topic. "What about you? How's work going these days?"

Like Jessica, Tara had left the practice of law shortly after getting her degree, and now worked as a legal recruiter at a boutique firm downtown. The two of them talked shop for a while, and then Jessica asked Tara how things were going with the new cute guy she'd been messaging on Tinder.

"I'm so done with this crap," Tara said, pulling out her phone. "I spent a week talking to him, and things seemed to be going well. Then this morning he messaged me to say that he'd had a dream about me last night, and that he woke up like this—" She held up her phone, showing Jessica a photo of a man's hand wrapped around an erect penis.

Hello. "He just sent you that out of the blue?"

Tara set her phone back down. "Oh yes. Because, apparently, in today's day and age, a woman saying, 'Hey, you seem cool, maybe we should meet for coffee,' is code for 'I'm horny, please send me a picture of your penis.' And what sucks is how normal these guys seem at first, so I'm thinking, 'Hey, maybe we actually have a connection here; maybe I somehow miraculously found a normal, single, thirty-something guy.' And then—*bam*—dick pic." Tara paused as the waitress stopped by their table. "Sorry, you caught me midrant."

"Tinder?" the waitress asked.

Tara turned to Jessica. "See? Be glad you can't be on it. I think I'd rather be single for the rest of my life than debase myself with any more of this shit."

Jessica smiled at the waitress. "Any wine recommendations? What can you pour the fastest?"

After they ordered drinks and some appetizers, Tara switched gears. "So. Tell me what's going on with John."

Prepared for this line of inquiry, Jessica shrugged. "He's gone. He left for Quantico two weeks ago."

"How are you doing with that?"

"I'm fine." Both Jessica's tone and expression were relaxed. "It's not like his leaving was a surprise."

"And how's John doing? At Quantico, I mean," Tara said.

Jessica paused, *not* having anticipated that particular question. "Actually, I haven't talked to him. But I'm sure he's doing just fine."

Tara raised an eyebrow. "I thought you said this Hostage Rescue Team is a big deal. You're not curious to know how it's going?"

"It's a very big deal. But trust me, if anyone can handle it, John Shepherd can. He's one of those people who are good at everything."

"Don't you hate people like that?"

Jessica chuckled. "Sometimes, yes. Although, professionally speaking, it's not a bad quality to have in one's partner."

"True. But if he's that good, maybe it's not entirely a bad thing that he's gone." Tara grinned. "Now you don't have to fight with him to be the superstar of your office."

Knowing Tara meant the comment as a joke, Jessica smiled. "Exactly. Good riddance."

But then, out of the blue, her eyes prickled with tears.

Quickly she looked away and cleared her throat.

Tara leaned in and squeezed her hand. "Aw, Jess. I'm sorry. I was just trying to be funny. I thought that's what we do when it comes to you and John."

"That *is* what we do," Jessica said firmly. Yes, the good-bye with John had been harder than she'd expected. And yes, maybe, she'd been working even more than usual to keep her mind off him. But if that was what she had to do, so be it.

John was gone. That was the reality of the situation, so these persistent sad feelings she kept having—or whatever they were—needed to hit the road pronto. Like a gray, early-morning fog that lingered past noon, they had long overstayed their welcome.

"I'll be fine," she added, seeing Tara's look of uncertainty. "Really. Joke away."

Tara seemed to consider that and then nodded. "Okay."

That settled, they both leaned back in their chairs as the waitress dropped off their glasses of wine. From her sheepish smile, it was clear she'd overheard the last part of Jessica and Tara's conversation.

"I swear we're not normally this dramatic. You've caught us on a very odd day," Jessica said.

The waitress chuckled. "It's all good. I'll check back on you guys in a few minutes."

After she left, Tara held up her end of the deal and kept the conversation light and fun. "So, I'm guessing you at least got some hot good-bye sex before John left."

Jessica shook her head at that. "Unfortunately, no. I'd been in South Carolina for an undercover assignment, and there were bad storms the night I was supposed to fly back to Chicago. I got stranded there."

"Ugh. That sucks. Did the airline at least put you up at a hotel for the night?"

"Actually, I didn't spend the night in South Carolina. I rented a car and drove home."

Tara blinked. "You drove from South Carolina? What'd that take you? Fourteen hours?"

"Twelve hours and twelve minutes," Jessica said proudly. If nothing else, she had, at least, made very good time that day.

"Twelve hours and twelve minutes. In a rainstorm," Tara said.

"Technically the rainstorms cleared up by Tennessee. But yes."

Tara looked her in the eyes. "All so that you could see John."

The bluntness of the comment caught Jessica momentarily off guard. But then she scoffed. "I mean . . . I just wanted to get home. I suppose, in part, that was to see him. We are friends, you know." She took a sip of her wine, going for casual.

"Hmm. Right."

Seeing Tara's mouth quirk upward, Jessica sighed. "Do not make a big deal out of this."

"Oh, honey, we are *so* past the no-big-deal phase. That ended the moment you said you drove halfway across the country, overnight, just to say good-bye to the man."

"I had a gift for him—a very nice bottle of bourbon. I didn't want to see it go to waste." When she saw that this only made Tara's smile widen—yeah, fine, even she couldn't sell that one— she regrouped and went for a more pragmatic approach. "Look, maybe it meant something. But it doesn't have to mean *everything.* John's in Virginia. I'm here. It is what it is." She looked at Tara pointedly. "And before you say whatever it is I can see you're dying to say, keep in mind that it's not like he's been blowing up *my* phone these last two weeks. I haven't heard from him once since he left."

"Maybe he's been pining away and avoiding the situation the same way you are."

A sudden ember of hope flared inside Jessica. Staying rational, she quickly stamped it out. "I'm not pining."

"Does John know you drove from South Carolina to see him?"

Jessica shook her head. "We didn't have a lot of time the morning we said good-bye. And I felt weird telling him, anyway."

Tara cocked her head, her expression curious.

Jessica frowned. "What?"

"Hypothetically speaking," Tara led in.

Jessica groaned. "Oh crap, not this again."

Tara ignored her. "Is there any way around the transfer rule with the FBI? Any exceptions, say, for badass undercover agents with top-notch records?"

"You're not seriously asking me this with respect to a guy that I slept with for *two weeks*, are you?"

"South Carolina, Jess. What's that, like, seven states you had to drive through?"

"Six. Three of which are very skinny," she shot back.

"Besides, you've known John a lot longer than two weeks. So, come on. Are there any exceptions to the FBI transfer rule?" Tara pressed.

"No. Two years is the minimum before I could even try begging for another transfer."

"Oh." Tara's shoulders slumped. "Damn."

A silence stretched between them, and Jessica knew she should simply let the conversation die there. Really, she should.

But something compelled her to keep going.

"However, the D.C. office is generally considered the easiest field office to get to as a special agent. It's filled with people who want to climb the ladder instead of doing the actual work. So while I couldn't officially transfer there, at least not for two years, I might—*might*—be able to get a TDY. Hypothetically speaking," she was quick to add.

"What's a TDY?" Tara asked.

"Temporary duty."

"I see." The gleam had returned to Tara's eyes. "And . . . D.C. is close to Quantico, isn't it?"

"About twenty-five miles away."

Tara's gleam grew into a full-fledged grin. "So there *is* an option, if you and John wanted to make a go of it."

Jessica held out her hands, incredulous that they were even having this conversation. "I mean . . . technically, yes. But it's not a *good* option. First of all, I wouldn't even request the TDY until I'd been in Chicago for at least a year. I can't keep asking to move around. That would mark me as trouble."

"All right, so we've got some office politics to work through. But still, now we're looking at only a one-year separation between you and John, instead of two or three."

"A year *minimum*, and one in which he and I would hardly ever get a chance to talk, let alone see each other. He'll be going through months of intense training at Quantico, and then they'll be sending him to specialty schools all over the country." Jessica pointed to herself. "And I don't exactly have a nine-to-five job, either. How are we supposed to build a relationship through all that? Hell, I couldn't make my marriage work with a schedule that wasn't half so chaotic."

"It wouldn't be easy," Tara agreed.

Jessica kept going, barely hearing her at this point. "And all of this is based on the assumption that I'd be willing to move to D.C. That I'd be willing to leave *my* home, even though I like being back and close to my family and to you. And despite the fact that my career is on a great track here in Chicago."

"That would be a lot to give up. Any guy worth all that would have to be very special."

Jessica looked her friend over. "Why are you so in favor of this? *You* were the one encouraging me to have fun with a Mr. Wrong who I would shamelessly use for dirty, no-strings-attached rebound sex."

"I'm not in *favor* of this. Heck, I don't want you to move to D.C." Tara sighed. "I don't know, maybe you've caught me in a funny mood here, after encountering yet another jerk on Tinder this morning. But as someone with a lot of experience with what's out there, I can tell you that finding somebody who makes you happy, and gets you, and respects you, is a special thing. And I guess I'd like to think that when two people feel that way about each other, somehow, some way, they can find a way to make it work."

Jessica said nothing at first, then shifted uncomfortably in her seat. "Christ, you get one dick pic and suddenly you're as sappy as a Hallmark movie."

Tara laughed. "So ignore me. We're speaking hypothetically, anyway, right?"

"Yes." The word sounded a little uncertain, so Jessica said it again more convincingly. "Yes."

Monday morning, Jessica arrived at the FBI office bright and early. She'd been feeling a little off all weekend, ever since her conversation with Tara, so she was eager to get back to the familiar routine of work.

The office was relatively quiet; most of the agents on her squad weren't in yet. She returned a few e-mails as she sipped her coffee, and then, as she had every morning for the last two weeks, she unlocked the top drawer of her desk, where she kept Ashley's cell phone—the burner she'd used while working undercover in the Jacksonville investigation.

Leavitt had e-mailed her last Thursday to let her know that the U.S. Attorney's Office had taken the Blair case to the grand jury, and that the mayor, as well as the eight developers who'd bribed him, had all been indicted. Leavitt expected they would be making their arrests imminently, as soon as they finalized the logistics. Because the plan was to arrest Blair and the eight developers all at the same time, it would be a coordinated effort by the Jacksonville field office, involving forty-five special agents grouped into five-person arrest teams.

She opened the desk drawer and turned on the phone, expecting to find the same thing she'd found every morning for the last two weeks: nothing. But this time, she saw that she'd missed one call and had a new voice-mail message.

From Blair's private cell phone.

Jessica listened to the message and played it back a second

time. Then she grabbed her own phone and called the Jacksonville field office.

"Are you sitting down?" she asked, when Leavitt answered.

"Yes . . . why?" he asked.

"I think you might want to hold off on Blair's arrest."

32

The following day, over seven hundred miles away, John and his six classmates lined up along the bank of the James River, just a few miles south of the Chesapeake Bay.

Standing in front of them while giving out instructions, per usual, was Tom Watts, their NOTS coordinator. In his clipped, brash tone, he told them that anyone who didn't want to partake in this particular activity was free to stay on the riverbank.

John exchanged a subtle glance with the guy standing next to him, Tony Rivera, a special agent from Nevada. Whether the activity was phrased as an option or not, he and his classmates knew this was another test. The James River jump was an annual NOTS tradition, an initiation ritual for all HRT operators.

No new recruit would ever lose the respect of his teammates by sitting this one out.

The task, as explained by Watts, was straightforward enough: climb sixty feet up a caving ladder to the gunwale of an old freighter docked in the river, wait for his signal, and jump.

"Keep your toes pointed down and your body straight and tight. Land wrong, and it'll be like hitting a brick wall at forty-five miles per hour. That won't be pretty." Watts nodded in Tony's direction. "Rivera, you're up first. Shepherd, on deck."

There was some good-natured taunting and trash-talking as the group made its way toward the freighter. Per tradition, they would be scored on their jump, so they were all pumped on a mix of competitiveness and adrenaline.

The rest of John's classmates came from around the country, with a variety of pre-FBI backgrounds: a civil engineer, a surveillance specialist, a Marine sergeant, an ICE agent, a cop, and an Air Force pilot. They were a solid group, each of them confident, athletic, and highly capable. So far, the seven of them got along well—which was a good thing, seeing how they spent sixteen hours a day together.

Their mornings began sharply at five A.M., with Watts leading them through a routine of agility drills, long-distance runs, high-intensity interval training, and close-quarter-battle sessions. Afternoons typically were spent on the shooting range, for combat firearms training, and then there were lectures in the evenings, after dinner. Intermixed with that over the course of the next eight months would be several types of specialty training: explosives breaching, knot tying, fast-roping and rappelling, fire training at the "hot house," high-speed evasive driving, and dignitary protection.

Every day, John and his classmates were tested. Their instructors pushed them to their limits and beyond, demanding that they move faster, run farther, hang on longer, shoot better, and trust themselves to take more risks. The days weren't easy, not by a long shot, but there was no complaining in NOTS. Every recruit had volunteered for the job, and, as they were frequently reminded, if they didn't like it, they were free to leave. These were life-and-death stakes they were preparing for, and nothing less than complete dedication to the team was acceptable.

And so John gave them exactly that.

As he had with Selection and as a Ranger, he threw himself

into every task, drill, and challenge. For those sixteen hours each day, he pushed himself physically and mentally, to the point of exhaustion. And he felt it, too. Every night, when he got back to the corporate housing apartment he'd temporarily rented and climbed into bed, his body was aching, bruised, and begging for sleep. By all rights, he should've passed out cold and been dead to the world for hours. But instead, he found himself lying awake in the dark, feeling restless and edgy.

So the next morning, he'd start again and push himself even harder.

John's mind snapped back to the present as Rivera hit the water with a splash. He and his classmates cheered from the shore when Rivera's head popped up in the water a few seconds later. A handful of HRT divers, hanging out on the river in a Zodiac boat with Watts, shouted out Rivera's scores.

And then John was up.

He scaled the caving ladder, climbing up to the cargo ship's gunwale. Heights had never bothered him, so when he got to the top he checked out the view while adjusting the strap of his helmet. The James River stretched out for miles, its shores lined thick with trees just beginning to show off their fall colors. Up here, he couldn't hear his classmates bantering on the shore, nor Watts and the diving team in the Zodiac—everything was quiet and still.

It was quite peaceful, actually.

Perched on the edge of the gunwale while waiting for Watts's signal, John took a moment to soak it all in. Six years ago, he'd come to Quantico with the goal of ending up right here, in this very spot. The men floating in that Zodiac, his classmates on the shore, and the rest of the operators back at the HRT compound were among the best of the best, part of a team—a brotherhood—that had judged him during Selection and decided that he was worthy of being included in their ranks.

He inhaled deeply, waiting to feel a sense of fulfillment.

But instead, as he stood there, sixty feet above the water, his brother's voice popped into his head.

If Jessica had been looking for something more serious, you would've had to leave for Quantico knowing that you might've actually had a chance with her.

"Fuck," John muttered.

Steeling himself when he saw Watts's signal, he looked ahead at the horizon and jumped.

Back at the HRT compound, in the locker room, the new recruits' spirits were high after the river jump. While getting dressed, John joked around with his classmates and joined in the smack-talk about everyone's scores. His undercover skills came in handy right then—to everyone else, he appeared as cool and relaxed as ever.

But on the inside, he was pissed off and giving himself one hell of a lecture.

He wasn't entirely sure what direction his mind had been heading in up on that gunwale ledge, but he *did* know that this wasn't the time or place to be distracted. After lunch, he and his classmates would be loading into a UH-60 Blackhawk helo for a rappelling exercise, and he needed to be crisp and sharp for that.

Whatever was—or more accurately, was not—going on in his personal life would have to wait. When he was here, at Quantico, the team came first. Period.

After pulling on his shirt, he grabbed his phone off the locker shelf and reflexively checked it before sticking it into the pocket of his pants.

Unexpectedly, he had a new message from Leavitt.

"You coming?" Rivera asked, on his way out of the locker room with the rest of the guys for lunch.

"I'll be right there." Not looking up from his phone, John

quickly skimmed Leavitt's message. Apparently, there'd been some kind of development in the Blair investigation, and the Jax agent wanted to know if John would be free any time that day for a conference call with him, Agent Todd, and the two Assistant U.S. Attorneys who would be leading the prosecution of the mayor and the developers who'd bribed him.

Jessica, too, would be on the call.

The locker room quiet now, John took a seat on the bench and read through the e-mail a second time, trying to glean any further information about whatever the heck was going on in the investigation. He'd gotten an e-mail from Leavitt last week, letting him know that the grand jury had indicted Blair and the developers, so he'd assumed the next time he would hear about the case would be on CNN, after word got out that the mayor of Jacksonville and eight prominent local businessmen had been arrested in a corruption and bribery scandal.

But now, apparently, there was a "development."

He briefly considered texting Jessica. What's the deal with this call? he could ask her, casually. But then, almost certainly, she'd ask him how HRT was going, and then there'd be some back-and-forth, and she would probably say something saucy and funny that would remind him of all the moments he'd spent the last two weeks busting his ass to *not* remember.

It was better to maintain some distance, he reminded himself.

That decided, he hit "reply all" to the e-mail, keeping his response short and sweet.

How about 6pm EDT?

During the dinner break before the evening lecture, John made his way to the HRT classroom, which was currently deserted. Cell phone in hand, he took a seat in one of the chairs and pulled up the e-mail Leavitt had sent everyone with the phone number for the conference call.

After he dialed in, a *beep* on the other end of the line prompted him to identify himself. He stated his name and was patched through to the others.

Leavitt immediately welcomed him. "John! Glad you could join us. How's NOTS treating you?"

"Not too bad. But ask me that again once we start fire training," John joked. He caught himself listening for Jessica's voice among the subsequent chuckles.

Huh. Maybe she hadn't dialed in yet.

"Well, we all appreciate you calling in tonight on such short notice," Leavitt said. "I'm sure they're keeping you busy up there at Quantico, so I'll try to move this along as quickly as possible. Agent Todd is here, too, and Mark Duffy and Kristin Loeffler are joining us from the U.S. Attorney's office—as I mentioned in my e-mail, they'll be leading the prosecution team. Unfortunately, Jessica had a last-minute conflict and won't be calling in. Something about a change in the trial schedule for one of her old cases, and she had to catch a flight out to Los Angeles."

Oh. Well, that was . . . probably for the best. John had wanted distance, and that's exactly what he'd gotten. "Sorry to hear she won't be joining us," he said, before exchanging hellos and small-talk with the two AUSAs.

Then Leavitt got down to business. "So, John, we should bring you up to speed on a couple of things. You already know that last week, the grand jury returned indictments against Mayor Blair and all eight developers. Our plan had been to arrest the nine of them this week. In fact, we'd just about finalized the details for that, when Jessica called me yesterday morning to let me know that Blair had contacted *her* over the weekend.

"From the sound of things, he's decided that Ashley and

Dave are a couple of cash cows. And now he's looking for another score. This time, he has his sights set on that second restaurant you guys told him about—the farm-to-table neighborhood bistro with a rotating special of gourmet scrambled eggs."

"I still say somebody needs to actually open that restaurant," Todd chimed in, getting a laugh out of everyone.

"In the message he left Jessica over the weekend, Blair said he knows of a location that would be perfect for the bistro: an abandoned building in the San Marco historic district," Leavitt said. "When Jessica returned the mayor's call and expressed interest in hearing more about the property, Blair told her that she could get it for a steal. And he's right—we looked up the address he gave her and the building is indeed listed below market."

John highly doubted Blair had brought this to Ashley's attention out of the kindness of his heart. "What's the catch?"

"The catch," Leavitt answered, a hint of excitement creeping into his voice, "is that in order for the building to be used as a restaurant, it would have to be rezoned by the city's Land Use Committee."

Ah. "Let me guess: and Blair would be willing to help facilitate the rezoning of the property. For a fee, of course," John said.

"He didn't expressly state that on the phone, but that was certainly the implication," Leavitt said. "He made a reference to the pizzeria and wine bar, and said he saw no reason why the zoning issues related to this second property couldn't be resolved just as easily."

Mark, one of the AUSAs, jumped in. "This is new for Blair. Assuming he's going where we think he's going with this, it's the first time he's ever *initiated* his own bribe. In the past, Morano had always arranged the deals. In a corruption case like this, we have to assume that Blair's attorneys might argue some sort of entrapment defense. I don't believe it would be a successful defense, but Kristin and I aren't taking anything for granted. Blair is a very popular mayor—if even one juror buys into some cockamamie theory that the FBI set him up, and that he was enticed into taking the bribes, we'd have a problem."

Kristin, the other AUSA, picked up there. "But if we have proof of Blair actually soliciting his own bribe, that essentially puts the nail in the coffin on any entrapment defense. Given how valuable that kind of evidence would be, Mark and I—along with Agents Leavitt and Todd—feel it's worth reopening the investigation. We discussed this with Agent Harlow yesterday, and she'll be going back in undercover to meet with Blair."

John went still. "When?"

"She's flying down to have lunch with him this Saturday," Leavitt said. "And Blair also suggested that, afterward, the two of them take a drive to the San Marco property so she could check it out."

I'm sure he did, John thought dryly.

"Obviously, we're all excited about this development," Mark said. "It's a credit to the work you and Agent Harlow have done on this case. If you hadn't earned Blair's trust in such a relatively short amount of time, we wouldn't be fortunate enough to be in this position." He cleared his throat. "There is one slight issue, however. While reviewing the audio recordings of your meetings with Blair, Kristin and I noticed that the mayor has been . . . making overtures of a personal nature to Agent Harlow."

"That's lawyer-speak for 'flirting,'" Kristin joked. "We know that the four of you discussed how to handle that situation, and we agree with the call you made. One potential concern, however, is that in a one-on-one scenario, Blair might take the flirting up a notch. Or several notches. That could put Agent Harlow in an awkward situation."

John opened his mouth to say that they could put Agent

Harlow in *any* situation and she still would do what needed to be done, but Mark the AUSA beat him to the punch.

"We have every confidence in Agent Harlow's ability to manage such a situation," he said. "But I think we all can agree that the best-case scenario would be to *not* put her in that position in the first place." He paused meaningfully. "As in the past, if someone else were at that meeting with her and Blair, it would force Blair to remain more business-focused."

"We can't bring in another agent at this point," Kristin said. "That would make Blair suspicious. And we can't use Morano, either—the mayor has deliberately cut him out of the loop. So, if there was going to be another person at Saturday's meeting, it would have to be you, Agent Shepherd."

There was a pause then, as everyone waited for John's response.

He said nothing for a moment. Technically, he didn't have a direct conflict with the meeting—even NOTheads got occasional weekends off, and as it happened, the only plans he had for Saturday were to go house-hunting. But regardless, this was a big ask on the part of Leavitt and the U.S. Attorney's Office, and they knew that. John was an operator now, and his responsibilities and dedication lay with the Hostage Rescue Team. Undercover work, Jessica, and the Blair investigation were all in his past, part of a life that he'd left behind.

As if reading his mind, Leavitt spoke. "We realize that this is asking a lot with you being at NOTS. If you can't do it, John, we understand. In fact, Jessica made me promise to pass along a message to you: She said that she can handle Blair on her own if need be, and that she knows a good leg move that'll keep him in line. I'm guessing that's some sort of inside joke."

Something inside John softened, and he smiled despite himself. "Yes."

And in that moment, he knew what he needed to do.

He might not have been a special agent anymore, and, yes,

he had a new life at Quantico now. But he and Jessica were partners in this. They had started this undercover assignment together, and now, with this one last meeting with Blair, they would finish it.

That decided, he gave Leavitt and the others his answer. "I'll book my flight tonight."

33

Sitting alone at a table near the back of Alexander's Grill, a crowded surf-and-turf restaurant in Jacksonville Beach, Jessica took a slow, quiet breath to calm her nerves.

The mayor would arrive any moment, although that wasn't the reason she had butterflies in her stomach. She knew how to handle Patrick Blair and understood exactly what she needed to get out of him during today's meeting. They would have a nice lunch with lots of schmoozing, a little shop talk, and, knowing Blair, some not-so-veiled flirting on his end. Following lunch, they'd drive out to the property the mayor had found for Ashley and Dave's second restaurant, where—after examining the building—they would agree that it was, indeed, the perfect spot for their farm-to-table brunch bistro with a rotating special of gourmet scrambled eggs.

Jessica doubted it would take much prompting to get Blair to spell out the terms of his bribe. In addition to his general propensity for bragging about his ability to get things done in "his" city, he was greedier now, and bolder, and believed he'd found an opportunity to score another quick fifty thousand in cash. He would be chomping at the bit to get the ball rolling on that front—of that, Jessica had no doubt.

What she was less certain of, however, was the thought of seeing John again.

When Leavitt and Todd had informed her, earlier in the week, that the U.S. Attorney's Office wanted to reopen the Blair investigation—and that they also wanted to ask John if he, too, could go back in undercover—she'd answered, as she should, like any other special agent in those circumstances.

"If John can make it work with his NOTS schedule, he's more than welcome to join the party," she'd said breezily.

Frankly, she'd never thought he'd say yes. She'd assumed he'd be far too busy at Quantico with the other HRT guys, scaling burning buildings with their pinky toes, playing with their flash-bang grenades, and running around with their helmets with the little bushes on their heads. And to let John know that there were no hard feelings, that she understood and respected that he had other commitments, she'd even passed along an inside joke via Leavitt.

But now, here they were, working side-by-side once again.

Or at least, they would be as soon as John actually showed up.

They'd had to roll with one minor glitch this morning: John's flight out of Virginia had been delayed, and as a result he would be about ten minutes late to the meeting with Blair. She'd been midflight when John had found out that *his* flight would be late, and then *he* had been in the air after she'd landed, but through a series of e-mails with Leavitt and Todd they'd worked up a cover story to explain why Dave and Ashley hadn't flown in from Chicago together.

Professionally, the delay wasn't a big deal; Jessica could chat up Blair until John arrived. But on a personal note, it meant that she wouldn't have any time to be alone with John before lunch, to get a read on him before they slipped into their Ashley and Dave personas.

Although what she'd been hoping for if she'd *had* the

chance to get a read on John was a question she wasn't sure she was ready to face.

The easiest scenario, obviously, would be if she saw John and felt something along the lines of, say . . . warm fondness. That had always been the plan, for the two of them to part as friends. After wrapping things up with Blair, they could grab a drink before catching their respective flights back home and jokingly toast to being really, *really* done with the investigation. He'd tell her about HRT, she'd tease him about being a hotshot operator, and then they'd hug—perhaps a moment longer than necessary, just because—and go their separate ways once again.

Her inner pragmatic was a big fan of the easiest scenario. In fact, she'd been praying for it all week.

But something deeper inside Jessica, a voice she'd been trying to shush since the morning she'd said good-bye to John, kept asking what her plan was if she saw him and felt, say . . . *more* than warm fondness.

The simple, scary truth of the matter was, she had no damn clue.

And the other simple truth was, she needed to momentarily table that and all other scary truths and what-if scenarios.

Because it was showtime.

The Honorable Patrick Blair walked through the front door of the restaurant, accompanied by the two police officers from the sheriff's office who were his personal detail. As the two officers settled in at the bar up front, Blair did his usual politician thing: smiling, waving, and stopping to shake hands with some of the restaurant patrons as he followed the hostess to Jessica's table.

When he got there, Jessica stood up to greet him. "Mr. Mayor," she said warmly, extending her hand.

He wrapped his hand around hers and stepped closer. "I thought we agreed you would drop the title."

332 · *julie james*

"But you wear it so well."

He grinned—not disagreeing with that—and took a seat in the chair across the table from her. Then he cocked his head, eyeing the two empty chairs next to them.

"Just you today?" There was a sudden gleam in his eyes.

"Dave's coming, he's just running a little late. He's flying in from Detroit, and his plane was delayed."

"Oh." Blair frowned. "What's he doing in Detroit?"

They'd chosen Detroit because it was a city John was familiar with, in case Blair asked him any questions about the trip. "He's scouting out potential restaurant sites."

Blair spread his napkin over his lap, sounding a touch haughty. "I wasn't aware Detroit had much of a culinary scene."

Neither was I, until an hour ago. As soon as they'd come up with their cover story, Jessica had done some quick research into the Detroit market. She'd e-mailed the information along to John, as well, so that they were on the same page. "Actually, it's really exploded in the last couple years. *Zagat* puts Detroit at number three in 'America's Next Hot Food Cities.' And the *Washington Post* just did this interesting piece about how the city is in the middle of a 'culinary revolution.' Apparently, statewide restaurant sales are expected to increase by 5.2 percent this year." She feigned a self-deprecating smile. "And that's probably more than you ever wanted to know about the Detroit culinary scene."

"Probably. But still, it's interesting to hear you talk about these things." Blair rested his forearms on the table, looking her over. "You're very good at what you do."

Buddy, you don't know the half of it. "I'm fortunate to have a job that I enjoy."

They were briefly interrupted when the waitress stopped by the table to take the mayor's drink order. After she left, Blair sat back and casually draped one arm over the back of the empty chair next to him.

He made no attempt to hide his appreciative gaze. Jessica had chosen to wear a slim-cut navy dress and heels, even though it was a weekend, because Ashley didn't strike her as the kind of woman who would wear anything less to a business meeting.

"Speaking of your job . . . what's happening with your pizzeria and wine bar?" Blair asked. "I drove by the building the other day and noticed you haven't started construction yet."

"We had to tweak the plans based on some recommendations from our general contractor. But we're hoping to get started next week," she lied.

"I would imagine you'll be in town more often once that gets started."

Jessica had a sneaking suspicion that comment was not as casual as it sounded. "Dave handles most of the day-to-day stuff, but I'll probably fly in a few times a month to help oversee the project."

"I'm glad to hear it." Blair's eyes held hers. "You'll have to let me show you around town sometime."

"You certainly would make a qualified tour guide." She used Blair's comment to buy some time until John arrived. "Here's a hypothetical question for you, Mr. Mayor. Let's say I'm a tourist in Jacksonville for a weekend. What things should be on my must-see list?"

As she'd suspected, Blair spent the next several minutes talking about his favorite things to do: going to the beach, kayaking along the St. Johns River, eating snake and alligator at Clark's Fish Camp, driving in a convertible along A1A from Jax Beach to St. Augustine, horseback riding on Amelia Island, and drinking craft cocktails in the speakeasy room of the Grape & Grain Exchange.

Apparently, they made a mean vodka/blueberry black tea drink.

Jessica nodded along attentively, thinking that, for all his faults, the mayor did love his city. It was a shame, really, that he'd strayed so widely from the straight and narrow path. When he wasn't renting out the power of his office for fifty thousand dollars, or making not-so-subtle innuendos and ogling women's chests, he had a natural charisma that probably would have taken him far in politics.

"Do you play golf?" Blair asked her.

"Not as well as I'd like," Jessica said.

Right then, John walked through the front door of the restaurant.

Seeing him for the first time in three weeks, Jessica immediately noticed something that made her want to smile.

He'd cut his hair.

Looking as handsome as ever in his gray suit and light blue shirt, John glanced around the restaurant and spotted her. His eyes met hers as he crossed the room, and for a split second, Jessica could've sworn they'd traveled back in time. Between the short haircut, his clean-shaven jaw, and the suit, he looked almost exactly the same as he had six years ago, that first day they'd met at the Academy.

Chicago, huh? We should team up, Harlow. I say we take down the three trainees from New York first.

Swallowing, Jessica stayed in character. "Ah, good. Dave's here."

Just before he arrived at the table, John gave Jessica a slight, private smile.

Let's do this, his look said.

It was exactly what she needed to see. Given their history, it was more than a little weird reuniting with John here, under these circumstances, without having spoken to him once in the last three weeks. There were so many things she wanted to ask him—how he was doing, and if NOTS was going well—and more than anything, she wished she could tell him how good it was to see him again. *God*, it really was.

But.

There were things happening in that restaurant that went way beyond her and John. They had a lot of people counting on them to do their jobs right then, so that was precisely what they would do.

"Look who finally made it," she said to John, with an easy smile.

"The joys of airline travel," he said. An inside joke—the same thing she'd said to him the morning after she'd been stranded in Columbia. Then he turned to Blair with a charismatic grin. "Mr. Mayor. My apologies for being late." After shaking Blair's hand, he took the seat next to Jessica.

Blair looked John over. "New haircut, huh? You look like you just stepped off the Navy base."

Thinking it was best to steer away from that analogy, Jessica was quick to change the subject. "How was Detroit?" she asked John.

"Promising. I can fill you in more during the flight back to Chicago," he said.

The waitress came by the table to take John's drink order, and for a while, the conversation at the table remained social. Blair continued to flirt with Jessica, but with John present the comments never got *too* forward, which left her free to do her thing and schmooze and pretend to be impressed and entertained as Blair told one personal anecdote after the other.

After their entrées arrived, however, Jessica steered the conversation toward business. As much as Ashley might have enjoyed hearing Blair talk about his golf game—or at least, she let him think that—she and Dave hadn't flown all the way down to Jacksonville just to shoot the shit over some steaks.

"Tell us more about this building we're going to see after lunch," she prompted Blair.

"It's in the San Marco historic district. Used to be a Laundromat and dry cleaner, but it's been vacant for five years now.

Great price," Blair added. "A couple of savvy entrepreneurs could snatch it up and really make something of the place."

"What's the neighborhood like?" John wanted to know.

"Generally, it's a mix of residential, office, and commercial space, but that particular corridor is almost entirely commercial. Boutique clothing shops, art galleries, that kind of thing." Blair took a sip of his dry vodka martini. "You'll see for yourself. It's a nice spot."

"Why has it been sitting empty for five years?" Jessica asked.

"As I mentioned on the phone, there are some zoning restrictions that probably have scared away potential buyers."

"Define 'some,'" John said.

Blair leaned in, appearing more than happy to do so. He spoke in a low voice, although the restaurant was crowded and noisy enough that no one could hear them anyway. "So here's the deal: The building is currently zoned as a CRO—Commercial Residential Office. To use the building as a restaurant, however, you'd need to get approval from the Land Use Committee to change the zoning to a PUD—that's a Planned Unit Development—that would allow you to serve alcohol and seat up to a hundred and fifty customers."

Jessica raised an eyebrow. "How difficult would that be?"

"Not difficult at all. If you know the right people." Letting that sink in, Blair looked at them both. "You know I can make this happen."

"For a price," John noted.

Blair smiled, all charm. "Well, I am a busy man, Dave. As I told y'all before, I can't help everyone who asks me for a favor. I have to choose those causes I feel most motivated about."

"You'd use this friend of yours on the Land Use Committee again? This Paul Ryu?" Jessica said.

"Yes. And again, he's not just *on* the committee. He's the director."

"That's my one concern," John said. "That Ryu gets suspicious and wants to know why you're now supporting a *second* zoning change on our company's behalf."

Blair shrugged unconcernedly. "So I'll tell him the truth."

"The truth would put us all in prison, Mr. Mayor," John said dryly.

"The *truth*, at least as far as Paul needs to be concerned, is that the building we're talking about hasn't had a tenant for the last five years. You have this beautiful neighborhood, with an empty building that sticks out like a sore thumb. Of course I'd support putting the property into reuse. Paul isn't going to ask questions beyond that."

Jessica paused, as if considering that. "All right, let's say we're interested. How much would it cost to get you motivated to help us out?"

"I'm not trying to gouge you," Blair snorted. He met her gaze. "Fifty thousand. Same as last time. And the deal stays between us—Morano never needs to know about any of this."

And there you have it, folks.

In her head, Jessica pictured Leavitt and Todd sitting in their car parked a few blocks away, high-fiving each other as they listened in via the microphone she had stashed in her bra. The Jax agents and the U.S. Attorney's Office had wanted evidence of Blair soliciting his own bribe, and now they had just that.

She looked at John. "What do you think?"

He took a moment. "If the building meets our needs, I think it could be too good a deal to pass up."

She turned, giving her answer to Blair. "I agree."

Blair grinned. "Good. We'll drive by the place after lunch. I don't think you'll be disappointed." He picked up his steak knife and dove into his filet.

Thinking she'd earned a sip of wine for a job well done—

hell, she'd earned more than that—Jessica reached for her glass. John picked up his drink, too, and Jessica mentally clinked her glass to his.

Cheers, partner.

And just when all was right with the world, the unimaginable happened.

"John Shepherd!" boomed a voice.

Heading straight for their table, with a huge grin on his face, was a guy in his midthirties. Wearing jeans and a T-shirt and an obvious look of recognition, he threw out his hands excitedly.

"Dude, what are you doing here?" he said to John. "Last I heard, you were working for the FBI up in Chicago."

Oh shit.

It was every undercover agent's worst nightmare: being recognized while on the job and instantly having one's cover blown. For that reason, Jessica always told her family and friends to never approach her if they ever randomly spotted her out in public.

But this kind of fluke happenstance was nothing any agent could prepare for.

To John's credit—even though he undoubtedly was sweating bullets right then—he handled the situation as best he could.

He calmly set his drink on the table. "Um . . . I think you've mistaken me for somebody else."

The guy laughed this off. "That's funny, Shep." He then noticed who else was sitting at the table. "You're hanging with the mayor? *Nice.*" He turned to Blair, gesturing to John. "We were in the 75th Ranger Regiment when the FBI came to recruit him. They told Shep he could put bad guys in prison for the rest of his life, and he couldn't sign up fast enough."

Oh my God, it just kept getting worse.

Jessica jumped in, needing to do *something*. "You have an FBI twin? How exciting," she teased John.

"Apparently," he said, his expression a mixture of bewilderment and amusement. "Sorry, but you really do have the wrong guy," he told his Ranger friend.

The other guy opened his mouth but then paused. "Oh." His face went pale, as if he'd just clued in to what was happening and how much he'd messed that up. "Sorry about that. You look a lot like him. But . . . yeah, my mistake." Shifting nervously, he gave them an apologetic wave. "Sorry for the interruption."

He turned and walked toward the front of the restaurant. Jessica didn't want to stare, so she glanced at John instead and remained in character. "Well, that was odd."

"I think somebody had a few too many drinks for lunch," John said.

It was the best they could do under the circumstances.

But Blair was no fool.

"FBI?" He spat out the letters, looking at both of them. Then his gaze settled on Jessica.

"You whore," he sneered.

"Watch it, Blair," John growled.

The mayor ignored him, continuing to focus on Jessica. "How the fuck is that possible? The guy who vouched for you has known Morano for years. They went to college together and he said—" He stopped, and a sudden look of realization crossed his face. "There never was any friend from college, was there? Morano is in on it, too."

Jessica kept one eye on Blair's hand and the other on his face as he leaned in toward her.

"That son of a bitch. Did he cut a deal with you to sell me out?" Blair demanded angrily.

"Put the knife down, Mr. Mayor," John said in a low voice.

Blair blinked and looked down at his hand, as if unaware that he'd been holding his steak knife and jabbing emphatically with it this whole time.

He stared at the knife for a moment, then looked back up at John.

John didn't so much as blink. "You'll lose."

Blair swallowed, then set the knife down on the table in front of him. He sat frozen in his chair for several seconds, then cocked his head as if something else had just occurred to him. "You're not armed. Neither of you." He looked at Jessica and John, as if waiting for them to acknowledge this. "You can't keep me here. I can leave this restaurant right now."

"Yes, you can." Jessica's tone was calm. She could see the cornered look creeping into Blair's eyes and wanted to de-escalate the situation. "You're free to walk out, Mr. Mayor."

The truth was, she and John were in no position to stop Blair from leaving. They were unarmed and had no handcuffs and no FBI credentials. On top of all that, this wasn't their case. Agents Leavitt and Todd were calling the shots, and they could hear what was going on through the microphone Jessica wore. Undoubtedly, now that John and Jessica's cover was blown, they were already on the move and had called in backup.

Blair locked eyes with Jessica. "And what happens after I walk out of this restaurant?"

Jessica remained silent, as did John, neither of them having an answer that would help.

"What? Are you going to *arrest* me? I'm the mayor of this city. I can't—" Looking shell-shocked, Blair stumbled over his words. "I was just . . . doing a few favors for some people. Everything I've done, all the deals I've made—that was part of my job. It's all been for the good of this city. Nobody gives a shit about these zoning restrictions, anyway." He scoffed. "Jesus Christ, with everything going on in this country, the FBI doesn't have anything better to investigate?"

As he reached for his glass, his hand trembled, belying the bravado in his voice. He took a sip of his drink, then stared them down. "I'm not going to prison." He waited, then slammed his hand on the table. "Say something, dammit."

Out of the corner of her eye, Jessica saw people looking over curiously.

"You don't want to do this here, Mr. Mayor," John said.

"Here's what we're going to do: Dave and I will stay and settle up the bill, and you'll get up and walk out," Jessica said.

"Just like that?" Blair said.

"Just like that," she answered.

He said nothing at first, looking her over. "You're wearing a wire, aren't you?" He swallowed, panic sweeping across his face. "I know what you're doing. You're signaling them. The rest of your FBI team. Telling them where to get me." His lips curled in a sneer. "Fuck you. Fuck you all. I told you, I'm not going to prison."

He stood up abruptly.

Reflexively, Jessica and John stood up, too.

She had a very bad feeling about this. "You still have choices here, Patrick. Don't do anything you're going to regret."

For a split second, a shadow crossed Blair's face. "I'm afraid it's too late for that, Ms. Evers."

Then, without warning, he pointed at Jessica and John and shouted at the top of his lungs. "They've got guns! They're going to shoot! Everybody run, get out of here now!"

Oh crap.

This was something Jessica had *not* been prepared for.

The panicked words—coming from the city's beloved mayor—caused the entire restaurant to erupt in pandemonium. People jumped up from their tables, screamed, grabbed their children, and ran for the door. Glasses and plates broke as tables were bumped in the fray. A chair tipped over, hitting the floor with a loud *crack* that sounded enough like a gunshot to elicit more cries.

"That son of a bitch," John growled, as Blair seized upon the distraction and pushed people out of his way. He hurried for the back of the restaurant, presumably in search of an escape route.

"He's heading out back," Jessica said to the microphone, for the benefit of Leavitt and Todd.

"Cops," John warned her.

Barreling through the crowd, heading straight toward them, were the two police officers assigned to protect the mayor.

Not taking any chances, Jessica and John immediately put their hands in the air.

"We're FBI. We're unarmed," Jessica shouted, and John did the same.

Unfortunately, their words were drowned out in the commotion. They each took a step back from the table, so that the police officers could see that they had no weapons on them.

The cops broke through the crowd, drew their guns, and pointed them at John and Jessica.

"Keep those hands up and get the fuck down *now*," one of them yelled.

John shifted a few inches closer to Jessica.

"We're FBI. We're not armed," he repeated. "We're going to get down on our knees."

And then everything happened in an instant.

Just as Jessica moved to comply with the cop's order, someone from behind—later, she would learn he was an off-duty security guard who'd been sitting at a nearby table—reached an arm around her throat and pulled her down to the ground. Startled, she let out a yelp.

John spun around.

"Stand down. She's FBI!" he shouted.

With John momentarily distracted, the two police officers didn't wait for a second chance.

Together, they lunged to restrain him, one cop grabbing for John's hands while the other shoved him down. All three men stumbled awkwardly, and as John fell—without the use of his hands to regain his balance—his head hit the edge of the table hard with a dull *thud*.

He slumped to the ground, motionless.

No.

Seeing him go down, Jessica struggled to break from the security guard's hold. "Let me go—get off me! We're undercover agents, goddammit!"

Apparently, her words sank in. The security guard let her go, saying something—an apology, maybe—that she barely heard. She scrambled up from the ground and hurried over to John. "Let me see him." Hovering over him, the cops made room for her as she knelt down at his side.

He still wasn't moving.

The older of the two cops was already on his radio, calling for an ambulance. ". . . we have a suspect down and request immediate—"

"We have a *federal agent* down," Jessica told him, then turned back to John.

Blood trickled down the side of his face, coming from a gash near his hairline. Bending, she put her cheek close to his mouth. "He's breathing."

Next to her, the younger cop—in his late twenties—looked shaken. "I heard you say that you were FBI, but with the mayor yelling about guns and shooting, I didn't want to take any chances." He pointed to John. "I just wanted to restrain him until we figured everything out. I didn't mean to hurt him."

The scene around them was beginning to quiet down, with several remaining restaurant patrons keeping a respectful distance back.

Jessica didn't want to move John in case he'd hurt his neck when he'd hit the table. Instead, she put her hand on his shoulder. "John."

He didn't respond.

She glanced at the cop who'd radioed for assistance. "How long before the ambulance gets here?"

"They're on their way," the cop said.

Jessica tried his name again. "John." She gently squeezed his shoulder this time.

Nothing.

Wake up, baby. Every second that passed felt like an eternity. What if he'd broken his neck? What if he never came to? What if she never again got a chance to talk to him, or tease him, or be annoyed by him, or hear him laugh, or—

He opened his eyes.

Thank God. Jessica smiled gently at him. "Hey, you. That was some hit you took."

He stared at her blankly.

Say something, she silently pleaded. *Anything.*

Then he blinked.

"How do I keep ending up on the ground in front of you in the stupidest ways possible?" he groaned, lifting his head up.

Tears sprang to Jessica's eyes as she choked back a sob of relief. "Just my dumb luck, I guess."

When he started to push himself off from the ground, she protested. "I really don't think you should move until—" And . . . he was doing it anyway.

All around them, people were clapping and cheering as John sat up and leaned against a chair. Jessica grabbed a napkin off the nearest table.

She moved closer to him and pressed the napkin against the gash on his forehead. "You're bleeding."

He winked. "Adds to the authenticity of the scene."

Seriously.

He grinned at her unamused look. "Give it time. That joke will be a lot funnier in a couple hours."

Jessica checked the cut on his forehead. "You might need stitches. How bad does your head hurt?"

"Not as bad as my pride," he said dryly. As she pressed the napkin to his skin once again, his expression turned cheekier. "Although it certainly helps having you—"

She cleared her throat pointedly, glancing at her chest. She still wore the microphone in her bra.

"—here to wipe the blood off," John finished chastely. He pushed himself off the ground and stood up, then held out his hand to her.

She tossed the napkin to the ground—apparently, they were done with the taking-care-of-the-man-who'd-just-been-knocked-*unconscious* portion of the day—and slid her hand into his. He helped her up.

"Any dizziness?" There was more she wished she could say right then, if (a) they hadn't been surrounded by a crowd of people, and (b) she hadn't had a microphone in her boobs that was transmitting her every word.

Not exactly a private moment.

"I'm okay. What happened to Blair?" John asked.

From behind them, a familiar voice answered that.

"He must've escaped out the back door." Wearing his FBI jacket, Leavitt stepped around a pile of broken glass and made his way over to them. "Todd has twenty agents and two SWAT teams looking for him. Blair won't get far."

"You should be with them, too," John said.

"What? And miss all the excitement here?" Leavitt reached out and clasped John's shoulder, his tone turning more serious. "You had us worried there, Shepherd. Hell, even Jessica sounded nervous. I didn't think that was possible."

John looked at Jessica.

She blushed and went for a joke. "On the upside, John got to catch up with one of his old Army buddies."

"You should've seen me and Todd in the car when that happened," Leavitt chuckled. "I looked at him and said, 'Holy shit, did somebody just yell *John Shepherd*?'"

They went through the postgame analysis, all of them needing a little levity after the high intensity of the last several minutes. More FBI agents arrived on the scene, and more police officers, too, both from the Jacksonville Beach Police Department and the Jacksonville Sheriff's Office—including the sheriff himself.

"Who the fuck is responsible for this shit show?" the sheriff demanded, storming through the front door with the undersheriff at his side.

Leavitt looked at Jessica and John. "I believe that's my cue." He headed over, all charm. "Sheriff! Special Agent Ben Leavitt, Federal Bureau of Investigation. How are you today?"

Jessica watched Leavitt walk away. "I have never been so glad to *not* be the case agent in my life."

John turned to her, with streaks of dried blood along his face. "Yes. Thank goodness we got the easy job."

Jessica smiled—God, she'd missed his dry sense of humor. Feeling all sorts of emotions, she reached up and touched his short hair. "You look like you should be on a Wheaties box with this haircut."

His expression softened for a moment just before the paramedics hurried in through the front door. Then he sighed. "Are you really going to make me do this? Can't you just drive me to the hospital?"

"Humor me, big guy." She'd seen how hard he'd hit his head against the table, and she wasn't taking any chances.

The paramedics agreed to let her ride with John to the emergency room—not that she gave them much choice in the matter. Leavitt followed them out to the ambulance, promising to update them as soon as they'd found Blair.

Before climbing into the ambulance, Jessica reached into the front of her dress, pulled the microphone out of her bra, and handed it off to Leavitt.

Ashley and Dave were officially retired.

34 ⁓

At the hospital, once they were in a private room, the doctor did a thorough physical examination before removing the cervical collar the paramedics had insisted John wear around his neck as a precautionary matter.

"Finally." Sitting on the examination table, John tilted his head to stretch out his neck.

"Well, you're not showing any symptoms of a concussion." The doctor looked at Jessica, who sat in a chair across from the table. "How long was he unconscious?"

"About three minutes." One hundred eighty seconds that had felt like a lifetime.

"Was he dazed or disoriented when he came to?" the doctor asked.

Jessica felt John's eyes on her as she answered. "He didn't seem to recognize me when he first opened his eyes. But as soon as he started talking, he was lucid."

The doctor nodded, turning back to John. "I'd like to do an MRI, just to be certain there's no concussion. As for the cut on your head, I don't think stitches are necessary. I'll have the nurse put a skin adhesive on it—that should do the trick." He smiled. "All in all, from the sound of things, you're a very lucky man, Agent Shepherd." After scribbling a few things in John's file, the doctor headed out.

Leaving Jessica and John alone for the first time that day.

Jessica exhaled, feeling shaky now that the adrenaline was wearing off. "The doctor's right. You are very lucky." She met John's gaze. "I saw what you did when the cops pointed their guns at us. You moved toward me." She paused meaningfully. "So you could block me, if they fired."

His expression was momentarily unreadable, and then he shrugged. "Seemed like the gentlemanly thing to do."

Getting up from the chair, she walked over to stand next to him at the examination table. "If I believed that patronizing explanation for one moment, I'd be even more pissed at you," she said, without any real heat.

He raised an eyebrow. "You're pissed because I wanted to protect you? Before, you said that was *cute.*"

"No, I'm pissed because you got *hurt* trying to protect me." She looked him in the eyes. "If you hadn't moved closer to me, you would've cleared that table when you fell with the cops. You hit your head because of me."

His expression softened. "Jessica . . ."

"Don't 'Jessica' me." She pointed. "Do you have any idea, John Shepherd, how close you came to turning my life into a Nicholas Sparks book? I never would've forgiven you for that."

John laughed hard at that. "I have no clue what that means. But if I had to guess, I'd say that what you're trying to tell me—in your saucy, Jessica Harlow way—is that you would miss me if I were gone."

She threw him a look. "Of course I would miss you if you were gone."

His expression turned more serious, and he cocked his head. "So . . . *do* you miss me?"

The air between them suddenly seemed to stand still.

She could make a joke. That was her thing, after all. But

after seeing him hurt, after being *this* close to potentially losing him forever, she no longer felt like joking. Or avoiding the truth, even if it was scary and invited questions to which there were no easy answers. Because she'd known the truth, in her heart, the moment he'd walked through that restaurant door.

Her feelings went way behind warm fondness at this point.

In fact, she'd dare say she was in love with John Shepherd.

"Yes." Her voice cracked with emotion. "I've missed you every day you've been gone. So much that it hurts."

He went still.

And just looked at her.

Okay . . . that was not the reaction she'd been hoping for.

There was a knock on the door, and a nurse with a bright smile strolled into the room. "Mr. Shepherd . . . or I guess I should say *Agent* Shepherd. It's time for your MRI."

John held Jessica's gaze for another moment, then looked at the nurse. "Right." Taking a deep breath, he stood up.

"He'll be back in about forty-five minutes," the nurse told Jessica, before smiling at John again. "Right this way."

After John left the room, Jessica sank against the examination table.

Oh God.

Her hands shook as she ran them through her hair. Okay, he obviously didn't feel the same way, but she could salvage this; they could at least still be friends. She could lie—she was damn good at that—and tell him she'd gotten swept up in the moment.

"Sorry. Could you hang on for a second?" she heard John say to the nurse, his deep voice carrying in from the hallway.

Jessica looked over.

When John appeared in the doorway, her heart began to pound.

With hope.

He stepped into the room and strode toward her, determination etched on his face. Then he grabbed her, pulled her into his arms, and kissed her.

His mouth swept possessively over hers, hot and fierce. Cupping his face in her hands, she kissed him back, all the emotions she'd been trying to hide these last three weeks—hell, probably longer—pouring out right then, in that moment.

When they finally pulled back from the kiss, he touched her cheek.

"We need to talk," he said huskily.

She nodded, finding herself uncharacteristically overcome right then. "Yes."

He traced his thumb over her skin. "Do you know how long I've waited for you to look at me this way?"

She assumed he was teasing her. "What are you talking about? You didn't even like me for most of the time we've known each other."

He bent his head before turning to go, his voice low and confident in her ear. "Or maybe I'm just that good of an undercover agent."

Unfortunately, when John returned from his MRI, he found half the damn population of the thirteenth-largest U.S. city waiting for him with Jessica. Or at least, it seemed that way.

Among his visitors were the public corruption squad leader and the Special Agent in Charge of the Jacksonville field office, both of whom had dropped by to personally check on John and to let him and Jessica know that Blair had been apprehended.

"We caught him at a marina on the Intracoastal Waterway, with the keys to a friend's boat and a duffel bag of cash. Apparently, his plan was to make it all the way to Cuba," the SAC informed them. "Agents Leavitt and Todd have the mayor in custody now and were quite pleased to inform him that the FBI will be adding 'incitement of a riot' to the list of criminal charges against him."

Also there to check on John's status were the two police officers who'd tackled him, both of whom seemed extremely relieved to hear that John was doing okay.

"No offense, but even though you were *saying* you were FBI, you had this look on your face, like—" The younger cop made an angry face, demonstrating.

John held out his hands innocently. "You told me to keep my hands in the air and get down. That's exactly what I was doing."

The older cop cocked his head. "Yeah, but when you do that, you somehow still give off this vibe that's particularly intimidating."

Jessica smiled from her corner of the room as John glared.

Yeah, he'd heard that one before.

Next to knock on John's door was Dan Frazier, his Ranger friend who'd unknowingly blown his cover at the restaurant.

"How'd you know where to find me?" John asked, after the two men exchanged back slaps and man hugs.

"They said on the news that a federal agent had been brought to the emergency room here." Dan pointed to Jessica. "Your partner spotted me in the waiting area, asking about your status, and told me where I could find you." His expression was filled with guilt. "I can't believe how bad I messed that up for you, Shep. I didn't even stop to consider that you might be working undercover."

Jessica made her way toward the door. "I'm going to step out for a few minutes. Let you guys catch up."

No. John resisted the urge to growl and block her way as she walked out. He knew she didn't want to intrude, and he appreciated that. Just like he appreciated that Dan and everyone else simply wanted to make sure he was okay. And on any other day, he'd be more than glad to catch up with one of his Ranger buddies and shoot the shit for old times' sake.

But if he didn't get Jessica alone soon, heads were going to roll.

Dan watched, too, as Jessica left the room. Then he turned to John with a sly expression. "By the way, your partner? *Wow.* Is she from Jacksonville? Any chance you could help an old friend out by hooking us up for coffee or something?"

Whatever "particularly intimidating" look John must've displayed right then made Dan smile sheepishly. "I'm thinking maybe I should just stop talking today."

Twenty minutes later, after Dan left, Jessica walked into John's room carrying two cups of coffee. "It's from the cafeteria, so drink at your own risk."

Without saying a word, John walked over and took both cups from her. He set the coffee down next to the sink, then drew the privacy curtain closed.

Jessica raised an eyebrow. "That'll look suspicious to anyone who drops by."

"It'll look even more suspicious if they see us doing this." John hooked one arm around her waist and pulled her in for a long, hot kiss.

"We're leaving," he said, in no uncertain terms, when they finally pulled apart.

Her lips curved. "Not until the doctor clears you."

Her concern for him touched something deep inside him. Sliding his fingers through hers, he lifted her hand to kiss it. "You're cute when you're protective."

There was a tentative knock at the door.

"Um, Agent Shepherd?" the doctor said, on the other side of the curtain.

Jessica yanked John's shirt out of his pants, covering his erection. Moving just as quickly, he adjusted the skirt of her dress so that it lay straight again, and then they stepped apart.

"Come on in." John smiled casually when the doctor pulled the curtain open. "Sorry. There's been an endless line of visitors. Figured the curtain would buy me a few minutes of quiet."

"I think we can buy you more than a few minutes," the doctor said cheerfully. "You're free to go. I got the results of your MRI back, and there's no sign of a concussion. Nevertheless, I strongly advise that you have someone monitor you tonight and wake you up every two hours." He turned to Jessica. "All you need to do is ask him a couple questions, just to make sure he's lucid."

Jessica blinked. "Oh. Uh . . . I think you misunderstood the situation here. I won't be with John tonight. *No.*" She chuckled, gesturing between them. "He and are I just partners."

The doctor smiled. "Sure you are." He looked at John on his way out the door. "If you need something for the headache, stick to acetaminophen. No ibuprofen or aspirin."

After he left, Jessica shook her head. "That's the *worst* cover I've ever done."

"You do seem a little off your game." John's tone turned teasing. "I heard you were even nervous earlier."

She looked up at the ceiling and sighed. "I knew that was coming back to haunt me."

During the short drive to the hotel, John switched his return flight to Virginia to the following day.

"What time's your flight tomorrow?" he asked Jessica, who was driving.

"Four forty-five P.M." Originally, she'd been booked on an early flight, but she'd moved it back while John had been getting his MRI.

"I'll take the five-fifteen," John said, speaking on his phone to the airline's customer service rep.

Jessica glanced at the clock on the car's dashboard. It was almost five o'clock now, so that gave them less than twenty-four hours together before they had to return to their separate lives that awaited them in Chicago and Quantico.

It wasn't much. But at least it was something.

When they got to her hotel room, John grinned when he saw the ocean view. "They finally upgraded you."

"Apparently, the fourth time's the charm." Jessica set her purse onto the desk and kicked off her heels. "Do you want to go to the gift shop now?" Because John hadn't planned to stay overnight, he hadn't brought a suitcase with him and didn't have a change of clothes or toiletries.

"Later." John took off his suit jacket and set it over the back of the chair by the balcony door. "Right now, we have a few issues to address. Like the fact that I'm pissed at you."

She pulled back in surprise. "You're pissed at *me*? What did I do?"

He folded his arms across his chest. "Do you know the real reason I was mad at you the day we had to fight at the Academy?"

Jessica paused at the non sequitur, not sure why they were suddenly rehashing this. "Because I resorted to tricks to get you in a hold?"

"Actually, I thought that was brilliant," he said. "I was mad because I saw how nervous you were before the fight. As if you thought there was a chance I might actually hurt you."

She softened, hearing that. "Mostly, I think I was nervous about making a fool of myself." She cocked her head. "But why are we talking about this now?"

"Because, six years later, you still don't get it."

She wasn't following. "Get what?"

"You lectured me today about moving closer to you when the cops were pointing their guns at us. As if there were any other possible way that situation could go down." He moved closer to her, his eyes a warm, deep blue. "Jessica . . . you have to know that I would step in front of a bullet for you without even thinking about it."

Her throat tightened, and she found herself momentarily unable to say anything.

"And no, not just because you're my partner." His eyes held hers. "Because I love you. I think I've always loved you, from that very first morning in the auditorium, when you stood up and inspired our whole class with your speech. You amazed me every day at the Academy, and now that we've reconnected—and you're actually being nice to me for a change," he added with a smile, "those feelings have only gotten stronger."

Her eyes had filled with tears. "I didn't know you felt that way."

"Well, I had a hard time accepting it myself," he conceded. He reached up and wiped a tear from her cheek. "Especially once I found out I'd made HRT. Because I was leaving, I convinced myself that it was better to keep things casual between us. But when you told me at the hospital that you'd missed me, it was like everything else fell away. I knew in that moment that the thing I want most is to spend the rest of my life with the one person who drives me crazy in all the best possible ways."

She wiped away another tear, complete *mush* by this point. "For the record, you are knocking it out of the park with this speech."

"You always did make me up my game, Harlow."

Ditto. She laced her fingers through his. "We have a geography problem. About seven hundred and fifty miles, to be specific."

He nodded, his expression turning more sober. "Yes, we do."

She squeezed his hand reassuringly. She'd thought a lot about it at the hospital, while John was getting his MRI. And apparently, Tara wasn't the only one who was as sappy as a Hallmark movie these days.

I'd like to think that when two people feel that way about each other, somehow, some way, they can find a way to make it work.

Damn straight they could.

"Obviously, I'm stuck in Chicago for the short term. But I

was thinking that we could do the long-distance thing for a while, and then, after I've been in Chicago for a year, I'll put in for a TDY at the D.C. office."

He studied her face. "You'd really be okay with that?"

"I'd really be okay with that. More than okay. I can be a special agent anywhere. Well, not *anywhere*, anywhere. In one of the fifty-six metropolitan areas across the U.S. and Puerto Rico where the FBI has field offices." When John's lips curved, she slid her arms around his neck. "But I won't find another you. And I know I'll never find anyone else who makes me happier." She peered up into his eyes. "So where you go, I go."

His voice was thick with emotion. "You don't know how much it means to hear you say that." He tucked a lock of hair behind her ear. "But I've already decided to quit the Hostage Rescue Team."

"What? *No*." Pulling back in shock, Jessica shook her head. "You can't give up HRT, John. So few people can do what you can."

"True. But just because I *can* do something doesn't mean I should. That's another thing that took me some time to figure out." He cocked his head. "You'd be surprised how much becomes clear when you're standing sixty feet above the water on the gunwale of a ship."

"But this is the Hostage Rescue Team," she emphasized.

"Yes, it is. And for the team to do what it does, every operator has to be one hundred percent committed." He looked at her without hesitation. "I'm not there. And I'm never going to be there. Not when I think about everything you and I could have together."

She stepped forward determinedly, closing the gap between them. "You don't have to choose. I'll come with you."

"But I'll be gone. A lot. And you'd be left alone, in a place that neither of us thinks of as home. It's one thing when I only had myself to think about, but it's not the life I want for us."

He smiled tenderly. "Somebody has to be around to teach our gaggle of towheaded girls how to make fire with the ass end of a lightning bug."

And here she thought she'd been total mush before. Swallowing, she took a moment. "I'm so afraid you're going to regret this. And that you'll end up resenting me."

He cupped her face in his hands and looked straight into her eyes. "Trust me to know what I want."

She nodded. She already trusted John with her life. If they were going to do this—really do this—she needed to trust him with her heart, too.

"Okay," she said softly.

"Okay," he repeated.

She knew that look. "You're going to kiss me, aren't you?"

He pretended to consider this. "Well, with all the emotions flying around, it just feels . . . expected."

She smiled as he lowered his head and claimed her mouth in a deep kiss. He guided her back toward the bed, his hands already working the zipper of her dress.

"I need to come clean with you about something," Jessica said, walking backward. "That morning we said good-bye, I lied when I told you that I took a cab to your place. I actually drove there in my rental car—the rental car I'd picked up in Columbia the night before."

He paused. "You drove all the way from South Carolina that night?"

"Yes."

"Why?"

Because I didn't want to depend on the airlines, she could've said. Or even, *Because I wanted to make sure I had the chance to say good-bye*. But really, it boiled down to one thing.

"Because I love you," she said.

His mouth curved in a smile. "Took you long enough to figure that out." He stepped closer, his eyes a deep, heated blue.

"In my defense, I might've realized it sooner if you hadn't spent our first six months together constantly hounding me."

He slid her dress off her shoulders and it fell to the floor. "Not hounding. I told you—I was trying to motivate you." He scooped her up, climbed onto the bed, and set her down against the pillows.

"We'll still have to agree to disagree on that one," she said.

He leaned down onto his forearms, trapping her between him and the bed. "I have a feeling that's something you and I will be saying a lot over the course of our lifetime together, Harlow."

She linked her fingers behind his neck and pulled him closer. "You can bet on it, Shepherd."

And she couldn't wait.

35

John parked the car on the tree-lined street, and Jessica looked at him before opening her door.

"Ready for this?" she asked.

This would officially complete their meet-the-friends-and-family tour. After quitting HRT and being reinstated as a special agent with the Chicago field office, John had packed up his things and come home. Jessica had asked him to move in with her, and he'd said yes. No messing around, no hesitation—they both knew this was a good thing, a really good thing, and they wanted to be together as much as possible.

Then they'd realized that the majority of their friends and family didn't even know they were *dating*.

Clearly, they had some 'splaining to do.

They'd tackled John's side first, thinking that would be easier since Jessica's family (with the exception of her mom) had no clue John existed. She met his brother and his friend Wes on the day John returned to Chicago. Since he was paying his own moving expenses this time—and also had to reimburse the Bureau for his moving expenses out to Virginia—he needed two people who would be willing to help him unload a U-Haul in exchange for a couple of cold beers.

Apparently more than willing, Nate and Wes had shown up on Jessica's doorstep with grins on their faces.

"The infamous Jessica Harlow. At last, we meet," Nate said.

"We've heard all about you." Wes cocked his head, looking her over curiously. "Huh. John's right—you do seem taller in person."

"Before leaving town, my brother showed off this photo of you from the Academy," Nate explained.

"'Showed off'? That's not exactly how that went down," John said dryly, standing next to Jessica.

Nate breezed into the condo and patted John on the shoulder. "You're moving in with her. I think the game's up, bro." He turned to Jessica, whispering faux-dramatically, "Spoiler alert: He likes you."

When John looked up at the ceiling and shook his head, Jessica had a feeling she was going to like these two very much.

That Sunday, she and John went to dinner at his father's house. She'd been a little nervous while getting ready, which John seemed to find amusing.

"I just want to make a good impression," she told him, changing her outfit for the second time.

John watched her undress from the closet doorway. "You're smart, know how to shoot a pistol, and have a whole cache of stories about catching bad guys. Tell him you're a Cubs fan, and you're pretty much his dream daughter-in-law."

"Daughter-in-law?" Jessica's pulse skipped a beat. "You and I haven't had that conversation yet."

"You should probably brace yourself, then."

She gestured to herself. "We're going to talk about getting married while I'm standing in my underwear?"

"That's the best time to talk. About anything." His gaze heated, he stepped into the closet and pulled her close.

They ended up being fifteen minutes late to dinner at his dad's house.

Managing the situation with their co-workers took a little more finesse. Because they didn't want people knowing they'd hooked up while working together—nor did either of them want "John Shepherd gave up HRT for Jessica Harlow" to become part of the office gossip—they devised a plan to control the narrative.

On John's second week back in the office (his first week having been spent convincing his shocked squad mates that, no, he hadn't been "kicked out" of HRT, he'd simply decided it wasn't the right fit for him), he just-so-happened to be working out in the weight room of the gym with several of his squad mates when Jessica just-so-happened to walk in.

She spotted him and headed over. "I heard a rumor you were back in town, Shepherd. Couldn't resist the lure of undercover work?"

At the sound of her voice, his five squad mates instantly peeked their heads up from their weight machines.

"Apparently not," John said to Jessica, with a self-deprecating shrug.

"At least, that's the 'story,'" Jin told her, making air quotes while lying on a bench to work his hamstrings.

"They think I washed out," John explained to Jessica.

"Ah. Well, I'm sure you had your reasons for leaving," she said, as if being diplomatic. "Ooh, the leg machine just opened up."

"Hey, we should grab coffee sometime and catch up," John said, as she turned to go.

"I'm around all day tomorrow. Text me when you want a break." With a smile, she headed off.

John deliberately let his gaze linger a moment, then turned back to face his squad mates.

All five of whom were grinning at him.

"Nice move," Jared said approvingly, as he did another shoulder press.

"It's only coffee." John glanced one more time in Jessica's direction, then looked slyly at his squad mates. "Has she always been this cute?"

Brandon snorted. "You just figured that out now?"

They turned back to their workouts. All except for Ryan, who'd been spotting John at the bench press.

He studied John carefully. "Over two months she's been at this office, and I've never once seen Agent Harlow working out at this time. How curious that we just happened to run into her today."

"Good timing for me, I guess," John said casually. When the other agent gave him a highly suspicious look—*dammit*, Ryan always had been the cleverest one in the bunch—John switched to plan B.

He lowered his voice. "She has a friend named Tara who's single and the spitting image of that actress who plays the green girl in *Guardians of the Galaxy*. You stay quiet and I'll arrange an introduction."

Ryan smiled. "Done."

John reached around to the backseat to grab the flowers he'd bought for her mother, and the bottle of wine that was one of her parents' favorites.

"So, we've got your mom and dad; Finn, Kim, Kayla, and Andrew; Maya, Camila, and Oliver. Anyone I'm forgetting?" he asked.

"Nope, that's everyone." She glanced sideways at him. "Don't tell me *you're* nervous now." She hadn't thought that was even possible.

"I'm just wondering what your family must be thinking. They've never heard of me before, and then, out of the blue, I'm the guy who's moved in with you."

Admittedly, her family had been surprised when Jessica had first broken the news. She'd talked to her parents over the phone so she could explain the situation, but for kicks, she'd merely sent Maya and Finn a text message.

Bringing a date to Mom and Dad's on Sunday. BTW, he and I are living together. Catch ya later! ☺

They'd lit up her phone for an hour straight after that one.

She shrugged in answer to John's question. "Well, seeing how I'm a pretty levelheaded person, and a good judge of character, too, I guess my family will just have to assume you're that damn good a catch."

John grinned, looking quite pleased with the compliment.

"We don't have to make a whole thing of it," she added.

He laughed and leaned in closer, tangling his hand in her hair. "Still so saucy."

"Always, with you." As they kissed, she touched her hand to his jaw. Seconds later, she heard her phone chime with a new text message. And then another.

Pulling back from John, she checked her phone to make sure it wasn't a work emergency.

Stop making out with the man. We're dying to meet him, Maya wrote.

Please tell me you brought those salted caramel brownies, added Finn. If I have to stand out here watching you kiss your new boyfriend I better at least get brownies.

Jessica looked up from her phone. They'd parked two houses down from her parents', and through the car windshield she could see her entire family standing on her parents' front lawn. They waved collectively at John and Jessica, and the kids yelled, "Aunt Jess!"—which got the dogs all excited and barking and racing around the yard in chaotic circles.

"Yep. That would be my family," Jessica said.

John winked at her. "Let's do this."

They got out of the car and walked over. Her family welcomed John warmly, hugging him and joking with him about being Jessica's "mystery man." She sensed they liked him right off the bat—a feeling that was confirmed later, when they were all hanging out in the backyard.

"So, your guy?" Maya cocked her head in the direction of the grill, where John was talking to their dad. "Blows my guy totally out of the water."

"My guy, too. Even without the Maserati. And that's saying a lot." Finn put his arm around Jessica. "So why all the secrecy?"

"It wasn't supposed to be serious between us, but then . . ." Jessica trailed off, watching as her three-year-old nephew walked up to John and matter-of-factly handed him a pretzel rod. Getting down on one knee, John broke off half the pretzel, handed it to Oliver, and they each took a bite.

"Oh my God, you are so smitten," Maya said to Jessica.

Finn laughed. "Your eyes literally just turned into hearts, Jess."

Seriously, *three* moves and she'd have both these clowns on the ground before they even knew what was happening.

Just saying.

When the food was ready, the kids sat on a picnic blanket in the yard, surrounded by the dogs, while the adults gathered around the patio table. As they ate, Jessica's dad asked John about the kinds of cases he worked on.

"I'm on the organized crime squad. I do a lot of undercover work, like Jessica," John said.

Maya pointed at them with a kebob. "And that's how you two met, right? Working undercover? By the way, I would know this already if *somebody* had done more than merely send a *text message* to announce your relationship." She threw Jessica a pointed look.

"That *would* have been more informative. But less fun," Jessica said.

"Actually, we first met at the Academy. Six years ago," John told Maya.

Finn looked intrigued by this. "Really? I didn't know that." He threw Jessica a cheeky look. "Did you make heart eyes at him there, too?"

"'Heart eyes'?" John chuckled. "Ah, no. More like daggers."

"John and I weren't on the best terms at the Academy," she explained to her family. "There was a bit of a competitive thing going between us."

"Hmm. Sounds like there's a story there," her mom said.

Jessica shared a look with John. Yes, there was a story there—one about a valiant heroine and an ex-Ranger hero who'd come a long way from their days together at the FBI Academy. They'd hit a few bumps in the road, but six years later they'd ended up right where they were meant to be.

"Come on, Jess—don't leave us hanging. Tell us the story," Finn urged.

Underneath the table, she slid her hand into John's. His lips curved as he linked his fingers through hers.

"I think you have to tell them now," he said.

And so she would. Which left only one issue to be resolved.

Jessica smiled coyly. "Your version or mine?"

the thing about love

JULIE JAMES

questions for discussion

1. There's a he said/she said dynamic in the story. Did you agree with both John's and Jessica's points of view about what happened at the FBI Academy, or did you side more with one character?

2. Both John and Jessica envy the strengths that the other has at the Academy. Why is it so important that they each be the best? Is that simply part of their personalities, or do they each feel that they have something to prove?

3. Jessica works in a very male-dominated field. Do you think her gender is an advantage or a disadvantage in her job as a special agent?

4. John and Jessica start out hating each other. In which scene do you think this begins to change?

5. What do you think John finds most attractive about Jessica? And vice versa?

6. John refuses to forgive his two friends Lucas and Matt, who knew that Rob was sleeping with John's then girlfriend, Alicia.

If you were John, could you ever forgive them? Do you think Lucas and Matt should've told John what was going on, or were they caught in the middle? Have you ever been in a similar situation?

7. If you were in Jessica's shoes when she finds out that her ex-husband is getting remarried, would you want to know whether he cheated, or would you prefer to never know?

8. Why do you think Jessica is so reluctant to admit her feelings for John? Is it because of her recent divorce and a fear of opening up again, or is it that she's afraid to fall in love with someone who's moving halfway across the country?

9. A recurring theme is the strain that undercover work can put on the agents' personal lives. Often people's jobs strain their romantic relationships. How is undercover work both similar to and different from a nine-to-five job? Has work ever stressed your relationship?

10. For the sake of her job, Jessica has to put up with Mayor Blair's flirting. Do you think this is something a lot of women encounter and have to deal with in work situations? What do you think about the way Jessica handled it? Have you ever been faced with a similar situation? How did you navigate it?

11. Jessica doesn't want John to know that she drove through the night from South Carolina to say good-bye to him in person. Why do you think she keeps this from him? Do you think it would've changed John's decision to leave for Quantico if he had known that she did that?

12. At the end, both Jessica and John are willing to make sacrifices in order to make the relationship work. What do you think about John's decision to quit HRT? Do you think making the team was something he genuinely wanted, or do you think it was more that he felt he *should* join the team since he could?

13. If this were a movie, who would you cast as Jessica and John? How about Mayor Blair? What about Nate and Tara?

After graduating from law school, *New York Times* bestselling author **Julie James** clerked for the United States Court of Appeals. She then practiced law with one of the nation's largest firms for several years until she began writing screenplays. After Hollywood producers optioned two of her scripts, she decided to leave the practice of law to write full-time. Julie's books have been listed on the American Library Association's Reading List for Top Genre Novels and *Booklist*'s Top 10 Romances of the Year, and have been featured as one of *Cosmopolitan* magazine's Red-Hot Reads. Julie's books have been translated into seventeen languages, and her most recent novels are *The Thing About Love*, *Suddenly One Summer*, *It Happened One Wedding*, *Love Irresistibly*, and *About That Night*. Julie lives with her husband and two children in Chicago, where she is currently working on her next book.

Visit her online at juliejames.com, facebook.com /JulieJamesfanpage, and twitter.com/juljames.